W9-AVY-448

The Witness

DEE
Henderson

DOUBLEDAY LARGE PRINT HOME LIBRARY EDITION

Tyndale House Publishers, Inc.,
Carol Stream, Illinois

The Witness

This Large Print Edition, prepared especially for Doubleday Large Print Home Library, contains the complete, unabridged text of the original Publisher's Edition.

Visit the author's Web site at www.deehenderson.com

TYNDALE is a registered trademark of Tyndale House Publishers, Inc.

Tyndale's quill logo is a trademark of Tyndale House Publishers, Inc.

The Witness

ISBN 0-7394-6500-7

Printed in the United States of America

This Large Print Book carries the
Seal of Approval of N.A.V.H.

The Witness

Chapter One

Stopping at the mall to pick up a cut-glass vase for his sister's birthday, a mystery novel for his day off, and a few items needed for the house had seemed like a good idea an hour ago, but Luke Granger was still short two items on his shopping list, and he had no desire to try another store.

"Officer."

He turned.

The lady clutching two Bergner's shopping bags and the hand of a three-year-old girl looked worried. "There's a woman in the restroom who needs help. She asked me to find mall security."

He was city police and off duty, still in uniform after a day in court; she was close enough. "Anyone else in there?"

"No."

He nodded and crossed the corridor into the hallway with pay phones and restrooms. A cleaning-service cart sat outside a door marked Utilities. He pulled it over to block the entryway to the women's restroom. "Police officer coming in," he called in warning. He walked through the sitting area with four chairs and a stroller station and into the lavatory area.

He saw the lady: early forties, sick, her face alabaster white, the counter doing more to hold her upright than her legs. He turned, set down his purchases, and returned with a curved-back and cushioned chair. "Sit down, ma'am."

He shut off the water streaming over her hands in the basin and eased her back into the chair. She wore a white tailored blouse and black dress slacks, the retailer version of a uniform, and they were no longer neat or straight. He wondered at sexual assault even as he stripped off his jacket and bundled it around her to deal with the chill he could feel. He was a big man, broad shouldered and tall, and the jacket swallowed her slim frame.

"His eyes were caramel, cold." A shudder rippled through her body.

"Okay." He swept hands down her midsection looking for the source of the smeared blood on the front of the sink counter. Blood darkened her slacks at the right thigh, but it hadn't soaked through the fabric from a wound.

"Bressman's Jewelry, the storeroom."

His gaze shot to hers.

"They're all dead. I checked."

He briskly closed his jacket snaps up to her neck. "Stay right here."

She gave a jerky nod.

He left her there.

●●●●●●

Luke walked into Bressman's Jewelry. The sign turning above the front display counter advertised 30 percent off diamond pendants this week only. No salesclerks were in sight. He walked around the counters and into a small back office, then turned down the narrow hallway that paralleled the public restrooms. A door moved back and forth in the breeze of the overhead air-condition-ing, and a radio tuned to a country station began a new song; nothing else spoke of life.

He looked.

And because he was a cop, he stood. The horror took a good minute to wash through his system as he cataloged the killings. Four store staff herded back here and shot as a group, the blood splatter staining the storage shelves. The youngest looked to be barely out of high school with her makeup perfect and her nails painted a soft pink. A lady his mother's age had been shot in the head. The store manager and a third sales associate, both middle-aged men, had died in front of a holder for gift boxes. The blood hadn't attracted more than a couple flies yet: ten minutes? twenty?

The fact it had been done in his town, within his reach, and as deputy chief of police he hadn't been able to prevent it, chilled his anger to a hard, sharp edge. Luke reached for his radio. "55-14."

"10-2."

He recognized the dispatcher's voice in the brief answer. "Janice, there's a multiple 187 at Ellerton Mall, Bressman's Jewelry." He mentally ran through the list of detec-

tives on duty. "I need Connor, Marsh, Mayfield, and St. James. Tell them minutes matter."

"Yes, sir. Priority calls are going out."

"Assign a band for this case."

"Four."

He switched over his radio frequency.

"Emergency Services?" Janice asked.

"Dispatch forensics code orange to the
scene and alert the coroner. I'll need forty
officers pulled in. Locate as many as you
can in-house, tap the Westford district, and
then start calling men back to duty. Marsh
will be handling assignments on scene.
Where's Paul Riker right now?"

"His schedule shows a Q&A with print
journalists."

"Have someone pass him a message. I
need him on scene."

"Yes, sir."

"Questions?"

"I can handle it, sir."

"Good. I'm code four."

Footsteps had him turning. Two mall security officers, both hurrying.

"Stay up front." Luke left the door swinging in the air-conditioned breeze and
walked back to the showroom. "There's

been a shooting. How many security officers does the mall have on duty?"

"Four."

"Okay. I want the two of you to close this storefront. Parker, once the gate is locked, I want you to sit at the side entrance to this store. No one but Brentwood or Westford officers enter or you won't be employed tomorrow, you understand?"

"Yes, sir."

"Richards, I want you to get the other two mall guards and start working the parking lot starting at this entrance. I want a list of license-plate numbers for every vehicle on the lot."

They stood there.

"Move."

They rushed to bring down the security gate, pulling the first panel from the ceiling to cover the main section of the store entryway.

Luke walked over to the east wall of the display area and took down the sixth framed picture. His witness looked better in her official photo. *Kelly Brown.* It didn't sound like a forty-something's name. Her hair had changed—it was now a couple inches longer and a shade darker auburn—but the blue eyes were the same.

He kept the photo and walked the display cases. Nothing appeared disturbed. A robbery with multiple murders and no jewelry taken? How much would be here in inventory? A hundred thousand? More? *Do you have a special sales area, Kelly Brown? Rings, watches, the necklaces that would cost a year of my salary? You were wearing no jewelry today, not even a ring. That surprised me.* The cash register also appeared untouched.

Luke looked up as the first officers he had requested began to stream in. Connor was in the lead with his partner, Marsh, towering over him a step behind. Connor was all of five nine, wearing the black jeans and sweatshirt he favored for days working the streets. Marsh, at six four, still looked like a hungover drunk after too many days staking out alleys, and the dark shadows under his eyes were more pronounced than normal. Luke considered them to be among the best officers in the department, even though neither would like to hear that commendation repeated in public for fear they would end up in management one day.

"What do we have, Boss?"

Luke pointed to the back hallway. "I'm leaving the scene to you, Connor. Marsh, you're coordinating the officers coming in to assist. I've got a witness to deal with. I need names and addresses of the victims fast, because I'm not seeing robbery as the motive. We're still in the first hour, so light a fire under everyone."

"Will do."

"Keep the traffic on channel four. As soon as Riker arrives, page me. The press is going to be a problem with this one."

Trying to clear the mall of all shoppers wasn't a workable option, and sending a SWAT team searching for the shooter in a crowded mall would only end up with public panic and injuries. The shooter had come in, herded store staff to a back storage room, and shot them there. The scene presented said the shooter had left without trying to attract attention, and the timing of the shootings said he was already gone. For now they would work it outward from the shooting scene and try not to amplify the problem they faced.

Already a crowd of shoppers was slowing, stopping, and asking questions of each other. Luke walked through them and around the corridor to the restrooms. The cleaning cart remained where he had left it. Luke stepped around it and into the ladies' restroom.

The chair sat in the lavatory section, empty but for his folded jacket. "Ma'am? Kelly Brown?"

He left the lavatory and walked through the stalls. The restroom was empty. She'd left. As shaky as she had been, she'd still managed to leave.

He walked out of the restroom and looked around the corridor. She wasn't watching the officers at the store, propelled there by the awfulness of what she had seen. *There wasn't a need to run, Kelly. You were safe now.*

"I need an address and a vehicle make for Kelly Brown, early forties. Give me any DMV records close to the name and age registered in the city." He started the trace and then flipped through the phone book to locate the main Bressman store. He tore out the page. Five branches. Why this one?

Luke reentered the jewelry store and moved into the small office area; the hallway had begun to fill with forensics people.

Connor looked up from a file. "Your witness?"

"Skipped. And from the sound of it, she saw the shooter. I've got a trace running for her car now. Anything here show addresses, phone numbers of the staff?"

"I've got customer information—jewelry repair and special orders—but the best I've done so far on the staff is an index card taped by the phone. The main store has all the personnel files. I've got an officer bringing them over."

Luke checked the index card. Just first names, but only one Kelly. He touched his radio. "I need a reverse lookup on a phone number." He read it off and got an address back. "She's close by; I'm heading over there. You're good here?"

"The photos and phone numbers give me a place to start, and forensics has a priority to tell me the weapon used. I'll have preliminary inventory confirmed in twenty minutes. Right now you're right; it looks like everything is here."

"Former staff, recent firings—this types as a workplace shooting, not a robbery. Station a patrol car and officer at the other Bressman stores; there's no reasoning yet for why this branch. Let's make sure it's not simply the first."

"Marsh had the same thought; he's got officers on the way to the stores now."

Luke stopped at the restroom to retrieve his jacket and his purchases from an hour ago. He headed toward his sedan. He could send other officers, but Kelly was spooked enough, and what she had seen was their strongest lead right now.

The trip took seven minutes, three of them spent idling at red lights. He turned on Amber Road. He wasn't sure he would personally like to live this close to where he worked. He slowed as the house numbers counted down to the address he sought and he stopped: an old two-story red brick with a massive front porch and a narrow lot. The oak tree in front towered above the house and shaded the yard. No vehicle was in Kelly Brown's driveway, and a slow drive past showed the garage had a blown-over trash can rolling back and forth in front of the door, suggesting she hadn't pulled through into the garage.

"55-14."

He touched his radio. "10-2."

"DMV records for Kelly Brown at that address show only one vehicle registered, a Honda Odyssey, plates alpha-bravo-nine-two-five."

"Alpha-bravo-nine-two-five. 10-4."

Luke circled the block and saw no sign of her vehicle. He parked on the street. Picking up his jacket, he slipped it on. He lifted the collar closer to his face and caught the faint trace of her perfume. A lady's scent: welcoming, a touch elegant. He walked up the sidewalk to her front porch. Mail jammed the mailbox, and potted plants lined inside the front window. Lights were off. He rang the doorbell and opened the screen door to also knock. "Ms. Brown, Kelly, please come to the door. It's Officer Granger."

He didn't get an answer.

He walked around the property and knocked on the back door. The house appeared locked and quiet.

He hadn't seen her purse in that lavatory, and she hadn't reentered the jewelry store. If she wasn't home, then where? He touched his radio. "Connor, get the mall security guard Richards on the radio. Check if a Honda Odyssey is still in the mall parking lot. Plates are alpha-bravo-nine-two-five."

"Hold on."

Luke checked windows around the property, but what he could see of Kelly Brown's life were plants, books, one bowl in the draining rack beside the sink, and a jacket lying over the back of a chair. He checked the mail and found it all addressed to *K. Brown* or *Kelly Brown*. She lived alone.

"The vehicle is parked in section G, aisle five."

"Tell Richards to keep an eye on it. Have you found any purses in the office?"

"No. There's a locker in the storeroom that may be for coats and such. I'll check just as soon as forensics gives me access."

"I'm on my way back to you."

He had left her at the mall restroom. If she didn't have her purse, she didn't have car or house keys, and she would have no cash beyond what she might have slipped into her pocket. But if she'd worked at that mall branch for three years, as the photo indicated, she likely had friends on staff at other stores. Lack of keys or cash wasn't going to slow her down. And if she was running scared—*come on, honey, the last thing I want to do is go knock on the doors of your friends and leave them worried when I can't tell them for sure you're okay.*

She'd seen the shooter well enough to know his eye color. She hadn't been killed. The two facts were incongruent. Someone she knew? Someone she recognized on sight? Then why hadn't she just said his name as the person who shot her coworkers?

Kelly Brown, I need to find you or you need to find me, and it has to be soon.

Luke parked beside responding squad cars at the mall and walked back inside. Marsh had set up shop east of the jewelry-store entrance in a small storefront available for lease, officers streaming in and out with information and new assignments.

Luke handed Marsh Kelly's photo. "I need a canvas of the mall, staff at the stores, anyone who has seen her or knows her. She's going to be wound pretty tight, so have me paged rather than approach her if someone spots her. She may have already left with a friend, so also be asking at stores for the names of who got off duty in the last hour and a half."

"You'll have it." Marsh passed the photo to the officer behind him. "Thirty duplicates, color. Tom, get me another stack of mall maps to mark store assignments. What's the latest count on the mall security tapes?"

"Nine scanned so far," Tom replied. "They just brought down another six."

"Your witness is going to turn out to be our best lead on the shooter. The initial interviews of those around the jewelry store are coming up dry, and the security tapes from the store and mall aren't offering much."

Luke suspected that too. "She saw enough to give us the shooter—I'm convinced of that. Stress that 'do not approach' when she's spotted; have me paged."

"Will do."

Luke stopped beside the mall security guard Parker. "Does the mall have a regular bus stop?"

"One by the movie theater and the other by Sears. The blue bus line stops at both every thirty minutes."

Luke headed over to the movie-theater entrance. The bus was on time. He stepped aboard, confirmed the driver had been on this route the last two hours, and got a negative when he described Kelly Brown.

Luke stepped back off. It had been a long shot. He flagged down a mall-security patrol car and got in beside Roberts. "Show me the van I tagged." As they drove the lot, Luke flipped pages in the license-plate list. They'd been recorded by section. "Three hundred cars, give or take?"

"Yes. The lot can hold seven hundred, and we've been under half most of today. That's it." Roberts came to a stop behind the vehicle.

Luke got out. The windows showed him two white shopping sacks on the passenger seat and an open soda in the cup holder. Nothing suggested she had been back to the vehicle; nothing suggested someone else had carpooled with her to work. "I'll walk from here."

Roberts nodded and returned to recording license plates.

Had Kelly headed out into the parking lot only to change where she was going when she realized she didn't have her keys? Had she tried for a cab ride to a friend's who could pay the bill for her?

Luke rejoined his officers. "Marsh?"

"Sorry, Boss, so far the canvas is coming up dry. Her friends working at other stores have caucused and can't come up with a name who might have given her a ride home. She didn't catch a bus?"

"No."

Connor joined them and passed over the list of victims' names and addresses. "She lives nearby; she could have walked home. Or she could have called someone to come get her."

"She could have. Or the guy who did this was waiting for her to reappear." Luke didn't like the time passing on him. Whatever was going through Kelly's mind right now was going to be dominated by the image of coworkers dead, and that shock wasn't going to pass easily. Besides the fact he needed her help to move this investigation forward, he personally needed to know she wasn't sliding into a worse shock reaction than when he'd last seen her. He scanned the list of victims. "Have next of kin been identified for the victims?" Most would have spouses and children; some would have parents and siblings still living; all would have friends. Which one also had an enemy?

"Next of kin have been located for two of the four," Connor replied. "We've set up a secure conference room for family members who feel they need to come to the scene. Riker is five minutes out, and he's bringing enough staff along to set up for a briefing outside the west entrance."

Luke nodded at the news. "Profiles on our victims?"

"Not as far along as I would like. Give me another thirty minutes and I should have preliminary workups done. The personnel files gave us five former employees that raised concern, two of them red flags for having made recent threats. Mayfield and St. James are heading out to check them personally, and Marsh has got officers working the rest as priorities. Forensics pulled a slug from the wall and should be able to tell us within an hour if this gun has been used in other shootings."

"Good. Did you find Kelly's purse?"

"Yes. Hold on." Connor went to get it.

The bag was basic black, soft sided, and smaller than Luke had expected. The wallet held thirty-two in cash, her driver's license, two credit cards, and a handful of business cards for the local bank, florist, insurance agent. The checkbook had a few checks remaining on the pad; the check registry went back three years and showed a couple thousand currently in her account. Luke opened an address book and found most pages covered in names and phone numbers with only a few addresses. A number of the entries had been marked through and updated with new phone numbers. Luke had a feeling he was holding most of Kelly Brown's life for the last several years. "This will help."

A look through the first page, the last, and the tab marked *B* showed no other Browns listed. *No family, Kelly? Or are they listed here under married names?* He glanced at his watch. "This lady went to somewhere she felt safe, and we need to find it. Keep working the mall canvas: employee lounges, dressing rooms, restrooms, anywhere she might go to get out of view. I'm going to check her place again. If we don't locate her in the next hour, I'll want her photo going out to the public. Marsh, you've got enough hands to get the former employees tracked down?"

"Yes."

"Call me if you hit any roadblocks."

"I'll do that, Boss."

Luke took the purse with him and headed back to his car. He drove toward Kelly's home again. He remembered the look in her eyes—*where do you feel most safe, Kelly? If not home, where?* When traffic paused, he tugged out the address book and flipped pages. If she wasn't found soon, he'd be calling most of the people she'd listed. If he put her photo out to the public, he risked the shooter finding her first. Time was not an asset right now.

Her driveway remained empty. This time he pulled into the drive and parked there, intentionally blocking the garage. The possibility existed that she'd acquired a rental car or borrowed a friend's car, and if she didn't wish to speak to him, leaving was one way to accomplish that. He walked around to her front door.

The frog planter had moved from the top step down a riser since his first visit—a subtle change, but he noticed the brushed-away dirt on the step. A spare house key hidden underneath? She could exit on him out the side door by the kitchen, but her house had no alley and her neighbors' yards were fenced. She'd have to come within view.

He pressed the buzzer and then opened the screen door and knocked. "Ms. Brown.

Kelly. It's Officer Granger. Please open the door. I know you're home."

He waited.

The dead bolt finally slid away. The door opened enough for him to see her. Wary. Haunted. Stressed. But no tears showing.

She was his age, but he had no idea how to relate to this woman. "May I speak with you?"

She stepped back and let him enter her home.

She'd changed from the blouse and slacks to a red sweater and faded jeans. A slender woman, the clothes hung on her. She walked back into a room off the hall. He followed, only to stop at the door to her bedroom. The bed had a rose-print spread neatly tucked under matching pillows and a large open suitcase sitting on the left side.

She picked up a shirt from an open dresser drawer. "It was Paula Grant's ex. I saw him leaving the store, and I saw the gun. She had a restraining order against him—what good that did her. He came out of the back office and hallway, walked past the ladies' watches, then turned east in the mall toward RadioShack. I saw the butt of the gun as he closed his jacket." She stopped moving. "I went to look." She stood still as the image hit her again, then briskly resumed folding a shirt for the suitcase.

"Why didn't you stay?"

"Because I've got a guy in my life not unlike her ex who is going to love to hear where I'm now living." She crossed to the closet and pulled out items en masse.

"Ms. Brown—"

"Please, it's miss or just Kelly."

"Kelly—you can't run. You're a material witness to a multiple murder."

"My name is going to be in the news soon if it isn't already. A dead witness isn't going to do you any good." She reached over to the dresser and tossed him the area phone book. "You pick the town and hotel. My cab arrives in five minutes." She shoved aside the mattress and pulled a thick envelope taped to the box spring free. "I'll stay put for forty-eight hours while you figure something out. That's all I'm promising. But you give me your word you're the only one who knows that information."

"Who's the guy you're running from?"

"I give you the name, you're going to run

it, and that curiosity is what got the last cop in my life killed."

He would have said she was overblowing conclusions, but watching her pack and the matter-of-fact way she'd delivered the news suggested it was merely the barest of the facts. There hadn't been a cop killed in his city in twelve years; she'd moved here from where? He'd know before the evening was out. "The Radisson in Park Heights."

"I'll check in under the name Ann Walsh." She shoved money from the envelope into her pocket, then looked at him. "I'm sorry about what happened to them. They were friends. But I have to go."

"Order room service and don't call people."

"I've been this route a few times now." She closed her suitcase. "I've got to go."

"Why didn't you say who it was earlier?"

The question stopped her. "I thought I had." She sighed. "I remember the running water, your blue eyes, and being cold. It's blurry from when I left the storeroom."

"Okay."

"Lock up behind me please; use the key that's on the kitchen table and put it back under the frog."

"I've got your purse in my car."

"If I have it I would just use something that could inadvertently get me tracked down." She walked out to catch her cab.

He watched her go and wondered just what he'd walked into today. The multiple homicide might turn out to be the easier of the two problems to solve.

Luke locked the house and restored the key to its guardian frog. From his car he placed a call to Marsh. "You can call off the search for Kelly Brown; I found her. She saw the shooter and knew him. We need an all points for Paula Grant's ex. There's a restraining order against him. Find the paper on it. Get the vehicle information and put it out as armed and deadly. We've got an arrest to make tonight."

"10-4."

He set down the radio, knowing the flurry of activity he'd just triggered. He headed back to the mall. If Paula's ex was still in this city, odds were good they would have an arrest in twenty-four hours. And unless they got a confession and a guilty plea, this case was going to need Kelly's testimony. In the next forty-eight hours he had to make sure he understood the trouble that she was in and how he could best neutralize it. He didn't need her bolting on him again.

There were problems. Kelly Brown wasn't her name any more than Ann Walsh was. The phone book she'd tossed him now rested on the seat beside him, and a full set of fingerprints should help him with her name if he could figure out a safe way to run the check. A list of cops killed in the Midwest was a phone call away. The employment application she'd filled out and her address book would close a few more loopholes. The lady was running scared, but running smart. Piercing the secrecy of her past without also piercing her carefully constructed anonymity would take some care. Staying under everyone's radar screen had probably been keeping her alive.

She would be hiding out in a strange hotel room tonight, trying to sleep after walking into that storeroom to confirm her friends were dead. *"They're all dead. I checked."* She'd checked. She wouldn't be sleeping much tonight.

And neither would he. Arrest this guy, then he was going to drive out to Park Heights. It didn't really matter what her name was. She had landed in his life and become his responsibility. She probably wouldn't like it much, but it wouldn't change things. She was running from someone, and he'd never been one to avoid trouble. To listen to his sister, he went looking for it.

God, there are times I wish I was better at this job; this is one of them. Figuring out what I do next is going to take wisdom I don't have right now. How do I help her without causing more trouble for her? She reminds me of Renee Lewis, and that case still bothers me. I'll need ideas before I see her tonight. I've got to ask about the shooting today and then double the stress on her by asking about her own situation. That's not exactly the way to help a lady end a traumatic day. My job is colliding with how I'd handle the situation if I were off duty—and I don't want to be making her situation worse just to do my job. There's got to be some options.

She carried herself well; under stress she had pushed past the shock to make decisions and move fast—that spoke of a lot of internal strength. He remembered faces easily because it went with his job, and he already knew her face was going to be lingering in his mind for a long time to come.

Maybe it was her age or the fact she was on a course of action that meant trouble was around, but she'd already clicked as someone to worry about. It was why he'd long ago chosen to be a cop: to do some good when it needed to be done. He'd have to figure something out in the next couple hours.

He pulled into the mall. Paul Riker waved him over to where the press had assembled. Luke pocketed his car keys and made his way toward the department's press spokesman. The reporters' shouted questions arrived as the microphones on long booms did, and Luke knew his face was going live across television sets throughout the city. This trouble he would gladly avoid if possible. "Just a moment, people. Riker and I talk privately first."

He walked through the crowd, and they parted out of habit. He'd been around this job too long; he recognized nearly every face in the crowd. A few were vultures out to exploit the story for the local and national tabloids, but most were solid reporters wanting to be first with the news. Luke walked with Riker away from the podium, saw Connor coming toward them, and he changed course, taking Riker with him to meet up with his detective.

Connor offered a folder. "We've got a decent photo on the shooter, and we've confirmed he did not return to his residence. I vote we put it out on the air now."

"Riker?" Luke looked at the photo, memorizing the guy he was after.

"Yes, let me broadcast it. We're set up to absorb the call volume. And for what it's worth it may keep the press busy enough to help us suppress the witness information with a cover story—we've got security video now and can use it as the way we made the ID."

Luke appreciated the suggestion, for while keeping Kelly's name out of the paper wasn't a concern, keeping her photo from being published was. He would prefer another hour of just officers searching for the shooter, but his name would be out on the rumor mill already as reporters talked with friends of the victims and learned Paula had a restraining order against the man. "Stress the do-not-approach warning. I don't want another civilian crossing paths with him."

Riker nodded and accepted the folder. He took it with him to the podium.

Luke tucked Kelly Brown back into the corner of his thoughts and turned his attention to the manhunt before him. One problem at a time. For now she was safe.

Chapter Two

Luke knocked on the hotel door for room 202, aware the time was uncomfortably late. He'd been at the office at 6 a.m. before a day in court, and the shooting and manhunt had layered adrenaline in on top of already long hours; this day needed to end sometime soon. He knocked again. He suspected the hotel-room location on the second floor next to the stairwell was no accident. "Kelly, it's Officer Granger."

She opened the door a few inches, her foot braced behind it. "You're the deputy chief of police. What are you doing babysitting a witness?"

Over her shoulder he saw the television on and muted. It was a reasonable question, but he could do without the combative tone. "Making a choice."

She looked coiled up to him, tension having tightened the lines around her face, and doubts clouded her eyes. She looked at him as if debating the value of that answer, then opened the door and stepped back. "I'm sorry; I just didn't need the surprise of seeing you on TV with reporters shoving microphones in your direction. Anonymous you are not."

It was the first time he'd ever had a lady complain about that fact; he let himself smile at the charge. And because he understood the reason and knew it wasn't personal, he chose to overlook the raw mood she was in. "I wasn't followed here, and the night shift downstairs doesn't look old enough to care about the news," he reassured. "I brought salad, breadsticks, and lasagna. It will beat whatever room service offered."

Her gaze shifted to the sack. "It does." He saw her begin to relax, her weight shifting on her sock feet and the tension in her face fading toward deep tiredness. She offered a smile. "What would you like to drink? Vending is at the end of the hall."

"Something diet and caffeine free."

She nodded and left the room. He watched her walk away, wondering briefly just how deep that fatigue he could see went. She didn't reach a hand out to run along the wall for balance, and at its worst she probably would have. They both needed this day to be over.

He turned his attention back to the hotel room. A small, round table and chairs overlooked the parking lot; he walked over to the table and set down the briefcase and sack he carried. He moved aside the jacket tossed over a chair and set it down on the nearest of the two beds. She'd folded a newspaper back together into a rough neatness, and he moved it from the table as well.

The aspirin bottle on the nightstand looked new, the broken seal resting beside the alarm clock. She'd been for a walk to one of the area stores, he suspected; he'd seen a couple down the block from the hotel. He was surprised to see a thriller resting facedown on the bed—reading to pass the time didn't surprise him, but the subject matter did.

He began unpacking the sack he had

brought. She came back into the room and set cold sodas on the table, then slid into the chair opposite him. He studied her, trying to get a read on her underlying mood. Brittle was going to take a finesse he didn't naturally have. "It's late, but I didn't figure you would be sleeping much yet."

"Safe guess." She cracked open her soda and took a long drink. "You have an odd profession, standing over dead people, going home to family, playing with your kids, watching the late news, getting up in the morning to a bowl of cereal for breakfast and the newspaper, as if the day part of your life were normal."

He paused. She'd seen violence today; she knew he saw that kind of violence often. He found it oddly touching that she was trying to square it up in her mind—how he handled it. "It's the fact the job is so abnormal that makes the rest of the day reassuringly normal. And in my case, it's two dogs, a cat, a nearby sister, her kids, and a preference for bacon and eggs."

She smiled. "I never outgrew the preference to skip breakfast and catch the extra sleep."

He handed her a plate. "What's your real name?"

She blinked; then her smile softened. "Amanda Griffin. Amy to friends. It's been years since I used it; the name feels stale."

"Thanks."

"You'd run the prints anyway. I was in the army for quite a while, so I'm on file."

The fact she'd just handed him the information shifted around his perspective on her. She filled her plate and he filled his. The army was an unusual career choice—either she was an army brat who grew up around the service or she probably had an older sibling who had entered the army ahead of her. "Did you enjoy the army?"

"Yes. I'm very good at logistics."

He tucked away the direct way she said it and liked it. Confidence wasn't this lady's problem. He nodded to the television and turned the conversation back to the present. "We don't have him yet."

He saw her tension begin to return. "I've been watching the news. It's been quite a thing to see from a distance, the manhunt going on. You'll find him."

"We will." He picked up a breadstick. "I

need you to go through what happened for a formal statement."

"I know. After we eat."

Her attention shifted away into her memories, and he waited until she resumed her dinner. "I'm sorry you had to see it. Not much will take that image away."

"Paula was twenty-two going on sixteen. There should be angels protecting people that innocent from making bad lifetime decisions."

"She married young?"

"Seventeen. He gambled and she didn't know it. The marriage lasted until she was twenty, and it was already a year too long." She shook her head. "Sad all around."

"Are you running from someone in the military days?"

She set down her fork. "Would you let me not answer and not go probing?"

"In forty-eight hours you're going to disappear on me, and I need to know how that decision can be changed."

"Knowing won't change reality. It will just put you personally at risk."

"It's my choice."

"And mine to live with for having told you." She broke a breadstick in two and studied the broken bread, and while it was obvious the mere topic had brought back bad memories, she seemed more reflective than afraid. She set the breadstick pieces on her plate and looked over to meet his gaze. "Let it go for now. Until I've slept on the events of today I'm not going to consider answering questions about my past. You've got enough to ask tonight just on the facts of today."

He studied her, the face pale, the hair slightly messed, but at ease with herself and clear in her words. She was segmenting the problems in her life and coping; he admired that fact even as he wished he knew what was driving her. Whatever her past—and he could make a few pretty clear guesses—it was going to be a lot deeper hurt than what she'd seen today. But trust was a tenuous thing, and for now the answers he sought were going to stay protected. He stabbed a leaf of lettuce with his fork as he nodded. "Fair enough."

"Thanks."

He thought she might push away her plate, for she'd been eating some but toying with the food more, but she picked up her fork and turned her attention back to the meal. She was either hungry under that overwhelming tiredness or wise enough to eat a good meal while she could. He wasn't going to speculate on which it was; he didn't think he'd like the answer.

He talked her into taking seconds on the lasagna and between them they finished the take-out container. "Have a preference for ice cream? I'll stop at the corner deli tomorrow."

She smiled as she tore open one of the chocolate mints that had come with the carryout meal. "I hear a small bribe in that offer. Fudge ripple, cookie dough, chocolate cherry—I'm easy to please. I appreciate this; not many guys would have thought to stop to bring a meal."

"I was hungry and not in the mood to cook once I got home. And while I'm sorry for the occasion, it is nice to have company for a meal for a change." He opened the other mint package and considered what the chocolate would do to his sleep when it finally came. Coffee didn't bother him, but chocolate for some reason tended to keep him awake. A stop at the office was still in his immediate future. He ate the mint.

"Were you able to stop at home at least long enough to walk your dogs?"

He smiled. "Chester and Wilks are fine; they've got a dog door into a fenced backyard to come and go as they please. A burglar wants to try and get past those two, let him try." He motioned to the containers. "Finished?"

She nodded.

He stored away the remaining salad and the plates in the sack and wiped the table while she threw away the trash. He opened his briefcase and retrieved the laptop he used when he was on the road and a pocket cassette recorder.

Amy didn't sit down. "Would you like another drink?"

"Sure."

She left for a minute, returning with two more sodas. She settled back into the seat across from him, the smile no longer near, stiller now.

He watched her, calculating the best way to handle this. "Have you given a police statement before?"

"Yes."

He absorbed that quiet answer and wondered not that it had been done but the number of them she'd probably given. He was more accustomed to seeing nerves during an interview rather than this stillness. "Since it's just a matter of time before some reporter has a copy of this, I'm going to use your name, address, and personal information off your employment application. I'll make the officer or clerk who shares the statement regret it dearly, but I'm not going to assume I can prevent it from happening."

"Matching the application information will help me out, thanks."

He turned on the cassette recorder and noted down date and time and witness information for the record. He'd thought about what he most needed from her, knowing the odds were still strong that this might be the only evidence they had to present to a grand jury if she disappeared on him, and made a decision. "I want you to talk through what you did and saw today from about noon on until I met up with you at your home. I want you to stop there and then tell me everything you can remember about Paula Grant and her ex. Things Paula said, the date you first met him, what you know about the situation between them."

She closed her eyes and let out a deep

breath, then nodded and began. "I took my lunch break today just before 2 p.m., ate at the food court, and then returned to work."

Luke started typing, appreciating her steady pace.

"I rearranged the ring display, helped three new customers who bought earrings, a necklace, and a ring, respectively, and wrote up two repair orders for a longtime customer. Shortly before four Jim asked me to take the day's cash deposit to the bank; the branch office in the mall is near The Limited clothing store. I left the bank about 4:15—the time is on the deposit receipt—and walked back to the jewelry store." She hesitated and reached for her soda. She took a long drink. "I saw him when I came around the candy display out in the center mall aisle." She went on in the same steady voice, and Luke kept with her, not pausing to correct the typos or the punctuation.

It took her more than five minutes to get the narrative out, and when she again paused he clicked off the recorder, rose, and went to get a washcloth from the towel rack. He brought it back cold and wet.

She pressed it against her eyes.

"We can take a break before you finish."

He was leading her back through rough terrain, and he knew the cost it was taking to keep her composure. There was a brutal rawness to remembering blood and death, and that reality was only hours in her past.

She shook her head. "Thanks, but no. Let me get this done. You need the words, and I'm going to be better just getting them out and having it over."

Courage, but maybe a little too brave, he thought as she pushed back the tears and the reaction and didn't let herself grieve. He waited until he thought she'd gotten a few deep breaths and taken at least the first steps back from the roughest memories.

He set a new section in the file, then clicked on the recorder again. "Okay."

"I first met Paula's ex on August ninth. I remember the date because we were taking inventory, and her ex shoved a display being put together and sent rings flying."

Her voice was husky now, but her words were solid and flowing. Luke typed, and as the story unfolded he knew the signs of what had happened today were in the history. He wished someone in his office had put it together before the explosion.

Her words came to an end. He watched,

concerned, as she twisted the cold rag around her hand and then back off, the motion just a place marker for the fact that mentally she was remembering more than what she was saying. She was feeling the events of today now as she spoke of them, really feeling them for the first time, he thought, for her emotions had been too numb for that before. They were friends who had died, and nothing he said could touch that pain.

He shut off the recorder and returned it to his briefcase. He turned back to the start of her narrative and read for content and corrections, giving her time. "Did you notice shoes?"

She blinked back at him for a moment, then nodded. "Black tennis shoes."

Luke printed the document. Her statement ran six pages. He handed it to Amy. "Read it through, note any changes you want to make, and I'll print a revised copy for you to sign."

"Okay." She started to read.

He picked up the soda she had brought him but didn't open it. Her words had stayed steady, but there was a fine tremor in her hands making the pages flutter just a bit. Sleep was going to be hard for her in the weeks to come, her mind having to process the images enough times to wash out the emotions attached to the event.

What gave you the courage to go see, Amy? to make that awful effort to confirm that none of your friends were still alive before you left them there? You're shaking, but you had the courage to stay and check and to know before you bolted. You did something even cops struggle to do.

She set the statement on the table. "It's okay as is. Where do I sign?"

"Initial the corner of all the pages, then sign and date the last page."

She reached for his pen.

He accepted the signed document. "I'll have a copy for you tomorrow."

"Thanks." She rubbed her eyes. "Now what?"

"We get him off the streets. Tomorrow we'll work on how to make your testimony safe for you to give." He initialed her statement, checked his watch, and recorded the time. He looked at her and didn't have a solution to offer that could make things better for her tonight. She would be alone with the memories of this day and her own past that she hadn't shared yet, and that worried him in a quiet way, how very alone she was in this. "Sleep with the television on tonight and don't set the alarm." He repacked his briefcase.

"I'll take that advice and also leave the Do Not Disturb sign on the door so housekeeping doesn't come by." She rose. "Thanks for dinner."

"I wish it had been under different circumstances." He hesitated but let what he wanted to say be left unsaid. "I'll see you tomorrow, Amy."

He wondered if she thought of that as a promise or a threat, knowing how much had not been said tonight, but she merely nodded. She followed him to the door. He waited in the hall until he heard both locks click in place.

Amanda Griffin: former army and now in her forties. That timing probably put her in at least one war. One very bad relationship in her past. He wouldn't guess which experience she found worse. Luke dug his car keys out of his pocket. He wasn't going to let the signs of another coming tragedy slip past him. He wasn't even sure who would be dead in the encounter: Amanda or the guy she ran from. The lady was civilian and yet not, running scared but with purpose. She might be ducking the collision, but when it came—and it eventually would—

Luke unlocked his car. Amanda Griffin struck him as a survivor. Tomorrow he'd get the details from her or start searching them out on his own. Trouble was here. He was inclined to stand in its way.

Chapter Three

"You're far away this morning."

Luke turned at his sister's touch and accepted the glass of orange juice she offered. "Yes, I suppose I am." Breakfast was a tradition on her birthday since evening meals tended to always be interrupted, but normally he was the one fixing it. The message on his machine last night had suggested he just plan to come over if there was time or they could try for another morning. He should have suggested another morning for all the good he was today.

Susan forked out two more waffles to add to the pile. "I don't mean to pry, but what time did you get in last night?"

"About 3 a.m."

"It was a rough day."

"Yes. I'll tell you about it on a day not your birthday." He rubbed her shoulder and reached around her for the basket of muffins. She was a small woman, his sister, largely sheltered from the job he held and what he saw, but he knew she was equal to the task of absorbing about anything when he did need to talk about one of the rougher days.

"You'll catch the guy?"

"We'll catch the guy." He crossed to the stairs. "Come on down, you two. I can hear the school bus rolling this way."

His nephew appeared first. "It's not for another thirty minutes, Luke."

"It might be early today. Pancakes or waffles?"

"One of each," Jack replied, dumping his backpack by the door and coming to the table by way of the refrigerator.

"Jessica, he's going to take the last of the blueberry syrup. You'd better hurry."

"Don't bother," Jack said. "She's curling her hair; it will be a while."

Luke looked over at Susan. "When did that start?"

"This summer."

He tended to notice details, but he'd missed that one. "Getting everyone seated for this breakfast is not as easy as it used to be. Want more coffee?"

"Please."

He topped off his sister's coffee and then turned the stack of gifts beside her plate to hide the fact he'd flubbed the tape job on his gift. "Where's Tom this morning?"

"South of Australia. He's calling from the boat at noon our time."

"The guy gets seasick; I bet this has been a great trip."

"A ten-million-plus investor, he'll take Dramamine from an IV. One more backer and the lab starts building."

"Has this car been named yet?"

"Hot Lightning, I think."

"I voted for that one," Jack added.

"It breaks every speed limit in the world—Hot Lightning sounds appropriate." Luke pulled out a chair for his sister and, once she was seated, shook out a linen napkin to place in her lap.

"Thank you, Luke."

"Why do you do that every year?" Jack asked.

"Courtesy, young man, you'll learn," his mom replied.

Jessica joined them in a flurry of hair bows and jacket choices.

Luke caught the pile before it slid off her arm. "Go with the red—they make you look intimidating."

"Ignore your uncle. Blue jacket, red bow, and add that scarf you bought last weekend," Susan suggested.

"Okay." Jessica leaned over and kissed her mom. "Happy birthday. One waffle, please." She darted back for the stairs.

Luke moved a waffle to safety on Jessica's plate. "Where's Tom taking you this year when you leave the kids with me?"

"I'm pushing for a tour of the eastern US this time, no flying, just miles of roads and thousands of places to shop."

Luke laughed. "He'll love it." He cut into the stack of pancakes on his plate. The guy might have chosen to focus his talents on building rockets and fast cars, but for Susan he'd occasionally slow down. Luke liked his brother-in-law.

His pager sounded as he ate. Luke offered a smile in apology to his sister and stepped away from the table to answer the summons. His quarry of the day had been spotted east of town. Luke didn't know if he was sad or sorry to be missing the wrapped gifts. He closed his phone. "I've got to go."

"Don't look so annoyed. I have another birthday breakfast next year."

"I know." He hugged his sister and kissed her cheek. "Happy birthday, Sis."

"You too. Jack snuck your present into your car."

"Did he?" His nephew looked entirely too pleased with himself. Luke paused by the boy's chair long enough to wrap him in a headlock. "Thanks, buddy. Study hard today. This weekend we'll go try out those golf clubs again."

"You're on."

Luke tried to break the twin birthday bond with Susan by the fact his birthday was minutes before midnight and hers minutes after, but she always snuck it in on him. She liked to celebrate hers, and he did his best to forget his. "Say hi to Tom for me. I'll be back this evening sometime to put together what he's going to tell you about at noon."

"Luke, you can't leave me in suspense like that for hours," Susan protested with a laugh.

"Sure I can." He hugged the returning Jessica. "Very sharp, young lady. You're still not dating until you're twenty."

"But I—"

"He's right," Susan added. "Come eat."

Luke pulled out his keys. "I'll see you all later." He left the threesome laughing around the breakfast table and headed out, wondering just what Jack had put in his car.

●●●●●●

Shortly after 6 p.m., Luke shifted the items he carried to knock again on the hotel-room door. Amanda Griffin had bailed on him before the forty-eight hours she'd promised? She wouldn't be down at the hotel pool, where she could be noticed, and if she had stepped away from the room to go to the vending machine she'd have been back by now. "Amy, it's Officer Granger. Please come to the door."

While he waited he slid another one of the cookies from the tin he held. His sister never said she understood his preference to keep the birthday low-key, but her gifts always conveyed it. The cookies had been home-made and carefully stacked, the book underneath the tin one of the mysteries he favored. She knew him very well indeed. He reached to knock a third time. The door opened under his raised hand. The sight of Amy paused him midmotion; her blue eyes were half open, the lashes framing them heavy with sleep. "I woke you up."

She gave a nod as she stifled a yawn with the back of her hand. "Yes, sorry. I didn't sleep well last night." She stepped back to let him into the room. "I just saw the news scroll by; you arrested him."

"The next town over did: shortly after 1 p.m. at his cousin's home." She was slow coming out of the sleep, her eyes a bit puffy and her attention not very focused, but it was rather nice to see the lack of the tension he had feared. "I brought pizza this time with cookies and ice cream for dessert. Although maybe in the circumstances I should have brought breakfast."

She laughed. It was the first time he'd heard the sound, and he rather liked it. "I love it all and I'm starved. What kind of pizza?"

He pushed the room door shut with his foot, wondering what she'd think if he mentioned she looked very young at the moment and he felt very old. Her feet were bare, and the faded blue sweatshirt she wore was from a college in Texas. "Half with everything, half cheese and sausage."

"Both work for me." She disappeared into the bathroom. He carried the items he held over to the table. She reappeared with a hairbrush, tugging out sleep knots in her long hair.

"This won't go to trial, Amy; he'll plead out to avoid the death penalty. When I left he was already talking with the district attorney."

She lowered the brush and tossed it aside with a sigh. "I'm not sure I like that outcome for what he did, but I guess I can understand it. And that kind of news you could have sent someone else to tell me."

He watched her, assessing her mood, and felt relieved enough to let himself smile a bit: not coiled so tight today, finding her footing, and beginning to regret her promise that he could have forty-eight hours; he should have expected that. "This case might be sorting itself out, but we've still got an unfinished conversation to have." At the end of this particular day he wasn't looking forward to it, but it was going to be had. There were times when the job had to dictate when he could ease back and when he couldn't, and this was one of those collisions.

She joined him at the table and accepted the plate he handed her. She chose two pieces of pizza from opposite sides of the box and settled back in her chair to eat. "Why do you have to dig? Why do you have to know?"

"Because you're running."

She shrugged, her slim shoulders making the gesture an eloquent answer. "Running isn't so bad. I had three good years here before chance put me in the spotlight. Maybe the next place I'll get five or more. That's a better alternative than another cop being dead. Your sister isn't going to appreciate that need of yours to know when she's burying you."

She was pushing him away incredibly hard. That resistance told Luke a lot about her past in itself. "Either talk to me or I can run your prints to confirm your name and do my own looking." He wanted her to trust him, but that wasn't in the cards. She'd already taken too many hits in life that he knew about to easily trust. He'd settle for a neutral interview. "I'm not asking just to drag up grief for you. You're in my town, running from a guy that scares the daylights out of you, and I care about the job and badge enough to do what I think needs done."

She pushed away her plate. "It's not that simple, Luke."

"Nothing ever is."

She rubbed her face and finally nodded. "Fine. Ask your questions. I'll give you the abbreviated version of the answers."

"Who wants you dead?"

"A guy named Richard Wise. He introduces himself with the phrase 'Call me Rich, not Wise' and laughs as he says it."

"Why does he want you dead?"

"I have his money. He wants it back."

The simplicity of it was startling. Luke looked at her and suspected where this was heading. "Go on. You said the guy killed a cop," he reminded her gently.

The jump in her nerves was instant, working the fine muscles around her mouth, around her blue eyes. "Had killed, but yes, he ordered it. The cop got curious, asked questions, and was found beaten to death in his living room forty-eight hours later."

"Why?"

"To have asked the questions he did the cop would have had to meet me. And they wanted to know where I was. So they beat the answer out of him. I was already a state away."

"Where did this happen? When?"

"Detroit, four years ago."

"You sound certain of what happened."

"Certain enough to have bailed out and run for my life again." She reached for her drink and just held it, lost in the thoughts that absorbed her. She shook her head. "I hate talking about this, Luke."

She got up and paced across the room, finally stopping to lean against the dresser, her arms crossed protectively across her chest. "I got out of the army when I was thirty-three. That was mistake one; I should have made it a career. I rented a place in New York from a friend while I looked for a job I might like. That was mistake two. I'd been in town about a month when I met an accountant at a party and liked him. Greg Southerland—rich family, ambitious, loved to laugh. We started dating. That was mistake number three."

It wasn't what he expected, her expression. Not nervous or worried, but sad, heartbreakingly so. "Over time I began to realize he worked at home a lot, that he'd have business meetings at odd hours on short notice. After a while I suspected Greg was doing work for a bookie on the side, but he'd wave me off or have explanations. His family seemed entirely aboveboard, not the kind to have raised a guy who would skirt the law. But he died, I was concerned on the how, and I knew where the books he worked on at home were kept. I took them."

"Greg had only one private client: Richard Wise."

She nodded.

"You didn't turn the books over to the authorities?"

"It wasn't that simple. Everything is in those books: serious-sized bets, bribes, payoffs, fixed cases. Richard Wise would take a bet on anything, or for a price get you out of whatever trouble you were in. Cops are implicated—federal, state, local—whoever Richard Wise needed to manipulate who had a price. Including Greg's father." She looked over at him then, and the cop in him understood the trapped look in her eyes.

"That just made it worse, Luke. Greg was

in deep at the end by his own choice, but somewhere along the way it must have started because his father crossed with Richard Wise." She walked the length of the room again, stopping to shift her jacket back onto the bed where it had half fallen off. She finally turned back to him. "I have been turning the information over to the federal authorities. Very carefully, and only as they are able to use it. I turn that pipeline of information on too fast and someone carrying a badge who's dirty comes back to slap at me. Or Greg's father realizes I'm still alive, and I get squeezed by the one person who could probably influence me to forget what I have."

"You've been doing it a long time."

She nodded. "Long enough. The entries are getting old enough the information has almost run its course. Which is one reason Richard Wise is so desperate to find me. The last step in the process is to seize his money; the accounts have sat out there while the people he's corrupted are slowly brought down."

"That's your hold on his money? The account numbers?"

She bit her lip as she nodded. "It took a

year to realize the only lists of account numbers in existence were in the books I had. Greg had moved most of the money the week before he died. Maybe that was part of their normal security steps to keep the accounts below the radar of authorities. Maybe it wasn't. But without the account numbers and authorization codes the money might as well not exist; it's unreachable. But until Richard's organization is fully rolled up, turning the account numbers in to the authorities is not something I'm willing to do. The numbers pass through the wrong hands and that money is gone without a trace. Too much money sits there, just a breath away from this guy's reach."

Luke understood those risks as well as the reality. "The fact that you are the only source for the account numbers has helped keep you alive."

"Yes. He'd have sent a sniper after me a long time ago if he didn't need what I alone have. This plan has worked for years and it's entering the endgame. We wait until all the people are identified; then the money is swept in. The books come into a trial—authenticated, original, and many entries in Richard's own handwriting—and there won't be a place left for him or the people he's corrupted over the years."

The location of the books and account numbers was something Luke was not ready to ask. "I need to walk for a while and think." He wanted to promise her it would be okay, that there would be answers for this, but he wasn't one to make hollow promises. Bad cops meant trouble at a level he hadn't even considered. He picked up his jacket. "Catch some of the news; finish dinner. I'll be back in half an hour. You're not going to be moving on me?"

"I'll be here."

"Good enough." He tugged the hotel-room door closed behind him and took the stairs down. He pulled out his gloves. The air was cool tonight, and it would rain again before morning, he thought. He walked east.

He turned her story over in his mind. He'd been a cop a long time. Truth or fiction? Every story had that kind of basic check to it. His gut said truth. Even the part with her not suspecting the guy she was dating was dirty. Innocence made even normally smart people blind. She hadn't thought Greg could be breaking the law, so she didn't see all the pieces until after it was over.

God, she's in a lot tighter place than I'd imagined. A man after money he sees as stolen from him, with no conscience for what actions he'll take to recover it—I don't see the defuse point. Most situations have one, but this has spiraled on for so many years that even putting Richard Wise behind bars isn't going to address the threat she has run from for so long. He'll want her dead. Behind bars or not, he'll want his justice. And there is nothing that can be done to keep an evil man from plotting evil.

There were times being a cop meant knowing how limited the law and justice could be. Justice was possible, but safety for Amy—she'd been right to run. If there were enough bad cops under the influence of Richard Wise, then Amy had been right to assume she was more safe long term out on her own than under the protection of the authorities. At least she was turning in the evidence she had, helping good cops clear away the turncoats lurking in their midst, helping end the corruption Richard Wise had created.

Amy hadn't told him everything. He'd

been a cop too long not to accept that and factor it into his thinking. She'd touched on the important points; he was reasonably sure the core of her story was in front of him, but the rest of the story she hadn't said would be the worst part. It was human nature to tell the hard and painful stuff in order to try and create a barrier to keep from touching the deeper agonies. He accepted that reality because he had to and wondered who, if anyone, she'd ever talked to about the fullness of what had happened.

Fixing the problem wasn't a reasonable expectation given what he'd heard; so what did he do with what she had told him? Luke walked for blocks, lost in his thoughts, and then retraced his steps.

Amy opened the hotel-room door for him when he knocked, and then she walked back across the room to where she was repacking her suitcase.

Luke closed the door and leaned against it, watching her. "Why haven't you taken the money and disappeared with it yourself?"

She stopped to look over at him. "I see why you made deputy chief. You don't miss much."

"How much is there?"

"Just over twenty million."

She folded a top and added it to the case. "I've thought about it. I've also thought about giving the money back to Richard to buy my freedom, but he'd just kill me for having taken the books in the first place. I've thought about tapping the cash so I could better disappear, changing my name again and again, disappearing into Europe somewhere with the best security money could buy." She shrugged. "It's blood money. Call it an oversensitive conscience or the fact I believe in heaven and hell. I take the cash, and I'm on a moral path I could probably never come back from—the money is too seductive."

She opened a drawer in the dresser. "There's the practical reality too. I'm a dollar sign for whoever finds me first, and with all the money or just part of it, I'd always be hunted as a means to the cash. I trusted a guy that turned out to be the bookkeeper for a criminal—my sense of self-protection hasn't been very good in the past. I just want to be free again to start over. I've paid for my mistake for half a decade; it's long enough. Another year and the cops will safely have everything I do. Freedom is worth more than any amount of money when it's the one thing you don't have."

"Why did you tell me? You could have stopped anywhere along the way with less information or wrong information—enough to put me on a wrong track while you left town."

"I made a choice." She gave him a weary smile as she echoed his words of yesterday back to him. "I could have been dead in that shooting yesterday. If I die, those books, the account numbers, are gone for good. There are no fail-safes, no people who know bits and pieces, no lawyer holding an envelope with instructions on it for if I die. Over the years, that hasn't bothered me because we were so far from the endgame. A lot of the people bribed in those records have been on the fast track to the top—I never thought they could be brought in. But the end is in sight now, and I'm not so comfortable having no backup plan."

"So I'm your backup plan?"

"If I write that 'if I die' letter, I have to leave it in safe hands and address it to someone. Think about it hard for a couple months, if you want a lawyer holding a letter like that addressed to you. Just the existence of the letter could be life threatening. If they find me I'm under no illusions I will keep my mouth shut. They'll get the location of the books from me. The day my body is found you get a letter, and now the both of you are racing to the same place. I personally wouldn't want to be on the receiving end of such a letter. But I'll ask if you want to be and let you think about it long and hard."

"The premise of it is your being dead— that doesn't sit well."

"I appreciate the vote of support."

She'd been dealing with this on her own for years, and that convinced him more than ever that he was still missing some significant facts. She had to be balancing something else in her decision making to conclude that dealing with this alone was the only answer up to this point. How had the man she dated died? It wasn't such an easy topic to probe. "Why me? Why not make arrangements to send the letter to the cop you've been passing information to?"

"He's had a few years to think about twenty million." She closed her suitcase. "Think about the offer."

"You're already regretting having made it," he replied, knowing it was true.

She looked up in surprise, holding his gaze. "Yes, some. You have a good quiet life here, and I know better than you what it would mean if you got such a letter." She slipped on her jacket. "I'm going to go rent a car, then buy a used one, and come back here for my things. You'll do me the favor of not watching that happen or noting down the details on the car."

He felt like he was losing something—a chance, maybe, to put things right for her. This wasn't the way it should be ending tonight. "We'll say good-bye here," he agreed, not wanting it, but understanding it. His forty-eight hours were closing, and she was moving on.

She stopped in front of him. "Thank you."

"Where are you going next?"

"Does it matter? West probably."

It mattered terribly, but he couldn't find the words to explain that. "You've got a new ID, a way to safely settle again?"

"It's available with a call. I'll make that contact from a state or two away from here."

"If I need you for any reason, I'm running an ad for Ann Walsh in the *New York Times* Sunday classifieds. You'll get in touch."

"I can do that." She rested her hand flat on his chest. "It's important, Luke, the job you do. But this town needs you more than I do. Don't be a hero just because you can be."

"I'm an old cop for a reason, Amy. I know my limits and how to evaluate a risk." She would be worth all those risks, if she'd trust him enough to let him help. But he knew he wouldn't be convincing her to stay, and he didn't try to fight a battle he knew he had already lost.

She stepped back with a nod. "Then I won't worry about you."

"Write that letter. And if you ever need my help or you just want to talk—" he scrawled two private numbers on his business card— "call me."

She didn't say yes; she didn't say no, but she did put his card into her pocket. "Thanks, Luke." She picked up the newspaper. "Give me five minutes before you leave, please."

He nodded and she was gone.

Three Years Later

Chapter Four

"Chief."

Luke Granger looked up from his call sheet to see Connor Black, one of his lead detectives in homicide, standing in the doorway to his office. Three years as the chief of police hadn't made the days different: they still started with the officers who worked the cases no one wanted in their days. "Come on in, Connor. How's the vacation going?"

"Too short, but I felt the need to stop in and see the state of my in-box. I got your message."

Luke smiled. "One of the problems with being too curious about what is waiting for you on your return. Marsh isn't due back for another couple days yet?"

"Monday, he said. He was taking his girlfriend skiing."

"Then I'll let you have first pass at this." Luke searched his desk and handed over a thick file. "Résumés, to find us a replacement for St. James. I want your top five prospects and one recommendation after you do the interviews. If you don't see a fit in that group, ask personnel to throw a larger net for the résumés."

"It seems a shame to replace the best homicide cop we've got, personal skills notwithstanding."

"I'm still working to get Caroline to reverse the retirement decision, but I doubt she'll agree to return to homicide even if I can talk her into coming back. The best I can probably hope for is to get her to take major cases."

"That's not a bad second, and she always did like a challenge."

"Does Marsh have any pull with her? I know they've been close over the years."

"He's tried, Chief, and I've even had a run at her in the last month, but the shooting shook her more than she's saying. I don't think she's held, much less fired, her weapon since then."

"Having cause to put two bullets into a cop does that." Luke wasn't going to let himself dwell on the memory. He'd had a beat cop commit suicide by shooting at one of his best officers, then turn to shoot at civilians so that Caroline had had no choice but to return fire and kill him. It rattled a department and it rattled the cop involved, enough to mess with her head and her confidence. The fact it had come just after she'd solved one of the worst murder cases they'd had to deal with since the Bressman's Jewelry store deaths hadn't helped matters.

Connor held up the file. "A couple weeks okay on this?"

"Yes. And get out of the office before they tag you for lead on a new case; it's Thursday and you've still got till Monday on that vacation."

"That order I can take, Boss." Connor paused in the doorway. "There's a rumor around that someone in this town is about to become very wealthy."

"Where did you hear it from?"

"A secretary who knows the secretary for the lawyer drafting the paperwork."

"I heard it from a courier at the courthouse where the paperwork was filed. I'll give it half a day before reporters have the name."

"It's not you?"

"I was about to ask you the same thing," Luke answered, smiling.

"As long as it's someone who owes me a favor or two I'm going to be happy."

"And just as long as it's not my secretary or one of my officers, I'm going to be thrilled for the person." Luke picked up the phone. "Tell Margaret she can quit waving at us both. I'm returning the mayor's call now."

He held up a hand to acknowledge Connor's farewell. The call regarding the budget was going to consume twenty minutes and accomplish nothing, but at least it would keep his secretary happy. There were days he regretted becoming police chief rather than keeping the much more coveted job of deputy chief. Between the politics of this office and the constant budget pressure, the fun of the job was wearing thin. The department had a hundred thirty-two officers and needed a hundred sixty to do the job adequately, and the struggle for resources never ended. After lunch he was getting out of this office and not returning; patrolling with two of his officers would at least shake his headache even if it would leave the officers he chose to ride with nervous.

After the mayor's call, Luke walked down to talk with his deputy chief, and then he took a long walk back through dispatch and the beat officers' bull pen to make sure he knew what was happening down in the ranks. But the budget couldn't be avoided. He was back at his desk by nine-thirty to proof the copy Margaret had pieced together from his notes written the day before.

Alerted by his secretary to the fact his 10 a.m. appointment was on his way up, Luke rose from his desk chair as his guest arrived. "Daniel, come in. Margaret said you were stopping by."

Luke pulled on his suit jacket, feeling like the meeting warranted the formality if only to show respect for a man in mourning, and walked around the desk to shake hands and take a seat on the same side of the desk as his friend.

Daniel looked tired, that was Luke's first impression, and as impeccably dressed as ever—the business suit conservative, the tie blue silk, and the white shirt crisp to the open collar and tight cuffs. The town paper still chose Daniel as their most eligible bachelor in Brentwood each year, selecting him for more reasons than just the money and political reach that stretched through his family and up to the governor's office. The recent death of Daniel's uncle had been reason enough to bring Daniel's photo back into the newspaper pages again.

"What can I do for you today?" Luke asked.

"My uncle, God rest his soul, left two daughters that he's just acknowledging for the first time in his will."

Luke blinked and then sighed. "I guess I should have seen that coming. I heard someone in town was getting rich, and the only person in the obituaries lately who could cause that kind of stir was your uncle."

"Henry loved his work, poured all his money into the Benton Group, and rarely mentioned his personal life. As Henry's nephew I now find myself in the awkward position of inheriting most of his fortune along with management responsibilities for the Benton Group and being joined by two daughters who never knew they had a wealthy father. I would have said he had been faithful to his wife, but the daughters are in their thirties. It's either going to go down smoothly or be a royal mess."

The implications of that kind of news into the social circuit of the town would prompt lots of second-guessing about the man they had honored and applauded over the years, hoping to get his contributions to their boards and charities. And the arrival of two new ladies in classic Cinderella fashion to the world of the well-off would cause its own stir. Luke thought of the rumors already flying around, and he didn't envy the two daughters. "You're just finding out about their existence?"

"Henry clued me in about a month ago when it became apparent he wasn't going to be leaving the hospital after his fifth heart attack. He apparently had an agreement with the aunt who was raising the girls that he'd not approach them until after the aunt died, and by the time that happened Henry was dealing with the third of his five heart attacks. So he left it simply a matter for his will and for me to deal with."

"Nice of him."

"Thank you. I thought I was the only one

who noticed the unpleasantness of that abdication of responsibility."

Luke could see the strain the last weeks had taken on his friend; honor defined him, and his uncle's conduct would have been bitter news to swallow. Daniel had always cared deeply about what was right; it was something Luke admired about him. The fact Henry had been a Christian and yet done this—Luke grieved that fact, knowing it would make his future conversations with Daniel about God that much more difficult. "Have you met them, your new cousins?" he asked quietly, not sure how to best help his friend right now.

"Henry had a private investigator keeping track of them. The older sister, Marie, owns a gallery here in town, and the younger one, Tracey, attends college at the next town over, finishing work on a second master's degree. I'll admit to having checked them out at a distance shortly after I got the file— curiosity got the better of me—but I haven't introduced myself as their cousin yet. Henry didn't want to face them, and part of me understood that; so I let the man die in peace."

"Where does it leave you now?"

"Hoping for a favor from a friend. I've got

two ladies to tell today that their lives are forever going to be different, and if you've heard the rumor, the press will have the details soon. There will have to be a press conference tomorrow to deal with the announcement if only to try and deflect some of the reporters who will be on their doorsteps. And I've reason to believe the younger sister is dating one of your officers."

"Oh?"

"Marsh. A good man when you need a shooter at your side, not so easy to figure out off the job: at least that's the private investigator's take on the man."

"A pretty accurate assessment, I'd say. Who was Henry using as his investigator?"

"Sam Chapel, of the Chapel Detective Agency."

Luke was relieved at the name. "I know him well; he's one of the best." Sam hadn't been able to find Amy either, but he'd at least been able to track her to Colorado before the trail entirely disappeared. There had never been a letter or further contact from her, and Luke had eventually accepted the fact she'd changed her mind. It was that or worry trouble had found her, and he preferred the easier answer of her choosing to continue going it alone. "You can be sure the leak isn't coming from Chapel's folks."

Daniel waved it away. "I never expected the news to last more than a day or two once the will began to work through the legal process. There is only so much the lawyers' office handling my uncle's estate would be able to keep quiet. But I'd hoped for another twenty-four hours before the press arrived in the picture."

"Caleb Marsh works homicide. I'd trust the man with my life; and he'll take less grief than most from the reporters, so the younger sister's got a good guy in her life when this hits. And the money isn't likely to mess with his head like it would some."

"That's good to know. I meet with the older sister in an hour. What am I supposed to tell her? 'Your father didn't mention your name until he knew he was about dead'? That's going to go over well."

"Start with welcome to the family and from there take it pretty slow. Just how wealthy are they about to become?"

Daniel gave a small smile. "Thirty million apiece, give or take a bit. Let's hope it smoothes a few headaches for them."

"How much did Henry leave you?"

"Four times that."

"Stressful day, Daniel."

Daniel sighed. "Thank you again. Everyone else has assumed the cash is something I would be thrilled to receive. Not that I'm not going to enjoy it and heading the Benton Group, but it is not all good changes."

"You were content with life when you were talking me out of investing that first ten thousand with you back in our college days. You'll see that kind of money as a burden to manage properly. But you'll do some good with it, which is more than your uncle did in the years he accumulated it."

"I hope to. My uncle did like to hold on to his wealth."

"I believe Marsh is skiing with his girlfriend this weekend and they are due back in town late Sunday, so you may have caught a break regarding the younger sister. I'll get that confirmed for you before you meet the older sister."

"I'd appreciate it. Marsh's partner is still Connor Black? I know Connor pretty well."

"Yes. They're close off work as well as on, so if you need to get word to Marsh, don't hesitate to give Connor a call. He's on vacation at the moment and around this weekend."

"I'll do that, if only because there needs to be as many people helping smooth this out as I can find."

"Come over for dinner tonight, Daniel. I'm putting steaks on the grill, and my sister is bringing her famous chocolate cake. You can tell me about how it went today, and we'll talk about how I or this office can help you out. I can already envision a few unpleasant people crawling out of the woodwork at the news of that kind of money."

"Sam Chapel is bringing in Silver Security, Inc. to help out with the press conference, so I'm starting to gear up for those realities. And I'll gladly accept the dinner invitation." He rose from the chair. "Tell Margaret thanks for fitting me in on short notice."

Luke rose too. "I appreciate the heads-up on what is coming."

●●●●●●

Daniel watched the older sister circle his small office, looking at the artwork on the walls, and knew a profound relief that his first impressions of Marie were unqualifiedly positive. He liked her.

"Did you choose this one too?" She turned from the painting to look at him.

He liked her smile. It lit up her face and touched her brown eyes, and there were an appreciation in her words and a warmth that was more personal than formal. She'd swept her hair up and caught its long blonde tresses in an elegant rainbow bow. She was neither tall nor short, her moderate heels chosen for comfort, and the elegance of her deep blue dress suggested that her love of color and style was part of her personality. He leaned back against the front of his desk, relaxed and in no hurry to move her away from the comfort zone of art that was at least a passion they shared.

He indulged her with a study of the painting he had picked up in Texas years before and thought about the gallery owner he'd haggled with for a good half hour before winning the tussle on price and wished he'd had reason to shop Marie's gallery before this day arrived. "I did, and it cost me almost my last farthing at the time." He'd sold some old British coins to make way for the painting into his private portfolio and hadn't regretted the change.

"You've got very good tastes, Mr. Goodman."

"And occasionally the money to indulge them." He smiled at her. "If I'm buying that Denart in your display window you can at least make it Daniel."

"I'm not sure I'm selling. It's not priced yet for a reason."

His smile widened. "Yeah, I like that about you too. You know a very good painting when you have one."

He waved his assistant in and took the note she carried. "Thanks, Virginia." He scanned it and folded it over to slip into his pocket. "I said lunch and I meant it. Would you join me? We have some other business to discuss, and I've found a nice meal a better way to talk than sitting around a desk."

"I'd enjoy that."

She was being patient with the reason for this requested meeting, but it couldn't be delayed any longer. He wanted a few things for them both—privacy, a place to walk, and time. It was the time that was running out on him. "Then let me escort you. This place has spacious grounds to walk, and we turned one of the walk paths to the next building into a year-round covered retreat and hot-house for roses with several niches set in for tables and private conversations. Consider it one of the perks of having had an archi-tect in the family as my aunt."

"Linda worked here too?"

Marie knew something of his family; good prep work before a meeting with a prospec-tive buyer or something more than that? Daniel chose not to ask just yet. "One of the firms on the first floor bears her name."

"I haven't said yet that I was sorry to hear about your uncle; I was, Daniel. Henry was a nice man."

"You met him?"

"A few times. When his wife was alive he liked to stop in and shop for an anniversary gift." She gave a small smile. "He'd want to discuss the purchase price over coffee and invariably find the number he had in mind to begin with."

"I didn't know that, although the choice of paintings fit what Linda would have loved. Linda passed away three years ago, Henry last week, and it's going to be a different place here without them both around."

"You'll miss them."

"Yes." There was also relief that some of what he would need to tell her would not be so much about strangers as about human failings.

He led her down the wide, curved staircase and back through the building that was an office building and yet in places carried the feel of a warm museum display gallery. His aunt had chosen well how to soften the marble and wide hallways and business-suite entrances with nooks of casual seating and lighting and carefully arranged art. A constantly changing display of fresh flowers from the hothouse added to the elegance.

Daniel led the way out into the covered walk path. The catered meal was being set up on a linen-covered table past a terraced display of baby roses cascading down in blankets of pink, red, and white. Daniel held a chair for Marie.

"It's restful here, Daniel. And quite lovely."

"I admit I often retreat down here to read the morning paper."

"I can understand why."

The caterers departed.

He'd left the meal simple, splitting the difference between the sandwich of an infor-

mal lunch and the elegance of a formal dinner plate, to request salads, oven-hot
bread, and lots of Texas grilling. "You'll find
the beef strips have a touch of spice and
the chicken strips less so."

"It all looks delicious."

Daniel lifted back the towel from the basket of hot rolls and offered her one.

Marie settled in to enjoy the meal. They
talked of inconsequential things for a while
and then Marie smiled. "The Denart was a
pretty nice opening diversion. Would it be
easier if I just asked why you really called?"

"Why do you think I did?"

"Your uncle recently passed away; it
might have been expected, but it's still a
substantial impact for you. There's your uncle and aunt's home to deal with and this
business. Since paintings are the one thing
I deal with, I'll assume you're making decisions about the estate."

Daniel nodded. "Could you handle placing a few paintings if I did decide to let go of
some my uncle owned?"

"You'd be better off taxwise placing them
with a charity or a museum. The upper end
of the art market is soft right now."

He chuckled. "Marie, that was spoken

like a wise dealer. Set expectations low and never oversell what is possible."

"Your uncle owns some magnificent works; I don't have to see them to know that. He was a man who did his homework before he made a purchase. But placing even three or four of those in the next year isn't something to be done in this state if you want the best price they can bring. I'll be glad to recommend a dealer in New York who can do better for you than I can."

"We'll discuss it. I have a feeling my uncle landed more often at your number than his own."

She offered a small smile. "Maybe that too."

"Did you know your father?"

She blinked at the question asked so out of the blue, but she finished the beef strip she was tasting and then shook her head. "No. My mother died when I was six, an aunt raised us, and I never knew my father."

"Ever know his name?"

"No. I never asked."

He wondered at that and the hurt it meant lived inside. The last thing he wanted to do was cause the pain he was about to. He opened his wallet and pulled out a very old black-and-white photo he'd carried for a few weeks now. "This is why I called you."

He offered the photo to Marie. She set down her fork after the first glance and soon pushed back her plate to set the photo down on the table. She didn't say anything for a long time. She was looking at a photo of two people, one of whom would be unmistakable to her. "Henry knew my mother."

"Yes."

She turned over the photo, but there was no date. He knew the lady was sharp, quick to put together details, and she'd made the connection. He saw it in the way her expression subtly closed. And an awful pallor had begun to creep into her face.

"That was taken when she would have been about twenty-seven," he said gently.

"You've got my attention, Daniel. There's more."

He hesitated and then removed the envelope from his inside suit pocket. "Would you recognize your mother's handwriting?"

She reached for the letter as if she'd aged a few dozen years.

It was the shortest and tamest of the letters he'd discovered in the bank box, written in the good times between Henry and her mom, when he'd arranged to join her for the weekend about a year after Marie was born. The affair had lasted at least six years from what Daniel had been able to piece together.

He watched Marie absorb a hurt so deep it was killing her and tuck it away deep. The pallor had been joined by a hard set to her jaw, and she wasn't going to let tears come; they were threatening, but staying forced away.

"You'll have already done more than just speculate that I'm Henry's daughter."

"There were paternity tests run at the lawyers' insistence years ago. Marie, Henry names you and Tracey in his will."

"Mandy?" she whispered.

There were three sisters, and Henry's will named only two. "No. I'm so sorry, Marie." He'd just ripped her family in two. The oldest sister had a different father. The detective's report said she had passed away years before, and part of Daniel was relieved at that, to not have to tell a third sister that she was, in reality, only a half sister to Marie and Tracey. The fact their mother had never been married suggested both men in her life during the decade the three girls had been born might have already been married, but it was not something he wanted to speculate on.

Marie shoved back her chair and walked away.

Daniel watched her, understanding some of the turmoil she was in.

He rose as she eventually returned and knew she wouldn't be able to face more of a meal right now. And while the coffee might help, it would be simply patching over the awkward moment.

"Can we walk the grounds? I think . . . I need to walk."

"Then let's walk." He settled a hand on her arm and guided her down to one of the exits tucked away, which led out to the landscaped grounds.

"This makes me what, your cousin?"

He pushed his hands into his pockets as he nodded. "Yes. I'd say welcome to the family, but I know it doesn't feel like such good news right now."

"Not Mandy." Marie was still focused on the heart of the problem for her. "A six-year-or-more affair with your uncle, and my mom has someone else in her life before that?"

"I don't know, Marie. My uncle rarely

talked about his personal life, my aunt never hinted at past marriage troubles, and while I have information I've gleaned from a few saved letters and photos, it's not much for answers. That kind of time—for what it's worth it suggests they really did care a lot about each other."

"Mom died shortly after Tracey was born. I have memories of someone who was happy, who laughed a lot, who liked to dress up, and who loved elegance. Not much to rest a lifetime of memories on. And she was involved with a married man. Didn't your aunt know? suspect?"

"I honestly don't think so. She wasn't a wallflower, passive, or likely to stay in a marriage where her husband strayed. Even for those times and the turmoil of a divorce, she would have left him."

Marie bit her lip. "My aunt knew."

"Yes." Daniel hated this, being the one who had to break the news. "It appears Henry had an arrangement with your aunt and had helped her financially in the past. Henry mentions you and Tracey in his will. He did have a heartfelt desire to recognize his responsibility and name you and Tracey as his daughters; I know he was waiting to do that somewhat out of respect for your aunt. And about the will—there's money involved."

She dismissed the words with a shake of her head, not ready to deal with the mention of money yet. She wiped at tears as she walked in silence for long minutes.

"I'm sorry, Daniel. This has to be particularly cruel to you."

He was surprised at the direction she'd gone with her thoughts. "The one thing I know about family is that they tend to surprise you. And I can't say I mind the idea of having cousins. Christmas was going to just be me this year and pretty lonely."

"You're not married?" She stopped walking. "I'm sorry. I know so very little about you, or Henry, when it comes right down to it."

She didn't say Father and he didn't expect her ever to; Henry would do. "I'm single, a year older than you, and about the only family you'll have to absorb now that Henry has passed away. There may be a distant third cousin or two, but I'm it for close family." He smiled. "Why don't we walk awhile and you can listen and kind of mull it around while I give you a sketch of this side of the family history."

"That would help, Daniel."

"My aunt and uncle married in 1959 while my aunt was finishing her architecture degree and Henry was working his way up to be vice president of a local bank. Henry left to start the Benton Group in '67. I'd call Henry a venture capitalist; he would leverage other people's assets and his own to fund projects around the state where he could potentially turn a healthy profit. Henry had one sister—my mother. She taught at the local high school, and my dad built up a successful real-estate business here in town. My parents died in a car accident about a year before I went to work for Henry. Over the last five years, Henry had been slowly handing more and more responsibility for the business over to me as his health failed."

"Thank you."

"Are you seeing someone now, Marie? Someone who can help you with this?"

"No. I've had other priorities the last few years." She settled her hands into her jacket pockets. "I admit I'm not feeling much yet.

How much money? I think I'm ready for that shock now."

"A little over thirty million to you; just shy of thirty million to Tracey."

She blanched. "He was that wealthy?"

"Yes."

"What am I supposed to do with that kind of money? Thirty thousand I can use, but thirty million—it doesn't register."

"You can afford to keep the Denart if you'd like to."

She laughed, a bit broken, but alive again for a moment. "Thanks, I needed that perspective."

"Let's get some coffee. I'm afraid there's still a lot we've got to discuss today."

"Yes, the coffee would be good now." She walked back with him in silence, and he didn't interrupt her thoughts. She sighed. "The press know about this?"

"They're going to soon. How do you want to tell Tracey?"

"She won't be as shocked as I was; Tracey is the kind of person who can flow with where life goes. She's skiing with her boyfriend for a long weekend."

"We could fly out to meet them tonight for a late dinner."

Marie shook her head. "Let her stay skiing; they're planning to come back Sunday
night. Maybe by then the worst of the press
can be pushed off and I can get past the not
knowing what questions to ask. I'll talk with
her by phone and kind of ease into the news
of what's coming."

"I'm going to enjoy getting to know her."

"Are you wanting us to be family, Daniel?
We can be fine being holiday relations, seeing each other a couple times a year. You've
got your own life to lead, and we just got
dropped in your lap."

"I'd like us to be family, Marie, in the way
the best of family can be. I never had sisters, and I'll gladly take two cousins and enjoy the time getting to know you both." He
smiled. "It helps that I decided I already like
you."

"Same here," she replied with an answering smile, and he was relieved to see it.

He held open the door for her. "Let's talk
about the press, security, and how to handle all the friends that are about to show up
at your doorstep. Then you can have a couple hours of peace to adjust to this before
we plan tomorrow's news conference." He
laughed at her expression. "Giving back the

money is not an option. You'll get through this fine. I promise you that."

"And to think I thought just this morning that life was finally so peaceful. It's not going to be that anymore, is it?"

"Not for a while," he agreed, understanding the turmoil the change itself was going to cause. "You'll adapt, because it's necessary, because it is what is."

"Yes. I am glad I have more family."

"So am I." He was going to like having more family, and it was his nature to want to protect where he could. "Coffee first. Then we'll talk about details. Have you ever met the police chief? He's a friend of mine."

"Am I about to?"

"For dinner tonight, I think; his sister makes a fabulous chocolate cake."

Chapter Five

She was rich.

The thought clashed with years of feeling short of money, and the reality began to take substance as Marie walked the sidewalks back to her gallery. The Denart, a few of the other paintings she loved . . . she could collect for the first time in her life.

The sack she carried brushed her knee. She'd taken Daniel's advice and stopped at her favorite paint-supply store and bought the paints and tools she'd always wished she could afford. Her studio was about to be her safe haven and retreat from this uncertain place she was in. Security upgrades, unlisted phone numbers, background checks on future staff she hired . . . there were serious changes about to arrive in her life.

The gallery would become a visitors' stopping place, browsers hoping to meet her rather than buyers coming to shop, and the need for more staff would be immediate. The studio would be her place to push back against some of those pressures. Tracey would have it easier, Marie thought, for she'd left her job with a medical counseling group to continue her schooling. The changes in lifestyle necessary to accommodate the unfortunate facts coming along with the new wealth could be factored in without a problem.

The sidewalk in front of her gallery had a few people waiting for the crossing light, and against the brick wall a man in a jacket and jeans waited beside the door to her private entrance to her apartment above the gallery. He had seen her approaching and was watching as she walked toward him. A compact man, dark hair, and eyes that studied her with more than casual inspection, his hands holding leather gloves rather than wearing them. Her steps slowed.

"Marie?"

"Yes."

"Lieutenant Connor Black. Daniel sent me."

She flushed. "I'm sorry. I didn't mean to keep you waiting. Please come up."

"It's no problem; Daniel caught me on this side of town. And I hear shopping is good thinking time." He pushed away from the wall as he smiled, and she caught the change just that smile caused as it lightened the intensity of his face and made hazel eyes soften.

She smiled back at him. "Shopping for work: some paint supplies, and I still stood and debated with myself the prices for which kind of brush to buy."

He laughed. "I doubt that will ever change. Daniel asked for a quick answer on what kind of security needs you might have for the next few days, and I had an ulterior motive for agreeing with his request. Your sister Tracey is dating Caleb Marsh—my partner."

She turned from wrestling with her key in the old lock. "Marsh is—" She beamed. "Oh, I adore him. Do you have time for a cup of coffee first? I would say we have a good deal to discuss." She got the door to unlock, and he held it for her.

"I don't know that I've ever thought of Marsh as adorable, but lately the man has looked happy in a way I haven't seen in years; for that reason I already like your sister a great deal."

She led the way up the stairs to the second floor. The hallway turned and made its way across the gallery space below. "Storage rooms and utilities are on the east side, and we combined rooms on this side to create an apartment flat." She unlocked the middle door and turned on the flat lights. "Please come in. Lieutenant—"

"Make it Connor, please."

"Connor. It's been four hours since I first got the news. I admit I'm still in a bit of a fog about it all. You'll have to tell me what you need to see."

"I'd say that fog is understandable."

"I've been trying to figure out what to tell Tracey, but the words aren't there yet." She set down her packages on the dining-room table.

"It's not a small thing, finally putting a name to the father you didn't know," he commented.

She relaxed. Beyond a glance around the flat his attention had stayed on her, and his words were unexpectedly kind. "Thank you. That's been the bigger of the shocks; the money doesn't feel real yet. But I knew Henry in a casual way—he bought paintings from me, I served him coffee, and all the while I was sitting across from my own father."

"Makes you mad?"

"Yeah. Furious. But it's another emotion for after the shock of all this fades. Please make yourself comfortable. Look around. I'll start some coffee."

The apartment was large and open, the kitchen counter one of the few room dividers beyond the door leading into the bedroom wing. She found the canister of coffee and filled the carafe with water, glad to be back in her own kitchen and on her own turf. She set the coffee to percolating and pushed open lids to find something to share. She bit into a shortbread cookie and found it still fresh; she got out a check-patterned blue-and-white plate to set out the rest.

She watched as Connor walked around looking at some of the artwork she had displayed around the living room. She'd hung a set of small oil portraits capturing four generations of one family, and on the far wall a fascinating piece that tried to capture the feeling of an urban city market. She particularly loved the small watercolor beside the clock, the scene capturing water flowing over a cliffside and falling into the sea below. She tried to keep variety in the art around her, to keep her own perspectives ever widening for what was possible to accomplish with paint. Over one of the couches hung her newest addition, a bold study in cubes and lighting, its vivid reds and greens dominating the white-painted brick wall behind the canvas. Connor's expression was difficult to judge. "What do you think?"

"You've got good natural lighting, and the tall ceilings—it makes this space really great. And the paintings—those are pretty nice too."

She smiled at the soft teasing she could hear in his reply. "Tracey calls it our brick warehouse, but she laughs as she says it. She's the one who figured out how to get the stencils to work on brick."

He turned from studying the waterfall. "You've got a nice home. It's elegant, Marie, and at the same time comfortable."

"I think so." She pulled out a tray and when the coffee was done brought it over to the low table set between the two love-seat couches.

He took a seat in the barrel chair and accepted the coffee mug she offered. "Thank you."

"I can almost see the lists being written; you took one look at this place and nearly winced."

Connor smiled. "Actually, this place I love. It's that old door and lock downstairs, the dim hallway, the fire escape coupled with very old windows—there will need to be some work done in the next twenty-four hours to make it safe for you and Tracey to be here."

"I'm not willing to consider moving away from the only home I've known in the last decade just because I inherited some money."

He held up his hand. "Relax; there's nothing here that money can't deal with—new locks, doors, security system, and for the next bit, a security guard on-site for another layer of help. It doesn't do much good to have a security alarm sound trouble and have the cops still be five minutes away from arriving to help, not when the risk is more personal than just a robbery."

"What kind of risk?"

"With serious-sized new wealth? You'd be surprised, Marie." He settled back in his seat with the coffee and studied her a moment before answering. "Any former boyfriends in your life? They'll find reasons to want to pick up the relationship again. Anyone imagine they were once a boyfriend? How about former school friends who have hit a bad patch lately? Former or current business partners? There are dollars attached to your name now and all kinds of past grievances to imagine.

"And that's just the beginning, Marie. Then there are those who want to be near the fame and publicity of it all or be involved in creating it—the autograph hounds, the reporters wanting photos of you 'relaxing at home,' the admirers who would like to get to know you, the other lost children of Henry who will begin appearing wanting to claim a piece of the pie too, the financial advisors who will have sure things for you to invest in. Money brings out all kinds. And while most will be just a nuisance for you, there's going to be a couple that are the reason you should have—and need—some rapid security upgrades around here."

"At least it's no to most of those categories you mentioned." She sighed. "There will be others claiming to be Henry's kids, presenting themselves as also being my relatives?"

"It's inevitable," Connor replied. "Henry names you and Tracey in his will, and you can be sure he knew who his kids really were. So when the letters arrive, the phone calls, just pass them on and don't worry about it. Daniel and the estate have the resources to deal with all those who will come forward."

The thought gave her a pounding headache. "Paternity tests were run for a reason, I guess. Daniel mentioned Henry had already had them done for Tracey and me." She set aside her coffee.

"Any past boyfriends to worry about? an ex? the personal kind of trouble?" he asked again quietly.

She looked over at him and shook her head. Did that make her life boring or simple, that there weren't troubles in the back of her personal closet? She thought it made her sound like what she was: alone.

"Family?"

"Nothing closer than a very distant cousin or two. Tracey and I were all the family that was left."

"Then you'll survive this, Marie. It's those close to you who can do the hurting—the rest of the world will take care of itself. Marsh won't get rattled by the money, so Tracey is in pretty good hands. And once the gallery downstairs is secured, and this apartment, your day-to-day routine won't necessarily have to change much. You'll still have a business to manage if you want that."

"From the sound of it, I'm going to need that slice of normalcy. How long have you and Marsh been partners?"

"Six years. We started working homicide at roughly the same time."

"Marsh doesn't say much about work."

"It's his nature to leave it behind when he leaves the office; I carry it with me longer, I think. It's not enjoyable work, but we're good at it. We're fortunate the city has had fewer and fewer murders each year to deal with. When I started out it was like getting thrown in the deep end."

"This used to be one of those rougher

neighborhoods before the downtown-revitalization money came in. It's one of the reasons I was able to afford this amount of space for the gallery."

"How's the area been recently?"

"Quiet. Not even a robbery in the area in recent years." She refilled her coffee from the carafe she had brought over. "What's the police chief like?"

He looked surprised at the question. "Granger? Good boss, nice guy, a cop's cop. He's on the street more than he's behind the desk. Why?"

"Daniel apparently knows him. He wants me to meet him tonight."

"That's smart. Granger is the kind of guy who can smooth things around for you and Tracey without it being obvious. He does a surprising amount of socializing for a man who doesn't care to be out and about."

"He's networked."

"Like very few others are in this town. I think he takes it personally, the well-being of those who live in his jurisdiction, even the upper crust who tend to end up in trouble by their own choices or lack of attention to their surroundings."

It gave her a picture of the police chief,

and Marie thought she would find it interesting to meet him. Connor admired him: it was there in the tone of his voice. Marie studied the bottom of her coffee mug and wondered how much she could get away with prying. "Are you close to Marsh?"

"We're not brothers, but there are days we might as well be." He smiled. "What do you need to know, Marie?"

She looked up at him briefly and smiled. "Is Marsh serious about Tracey? Is he the type to want to settle down? So many things that would have played out on their own course are going to get badly disrupted right now."

"I don't think you need to worry about Marsh; he's a selective kind of guy. Your sister chose him, rather than the other way around, and that kind of smoothed the age difference between them. Not that Marsh ever tried to put on the brakes to the relationship. From all I've seen they are a very good match together. The money isn't going to change his opinion about your sister, and I don't think it changes your sister all that much either—I expect she'll still finish that degree and then rejoin a medical practice here in town. But this will likely slow down any plans the two of them have been talking about until this situation sorts itself out more, rather than speed up those plans."

"Yes, I think you're right about that." Marie sighed. "I worry about her, being married to a cop one day. He's a good cop, and oddly that makes it harder than if he wasn't so committed to the job."

"I know."

"You're not going to tell me not to worry?"

"Marsh and I carry guns; they don't give them to us because it's a desk job."

"I like you."

He laughed. "Because I'm honest?"

"Because you're sitting there drinking my coffee and answering my questions and being pretty patient with getting handed this task as a favor for a friend."

"Daniel's an old friend—that does make a difference." He got to his feet. "But it's probably best we get on with the task before you need to get changed to go meet Granger. I like my boss, but I do try my best not to keep him waiting."

She got to her feet too.

"Without wanting to invade your privacy, let me glance in bedrooms and the bath, get a count of windows; then I need to see storage rooms and access to the roof, any other ways on and off this floor. Securing the gallery floor will be the easier task."

She nodded. "This way." She wished she remembered how she'd left her bed that morning, how many clothes were still tossed around, if her makeup still sprawled across the bathroom counter. She'd been in a hurry to open the gallery and make the meeting with Daniel, not thinking there would be anyone up here today. Her Saturday had been planned to be her cleanup day.

Connor glanced around her bedroom, smiled at the mannequin she used to keep her coat and hat and longer scarves, and counted windows. He glanced into the second bedroom. "Does Tracey stay here often?"

"She rooms on campus when classes are in session. She'll be here for another ten days or so, and then she planned to head back."

"I'll make sure someone stops by her place on campus next week and gets its security tightened up."

"The third bedroom I use as a studio of sorts."

The room had the best lighting of all the bedrooms for it faced north and had three full windows. The room was pretty bare. She'd spent the night before setting out new canvases to work on, and her sketch board had been cleared. She'd left the furnishings as a simple arrangement of chairs and open display case for her paint supplies.

"You spend a lot of time here."

"More and more as the years pass."

"I like it. Someday I can say I knew you when."

She laughed. "I doubt my paintings will ever become collectible works."

"You never know." He added more notes to his pad.

Connor rewalked the living-room area, and she saw him studying where the heating and cooling came in, counting windows, and checking what doors inside had locks. "Are you particularly attached to any of this woodwork? It really would be good to have better frames on the windows and solid doors put in for the bedroom wing. Someone gets inside or someone's just hassling you, you've still got layers of protection and locks you can throw."

"I'm not going to quibble if you think it needs to be done. Daniel gave me a pretty good reality check even before you rattled off that list of risks."

He looked over, and she understood the gaze even if she didn't want to understand it. "Rattling you is okay, Marie—scaring you is not. Sorry about that." He counted doors. "The more stuff done now tends to mean less trouble later, and the carpenters can do it all as one rush job."

He jotted notes. "I've got what I need in here. Show me the storage rooms and utilities."

She picked up her key ring and led the way.

"You've got valuables stored up here?"

"I built a room downstairs to be secure storage for the paintings; up here is extra framing and packing materials, Christmas decorations, replacement panels to use when we have a showing, that kind of thing."

He walked past the storage shelves to the windows and tried turning the locks. "You open the windows during the summer?"

"Yes. I don't think any of the windows will

still be painted shut, but a few are tighter than others."

He looked at the fire alarm. "Cover your ears." He reached up and hit the self-test button. "You've changed the batteries recently."

"First of every month. Fire is the one thing I'm kind of paranoid about."

"That's not such a bad thing to be. Where's the electrical box for the building?"

"There are two—one for this floor, one for the gallery." She opened the utilities room and clicked on the light, then nodded toward the electrical box on the back wall.

Connor checked it. "Good, there's room. New lighting for the hall can include emergency floodlights as well as just better fixtures and higher watt bulbs. Someone cuts your electricity, the emergency lights will automatically come on in the halls. Amazing how many times that's enough to stop trouble in its tracks. And it saves you a lot of time if there is a fire or other reason to be leaving quickly."

"You're not doing a very good job cheering me up here."

He smiled. "Daniel gets the bills; just remember that. I'll have the carpenters replace that stairway handrail for you too; I noticed it was a bit shaky. You've got another staircase down to the gallery level, or do you always go out to the street and then back inside?"

"There's another stairwell at the other end of the hall. We use it just enough to keep the cobwebs down."

She led the way to show him.

"Nice." The stair treads were steep and narrow and disappeared with a sharp turn.

"The building was divided in half until about thirty years ago. This used to be the other entrance, but they bricked the former doorway and turned the direction of the final few stairs when they combined the building." Accustomed to the narrower treads she walked down first with her hands braced against each wall and turned the corner, stepping into the open storage room at the back of the gallery.

Connor joined her. "Doors at the top and the bottom and brick on either side of you— it has potential." He checked the lock. "If you had a fire, Marie, I'd use these stairs rather than try for the main stairway. There are no cooling or heat ducts to carry smoke in. I'll have them put in a steel-core door at the top—that will give you better security and a final bit of fire protection and emergency lighting." He jotted down a final note and then looked around where they stood. "Okay, what's down here?"

"This is general storage and where we pack paintings to ship." She pointed to the back wall. "The longer narrow storage room is climate controlled for the paintings and built to not let you get inside easily."

"I can see that; it's the first lock I've respected on sight so far."

She laughed and led the way into the gallery. "The gallery has four areas, loosely divided into themes, with two main brick walls forming the interior and the main support column for upstairs. I've also got my office down here and a more elegant seating area for when I'm talking with buyers over coffee and cake."

"I can see I should have been into art a long time ago; car shops might have the coffee but rarely the chance to sit in elegance to drink it." He walked around, studying the large windows that looked out onto the street, the pedestrians passing by. "You've already got a security system down here."

"Yes. Once the place is locked up it's pretty secure—break triggers on the doors, the plate-glass windows, enough for the insurance bill to come down some. The silent alarm contacts the police."

"You open and close the gallery most days? Or do you have staff that handles it?"

"I'm the one most often handling opening and closings. The posted hours are ten to six, and we're open on Saturdays but not Sundays; it's also pretty common to have private showings or special evenings with invited guests. I have one assistant who has been with me since I opened the gallery who works about thirty hours a week. She typically works the lunch hours for me and helps when there is a showing to put together or a shipment coming in. When she needs to be out of town, as she is today and I've got a meeting, I simply close the gallery for a few hours. It's not a good solution, but the business doesn't do enough volume to support more than the two of us."

"How do you handle the cash?"

"There's a safe on the premises in the office, and I bank at the branch across the street. It's not been a problem. Most of the sales are by check."

He walked through the gallery rooms, and while she wasn't disappointed exactly that he didn't comment on the artwork displayed, she was surprised he didn't seem to even linger to take a second glance at some of the works. The artwork available this month was some of the finest she'd ever been able to afford.

"Daniel will be after that Denart in the front window and that Gibson on the east wall," he predicted.

The fact he'd put the artists' names to their art without looking at the signature cards startled her. "He already asked about the Denart. You know his tastes?"

"Someone once swiped four paintings out of his office. This was before he worked at the Benton Group; it's how I first met him."

"I wondered."

"I learned enough about art working that case to at least know why he bought the paintings he did. Daniel and I play softball together in a league, and he's a pretty regular racquetball partner. Your cousin is the kind of friend you don't think twice about picking up the phone and calling to ask for a favor. Just so you know."

"Yeah, that helps. Not too full of himself."

"A pretty average guy for all the media attention. Where's your office?"

"Back here." She turned on lights.

He paused in the doorway. "Comfortable."

"I spend a lot of time here."

"I'm going to suggest another couple phone lines with at least one of them a very private number you give only to friends. And if you've got the power outlets to handle it, we'll bring one of the security monitors in here and probably another one tucked away near that front reception desk. Cameras on the streets, covering the rooms here, another two for the stairway and hall—they don't have to be intrusive to give you a lot more information about what is around you than you have now."

"I'll get used to them."

He nodded. "In a few weeks, you'll wonder how you functioned without them. No more deliverymen you don't recognize before you open the door."

He finished his notes and slid his notebook back into his pocket. He leaned back against the front of the desk. "Nothing on the list is going to be particularly hard to get installed. The window locks and frames are probably the toughest job—there are simply so many of them. And at least it's projected to be good weather tomorrow. Once it's all in, I'll walk you around and show you how to take maximum advantage of it all."

"I appreciate all this, Connor, even if I am a bit befuddled by it."

He laughed. "I haven't heard that word since about seventh grade. You'll get used to it, Marie. The changes are going to come in a bunch, but they'll level off after a while."

"How would you handle it, being wealthy?"

He thought about it. "I'd probably take better vacations." He shook his head. "I don't know. What I need, I have, and what I want, I enjoy dreaming about. I like my job."

"I wonder if I'm still going to like having this gallery after all the curiosity seekers come by."

"You've built this as a place you love, and you'll still love it a year from now." He paused. "May I?" He reached for a photo on her desk. "Your family?"

"My aunt and the three of us girls: Mandy, Tracey, and me. My aunt passed away in

'95, and Mandy was killed in '98. That's one of the last pictures I have of us together."

"Mandy was your older sister?"

"Four years older. She was murdered in New York."

His gaze shot up to hers. "I'm sorry. I didn't mean to open old wounds."

"It's okay." She leaned back against the credenza. "We've never been able to give her a funeral; they never found her body."

He stilled and looked back at the photo again. "I really don't mean to pry, but what happened?" When he looked back up at her she didn't understand the quietness in him, but she did understand the sympathy and appreciated it.

"She'd had dinner out with her boyfriend; they were on the way back to her place. The car stopped at a stoplight, and someone walked up and shot her boyfriend three times in the chest. They found Mandy's blood on the passenger seat, and a witness saw a woman being chased from the scene. They never found her body, but the police finally concluded she had been killed that night too. Her apartment was never returned to—pets abandoned, her credit cards never used, her bank accounts never touched, her car where she had left it parked. No one ever heard from her again. She would have called had she been alive. That convinced me more than anything that she was gone. We had a private investigator work with the cops, but what he found just confirmed what we knew—a pendant she never took off showed up at a pawnshop, that kind of thing. I wish her body had been found so we could have had a funeral. It's like an open sore without the closure. And I'm sure it will get dragged up again now that we are in the news."

"It's the kind of case a homicide cop dreads, the one that you can't fully wrap up. Did they identify the shooter?"

"They had some solid suspicions, but nothing they could prove. I doubt Mandy ever suspected her accountant boyfriend had some less-than-reputable clients. She was trusting that way, always assuming the best. She ended up at the wrong place at the wrong time. The guy they think probably hired the hit went to jail two years ago on an unrelated murder charge. I'd like more justice for Mandy, but it's not going to bring her back. And that's the hardest part to live with."

He carefully set the photo down. "I really am sorry for your loss."

"I'd have hated to tell Mandy she's just my half sister. We've been sisters all our life. Today would have been incredibly rough on her."

Connor shook his head. "Today wouldn't have changed anything; you're always family." He tugged out a card and wrote two numbers on the back. "Anything bothers you in the next few weeks, even a cat walking on the fire escape, give me a call. Marsh or I will be around."

"I appreciate it, Connor." She slid the card into her pocket.

"Show me out, Marie, lock up, and then get ready to meet Daniel. I'll give him a call before then with a list of items I think need dealt with. You'll like Granger; he's a good police chief. And if he suggests anything else tonight, take his advice."

"I'll do that." Marie saw the clock as she turned off the office light. Connor had been with her almost two hours. He was doing quite a favor for a friend.

Connor stepped outside and zipped his jacket, then turned to walk back to join her again. "Would you mind terribly if you heard Marsh proposed to Tracey?"

She blinked, then smiled. "I wouldn't mind at all."

Connor smiled back. "Good."

"You know something, don't you?"

He stepped away, pulling on gloves. "Nope. I swear. But my mom calls me a touch of a romantic. Let's just say I had hopes for this weekend before today arrived."

"I did too."

"Did you?" He grinned. "I'll see you around, Marie."

●●●●●●

Connor shoved the door closed to the police chief's office with his foot and searched for the item in the thick file he remembered. "Chief, I don't know what to think." Granger had canceled two appointments on the strength of his request for half an hour of his time as soon as possible, and Connor wasn't one to shy away from giving his boss a gut reaction to events, not when it was this serious.

"There are three sisters, not two: Mandy, Tracey, and Marie. The oldest everyone thinks is dead, murdered in New York eight years ago. Daniel thinks it, the two sisters do, the New York cops, the investigator the family had work the case. But I swear, Chief, I picked up the family photo on Marie's desk, and I was looking at a younger photo of someone I recognized."

Connor found the photo he sought and felt a punch in his gut; reality was even more vivid than his memory. He set it on the desk. "I will swear on my grandmother's grave that lady is the oldest sister, Mandy, and she was very much alive as of three years ago."

Connor watched the chief shift the photo over to his side of the desk and pick it up. He was quiet for an unusually long time. "The sisters, Marie and Tracey, their last name is Griffin? Daniel didn't say."

"Yeah."

The chief tapped the photo. "Meet Amanda Griffin; Amy to her friends, Mandy to her family."

Connor dropped into a chair. "I was hoping I wasn't right. The sister was staying in this town under the name Kelly Brown, while her sisters thought she was dead? What kind of oldest sister is that?"

"One afraid they'd be dead if she showed up alive."

That simple statement on the chief's part told Connor a whole lot of case was out there he'd never even had a clue existed. "I stepped into something I shouldn't have, didn't I?"

Luke smiled. "Well, for what it's worth, you caught a wrinkle others had missed." He nodded to the photo he held. "Kelly Brown, Ann Walsh—she's used those and probably quite a few more names over the years. The sisters believe she's dead?"

"They're absolutely convinced of it. They think she was murdered in New York eight years ago, and either the cops that worked the case did a really good snow job for some reason or they think she's dead as well. Marie said she'd even hired a private investigator to look at it, and he also concluded the sister was dead. Her body was never found."

"Then, Connor, you and Marsh are about to have a tough reality, because for now Amy is dead. And you two never saw the photo of Kelly Brown. Clear?"

"I can handle that part. So can Marsh. But she's got two sisters about to be seriously

rich. And I can tell you for a fact it's not going to take long before Marie and Tracey are
posting a major reward for information
about their sister to try to find the body and
get some closure. Marie calls it an open
wound, the fact they never were able to
have a funeral."

"Okay. I've got some calls to make." The
chief looked at his watch. "And I've got a
meeting with Daniel in just under two hours,
and he's bringing Marie with him. What's
she like?"

Connor smiled. "Nice. Pretty." He thought
about the last few hours, about the impression he'd been left with. "She's a little like a
pretty tiger shark. A little wary on the initial
read, pretty determined on what she wants,
and eyes that make you want to look back
a second and third time to figure out what
she's really thinking."

Luke chuckled. "Interesting choice of
comparison, but I know what you mean.
Amy was like that too. Confident, but preferring to swim alone. Keep your phone on
tonight. I'll be in touch, probably very late.
You've got a number for Marsh?"

"Yes."

"Call and tell him quietly to do the same."

"Trouble's coming?"

"Trouble's already here. Thanks, Connor."

"Anytime, Boss."

● ● ● ● ● ●

Luke's home office was quiet, and he didn't bother to turn on the radio or sit and check e-mail as he would have normally done. He unlocked the private safe and tugged out a folder. He shifted his coffee to the side and picked up the phone. He had wondered at the reason Amy had been in his town, staying under the radar screen in such an odd place as Brentwood. She'd had family here to watch out for, family to protect from Richard Wise trying to use them to locate her.

He should have seen it. The detective working for him should have seen it. Sam Chapel—Sam would have put it together, and he'd never said a word. Luke's eyes narrowed. Amy had turned to Sam. It was the only thing that made sense. Sam had been working for Amy either from the very first or from sometime after Luke had hired him, but one way or the other, Sam had been feeding him misleading information. Sam had never lied; he'd just stopped short of passing on all he knew. And odds were good the investigator Marie had hired to deal with the New York cops had also been Sam Chapel. Brentwood was a big town but not that big when it came to well-respected detective agencies. Sam had convinced the sisters Amy was dead—to protect them? to protect Amy? This was a big town, but still . . . the lady had been taking a risk working at a mall even on the other side of town.

While Luke waited for the phone to be answered, he looked again at Amy's photo. She was still pretty, still clear in his mind even after three years. Meeting Amy's sister tonight was going to be an interesting experience, if difficult, given the information he'd not be able to tell her.

The phone was finally answered. "Chapel."

"Sam; Granger. I'm meeting Marie Griffin in twenty minutes. I think you and I need to talk, don't you?"

His words were met by a puff of exhaled breath, and then the answering voice hammered back, "It's about time you called me. Ever since Henry died I've been waiting to get waylaid some evening and have the stuffing pounded out of me."

"You've been running on the wrong side of the street for too long: I'll just yank your investigator's license and stuff your gun permit down the shredder. Ten o'clock tonight, my place?"

"I'm in Texas, so it will have to be tomorrow night, but I'll be there. There's a lot more than you've figured out so far."

"I already figured as much. You were sourcing Amy the IDs, weren't you?"

"Among other things. Tomorrow, Luke. And think kind thoughts between now and then, would you? I dated the woman once upon a blue moon ago, and it was kind of hard to tell her no."

"When did you last talk with her?"

"That's one of the problems. She went cold twenty months ago."

"Bring everything you have."

"You've got my word. You ought to know now—Silver's in on it too."

"I should have seen that coming." Jonathan Silver of Silver Security, Inc. had been friends with Sam back to the days the men had been in grade school. This kind of job, Sam would have kept it tight to the vest when he needed help.

"Jonathan's got Silver Security guys sitting on both sisters at the moment, so you might want to tell Marsh not to get spooked and take an aversion to the guy watching his and Tracey's backs. Your cop is not the kind of guy to ask questions until after he's snuck up and crowned the guy watching them first."

"I'll pass the word on," Luke promised. "Tomorrow, Sam." He hung up the phone and rubbed a hand across his face.

Jonathan Silver knowing was probably a good thing, for the man had security resources that could be put on the task of watching for trouble without having to figure out how to budget such a thing into city resources.

Amy hadn't been heard from in the last twenty months; that was not good news. She should have already turned in the books and the account numbers by now. She'd said at the time he met her she thought that would be done in another year, and that was three years ago. He knew Richard Wise was in jail on an unrelated murder charge. Part of him had hoped Amy was safely past the trouble. But if she had went cold twenty months ago—that said trouble had found her. There would have been no reason for Richard Wise not to kill her once the money had been turned in.

Your sister was alive, Marie; she didn't die in New York, only she was killed twenty months or so ago by the man who was hunting for her. . . . And the guy who did it wants his money back, and he'll take it out of you and Tracey since he couldn't get it back from Amy—Luke winced at the worst-case thought for what he might have to tell Marie. There was not a good solution to this quagmire.

God, just don't let Amy be dead. I can handle about any of it but Amy staying lost out there somewhere, dead. He finally had the lead he had prayed for years to find, and it wasn't all that good of news.

"Luke?"

Startled, he looked around toward the door to see his sister standing there, his two dogs winding their way around her knees. They were his dogs until she came over, and their loyalty transferred in an instant.

"Everything okay?"

He sighed. "It will be."

"You were talking with Sam."

Susan didn't know what had absorbed him so much over the last years, but she

knew the edges of it. "The trouble's contained for now at least. How are the
steaks?"

"Ready for the grill anytime."

He heard the doorbell ring. "That will be
our guests."

He rose and joined his sister and went to
meet Daniel and Amy's sister Marie.

Chapter Six

What was she supposed to wear to a press conference? Marie knew she was stalling getting ready, but the rebellious part of her wanted an excuse to avoid today. This sunny Friday had one huge obstacle in her path.

"I've got a sister who it turns out is only my half sister, a father I met but didn't know was my dad, a cousin who has read private-detective reports on me . . . it gets mind-boggling how this day is ending compared to how it began, Luke."

Her words last night to the chief of police still echoed in her mind. She'd had the nerve to call the man Luke. He'd asked her to, but still . . . two days ago she would have demurred the invitation and left it at Mr. Granger if she'd dared even go beyond sir. She'd gone a bit mad yesterday: there was no other explanation for just about flirting with a cop who stopped by to check security or finding the nerve to call the chief of police by his first name. There was a reason her gallery was in the recovering part of downtown—she didn't like the wealthy and powerful as a rule; they made her nervous. Yesterday the nerves had been gone, numbed under the unexpected weight of what had happened. Today the nerves were back to normal and out in full force.

"Mandy, I wish you were here."

She whispered the words as she chose a dress to wear. If she was going down blushing and stammering before the cameras, at least it would be in one of her best outfits. Mandy had been a natural with crowds, with people, fearless and bold. Tracey would do fine at a news conference too—she liked public speaking. But Marie was glad Tracey was still skiing; there were going to be too many people seeing this news conference for comfort. She couldn't protect her sister like Mandy could have done, but she would do her best.

God, give me courage. I need to be able to get through this day somehow without falling apart and embarrassing my family. The whispered words were a plea, one of many since last night, but at least a reassurance she wasn't facing this entirely alone. She'd thought losing Mandy would destroy her, and for years her relationship with God had been more anger and tears and pain than conversation, but slowly the relationship was rebuilding. God was still with her, even after the losses of the last years. That mattered enough to trust Him as these new events slammed into her. She didn't know yet what to think of it all—whether this was a good turn or one that she would come to regret in the days ahead.

She brushed out her hair a final time and conceded it was the best she could look. She slipped on her long coat and made a point of locking the apartment door behind her before walking downstairs. Daniel had offered to pick her up, but it was just not in her to be focused and smiling and on as soon as she walked out her front door today. She wanted at least that drive time to get a handle on her nerves.

The street bustled with people on their

way to work, several carrying hot coffee cups steaming in the cool air, and she thought about stopping at the deli for a bagel and coffee for herself but changed her mind when her stomach again rebelled at the idea of food. Maybe saltines would stay down. She could stop in at the corner store on the way to her car.

"You look quite lovely this morning."

Her turn was too fast to be elegant, and her blush already too high in her face to avoid showing her embarrassment. She smiled at Connor because she didn't have words and wildly wondered what he was doing standing outside her building helping hold up the wall.

He held up keys as he pushed himself away from the wall. "Even if you want to drive yourself to the press conference, there's no way you're going to want to drive yourself back. So keep smiling and say yes when I offer to take you."

She didn't keep smiling, but she did shift her weight on her moderate high heels and let pleasure take the place of panic. "That's thoughtful of you, Connor." He looked good this morning, casually dressed in jeans and a button-down checked shirt. There was less fatigue in his face, she thought, noticing the small changes in a face she still thought she might like to paint. The wind was blowing his dark hair across his forehead and adding another wave to those already naturally there.

"So say yes."

"I'm supposed to meet the contractor coordinating the security changes at nine-thirty first. Daniel arranged it."

"I know. Peter Towns; he does good work. I just sent him off to get me a coffee. Got extra keys for him? And a list of anything else you thought of?"

She pulled a key ring out of her pocket. "Gallery, apartment, storage rooms—the works. And the list Daniel faxed me this morning was already breathtaking. Is there anything you didn't recommend changing?"

"I really liked that doorbell you've got—the screaming screech. That isn't changing."

"It does that because it's broken; it has been for as long as I've lived here."

"So maybe we'll compromise, and he can just fix it." Connor slipped his hand under her arm and turned her without making a big deal of it toward the deli. "We'll drop the keys off in passing. I'm parked that way anyway. You'll have new keys for everything tonight, by the way, and a couple extra sets."

"The contractors will be done today?"

"Sounds like it. The toughest job is the windows, but Peter brought along a full crew of guys. Four hours, five if the door-frames turn out to need to be rebuilt, and you'll have both security and comfort. No more getting surprised to find a guy lurking outside your front door."

She laughed at that, because the thought of a cop lurking struck her as funny. Anything would strike her as funny this morning, but he smiled with her laugh, and she let herself relax a bit more. "Is that the only reason you're picking me up this morning, because I might not want to drive myself home later?"

"Granger did mention he thought you might like someone absolutely normal around today. And I can do a really good bad-cop routine when the occasion demands it if the reporters should happen to get pushy."

He opened the door to the deli. "Peter's

the guy in the red jacket. He likes to stand out in a crowd."

The man in the red jacket stepped away from the counter carrying a tray. "I'm not hard of hearing yet, Connor, stand out in a crowd indeed. I had them put skim milk in yours; you've been gaining weight again."

Marie met a man close to being her grandfather's age as he handed the cop with her the second coffee on the tray. "For you, Marie, I got hot chocolate. Even if you don't want to drink it, holding something warm will mean he can't go reaching for your hand like a young courting man."

She bubbled in laughter because he winked at her.

"I built that building you're now occupying, laid a good number of those bricks when my hands were still too soft to have calluses. I figure I can fix it up for you while you're off being questioned by those reporters. Anything you want to add to the boy's list?"

She swallowed hard at the thought of Connor as a boy but gamely bobbed her head. "It's a good starting list, and you can feel free to add whatever else you think he has missed to it."

"Good answer."

Connor held out her key ring. "I do, how-ever, like the doorbell."

"Old screech? Sure, I thought you might. I put that in for the grandkids that used to spend their Saturdays pushing the button and darting away down the sidewalk. Now get going before you're late, and drive her nice, Connor. No sirens and speed just be-cause you've got the toys."

Connor leaned over and kissed the man's cheek. "Yeah. Bye, Gramps. She'll be back sometime this afternoon."

Marie kept her hands firmly around the cup of hot chocolate and didn't try to come up with a good-bye as Connor steered her out of the deli. "That's your grandfather?" she whispered.

"On my mother's side—when he claims me."

"I like him."

Connor grinned at her. "So now you've met two people who aren't going to care that you are rich. Think you'll meet a few more today?"

"Probably not."

"Then I'm in exclusive company. I like

that, and Gramps is too old to do much more than flirt."

She laughed so hard she nearly bobbled her hot chocolate. "Thank you, Connor."

"Nerves gone?"

"Entirely."

He nodded, satisfied. "We aim to please. The car's over this way."

●●●●●●

"Do you plan to challenge the will and the fact more was left to a nephew than his own daughters?"

Marie struggled against the lights to know which direction she should face to answer that question. The reporter who asked it had already shot four zingers her way, and she could feel the anger turning her stomach into knots. "No, the will provisions are fine. Next question?"

"Will the charity work you spoke about be concentrated in this community?"

"We'll coordinate with the already generous giving Daniel has announced and see what else we might do together, mainly in the area of literacy and the arts for youth." She smiled at the reporter she could see off to the right of the bright lights. "Yes, your question?"

"What's the *T* stand for? Your middle name?"

"I could say my mother never told me, and I think I wisely never asked; but I'll simply say it's not worth repeating."

Low laughter told her she'd at least made one clean answer. "Yes?" She nodded to the man beside Daniel.

"Would you characterize your reaction as grateful, stunned, surprised? How's it feel to be told you have a rich father?"

"I already have a very rich father in God; this just closes a loophole I wasn't aware of here on earth. And it is nice to know the man I met through the gallery was also the man my mother loved many years ago."

Daniel was moving toward the podium now, and she was relieved to have only a couple more questions to go in her self-imposed fifteen minutes of fame. "Yes?"

"Are you planning to settle in this area or are you going to travel the world for a while and choose somewhere more, say . . . warm and sunny . . . as the place you'll reside?"

Laughter met the reporter's question.

"While Hawaii has its appeal for the next month, this is home. I'm comfortable we'll stay in this area."

"Thank you, ladies and gentlemen." Daniel took over the podium with an ease she could only envy, one hand sliding into his pocket and the other resting against her lower back to keep her from immediately turning for the privacy of the hall. "As you've asked many times for more details on the trust and will arrangements of my uncle's estate, and given they will be public knowledge once signed by the judge, I've arranged for copies to be available today; please see my assistant, and she'll be able to provide them for you. On behalf of the family I'd like to caution again that interview requests should come through the Benton Group if you want to have any chance of hearing a yes. We'll be coordinating several over the course of the next two weeks. I thank you for your time and your patience; that concludes the press conference."

He nodded toward the back, and the technician killed the microphone. Daniel offered a smile and whispered, "You just survived your first trip into the lions' den." He shook his head at the reporters beginning to crowd forward and gestured toward the side door. "What do you say to a few minutes of walking through the roses to relax?"

He had her through the crowd before she realized he'd maneuvered them through. Once out of the small auditorium she took her first deep breath and smiled at him. "Thank you, Daniel. I couldn't have done that without you."

"You did great."

"Better than great," Connor added, and she turned to see him behind her. "Security needs you out front, Daniel, something about a legal filing?"

"The tender offer was arriving today; thanks, Connor. Keep Marie company? I won't be a minute."

"Not a problem at all."

Marie smiled at Connor and took the soda can he held out. "So I did okay?"

"Massacred them, Marie; though I thought that question about your dress was going to throw you."

"She's the fashion editor for the paper. I saw her early on and had prepared for that one. She's one of the few reporters I at least knew by name."

"Well, they all know yours now. I imagine

there won't be many quiet walks to the deli for coffee in the next few weeks without someone asking you a question about something."

She drank her soda and just smiled at him. "That's tomorrow's problem."

"Your nerves are gone again. I like that. My company seems to work wonders."

"I think it's called relief. I heard via the grapevine that it's your day off. Why did you stay? I know you were going to give me a ride home, but Daniel could do that."

Connor laughed. "And miss the biggest news event of the day?" He let her off the hook with a shift in the question. "As for the day off—I decided to spend it flirting with you. My grandfather is so far my only serious competition; I think I can take him."

She blinked and laughed. "Find me another soda, okay? I'm parched. Then let's enjoy the roses and walk paths that I apparently now partly own."

"See, wealth is going to fit like a nice glove sooner than you think. You want another diet soda or something flavored?"

"Orange if they have it."

Connor pointed to the bench by the trellis

of climbing roses. "Sit over there. I don't want to be losing you."

"Sure."

She watched him head back inside, and she turned toward the roses he had pointed out. It was lovely out here in the covered walkway. She was aware even as Connor left that she still wasn't entirely alone. The man Daniel had introduced earlier as one of the Silver Security, Inc. staff was standing off to one side of the door, near enough he'd be between her and anyone coming through those doors who wasn't on the cleared list. She smiled at him briefly, and he smiled back but stayed where he was at. She supposed she'd get used to that kind of quiet, polite watcher eventually. He looked deadly professional and had rather spooked her when first introduced; she'd noticed even Connor had given him a second glance to make sure he knew where the man was standing.

She walked around the trellis toward the waterfall. She was wealthy, she knew who her father was, and all those crazy if-only plans she'd thought of over the years were possibilities for her now. And she wasn't ready for this. Tears wanted to fall for no reason at all, and she pulled in a deep breath and then another. She trailed her hand through the water cascading down carefully stacked rocks and smiled rather sadly at her own falling sense of joy. All her dreams come true but one, and she was too overwhelmed to take it in and enjoy the moment.

She turned away from the water.

Connor sat on the bench by the trellis, patiently watching her. The second soda she'd requested sat on the bench beside him, and he looked to about have finished the one he had gotten for himself. He smiled and held out a couple napkins. "Your fingers are going to turn blue; that's practically ice water."

"You explored it earlier?" she asked, taking the offered napkins.

"This entire place is an exploration wonder. Did you know Daniel has heated lamps under the bench seats so they stay nicely warm on cold winter days?"

"That I didn't know."

"The gardener told me. And there are butterflies released within the walkway to help the roses grow, though I don't know about

that rationale. I think they're just pretty crea-
tures to go with pretty flowers."

She took a seat beside him on the bench.

"Want to spend the day exploring? This
place, maybe drive out toward the lake and
find some ducks to watch? You're not
dressed for walking far, not in those shoes,
and there's not a mall in the city that didn't
have a few hundred TV sets turned to that
interview, so wandering in to get new
footwear is probably not a good idea."

"Peter's going to be a while with the construction?"

"Even if he's done, I bet a good portion of
that reporters pool just moved to camp outside your gallery for your return home."

"Daniel already asked me to stay for a late
lunch."

"Ask him to make it for dinner instead.
He'll understand. It's not like you aren't going to be seeing him just about every day for
the rest of your life."

She smiled. "An exaggeration, but there's
a point in there. I'd like to change, but I can
do that at the gym where I keep a bag,
rather than brave the construction work going on at the gallery."

"Problem solved. Come on, Marie. Let's

blow this place and have some fun. It's not every day you announce to the world you're the luckiest lady around."

"Tracey is too."

"I guarantee she was watching that news conference and beaming with pride at your answers. She's probably got Marsh entirely too flustered at her joy."

"They're coming home early, she said. They'll be back tomorrow midday."

"Yeah, I talked to Marsh last night a few minutes after you did." Connor got to his feet and held out his hands. "Today there's no more business to deal with, just time to let it settle."

She slid her hands into his, wishing she understood this man and why he was willing to be the counterbalance to the craziness she had going on in her life. As far as she could tell he was doing it because he wanted to, and that hadn't often happened in her life with guys. And on him the money wasn't sticking as a fascination or a problem, and that just didn't fit.

"You're wealthy, Connor, aren't you? That's why all this kind of slides past you as no big deal."

He smiled. "I'm a cop, Marie. No one gets wealthy on what the city pays."

"You're ducking the question."

"My grandfather owns a few of the buildings we passed today; would that do? I'm not wealthy, but there's enough to do what I want, and beyond that, money isn't something I particularly worry about. Though I admit your cousin probably holds a few of the family pennies in that investment pool he manages. My grandfather was never a man to let a building project go by without betting a couple bucks on its success."

"You're one of those guys who drives a pickup truck, hunts on weekends, watches NASCAR races, and has a couple million sitting in the bank?"

He laughed. "Watching the NASCAR races I'll admit to. Quit trying to figure me out—my mom hasn't done it in thirty-odd years—and just take what you see as what you get. There really isn't a lot of layers to figure out."

"Right, and I'm a natural in front of cameras." But she smiled. "I'll quit trying so hard if you promise tomorrow I can wipe away all the embarrassing points of today and you'll kindly forget they happened. I get too chatty after a morning like this one."

"I can be as forgetful as needed." He directed her toward the walk path and gave a quiet nod to the security man. "How about a perfect rose to press into your scrapbook to remember today by?"

Marie glanced back, and the Silver Security employee was gone. "What was that about?"

"Transportation. They even do fill-ups if you ask very nicely."

"You're kidding me."

"Well, maybe a little."

"Connor—"

He squeezed her hand. "Cops and security guys, we do our own thing. It's best not to ask until we're somewhere over a very long meal. There's nothing wrong—I promise you that—just well-done planning clicking like it's supposed to."

"You'll explain that sometime."

"Yep."

"Then I'll ask later. I'd like a pink rose for the scrapbook. Something so pink it makes the color pink proud."

"And try to say that tongue twister ten

times fast." He chuckled and pointed out a rosebush. "There."

"Yes, that's perfect."

● ● ● ● ● ●

Connor tried to remember the last time he'd eaten a waffle cone with just plain vanilla ice cream and couldn't place it, short of maybe a state fair when he was a teenager and an occasion equally designed to impress a girl. "The fudge would have helped."

"It hides the vanilla," Marie protested. "They make the smoothest ice cream in the state, and you want to hide it under a layer of sugar."

"Tell me you at least like mustard on your hot dogs."

She laughed and reached up to wipe his chin with a napkin as the ice cream dripped. "I do. And I love corn dogs on a stick and saltwater taffy and cotton candy."

"So next time we'll come back to the fair when it's actually open." He hadn't known the fairground had a few concession stands open year-round to serve those who worked at the livestock barns and managed the grounds and staffed the weekend convention hall, but Marie had known. So he was wandering across the racetrack trying to avoid stepping in horse droppings while eating a very cold, very plain, vanilla waffle cone for an early dessert.

"Hold on; your sleeve is about to come down again." She stepped close enough to turn up the cuff twice.

He got in the last two bites of the cone while she finished squaring the corners of his shirtsleeve. The sun was warm on his back and the afternoon pleasant; it was good to be outside with her. And since it was incredibly hard not to just tip her head to the side and kiss her as he'd like to, Connor kept his eyes above her head on the clouds lazily floating past and thought about his odds of maybe talking her into canceling on Daniel for dinner too.

"There, that's better."

Connor rested his arms on her shoulders rather than let her step back and checked his watch behind Marie's head. His grandfather should be done with the security changes by now. He looked down to meet her startled gaze. "I'm seizing the opportunity presented to me."

She had a nice blush; he liked that about

her. "Want to find dinner to go with that dessert?"

"I promised Daniel I'd be there at seven."

"Phones are good for apologies; I can stick a pocketknife into a tire and give us a flat so you can have a real excuse."

"That wouldn't be fair."

"All's fair in love and war."

"He's my cousin; the analogy doesn't fit."

"Then how about time is of the essence? I go back to work on Monday. No more days off for way too long in my future."

She smiled. "Why not just say it was a great afternoon and we'll go out on top?"

He sighed. "We could do that if we must. I could even call you late, late tonight to chat if you give me that new private number you're not supposed to give out to any-one."

She rested her head against his chest and laughed. "I feel like a teenager on a date again, Connor. It's been an incredibly long while since I could say that."

"I'm kind of enjoying the flashback too. You, lady, can be very good company."

He dug out his car keys and pushed the button to remotely unlock the car doors. "Want to pull through McDonald's and order like a zillion french fries to go and pass them out to every kid we pass?"

"You're not a cop; that's got to be a fake badge or something. Your sense of humor never grew up."

"Or something. It's a nice gold shield, and they only give those out to boys that play well together. If you don't want to do the zillion french fries, how about finding a speakerphone and calling Tracey and Marsh? We can compare notes on who goofed off the most today. All they probably did was ski or something tame like that. We did duck calls."

She swiped the keys out of his hand. "I'm leaving while I can still breathe. I've been laughing so much my ribs ache."

Connor followed her, pleased to see the joy was real and all the traces of nerves were truly gone.

Those nerves would be back this weekend, when she realized the Silver Security guys were still around her, when the chief told her Amy was still alive, when the inevitable cutting words were said by someone who envied the money—he couldn't stop those things, but he'd done what he could. For a brief few hours he'd forgotten about being a cop and the murder cases on his desk, waiting for his return. And she'd forgotten about the risks that came with the changes in her life. He wouldn't have given this day back for anything.

He walked to join her. "You've got the keys, but I'm not letting you drive. It goes against the guy's code of honor or some such rule in life."

She perched on the hood of his car and held out the keys. "I changed my mind; let's stop by McDonald's for some fries."

"I was kidding, Marie."

"I know. I'm not."

He took the keys and flipped the ring around to find the one for the trunk.

"What are you doing?" She turned to watch him as he circled the car.

"Getting my bullhorn. If you want to attract a crowd of kids, just call, 'Free food.' It works every time, and I don't feel like shouting."

"You'd actually do it."

He smiled.

"We need cash."

"Daniel floated you a loan for the day; it's in your purse."

"What? And you didn't tell me?"

She retrieved her purse and spotted the envelope. "There's . . . oh my—" she turned an odd color of pale—"at least five thousand dollars in here. And it sat in the car with the doors unlocked most of the afternoon while we fed the ducks."

"Not many people think to steal from a squad car, at least not on this side of town."

"You really should have said something."

"Holding that much money makes you go kind of yellow pale; I don't think you're entirely sure it belongs in your hands yet. It was easier not to tell you than to see the reaction."

"I know it's just money, but it's not just money, you know?"

He came around to lean against the car beside her, and the teasing disappeared. "I know."

"What am I supposed to do with being rich? Leave it sit in a bank account when so many could use a helping hand? Give it away, and in a few years find I've done nothing but give it away? Spend it all on things I enjoy?"

"There's no right answer. God might be wise enough to judge the intents of your heart and what you choose to do over the next years, but the rest of the chorus of voices you'll be hearing saying do this with it or that will just be random noise. Follow your heart. It's your money, not someone else's, and uniquely your task to sort out."

"I wish the situation was reversed and you had inherited the money."

"I don't." He smiled at her. "You're a thinker; your gallery reflects that, your love of painting. Major money takes thinking to figure out what to do with it. I'd rather be out chasing car thieves and answering old ladies who hear cats and think prowlers have come by."

"And occasionally working murder scenes."

"Marsh and I take what comes with the days. You want to go get those french fries, or have you changed your mind?"

"The intent is good, but there's probably a better way to pass out free food to kids than hollering at them with a bullhorn. Maybe I'll sponsor a kids' night at the ballpark and give away hot dogs."

"With mustard."

She smiled. "With mustard."

He opened the passenger door for her.

"You're going to do fine being rich, Marie. You'll see."

● ● ● ● ● ●

Connor had been to the chief's house a few dozen times in his life, but it had never become comfortable ground, and coming by in the evening hadn't changed that. The barbeque pit out back was fine, but the private office tucked at the back of the house—the inner sanctum of the chief's territory—it was the place sheriffs from the surrounding area came to put up their feet and privately compare notes on crimes and cops and who was cutting it and who was not. It was not the place mere cops wanted to be, and he'd be sitting in that office soon.

Connor waited by the kitchen door while the chief opened the refrigerator and found cold drinks. "Are you sure I can't get you something to eat? I've got a few steaks set back and the grill is still hot; or there are sandwich fixings that can quickly pile together."

"I'm fine, Chief."

Luke found himself a soda and passed another one over. Connor studied the man he worked for as he opened the soda. The man had come up through the force from a rookie walking the streets to end up as chief of police. Connor respected the work and focus that journey had demanded, and he knew it had come with experiences Connor wasn't sure he would want to ever face himself. Granger looked tired tonight, like he hadn't slept much in the last twenty-four hours, and Connor wondered just what it really was he'd stepped into. The chief's call late last night had answered some of the questions, and the request that he help cover Marie today while they worked on the security picture—that had been no hardship. But what he was seeing tonight said there was more to it than that.

"Sam will be here shortly."

"It's no problem. There are few places I need to be tonight."

It was personal for the chief—that was the only thing that made sense, the fact this was being worked late at night, quietly on the side, said the case was not only sensitive but also personally important. To the best of his knowledge, the chief had met Amanda Griffin only once or twice and briefly at that three years before. It made him wonder. But he also understood some of it. If the oldest sister was anything like Marie in personality, it didn't take much time to form an impression that mattered.

"What's your opinion of Marie after today?"

Connor smiled. "Tiger shark wearing a lei."

Luke chuckled. "You had a good afternoon."

"She's roughly my age, remembers high school as I do, gets nervous in an endearing kind of way, and has a laugh that makes a guy want to dive into it. She's still pretty real for a rich lady—lots of layers, but not the hard-shell, polite kind of layers." He stopped talking, for he was trying to fit a whirlwind of reality into something that could be conveyed to another cop, and it just wasn't coming out right. "I like her."

"Can she handle the fact her sister is alive?"

"Alive, yes. That Amy's spent the last eight years running for her life—I don't think Marie has had anything in her life to prepare her for that kind of reality arriving."

"What about Tracey?"

"Marsh would have a better read. I don't know. I think it's all around going to be one incredible shock."

Connor felt a nudge and looked down to see Wilks looking for some attention. He reached down to rub the dog's head. Chester had met him earlier only to disappear out through the dog door to explore outside.

"Silver Security was covering Marie when you left her?"

"He put two of the best on her—James Anthem and Michael Tate. They were outside Daniel's place, and they'll stay on her back to the gallery apartment. The security improvements seem to have done the job for tightening the place up. Marie will be fine upstairs."

"You introduced her to the man who will be the visible security around the building and gallery?"

Connor nodded. "Jonathan tapped Tom Bryce for the job; he put her at ease pretty quick with that smile of his. She seemed satisfied that his presence around the gallery will be enough to keep the reporters and thrill seekers in check. The fact he could also take down a professional hit man we just kind of glossed over."

"Better that way, I think."

"The sisters can't stay in that cocoon for long; they'll slip coverage not even realizing why it's so important to have around."

"I know. This is at best a stopgap arrangement for a few days while we sort things out."

"Daniel knows?"

"No. You, me, Marsh, Sam, Jonathan—the world that knows Amy is alive is staying under a handful until I'm sure we understand the risks. Word gets out she's alive before we've found her again—you can be sure it will make the search we've made so far be like child's play compared to the effort it would take then."

Lights crossed the window. "There's Sam now."

The chief went to meet him and Connor waited. Sam Chapel was the kind of man a cop could respect and admire but also want to stay an uneasy step away from. Sam did the type of investigations that weren't illegal, just often distasteful. He found out facts that could form—if not a case which could hold up in a court of law—a slate of truth about a matter. When you had to know something, you called Sam. And one way or another he figured out what the answer was. The fact the chief had made the call to Sam on this case told Connor more than he probably should know. The chief didn't work off the books from his own pocket unless the information was both highly charged and extremely dangerous to know.

The men came in. Sam was still very much the broad-shouldered, thick-chested, powerful defensive tackle who could control his environment without much effort. Connor had to stop himself from stepping back to give the man more room.

"Connor."

He nodded a greeting in return rather than shake hands. "Sam." The investigator had come into his profession after a side trip through the navy, and his hands still had the strength of a man accustomed to wrestling ships into line.

Connor followed Sam and the chief back to the office. He was involved even if he wasn't sure he wanted to be, and about the only thing he knew for certain was the next few days were going to be a challenge.

Connor knew the reason Amy Griffin had run, the reason Richard Wise wanted her dead, but listening to the two men who had carried the knowledge of Amy's flight around with them for years made him feel like he was eavesdropping on a private conversation. He stood inside the door to the chief's office, one hand resting on the bookshelf and the other holding the cold soda, and he listened and he learned. This was now his problem too. Not only because his partner, Marsh, dated Tracey, but because he personally liked Marie.

Sam flipped back through his notebook and then simply closed it. "Amy's last known location was Minnesota, twenty months ago. There's no need to be more specific than that—you can safely be sure I've turned that lead upside down without results. She's been cold since then. Nothing passed to the federal officers she works with. No contacts or attempts to make contact that I can discover. No inquiries by third parties that would raise the concern. She just for reasons of her own dropped out of sight."

"Again," the chief added with a grimace.

"She does like to run solo." Sam shifted in his chair. "I do know she monitors what is going on in this town and with her sisters. The news conference this morning—odds are good she knows about it now or will know about it in the next twenty-four hours."

"And if Amy is watching for news—Richard Wise and his crew will be watching too," the chief said. "Maybe not quite as closely, but the fact Amy has two sisters is known to them. The fact those two sisters just came into a chunk of money—it's not *if* Richard Wise will act but when and where and how. He wants money out of this family; he'll take it from Amy first, but he'll go after the sisters if that's the only way to get it."

"Amy's going to be worried for her sisters' safety and with reason. She's going to be heading to this town; it's the only reasonable conclusion," Sam said.

"She'll contact you surely?" Connor asked.

Sam looked his way. "Maybe. Amy knows I'll already be doing what can be done to watch out for her sisters. She'll assume Richard either has my office bugged or has someone following me."

"Will he?"

Sam shrugged. "Years back he sent someone to break into my office in order to pilfer through the file after I'd been in New York, probably on the assumption I had a lead written down regarding where Amy might have gone. I used that fact to feed back some false information that may have bought her some time. I'll be hoping they use the same tactics again this time. Whoever arrives will have to get information from somewhere. You can be certain they'll have someone following the sisters, expecting Amy to make contact there. You can also assume they'll be paying for inside tips from anyone even remotely close to the family, their friends, the reporters around them. They'll be wanting to know movement times and places and who is important to them. Consider what is coming to be a case of information warfare. But if they locate Amy before we do—she's going to be dead."

"Assuming she's not already dead," the chief said quietly. "We don't know why she went silent. What was the longest silence before this?"

"Six months."

Connor winced.

The chief just absorbed the bad news and nodded. "Do you know how much of the money she had turned in? All of the accounts, some of them?"

"She still had one final batch of accounts and the oldest of the logbooks to deliver when she went cold. My guess, she's still holding something between five and ten million. The feds are hoping against hope she'll still make contact and turn them in."

"The oldest log—it's likely the one with information about what got the boyfriend's father in the sights of Richard Wise to begin with." The chief leaned forward in his chair. "We need to know a great deal more than we do at present about Richard Wise and his current organization. How much control he still exerts from jail, who in New York might be at the top of the list to see disappear from there and show up here."

"I know the New York cop to ask; I'll be flying out and back tomorrow."

"And if they don't send anyone?" Connor asked.

Sam looked back at him. "Then they already know Amy's dead. But even then I think they'd still send someone to come after the sisters for the money." He got to his feet. "I know Amy well enough to know it's not that easy a thing to get a jump on her. I believe she's still alive and she's going to be heading to town to watch out for her sisters. Jonathan's guys are in place for the security, so I'll put my focus on Richard Wise and getting the latest out of New York on who might be coming this way to cause that trouble."

"Thanks, Sam."

"I can find my way out—you two need to talk some more." Sam left the office.

Connor took the seat Sam had vacated. "What are you thinking, Chief?"

"If Amy's going to make contact, it's going to be in the next forty-eight hours."

"What's the plan if she does?"

"That I haven't figured yet." The chief tapped his pen on the pad of notes he was working from. "The Silver Security guys can cover Marie and Tracey for the most part— the gallery, their basic routines. The problem is if Amy contacts one of the sisters rather than Sam. If we've got one or both of the sisters trying to slip away for a private meeting with Amy and if Amy is the one giving them a list of steps to take to shake any tails—I don't think there will be enough Silver Security guys around the sisters, at least not in close enough, to be able to stop it."

"Tracey isn't going to keep a secret like that from Marsh. I have to believe that."

"Probably not, but Amy calling Marie is the more likely first contact. And if she stresses the danger—Marie may get convinced to go alone."

Marie didn't strike Connor as particularly foolish or suicidally brave, but her sister calling—Marie would go alone and never hesitate on it. The thought didn't sit well with him either. "We need to tell the sisters that Amy is alive."

"I know. But I'm not willing to raise hope only to have to tell them Amy spent years running and died twenty months ago. At least not for the next couple days. After that there may be no choice but to tell them."

Connor understood that. "Marsh and I can keep in pretty tight with them for the next forty-eight hours. The weekend makes that pretty easy to handle, and the number of reporters around does at least contain where the sisters are going to want to go. Daniel can help too. The sisters will be spending time with him at places where we've already got security established. The gallery and their apartment flat is covered. Is it enough?"

"The sisters have got money, and Richard Wise is going to want it; so how does the trouble come?" the chief replied.

"A kidnapping or threat of one," Connor finally said, dreading the very thought of it.

"That's what I think too. Forty-eight hours and we'll have to tell the sisters why the security bubble has to stay tight and close. I just hope Amy comes in before then." The chief pushed aside the pad of paper. "Are you okay with this, Connor? I realize it's turned into a pretty personal thing from the initial favor you were asked to do for Daniel."

"Don't worry about it. Marsh dating Tracey would have had me in the middle of this anyway, and I find I like Marie a great deal too. It's no hardship." Connor got to his feet. "Marsh and Tracey are due back tomorrow midday. I'll touch base after I've talked with him. Chief—" He hesitated to ask the question.

"Ask."

"You and Amy—it sounds very personal."

"She wrote an 'if I die' letter; my name's on the envelope. And I'm wondering if I'm about to get it in the mail."

Chapter Seven

Luke was waiting for the mail to arrive, lingering around the house before starting his Saturday errands until he flipped through what was delivered, but he didn't let himself dwell on it. He finished his coffee and walked through to his workshop to open the gun safe. Amy had disappeared twenty months ago, but the news of her disappearance was fresh, as was the real fear she was dead. He would be dreading the mail now until he knew one way or another where she was.

He tugged out a box of gear he'd stored years before.

That "if I die" letter had been written. Amy had hated the idea of disrupting his life by putting his name on the letter. She had asked him to think about it and then never got back to him to see what he thought—but the news she had sisters in his town had removed any question from his mind. Amy had written the letter, put his name and his title on it, and given it to someone she trusted to mail if it became necessary. She would have hoped by doing so she was providing him with enough ammunition to help him keep her sisters safe. If something happened to her she would have wanted him to understand why she was appealing from the grave for his help. The fact Sam had mentioned Amy had made an odd request for Luke's home address and Sam had passed it on just suggested the letter might be coming here rather than the office.

Luke listened for the vehicle with the rough exhaust to rumble by delivering mail into the street-side boxes while he cleaned and repacked gear he had rarely had cause to use since he had been promoted to deputy chief and then police chief. When he'd been down in the trenches he had headed vice, robbery, and then major cases, working when needed on the SWAT team, and while he didn't have the reflexes to be doing that SWAT job again, he figured the equipment and knowledge were going to be useful if this got ugly. If she was alive Amy had to have the news about her sisters by now; she was going to be on her way here.

Your sisters are adjusting to the news about their father, Amy—you'd be proud of them. Now I need to know you're alive before I have to tell them you have been on the run and may be dead. I don't want to be hurting your family that way. Call me; I know you've got the number.

Reality said he had to tell the sisters soon. Tracey and Marsh would be back in town today, Daniel would be meeting Tracey for the first time tomorrow, and Monday the public would be streaming into the gallery if Marie got up the courage to open for the day. Tracey and Marie needed at least one more day to adjust to the huge news about their father before Luke pulled up the past and made it a living thing for them again. But putting it off longer than Sunday night was simply too much of a risk. Luke carried the gear out to his personal car and locked it in the trunk.

The mailman was late this morning.

● ● ● ● ● ●

Marie could see the reporters and cameramen staking out space on the sidewalk below the apartment. They came and went from the deli and the corner store, but otherwise they mingled and talked among themselves or stopped people passing by to do spot interviews. Twice she'd been spotted as she looked down from the new window, and flashbulbs had gone off like fireworks below, as if a photo could be gotten at such a steep angle through a windowpane that was catching the sunlight.

Opening the gallery was not even a consideration today. Marie left it closed and dark and thought about trying to find an accommodation with the press to get them to call it a day, but her courage had deserted her. She didn't want to face more reporters. Connor had been good for her yesterday, making even that unreal day of the news conference workable. But he wasn't around today, the gallery was closed and would stay closed, and she was effectively hiding, waiting for her sister Tracey, who should be back sometime in the next hour.

Marie retreated to the spare-bedroom studio. She'd already spent two hours this morning on the phone talking with friends about the events of the last few days on top of three hours on the phone last night; she was talked out. She'd scratched out a list of things to do in the next month with the money, from changes at the gallery to art auctions she wanted to go see. It was numbing to consider further what she should do.

Find Mandy, fix up the gallery, collect a few personal works of art, figure out who is going to remain safe friends in the future, and get on with things. . . . It wasn't much of a plan, but it was what she had.

God, it's day two. Tell me this gets easier soon. The depression had been weighing on her since she woke. *I'm sure You'll help me figure out what to do with the money and the pressure that's come with it, but I wonder if it was such a good thing to learn my mother had a many-year affair with a married man. I'm ashamed for the family we were rather than the family I'd always cre- ated in my child's-eye view of our lives. It was easier with the fantasy than to learn the reality. I don't know what to do with that hurt at my mom and the father who didn't want to acknowledge me as his child. All those prayers growing up that my mom would marry so I could have a dad; all those painful days being raised by my aunt as other kids had moms and dads to be there for birthdays and holidays. This has brought it all back, and those memories are fresh and the pain still raw.*

Marie picked up one of her new brushes to prep a blank canvas. She couldn't change any of it; she could only try to find some peace to live with it. And it wasn't going to be an easy adjustment.

Her new cousin wasn't such a bad thing. She really liked Daniel and the way he'd handled this. Dinner last night had been filled with stories and laughter, and she thought his personal art collection first-rate. They'd found topics of conversation that were comfortable ground, and she felt a bit easier at the idea of picking up the phone now to hear him on the other end of the line. She thought Tracey would like him too. They'd spend the day with him tomorrow, and he'd promised to have the letters and photos he had of their mother available for them to take home.

It bothered her that Daniel didn't believe in God, but he'd been kind about it when she'd wanted to discuss one of the gifts she hoped to give to her church and how best it could be given. They had had very different lives growing up, and it was going to take a while to feel like she knew him well enough to understand him. But she was trying, and Daniel had met her more than partway, having been remarkably open in his conversation last night about his family and his relationship with his uncle.

And Connor—Marie knew she would have eventually met him through his connection with Marsh, but she doubted under different circumstances Connor would have chosen to spend his day off with her so soon after they first met. She had yet to spend an hour with him where it felt like she was being herself—the money, the situation, the pure shock of all the adjustments had left him seeing some convoluted form of who she really was. Even so, the friendship that had formed over the course of those hours felt like something solid. She could trust him to be what he seemed, and that mattered.

The doorbell screeched. She walked back into the kitchen and to the nook where the security monitor had been installed. It looked like a deliveryman waiting outside her apartment entrance, but then reporters could get disguised as about anyone. And if she opened the door she was just asking for microphones to push her way and cameras to go off. She thought about ignoring the doorbell, but it would be rude if it was a legitimate delivery.

She hesitated and then pushed the button Connor had shown her. "Bryce, I'm going to get a delivery at the street door."

"Thanks. Go ahead. I'll be around there."

She released the button and realized she'd just informed security for the first time of her movements. She wondered how long, if ever, it would take before the absolute strangeness of that wore off. She might have been told Tom Bryce would be around to keep hassles down around the gallery, but it didn't seem to change his plans having the gallery closed rather than open. He simply shifted his attention to watching out for her at the flat.

She pushed a bill to use as a delivery tip into her pocket and walked down the main staircase. Bryce would probably be standing next to the delivery guy, having already confirmed the package was safe before she got the new locks on the door undone, but at this point that kind of attention was fine with her. She didn't want unpleasant surprises.

She pushed open the door.

"I've got a package for Marie Griffin."

"Yes, that's me." She signed the form on the clipboard where indicated. There were flashbulbs going off and shouted questions from the reporters that she did her best to ignore. She thanked the deliveryman who looked ready to bolt with the tip. She got a good hold on the box and took a step back inside, letting the door close and giving her back some breathing room. Tom Bryce standing between her and the reporters helped—none were likely to want to challenge passing that man to get close to her—but still her heart raced with the panic of all those cameras. All for a delivery box. She regretted hoping for another scandal to appear somewhere in town if only to distract the tabloid press and give them some other story to chase.

She looked at the package. She hadn't been expecting anything today. In the upper-left corner of the box where the return address would normally be were the initials of Connor Black, written in a strong, confident hand.

She sat down right where she was on the stairs and opened the box.

A turtle.

A real, live, moving, breathing turtle.

She tugged out the card in the corner of the box, and her smile blossomed. *My advice—you should take life slow for a while. Connor.*

She turned the card to see what he had written along the side. *No need to go too slow though. What's your private, private phone number?*

Her laughter echoed in the stairway.

She looked at the turtle. "I'm going to name you Oscar. I have no idea if you are a girl or a guy and I don't really care because I don't like turtles, but you'll do."

She carried her new company upstairs.

"I'm going to paint and think, and when

I'm no longer in a tongue-tied mess, call him. What do you think of that?"

The turtle didn't move.

"Maybe waiting an hour from the time of the delivery would be long enough to convey I'm following his advice and taking it slow?"

The turtle still didn't move.

"You are alive, Oscar?"

She thought she saw one eye close for a moment.

Catatonic or in shock from the delivery guy moving the box around this way and that; either way, the turtle was having the same kind of week she was having. Marie gently set the box on the coffee table and decided it would take a turtle-care book to tell her what she was supposed to do next. Since Oscar didn't look like he'd be a climber, she thought it best to let him sleep.

She returned to the studio, but this time she caught herself humming as she picked up the brush to resume her preparation work for a canvas.

"Marie?"

"Back in the studio, Tracey."

She grabbed a rag to quickly wipe her

hands. She met her sister just inside the living room, the guy behind her taking a couple blinks before she realized it was Marsh with a good start on a beard.

She was swept into a hug by her sister. "A name for Dad, a new cousin, money, you gave a news conference . . . I only left you alone for like four days and everything happens."

Marie laughed as she returned the hug. "Sorry about that."

Tracey leaned back and studied her face. "You look . . . happy."

"Did you think I wouldn't be?"

"I figured you would be mad at Mom."

Having a clinical psychologist as a sister had its disadvantages. "I am, but it's a hard emotion to settle. So I'm just thinking about other things first."

"That works. Since it's now paid for, I'm staying in school for my PhD. What's your first money thought?"

"Buying Oscar turtle food."

Tracey blinked.

"I'll explain that later," Marie offered.

"Yes, I think you should. What's he like, our new cousin?" Tracey asked, moving to slip off her scarf and jacket.

"Nice, kind, a gentleman but I think touched, just a smidgen, with a bit of rogue."

Tracey glanced up from pulling off her boots, her grin quick. "Single child, responsible son, with humor and that 'going to do what he thinks best' habit already woven into the DNA?"

Marie laughed. "That was my first, second, and third impressions."

"I'm already going to love him."

Marie turned to their guest. "Marsh, can I get you some coffee? You can stay awhile?" He had yet to remove his jacket, and she wasn't sure how to read how things had gone for them this week.

"I told Connor I'd track him down at three. I would love that coffee." His voice was near a baritone, and with the beard starting he looked a lot more rough than usual. She'd always thought he'd looked like a particularly dangerous man and today was giving even more of that impression. That he had a soft heart under all those layers was a simple fact Tracey had known from the earliest days.

Marie moved around the kitchen counter

to start the coffee. "I gather the skiing was a good time?"

Marsh laid his jacket over a chair. "The snow was perfect; a nice powder. Tracey only took a few dramatic spills, thankfully. Your sister was trying to give me a heart attack a few times and laughing as she did it."

Marie smiled, remembering past trips with her sister. "I can believe it."

"I'm getting much better on skis," Tracey defended. She stepped back and into Marsh, who seemed to have grown accustomed to the habit, for he'd braced his feet apart. Tracey leaned against him while his arms settled comfortably around her. Marsh had a good six inches and nine years on her sister, but the two looked more like a couple every time Marie saw them together. She checked Tracey's ring finger just to make sure she wasn't wearing an engagement ring; her sister's happiness had a different quality to it now. "How did you two get past the reporters downstairs?"

"I called Bryce when we were getting close, and he arranged a delivery van to move in a large display board into the side entrance of the gallery. That blocked the sidewalk so we could walk up and into the gallery without being reached by the reporters," Marsh replied. "You look tired, Marie. I'm sorry we were so far away when this news came."

"I admit it's been a long couple days." She smiled at him. "I'm surviving. I met your partner."

"Connor told me. I hope he was on his best behavior."

She looked up and saw a distinct twinkle in the guy's eyes. "He's not quite the gentleman you are, but he tried," Marie replied, smiling softly. "His grandfather likes me too."

"Peter was by . . . that explains a few things." He nodded toward the hall. "I noticed the new doors."

"New doors, windows, locks, it was an incredibly long list. Tracey, before I forget. There're new keys to everything. I left yours on your dresser."

"Thanks. I promised Marsh I'd show him that new landscape we got in; can you give us ten minutes?"

"Sure."

Tracey tugged his hands. "A few minutes

of art, then coffee, and you'll still make it on time to meet Connor."

Marsh smiled. "Marie, she's starting to harass me about the fact I like to be on time. I don't think my trait is rubbing off on her like you had hoped."

Marie laughed. "I noticed." The phone ringing interrupted. "Tell Bryce he's welcome to come have some coffee too." She went to answer the summons.

• • • • • •

Connor shoved aside his gym bag and extra tennis shoes to make room at the bottom of his closet for snow boots and ski gear. Marsh renting equipment when Connor had a closetful hadn't made sense. He pushed the closet door closed and it stayed closed, and Connor decided it was neat enough to do. His partner was in an odd mood. Connor had picked up on it within minutes of his arrival. And he wasn't certain what to do about it.

Marsh was out on the small balcony looking over the traffic the next street over and the parking lot below; the apartment wasn't known for its view. He held a mug of steaming coffee in his hands rather than the cigarette Connor had wondered if he'd see. His partner had busted smoking two years ago, but on stressful days it would show again if life turned bad enough.

"So what's your read on their new cousin?" Marsh asked.

Connor leaned against the brick of the building, the day cold without a jacket. "I've known Daniel a long time; he's a straight shooter."

"He's going to be carrying a lot of influence over the two of them in the next few years. Not only the money, but everything they now relearn about their pasts."

"He's doing his best to protect them from trouble rather than walk them into more of it."

"Maybe."

Connor studied his partner. "What's got you so out of sorts?"

"Tracey didn't particularly take the news about her dad well. She's put on a pretty bright exterior for Marie, but it's not been taken as good news."

"I'm sorry to hear it."

"Yeah." Marsh studied the bottom of his mug and straightened. "They're spending tomorrow with Daniel."

"Marie mentioned it," Connor replied.

"Richer than two oil-well cats, and before I gave her the ring."

So that was the problem. . . . Connor wished there was an answer. "You can't turn back time."

"So we'll spend the rest of our lives defending the charge I married her for her money."

"You could not ask her."

"I might as well slit my own throat." Marsh smiled grimly. "Don't fall in love, Connor. It's not worth it. And what is the deal with that turtle?"

"I'm moving; I couldn't exactly put it in storage."

"You've had that thing since you were a rookie. You just don't give away your only pet and not have people worry about you."

"It was a turtle, Marsh, not a dog. And I figure if she didn't want it the worst that would happen is that I'd have him back. The last thing I needed was to end up with *two* turtles."

"A turtle. You couldn't think of something like roses?"

Connor took the point but bit back a smile. "Marsh, she's already got all the

roses you can dream of, trust me on that."
He pushed away from the wall. "You want to
hear the full story on Amy?"

Marsh sighed. "I think I'd better. Tracey
cries for hours about her dad; tell her the
truth about her sister and I don't think she'll
talk to me again. . . ."

Chapter Eight

Daniel smiled at the younger sister sitting across from him at the table. "Have you settled on what you think yet, Tracey?" He'd been aware that her study of him had been going on throughout their Sunday lunch together, and he was curious as to its reason.

Tracey was more petite than Marie, her face noticeably younger, the brown eyes and the ash blonde hair she had cut to frame her face echoing a strong resemblance to her sister. Daniel liked this sister too; he liked her smile, her laughter, the way she could easily tease Marie out of feeling nervous, and he liked the fact she enjoyed talking casually about so many topics that he got a lot of information about his cousins just by tagging along with the flow. But the study was getting unnerving.

She rested her chin on her hand and studied him some more. "You played band in high school, junior year, trumpet, I think."

He felt embarrassment start. "Of all the things you could have remembered, that one I could have done without. . . ."

"I had a crush on a high school football player; I was not even in junior high yet, but I went to all the games. You marched in those neat rows in those neat uniforms. I really do rarely forget a face, Daniel. But you had me stumped for a while."

"What happened to the guy you had a crush on?"

She chuckled. "Married someone from the math club, I heard. But not before I sent him at least a couple anonymous Valentine's Day cards."

He laughed, wishing he'd been around to know her then. "I bet you were a fascinating kid to know."

"Loyal to a fault and intensely romantic." Tracey looked over at her sister. "Remember that trip to Chicago, when we talked our aunt into letting us go grown-up dress shopping? I thought she was going to have a heart attack when she saw the prom dress number I had picked out. Classic black and designed to make a guy forget where he was at."

"You were dating Willard Graham back then if I remember correctly. No wonder that relationship broke up when you headed to college. You probably had him scared to death with visions of five kids and several dogs by the second date."

Tracey smiled. "You have to admit, the tactic does shake off the weak-kneed pretty quickly." She looked back at Daniel. "Did Marie tell you about the painting that was offered to the gallery? A classic Monet, for sale if she didn't want to purchase it herself. All the publicity she's having being the reason he thought she could get him the best price."

Daniel glanced at Marie. "Lots of changes coming."

"I recommended a dealer in New York. I might spring for better donuts and coffee for the browsers at the gallery, but I really don't want to replace my current clients who might wear boots and construction coats with a set who want champagne and marble floors."

"Judging a bit on appearances, I think, but I concede the point. There's a comfort level the gallery has right now that would be a shame to lose." He picked up his coffee. "I promised you both a tour of Henry's home. Would you like to head over now? It's worth the time if only to see how a prior generation solved some of those money decisions."

Tracey glanced at Marie. "Yes, now would be a good time, Daniel."

●●●●●●

Late Sunday afternoon, Luke motioned Connor and Marsh toward his living room. The cops paused when they saw Sam already there but gamely entered the room and perched on the armrests of the easy chairs.

"Anything seem off with the sisters this afternoon? Anything to suggest Amy has called them?" Luke asked, looking between the two men as he took a seat on the couch.

"Marie teased me about getting her the turtle; she didn't seem that distracted to me," Connor replied, looking over at Marsh for his opinion.

"Tracey was enthralled with some waterfall she saw built in beside the fireplace in Henry's living room—that's pretty conclusive she wasn't pondering very heavy thoughts," Marsh agreed.

Luke looked at his watch. The news conference had been Friday morning; they were past fifty hours now. Amy had already made town—he was sure of it. If she was alive, she was here.

"She'll call me, Luke," Sam remarked.

"I hope so. Is there any way we can find her if she's here and burrowing her way into town again? any pattern we can watch for? Names? Hotels? Anything that might be predictable?"

"I doubt she's using a name I would know, and she's a chameleon for how she changes up her behavior. Beyond someone spotting her near her sisters or the new cousin, there's not much hope of figuring out where she would have settled into town."

Connor ran his hand through his hair. "We've got to tell the sisters, Chief. We got through the weekend, but next week they are planning a private party for Tuesday night so friends can stop in and celebrate with them; Marie is talking about reopening the gallery for business; Tracey plans to head back to college toward the end of the week. . . ."

Luke knew it was necessary. "I'll ask Daniel to arrange something for tomorrow around noon, down at the office, and we'll break the news to the sisters then." He looked over at Sam. "Do we have anything else out of New York?"

"Richard Wise is trying to run his organization from prison, but his grip is sliding. Most of those still around consider this old business best forgotten, and as for leaving New York—they aren't in a hurry to do so. They go out of town right now, someone will use the opportunity to take their turf. But there are a few down in the ranks who would be of concern. I've got photos and names of the most likely dozen and a promise from New York to hear if they suddenly turn up missing from their normal haunts."

"The wiretaps giving anything?"

"They know they are tapped and aren't using the phones. I asked New York to probe. It's a whispered legend that Amy Griffin took Richard's money and got away with it. And they know the sisters have come into money. It's not the fact they know I'm worried about—it's what Richard Wise is still able to do about it. And that isn't entirely clear."

"The shooter they think killed the boyfriend—he's on the list?"

"Still alive, in his fifties, and semiretired from the business as best the cops can tell. Richard Wise went to jail, and the others in the organization weren't eager to take on the guy's services—afraid not only that he knows too much but that age might be making him sloppy and more likely to get caught. And he's probably got his own reasons for wanting a quieter life right now— the cops would love to convict him of at least seven hits they think he was involved with; he's staying out of the business for a reason."

"Amy was at the scene of that shooting; she could identify him." She'd never said that when giving her version of events, but Luke had read the report. A lady had been in the car and had been seen being chased from the scene: Amy. She'd seen her boyfriend murdered and been lucky to escape that night alive. "If they want to make a case against him, an eyewitness to a hit is a nice place to start. Tell New York he's at the top of our list for news of his movements. He'll have the most cause to want her dead."

"I'll convey it."

He could keep the two sisters alive if he surrounded them with enough security, but it was an open-ended problem. They had to figure out how to end this for good. They needed Amy alive and well and able to finally testify and put away those who were a threat to herself and her family. Any other route just left the sisters open targets.

He looked at Connor. "What else has happened since the news conference that might be trouble?"

Connor grimaced. "The tabloid reporters are getting aggressive. They tried to stop the car Marie and Tracey were in this morning to get a few quotes. Daniel had sent the car, and it was one of Silver's guys driving. He handled it without running one of the reporters over, so we'll call that one a wash. Bryce has the sisters at about two hundred phone calls now—the gamut of those seeking money and those wanting to help them invest it. One woman claimed to be their aunt's sister; another wanted information on why Marie looked like a twin of her cousin. Both are nonstarters. Two clear threats among the calls, but the calls were traced down to psychiatric hospitals and the appropriate staff notified."

"Do Marie and Tracey know about the calls?"

"No."

"Let's leave it that way."

"They won't be hearing it from us," Marsh agreed. He looked at his watch. "I'm taking Tracey out to dinner, and unless I'm mistaken Connor is hoping to take a slice of Marie's time tonight, so we'd best be making tracks."

"I only mentioned I was thinking about it," Connor informed his partner, but he was smiling.

Luke thought of the two of them one day being married to sisters and didn't know if he was personally ready for it. "Thanks, guys. I'll let you know what time Daniel arranges for tomorrow. Sam, stick around a minute," he requested as Sam rose too.

His officers headed out, and Luke waited

until he heard the door close. "Tell me more about the guy they think shot the boyfriend."

Luke's dogs were roaming his backyard, and his cat was wandering underfoot looking for more handouts. Luke lifted the lid on the grill and turned the steaks. Sam had declined staying for a meal, but the meat had needed to be used tonight so he was cooking more than he could eat.

He was getting too old to deal with the lingering tension that came with waiting for something to happen. It ate at a man, consumed his thoughts, and no matter how much he tried to push aside the fact in the end it really wasn't his decision that would matter, it still did. He wanted Amy alive and back safely with her family. For the man who had lost the money and for the shooter who knew Amy was a witness, there was nothing old and forgotten about this case. Luke grew more concerned with every passing hour that this was going to end in another tragedy, and he'd had enough of those in his town.

The phone rang.

He'd set it on the picnic table next to his glass of iced tea and the barbeque sauce. He reached over for the phone. "Granger."

"It's Amy."

The meat sizzling on the grill seemed overly loud, the dogs following scents through the bushes like crashing bricks. He pushed away the sensation of being pulled back in time and simply smiled, hoping it would be conveyed in his voice and help lower the tension he could hear in her first words. "Hey there, lady. You kept my card."

"Memorized the numbers."

Silence lengthened.

"You're not pushing. Thank you."

"I'm aware how hard it was just to dial. You okay?" he asked softly. He wasn't going to put her as crying, but she did sound at her limit.

"Yeah. They're safe?"

"Yes." He took the steaks off the grill and closed the lid to burn out the charcoal bricks.

"I need to see you."

"Just tell me when and where; I'll be there."

"You'll need a pen."

He already had it and his pocket pad of paper out. "Go ahead."

He wrote down the directions she gave him and searched his memory to put a location to the spot. Then it clicked. She was across the lake from his own hunting cabin, probably able to sit out on the dock and watch his place with binoculars. He'd inherited the cabin from his father and never had the desire to sell it. The land was registered a county over and only with first initials, but she'd done her homework and found it.

"You got the exact location from that?" she stressed.

"I did."

She'd chosen a good spot to meet. His place was remote, isolated, but several roads in and out of the area. And if car lights showed anywhere near the address she'd given him, she'd be long gone, knowing someone had been listening in to the call. The lady was more than just wary—she was frightened.

"It has to be tonight, after it gets dark."

"Three hours. And if you need to wave off, go; the second number you have will come directly to me until you can call in again," he promised.

"Thanks."

He held the phone for a good minute after it went silent, thinking, replaying her words. No signs it had been a forced call on her part, no signs she had a gun to her head at the moment. Just one very frightened lady who didn't strike him as easily frightened even after everything she had been through.

He could ask Marsh and Connor to join him; he could ask Jonathan Silver for some guys. He could, but he didn't call them. In the back of his mind was the fact there was a dead cop in Detroit. If someone came searching for information, he would rather have that fury directed at him than at one of his officers. His gear was already in his car. It might be three hours before she appeared, but he could do some looking around of his own in that time.

He brought out a metal pan for the steaks and covered them with foil, slid the tray into a sack, and added the dish of scalloped potatoes he'd had warming in the oven. He was spending his life feeding her, but it was a small way to at least offer her something tangible to help her relax.

He picked up his coat and gloves and whistled for the dogs.

●●●●●●

The cabin was cold, dark, and smelled a touch musty, but Luke knew that would soon change as it came back to life. So many good memories with his dad were here—the vacations fishing, hiking in the woods, trying to find a deer during hunting season. Luke slid the food into the oven, turned the temperature to keep the tray warm, and then set about checking the fireplace flue and lighting a stack of the dryer logs. They flamed quickly and soon roared, casting off heat. In an hour the comfort level in here would come up several notches.

He wasn't worried about someone getting close enough to be trouble; his dogs were out now, roaming around the cabin grounds. He'd offered the dogs the jacket Amy had left behind years before that he'd kept folded in a storage box to give them a hint of her scent, and they would treat her now as a friend. But anyone else coming near—he'd have warning.

Amy had walked away from so much after the jewelry-store murders—the house, the vehicle, her things—and left him dealing with a missing person's report filed by her friends, which he could only work in vague ways. His reassurances she had left town to get away from the press hadn't been adequate words for any of her friends. The bank had eventually taken back the house and auctioned off the contents; he'd used the key under the frog before that happened to let himself into the place one last time to retrieve a box of the things he thought she might want back one day. It had been more an act of hope than of planning ahead, but he was glad now he'd done it.

The fire going strong and the screen in place, he left the lights in the cabin itself dimmed and picked up the bag of gear he had brought in with him. Most of it was military gear, acquired through arrangements with the local national guard. Night-vision goggles didn't solve as many problems as civilians thought, but they were one of the tools that could help. Someone after Amy, following her, that was the real risk.

He settled outside on the back deck and began to listen and look. The night was cold, growing colder, but he sat in stillness and slowly his senses became tuned in to the smaller movements around him. The leaves rustling as small animals scurried across, the wind in the trees, the lighter sounds of water moving on the lake, and the occasional swift flight of a bird hunting at night.

It was peaceful out here, and as the time wore by he felt himself relaxing.

What's going to give first, God? Nothing happens without a plan and purpose behind it. That inherited money can either be a good thing or a very bad thing for the sisters' future. I worry about it being more trouble than anyone expects, of danger staying around and shadowing them for months to come. There has to be a way to put this family back together, to restore justice to events that are far from just. Amy needs a life back; she's lost so many years living on the run, staying one step ahead of the threat. It's time, God, time to answer my prayers and let me solve this. I'm not sure what step has to come next. Amy's got to have the courage to trust me, and I know that won't be an easy thing to ask of her.

Luke wondered at times if his life had come together for just such days as this— so many past tragedies and investigations had passed by that when there was a way to stop violence there was very little he wouldn't do to try and intervene. His sister had hugged him after hearing the news he had made police chief and then cried on him too. She understood the pressures of becoming police chief and the reality of what it would mean for her dream of him settling down to marriage and family. It didn't preclude it, but it did mean choices were being made for his time and energy and focus, and it would slide getting married further into the background and longer into the future. She loved him, and she understood what life took away even as it gave more responsibility.

And maybe because that was his past, Luke understood better who Amy was and a few of the sacrifices she had made for her family over the past years. She had set aside much of her life and a career to carry the responsibility of seeing justice done— turning in the evidence of those bribed, cleaning up a criminal organization because she'd unexpectedly been thrust into that responsibility. She hadn't abdicated the task, declared it too hard; she'd accepted and bore it as best she knew how. But everything had an ending, and she was entering that final chapter now. He just hoped he was going to be adequate help to her as it unfolded. There was being prepared and there was being able to prevent—and he knew better than to hope he could prevent the trouble coming. The best he could likely do was be in place to stop it.

He heard her before he saw her, because the dogs heard her and moved together to the edge of thicker woods. She'd come around the lake, it appeared.

"Are you Chester or Wilks?"

Luke smiled as the soft words drifted his way. She'd knelt to greet the dogs, and they were going ecstatic with the belly rubs. She walked his way, his two shadows having transferred their loyalties already. It had to be something about women—they did that with his sister too.

He waited until she was about fifteen feet out. "Hello, Amy."

"Luke."

"I see you remembered their names."

"I've a good memory that way." She walked up the two steps to the back deck to join him. She looked thinner than he remembered, the change obvious in her face and her hands, and her smile was there but not nearly as easy as it had once been.

"Why don't you warm up inside for a couple minutes. How many do you think were tailing you?"

"There's been two pretty persistently, on and off, for quite a while now. But I don't think they were able to pick up my trail coming toward town."

"Okay. The dogs can go in with you if you like."

She smiled and snapped her fingers. The dogs slipped inside with her.

Luke picked up the binoculars again and turned his attention back to the area, searching, thinking. She'd gone cold twenty months ago. She'd been dodging someone after her that full time, never able to shake them . . . that spoke more of an investigative team than the enforcer type who would want to be able to do his job in a matter of days, not spend months on it. Even if they hadn't caught her trail here, they would have seen the same news conference. There was no need to try and follow her when they knew exactly where she was heading. They would have just leapfrogged ahead and been patiently waiting for her to

appear. But there was always a chance—
Luke watched until he was certain the area
was quiet.

He held open the door. "Wilks, Chester,
guard."

The dogs moved outside in a rush, divid-
ing up as they went through the door and
none of the roaming-around behavior of
earlier anywhere in evidence. They looked
mean now in a subtle way, hair stiffer, patient, standing to smell the air for anything,
anyone. Former police dogs did come with
some useful training.

Amy stood by the fire, warming her
hands. She'd shed the coat and gloves.
Thinner, dressed for the cold, the sweater
cream-colored wool, the jeans new, the
boots polished. She looked nothing like the
lady he had met three years ago. "I think I
like you as a redhead."

She gave a slight smile. "It's closer to the
real me."

"We've safely got an hour, Amy. It will take
at least that long for someone to try and get
in near this cabin quiet enough to avoid the
dogs." He moved over to the oven and slid
out the tray. "I know, more food. But you
called my cell phone while I was just taking

the steaks off the grill, and it seemed the thing to do."

She laughed and he liked the sound of it. "I can't say I mind; it's been a long few days of traveling." She pulled out a chair at the table, which dominated the room.

"The steaks aren't going to be my best, but they'll do on a cold night."

He waited to see if she had any appetite at all or was simply being polite. Her answers were open enough, her voice calm, but she hadn't met his gaze for more than a moment since she had arrived. The tension in her was skimming just under the surface.

Not much appetite, he concluded within moments. The fact she wasn't looking at him told him more. "How close did they get?"

She turned the glass of iced tea he had poured her, looking at the way the firelight reflected through the ice cubes. "Waiting in my home when I came back from work one night," she finally said softly.

He wanted to reach over and touch her hand, to ask what had happened that night but knew there were some memories just better left alone. "I'm sorry."

"At least there wasn't someone dead left

in my wake this time. They had someone in-side the FBI group; that's the only thing that makes sense for how they got on my trail."

"You've been running since Minnesota?"

"You've been talking with Sam."

"Finally. I should have realized he was working for you years before."

"Sometimes keeping people safe can mean being very rude. I couldn't chance getting in touch, Luke. And Sam . . . he knew the dangers going in."

"I know."

"How are they? Marie and Tracey?"

"They're safe; they're getting accustomed to the news of their father and the will. They seem to get along okay with the new cousin."

"I remember Daniel from high school in a vague kind of way."

"He's been a friend of mine for a long time, Amy; he'll handle this right."

"That's good to know."

She toyed with her food, and he won-dered how long she'd been so tight on the edge of breaking. The confidence he'd seen in her years ago was a thing of the past; she had felt hunted for a very long time, and it showed in the strain around her.

"Richard will try to get the money from them," she said quietly.

"I know. The security guys around your sisters are aware how serious the threat is. No one is taking chances with this."

"I ran to keep them safe, and now trouble just walked in and swallowed them. Do they know?"

"No, but they're going to have to be told. For their own safety they have to know the threat out there."

She nodded and then picked up the glass and walked away from the table to return to the fire and the warmth being cast off from it. "What would you have said, if I had called all those years ago?"

He pushed away his plate before he answered. "Yes, with a condition: that you come in from the cold. That you settle around here where I can watch out for you. I'll keep you safe. And if I fail—if I can't keep you alive, then I'll accept the letter and finish what you began."

"I left myself open for that counter; I didn't think of it."

"Think about it now. Your choice of name, location, job. Just as before. But when you come, this time I'm watching your back. You

should say yes. It's the final steps to freedom, and for that you need to trust someone to help you. Let me."

He wanted her to trust him, wanted it
more than he could explain, but as he
watched her struggle with what to say, what
to decide, he knew it was still wishful thinking that she'd be able to make that huge of
a step right now. "Give me a chance, Amy.
This time the cops aren't going to let you
down."

She looked up, and there was uncertainty
in her eyes, a want to believe him and a
doubt fixed by experience. She offered a
quick smile. "You surprised me, and I didn't
think that was possible anymore."

He noted the change in subject but
wasn't going to press his offer and risk a no.
He couldn't afford a no from her, not when
that meant she'd be on her own as this was
wrapped up.

"I'm worried about the cop I already
pulled into this."

"Who is he? The guy you trusted with the
accounts?"

"An FBI agent with the Dallas office
named Jim Nelson. Fifties, a wife and two
college-aged kids; he worked narcotics

cases in the New York office before moving to Texas."

"Did you really worry about him taking the money if you turned over everything you had?"

"No. I worry about him turning up dead." She studied the burning logs in the fireplace. "There isn't much they could force him to say. The handoffs are always done with no notice to him, and I leave the state immediately afterward. He's never known where I was or when I would be back in touch. He doesn't know the name Ann Walsh or Kelly Brown or the other names I've used; he doesn't know I was ever in this state. But still I worry that somehow Richard Wise figures out Jim is the cop I've been talking to and turns his fury that direction. Jim's at risk, and as much care as the man takes, I still worry that it won't be enough. The guys on my tail—they showed up within days of my last handoff. The only thing that makes sense is they had Jim already under surveillance from the prior accounts I'd turned over or else someone in that office got turned."

"I'm sorry. You must see you can't run forever. You need more help than Sam can give you. And your sisters—it would destroy them to hear you'd been running all these years and then were killed. You can't do that to them."

"They're in enough risk without me showing my face and just adding to that risk."

"You came back to see them, didn't you? to know for certain they were safe? that they had adequate protection?"

She didn't turn her attention from the fire, but she nodded.

"Then let me do my job and help you out. Let me set up a reunion."

She violently shook her head, not looking back toward him.

He walked around the table and joined her, sliding an arm around her shoulders as she battled silent tears. He could feel her grief, and he wished he could end it. "They've thought you were dead for the last eight years; let's end at least one grief they've carried. We can go on the offensive to deal with the rest of it."

"I'd bring trouble right to their doorstep."

"Trouble's already here, and your presence won't change it. If anything, your being so hard to find makes your sisters the more attractive targets."

The words were cruel to be kind, and he felt her stiffen. "You can't drive your sisters into a life on the run too, and that's what this is going to come down to unless it is finally stopped. Let me and the officers working with me do our jobs; let us finally stop this."

"It can't be done."

He smiled. "Sure it can. Richard Wise is in jail. The guys who still have enough loyalty to him to do his bidding are less than a couple dozen. All it takes is one or two arrests and you and your sisters are suddenly not nearly so attractive a problem to take up. We'll win based on attrition, if nothing else."

She didn't answer him.

"Trust me, Amy. Please."

He felt the sigh that came from her as a soft acceptance. "I so want to see them again, just once."

He eased back a step and pulled out a handkerchief. He gently wiped at the tear traces on her cheeks. "Let me set it up. Let me show you it is possible to safely settle here near your family."

"If there's a mistake, one or both of them dies."

"Do you really have a choice? You leave them thinking you are dead, they'll resume the search for information. They'll slip security around them not realizing the risk. They'll let someone looking for you convince them you're still alive. It's not going to get better, Amy. It's not going to go back to the way it was."

"One time, Luke, one meeting. That's all I can offer."

"Then I'll take it." He tucked the handkerchief into her hand and smiled to lighten the moment. "Practical stuff first. What name are you using? Where are you staying?"

"I can't answer that. I can't," she whispered.

The words erased his smile and his optimism. The idea he was through this lady's fear was merely a shadow; he didn't have her trust yet. He pulled back the hope he'd felt and quietly settled for what he thought she could accept. "Are you okay for cash?"

"Yes."

"Got something to wear to a reunion?"

It got him a brief smile.

"I'll get it set up for Thursday night, somewhere private, easy for you to access, and far from the attention that is around your sisters. I'll make sure your sisters get there without a reporter or anyone else trailing them."

"They can't know ahead of time. The odds are too high I might have to wave off."

It was a reasonable fear. "I can wait until you are there, then give the all clear to their escorts. If it's waved off they'll never know it was ever being planned."

"Thank you."

"I brought a phone with me for you, never used; the number is not going to be in anyone's hands. Call me Wednesday night, eight o'clock. I'll give you the details for when and where. Are you set okay for transportation? I can arrange another car. . . ."

"It's covered."

He wasn't sure what to ask next, to say.

She looked away from him. "It's best I get going. Thank you, Luke. You can't imagine how much I want to see them again."

"Thursday's going to be just the beginning."

"We'll see. Thanks too for the meal."

"Next time we'll make it a dinner when you're feeling more able to eat." He helped her with her coat. His expression sobered. "No matter what happens, if trouble shows up, if you have to leave, promise you'll call me. Promise you won't just disappear again without a word."

"I'll call." She rested her hand on his arm, squeezed gently, and disappeared through the back door.

Luke heard his dogs greet her. He cleared away the dinner plates, put the remaining pieces of steak on two paper plates for the dogs, and when he moved to the back door to let them in, Amy was gone.

Chapter Nine

The ground wasn't frozen yet, but it was hard packed and ankle turning, and the walk took twenty minutes across rough pasture. She was a lone figure on the horizon with nothing around her but the fence she was working on and the tools she carried. The destination was easy, but what Luke would say was not so simple. It was too early for the coffee he carried even though the sun was up, his sleep something that had ended with the alarm clock sounding at 4 a.m. He could think of a lot easier ways to start his Monday morning.

"You're a hard lady to find, Lieutenant."

Caroline St. James looked around to see him, and he caught a brief flash of surprise followed by stillness. "Chief." She turned her attention back to the job at hand and tightened another coil of barbed wire, then stapled it to the post.

"I thought you were staying in the city this winter."

"My uncle needed a hand."

"Humm." It looked like she was rebuilding most of this pasture fencing. He set aside his coffee and put his weight against the next wire to be stretched and pulled it taut. She drove in the staples.

She'd grown up on this land. She'd learned to shoot in the upper pasture firing at old Coke bottles and learned to be still and watch by tracking deer through the woods. He'd thought when he first met her that the city and the job wouldn't be her cup of tea, but she'd turned out to be one of the best cops he'd ever had the privilege of working with.

"What brings you out to find me?"

"Trouble."

She paused long enough to read his expression. "Not a shot cop."

"Not quite that bad."

She picked up her tools and moved to the next fence post.

"Have you been following what's been going on with the Griffin sisters?"

"I'm not entirely cut off from the news out here, Chief." She smiled. "I've met the youngest, Tracey. Marsh is seriously attached to that one."

"There are three sisters: Marie, Tracey, and Amanda. The oldest, Amanda, you'll remember as Kelly Brown."

Caroline stopped working and leaned against the post to consider the name. She nodded. "Bressman's Jewelry store three years ago—the murders. The lady gave us the name of the shooter—yeah, I remember her. I was interviewing one of the former employees who had made a threat against the store manager when Marsh passed word they had an ID on the shooter. You've got me curious."

"Amy witnessed a hit in New York eight years ago and has been running ever since. There's a dead cop along the trail, along with a few other close calls, and a bunch of money a guy wants back at any cost."

"And her sisters just inherited money and became new targets."

"Yes."

Caroline winced. "I can see that would indeed be trouble." She secured the next loop of the wire. "What do you need?"

"A safe place for a reunion. The two sisters think Amy died in New York. They haven't seen her in eight years."

"She's back in town?"

He smiled. "She keeps her own counsel, kind of like someone else I know. She'll call me Wednesday night for details."

"There are a lot of reporters around the sisters. I've seen the news stories being run every day. They are making the two of them the main celebrities for the winter people-watching season."

Luke smiled at the way she put it but thought it pretty accurate. The events in Marie's and Tracey's lives were being made into something even bigger than their story already was. "I'll arrange the transportation to get them out of that spotlight. I need somewhere remote, absolutely private, with several roads in and out, and if you can add elegance and food and drinks and a lot of Kleenex it would help. Plan for Thursday night, and I'll bring them in after dark."

"I've been chosen for this assignment, I see; why?"

"Amy's former army too."

Caroline looked at him. "You always did like to go for the jugular when you needed to use it."

"Logistics, she said. And good at it. She was in a long time."

Caroline sighed. "It's going to cost."

Luke held out an envelope. "Blank checks already signed and you're authorized for all three cards; try not to max them all out, please."

She tucked the envelope into her coat pocket. "At this point I'm curious enough I've got no choice but to do it just to meet her. You know her well?"

"Not nearly as well as I would like." He reached for his coffee, satisfied the biggest objective of his day was covered. "You should think about coming back to take over major cases, Caroline."

"I retired."

"Unretire." He reached out a hand to rub her coat sleeve. "You're missed. And there is nothing you could have done differently."

"He left behind a wife and two kids, and I'm the one who put two bullets in him. He was breaking up under the stress in his life, and the officers around him didn't see and stop the spiral. I can't do my job when I'm wondering what is going through the head of the guy beside me and behind me."

Luke didn't dispute any of it; he—more than anyone—knew the pain she carried. She was tall and proud and comfortable with herself, but the shooting had taken a lot away from her. "You'll suffocate out here, in the absence of the job you wanted since you were a kid. You are a good cop, and nothing that happened changed that."

"I don't want the dream anymore, Luke. It's not worth the hurt."

He slowly nodded. "Think about it anyway. I'm keeping a slot in the payroll for you—any time, any job—you'll be welcome back."

"I appreciate it." She picked up her tools. "What of this do you want to approve?"

"I'll trust your judgment. I'll just need specifics before Wednesday evening."

"Who knows about the reunion?"

"Me. You. In a short while Marsh and Connor. That will be it."

"That's best."

"I think so too."

"I'll call you when I have something arranged."

"Thanks, Caroline. It means a lot."

She smiled. "I think you mean Amy means a lot. I'm glad for you."

"Don't get your hopes up; she won't even tell me the name she's using now." He smiled and finished his coffee. "I think someone is going to fall hard for you one day, Caroline, and they'll never know what hit them."

"I do have that effect on guys," she agreed, smiling back. "Get to work, Chief. This problem is covered."

Because he knew just a layer of the depths in this woman and the deeper waters inside her heart, he reached over and gently brushed a glove down her cheek. "I'm glad we dated all those years ago; I've been waiting for someone to match you for a very long time." She'd been in the army then and home between deployments. Caroline was one of the most fascinating ladies he had ever had the privilege of getting to know, as well as being one of the most beautiful. The years hadn't changed that impression of his friend.

"You'll find her sometime, maybe this time. And, Chief—" she smiled as she shared a secret—"Marsh already bought the ring for the youngest sister. Just so you know."

. . . . . .

Luke tugged off his coat as he entered his office and dumped it on the box of reading materials he had to get to eventually. His Monday was already looking to be a flurry of calls and meetings, and finding time wasn't going to happen, so he was making it where he could. "Close the door, Connor."

Connor closed the door, and he and Marsh took seats across from the desk.

Luke took a deep breath and knew how unusual his request was going to sound. "I need you two to arrange dates for Thursday night, and get Tracey and Marie over near Pliat County for the evening. Any problems with that?"

Marsh looked at Connor and back at him. "No, sir, there shouldn't be. They've got a private party tomorrow night for friends at the gallery, but otherwise their calendar was still clear."

"Amy called," Connor said quietly, looking for confirmation.

Luke nodded. "St. James is helping me set something up for late Thursday night;

we're going to try and get the sisters safely together for a reunion."

"I'll need a pay raise for all the Kleenex this is going to take. Amy's okay?" Marsh asked.

"She's got guys trailing her, and it won't take much to have her call it off. I need you to arrange it so if this aborts, Marie and Tracey have no idea it was ever planned. I'll call around eight Thursday night—if it's on, come to the location St. James arranges, but if there's been trouble, take the sisters straight home."

"Yes, that's probably best. Who else knows?"

"Me, you two, St. James. I'll tell Sam she's made contact but not about the meeting. If trouble's not here already, it will be anytime. The less people who might be followed or overheard the better. Amy said there have been two guys on her trail on and off for quite some time. They'll have seen that news conference too."

Marsh rose. "We'll talk to Caroline and make sure we're clear on the area where this will go down."

"Guys . . ." Luke hesitated. "Amy's fragile right now, very much on edge. Try to make sure the sisters have some perspective on it even if you can't tell them what is coming. Anything you can do will help."

"She not only called; you met her," Marsh said softly.

"Yes."

"This will go down smoothly, Chief. Whatever it takes," Connor replied.

"Thanks, guys."

● ● ● ● ● ●

"So what are you doing on this beautiful day?" Connor asked.

Pleased at Connor's call, Marie shifted the phone and looked down at the street. "My plans for opening the gallery at 10 a.m. look like a waste of time. There are six reporters and cameramen out there, Connor. I counted them. It's ridiculous."

"Bryce is around?"

"Yes. He's the only bright spot around here. They'd be pounding on glass and holding the doorbell button down if he wasn't out there making his presence loom large in their minds." She turned away from the window to resume her work folding laundry, the phone tucked against her shoulder.

"Daniel was arranging a pool interview to try and back them off?"

"Tomorrow morning at nine with both Tracey and me. Maybe it will help but I don't know. Most of them are from the tabloid press and are looking for dirt at any cost. They've been calling our friends, our former schoolmates, anyone with a story to tell. Did you see the paper today?" There had been another piece on the family with most of it being hashed over thirdhand quotes about her aunt and mother and her sister Mandy, but it had been deeply embarrassing just the same, more innuendo than fact and overly aggressive in the picture it painted of the affair Henry had had. Marie knew the article must have deeply wounded Daniel too. She'd like to tarnish that reporter's name in reply but had no means to fight back.

"Sykes is an aggressive reporter looking for anything that can get him promoted from the city daily to a national paper. He's filling space with whatever he can get to have the byline. Ignore him. It's not going to stay this way forever."

"I know. That's just easier said than done."

"Let it go. So what are your modified plans for today?"

She turned her attention to what she'd been doing when he called. "Finish the laundry, then work with Tracey on the party plans for tomorrow night. So far we've made a hundred thirty invitation calls, and not a one has said they can't make it. You would think someone in our circle of friends would have other more pressing arrangements for tomorrow night."

Connor laughed. "Yeah, right. You're inviting everyone you and Tracey know?"

"Pretty much. If I've got to explain everything and answer questions and plaster a smile on my face for a few hours, at least I want it over in one night. Not that I mind talking about this turn of events . . . I just get tired of doing nothing but talking about it."

"I know what you mean. I think the party is a good solution. What else is on your week?"

"Daniel wants us to meet with a couple attorneys Wednesday. He insists we have independent representation not associated with Benton Group or Henry. The rest of the day will be trying to get some order back into the gallery after the party. I'll keep the gallery closed for another week, interview two more possible staff on Friday, and adjust to thinking about maybe next week getting my life back into some order."

"Give it time, Marie. The days are going to be like this for a while, but they'll eventually return to normal. Would you maybe like to catch dinner and a movie some night this week, say Thursday? I've got a day in court so I should be getting off at a reasonable time."

Marie looked down the hall to where Tracey was singing with the radio as she sorted out her things to take back with her to college. She'd heard Tracey on the phone with Marsh earlier that morning and left to give them privacy for the call, but not before she had heard her sister confirm a date for Thursday night. Since the choice was staying at home by herself or going out, there wasn't much of a decision to make. She would enjoy an evening out. "I'd like that, Connor. As long as it can be somewhere I'm not going to get approached by hordes of well-wishers."

She heard Connor chuckle. "I can probably manage that. Any kind of movie you don't like?"

"Avoid the blood-and-guts kind, but otherwise I'm flexible."

"Easy enough. I'll call for you around six-thirty, and make it dress up. I've got a nice quiet place in mind that does wonderful Italian."

"I'll look forward to it. Thanks, Connor."

"You'll hear from me again today; I'm just catching ten minutes while I sit and watch for a guy that I suspect is already in Honduras by now."

She smiled. "You got stood up."

"Happens all the time in this profession, I'm afraid. Enjoy today, Marie, even with all the obstacles."

"I'll do that."

She was smiling as she set down the phone.

"That was Connor?" Tracey asked, slipping in earrings as she came in.

"Yes. It looks like I'm going out Thursday night as well."

"Marsh said dress up, so I was thinking of a shopping trip this afternoon. You want to risk it? Maybe head over to those shops near the college?"

"Yes, let's do that." Tracey had a great eye for clothes and what accessories went well together, and Marie would enjoy hearing her opinion on what she found. "Let's splurge on new outfits for the party tomorrow night as well."

Tracey headed back to get her purse and jacket, and Marie smiled as she thought about what she wanted to look for in a dress. Dates were special occasions and called for special things.

Mandy, I wish you were going shopping with us. These are big days in our lives, and there's a void that never fills when you're not here to join us. I hope heaven is nice. You are missed here.

With the will and the new wealth had come the possibility that they could finally get some closure regarding her sister. Sam had agreed to meet her and discuss what could be done to learn more about what had happened in New York years ago. There had to be a solution to this hurt.

Does peace ever come, God? So many years grieving the loss with You and it never really seems to get better or less sharp. I don't know what I expected You to do for me about the hurt, but the fact it's still so raw—I guess I didn't expect that after all these years. Tracey's going to pick up on my mood if I'm not careful, and I don't want that. She deserves the happiness she's found with Marsh, and I am looking forward to going out with Connor. He strikes me as a nice guy to have as a friend if not something a lot more. Please help me shake this sadness, at least for today.

Facts couldn't be changed; she'd long ago accepted that. But they still hurt—and badly—in the memories that did not fade.

Marie went to join Tracey, forcing a smile in place and pushing back the sadness.

Chapter Ten

The sharp cold had eased by Wednesday morning, and the chief appreciated that fact as he walked with Caroline St. James through the grounds of a private home on the border of the next county east of town. "You're comfortable with the security?"

"I put a guy on it yesterday afternoon to confirm things, and it came back as solid."

The location was perfect, and the place—he would have never thought the ambassador to Denmark lived in the area, but then he hadn't expected Caroline to find him something ordinary. "How'd you arrange it?"

"I asked a favor, and he had the keys dropped off. I know him from my army days when he was on the NATO staff."

"Dated his son?"

She smiled at him. "A friend did. I knew the place was empty while he was abroad. His son stayed here most recently, but he got deployed to Guam a few months back. It will do?"

"In spades. Secluded, good security, solid-rock walls on the perimeter—it's probably as close to a fortress as this county has for an estate."

"I've still got some work to do to make sure there are safe secondary locations nearby if needed and arrangements made to have dogs on the grounds, but that won't take much beyond your money to solve."

"Spend it, as much as you need."

"I will. I'll pick up food from the caterers at four and have it set up by, say, six. Nothing fancy, just stuff that can keep hot easily on warming trays that will taste better the longer it heats. The living room will have both fireplaces lit, and I'll see about some music. It should be comfortable enough to give a few conversation points if there's a delay between when everyone arrives. The only room in the house that would be considered off-limits is already securely locked. If they end up wanting to talk until 3 a.m., push them toward guest rooms—there are several—and I'll have breakfast stuff on hand. Amy can leave the next evening once it's full dark. It won't be a problem to take the extra day. I didn't tell the ambassador what was going down, but he's had enough under-the-radar meetings to appreciate the request and why I made it."

"I appreciate the possibility. The sisters will want the time, so it's just a matter of how Amy's handling it."

Caroline handed over a slip of paper. "Security codes for the front gate that I've already changed now for our stay. I'll revert them back before I return the keys. Tell Amy to pull all the way around and into the garage. I'll make sure there are open slots. She can walk through the breezeway into the house without having to step outdoors. There's half-a-mile visibility on the main road approaching the gate. If she's got a tail when she makes that last turnoff, let her know there's a maintenance road just past the larger of the three boulders, and it's possible to make that turn and speed east. She'll knock around the car shocks, but it's a clear shot right to the interstate, and for busting a tail that's where I would head."

"I'll pass the word."

"When is she calling again?"

"Eight tonight."

"I'll have the secondary locations arranged by then at the local hotels, probably an apartment building too, if she wants to use one earlier in the day to help ease her way this direction."

Luke nodded. The arrangements for the meeting were tight. Now it was down to things no one could control—how the sisters reacted, if they could handle having to be silent about the truth in the future days, whether Amy accepted staying around the area or this really did become the only time they would see each other until this was resolved . . . so many factors that would have to simply be dealt with as they came.

"She'll stay this time; Amy will stay."

He smiled at Caroline's confidence. "I'm smart enough not to take that bet, but I'll hope." He put the slip of paper into his pocket. "Anything I can do for you in return? This was mountain moving in forty-eight hours."

"I'll call you for lunch one day, and you can take me someplace extra nice."

"Consider it a standing invitation. How's your uncle doing?"

She shrugged. "Old enough he'll accept help but not old enough yet that it doesn't bother him to need the help. We get along fine and always have—I just smile and pester him about what needs done next until he gives me another item on the list of what is bugging him the most. My cousin's going to come back and work the farm with him next year, and that will solve a lot of it. Most of the problem was simply the fact he was lonely and wasn't going to admit it to anyone. And it wasn't like I didn't have some time to share."

"Just don't get too settled out there, okay? I really do want you back."

She smiled. "It's nice to be wanted. I'll think about it, Chief. That's the best I can offer. Where are you heading next?"

"To see Sam. Anything you want me to pass along?"

"I had breakfast with him this morning; I think I know what he does on the threats out of New York. You might want to check on the change of ID he was arranging for Amy. She really needs a new ID already in her

pocket, given the speed this has been un-
folding."

"I'll do that. Thanks, Caroline."

"Anytime, Chief. I'll admit it has been nice
to briefly get back into the game."

●●●●●●

Marie sorted out her jewelry Thursday as
she dressed for the evening out. Connor
had said elegant, a nice restaurant out of
town, a movie. The elegance was not hard,
for spending enough money had solved the
dress problem, but the rest of it—the jewelry, the perfume, how she wore her hair—
she didn't want to overplay the fact it was
their first formal date. Connor coming over
Sunday night and working with her in the
gallery moving paintings around from storage and debating with her the best way to
do the displays didn't count as being a date
even if they had ended up sharing deliv-
ered-in Chinese food.

She elected to wear her newly bought
bracelet and a locket kept on a thin gold
chain—Mandy's locket, retrieved by the investigator from a pawnshop and returned to
her with his apology that he couldn't bring
good news. Having something of Mandy's

with her helped settle her nerves. If her oldest sister was alive, she would have been perched on the bed and laughing with her about the nerves before a date, doing it kindly and talking about guys and how incredibly nice it was to have one decide to focus on you. Marie chose medium-height heels and found a small clutch purse for her keys and a comb. She leaned toward the mirror and checked her lipstick one last time.

"Oh yes. *Very* nice."

Marie smiled at Tracey in the mirror. "You look quite elegant yourself."

"Marsh told me we're going ballroom dancing, as if that was something he really would like to do."

Marie smiled. "He's kind that way."

"At least willing to take a risk just because he knows I'll enjoy it," Tracey agreed, leaning against the edge of the dresser. "You'll be okay tonight?"

Marie lifted one eyebrow.

"Connor isn't going to be making a serious pass or anything?"

Marie chuckled. "I doubt it; I expect he might want to hold my hand. He's nice at preferring this doesn't rush past the finer points of dating. He brought me chocolates Sunday and daisies."

"Marsh took me out to eat and then insisted we go see a musical that wasn't really his cup of tea. You could tell he was overtrying, kind of like tonight. I've wanted him to propose for so incredibly long . . . the money kind of destroyed any hope of that anytime soon."

"He'll get over it."

"Probably. But I'm miserable while I wait. Not that I don't like sharing this place with you, but knowing Marsh, he'll propose and then want to wait a year for the wedding or some such nonsense."

Marie laughed and hugged her sister. "I doubt it will be more than a couple months. Maybe tonight."

"He hasn't even dropped a hint." Tracey forced a smile and stepped back. "But I'm not giving up hope. Have a good time tonight, Sis. I like Connor."

"So do I."

The doorbell rang, and Tracey disappeared to answer it. Marsh had said six and Connor had suggested six-thirty. Marie finished her makeup touch-ups, letting her sister leave without a lot of polite conversation to slow them down.

I hope you do propose soon, Marsh. She's on the good side of impatient right now, wanting so much to be your wife. You'd be wonderful for Tracey, the kind of guy that will love her forever.

She closed her purse and walked into the living room to wait for Connor to arrive. She'd have to ask a few subtle questions over dinner and see what Connor thought was going on.

● ● ● ● ● ●

The movie was too serious a drama for much laughter, but at least the romance in it was subdued to not be embarrassing to watch with a guy she was just getting to know. Marie liked watching the story unfold, the way the director had put meaning into the simple facts of life that went with being married—the grocery shopping, the mail, the phone calls when it was family checking in. She shared popcorn with Connor and thought about how long it had been since she had last shared a movie with a date. Way too long. As nice as dinner had been, and she'd remember it for a long time, this was even nicer. Connor had been holding her hand for most of the movie.

Connor handed her the popcorn box and shifted in his seat to unclip the pager from his belt to read the text message.

"Trouble?" she whispered as she saw him clear the message and return the pager to his belt.

He reached over and gripped her hand again, and she was surprised at the sense of tension she felt in him. "No trouble, just good news."

She turned her hand to settle it more firmly in his. He hadn't talked much about his job and the fact he had returned to work this week. But it was there, skimming just under the surface. She'd sensed the tension in him when he had called in the evenings to chat. He had mentioned he didn't leave work behind as easily as Marsh did, but he ducked her questions about it. Good news that left him tense—she rubbed her thumb alongside his and wondered who it was that had been arrested.

Chapter Eleven

"They'll be here, Amy," Luke reassured softly. He had made the two pages a short time ago and thought the first of the sisters was no more than ten minutes out.

She turned from watching the moonlight shimmering across the frosted ground. "I know."

He had expected the nerves and the uncertainty. He hadn't expected the sadness. It seemed to press in on her like an enfolding blanket. Amy wasn't ready for her sisters' arrival, and he didn't know what to say to help her.

The music clicked over to something softly romantic, and he nodded toward the food. "You ought to eat something or have a drink. I know it's hard to wait, so let me be a bit of a distraction."

She smiled at him, and it was the full smile he remembered from years before. "Trust me, Luke; you don't need help to be a distraction. It was very nice tonight, stepping out of the car and seeing you waiting for me. I appreciate all the arrangements."

"Caroline helped me out." He saw her lifted eyebrow. "Former army, former cop, a very good friend when you need someone to trust. I'm doing my best to convince her to unretire."

"Bad shooting?" she asked softly, anticipating the cause.

"One of the worst the department ever had."

"I'd like to meet her."

"You will. She's around here somewhere; she simply excels at being discreet."

Amy smiled. "I wonder what she'd say if she knew reality. I'm trying to trust you, Luke. It's just not that easy anymore to trust anyone. Without that—" she shrugged—"it kind of precludes about anything else, even the friendship we've been skirting around since we first met."

He served himself a plate and nodded for

her to join him. "Eat something or those aspirins you've been popping are going to just
make the headache worse." She joined him,
and he considered her thoughtfully a moment. "Do you still trust God?"

She looked over, startled.

"I understand entirely the doubts that surface when you look at someone and can't
totally be sure if what you are seeing is the
real story. You ran into a lot of people with a
dark, dangerous side. But is it trust that is
the problem, or is it discernment of who is
safe and who is not?"

"Good question. I've never really thought
about it in those terms." She stuck toothpicks into a couple meatballs and two of the
sweet pickles. " 'God is in heaven; He does
whatever He pleases.' " She shrugged.
"That was the only verse in the psalms that
made the most sense over the years. He let
me get hurt, and maybe I was naive, but
that didn't fit what I thought was the expectation about being a Christian. Not the kind
of deep, damaging hurt I took after I spent a
lot of time praying about dating Greg. I
never really even sensed a back-off check
in my spirit about the relationship. Maybe I
was deaf, but I didn't get the warning I

thought I would for what was coming. I assumed there would be protection or at least an end to the harm in a reasonable time, that God would keep me safe. Eight years and a dead cop later—that kind of changes things."

"God is against you? or unconcerned about what happens?"

"That's probably where my head was at the first few years. I was in too much panic and stress to be anything more than horrified that even prayers for safety didn't seem to be getting answered." She walked over toward the couch and sank down into it to enjoy the warmth from the fire. "Maybe time changes things, but I'm past the worst of that reaction now, I think. I know the evil is not past yet. But this is earth, not heaven. And the reality on earth is it's the good days that are the exception in this life, not the bad. Once that settled in, it changed my perspective and made this easier to face."

She turned to face him as he settled into the chair to her right. "Now . . . God hasn't changed. He's still loving, righteous, and in charge. And evil and free will still exist. God could change this, but it doesn't necessarily mean He will. I still pray He'll end the dilemma I am in, but I gave up expecting it to happen tomorrow. Everyone gets their own unique mess to try to survive in life, and mine came when I was in my thirties."

"You have survived it, Amy. It hasn't knocked you into pieces and left you unable to function, unable to cope. And even in all this—God hasn't forgotten you. He cares about your days, every one of them."

"I know. I've grown up quite a bit, I think. There were many days I wondered if I could take even one more hour of it, let alone another month. I don't like to run, Luke. I don't like to be afraid. But part of me has started to cope with the fact I'm doing both. That's been by God's grace. Accepting where I'm limited and figuring out there will be some way through the latest wrinkle. Someone wants me dead; that's the stark reality that leads every other one. The hatred is too strong now for it to ever disappear, not even after the money and last ledger are turned in."

She looked toward the window and the night. "I worry about what this will do to Marie and Tracey when they know the truth. Sometimes it's a whole lot easier to live with what you think is the truth than to have to face what is the truth."

"As bad as the truth will be, you'll still be comforting them just to let them know you aren't dead."

"And when they spend the next weeks and months worrying every day about my safety?" Amy shook her head. "It's like asking them to drink poison, not enough to be lethal, just enough to haunt their days. When I have to go silent, when I have to run—what then? They live afraid for me, frantic to know where I went and if I'm okay. When I run I can't have them coming after me."

"When you run, they become the easier targets. That's reality too. Protection that encompasses only you won't help them, and protection that encompasses only them won't help you—not really. You need to come in from the cold and let this be managed properly."

She turned her head to look at him, and while he knew she was accepting his argument, it didn't mean she was agreeing with it or accepting the implications of that. She wasn't ready to cross that line and face what it would mean to totally trust someone else for her safety, and he could understand that fine line. "You'll have to trust me as a simple leap of faith. Just like you've chosen to keep trusting God. I'm not infallible, but I'll promise you my best. There's no other way for you to cross that threshold to trust me but to just risk it."

He saw lights cross the windows and so did she. She rose, and he took her plate for her. "You want to do this alone or with some company?"

"Stay . . . please."

He rested a comforting hand on her shoulder. "They love you. Remember that."

● ● ● ● ● ●

"This isn't the way home," Marie realized as Connor turned off the interstate. "Where are we going?" She looked over toward him.

He turned his head to briefly smile at her before looking back at the road. "There's been a stop added to the evening that I think you might enjoy. We're almost there."

"What?"

He reached over and squeezed her hand. "Trust me. It's in the category of being nice."

"Daniel set something up?"

Connor shook his head. "You're welcome

to turn on the mirror light and check your makeup if you like. You look gorgeous, but you can fuss a few minutes anyway."

"Now I'm really wondering." She picked up her purse.

He turned again, and in the night it looked like an expensive area of homes, vast expanses of land stretching between gated entrances; the home that must be back on the private roads so far back as to not be visible from this road.

She brushed out her hair and touched up her lipstick. Someone Connor wanted her to meet? Surely his parents didn't live out this way; surely he'd warn her before a meeting like that. Meeting just anyone when it was after nine o'clock didn't seem likely. Was there a place back here he knew about? Cops did know a lot about the area. Something he wanted her to see? The moon was bright in the sky, and it was a nice evening to walk if you bundled up well.

He was driving toward the home ahead, this road leading back to an imposing gate set into what looked like a massive wall of stones. "Connor, I don't like surprises," she whispered, worried now as he pulled up and lowered his window. The fact he knew the security code to punch in put her even more on edge.

"Relax, honey. An hour from now you'll be hugging the breath out of me, I suspect," he teased, but his hand was gentle as he reached over to take hers again.

The gates opened.

He followed the drive, and a massive home appeared, three stories, huge windows. Lights were on and she could see smoke lazily rising in the still night air from two chimneys; the home was occupied. Connor circled the home and parked before a four-door garage.

A possible client for the gallery? If they can afford the house, they can afford some very nice artwork. Marie settled with that thought, for that might make sense, given how Connor was treating this stop.

He came around to open her door, and she let him take her hand. He locked the car behind them and nodded toward the breezeway patio doors. "Let's go inside."

The breezeway had marble floors. Already clued in to the wealth in this home, it was still a startling realization. Another set of glass doors automatically opened for them, and they stepped from the wide breezeway into a great room with soaring ceiling, comfortable couches, and a grand piano tucked into the corner. The room overlooked part of the backyard, and it was as landscaped as she had suspected, soft lights illuminating walkways.

"Go on through to the more formal living room," Connor suggested, nodding to the wide arched doorway into the adjoining room. She could hear music.

She didn't ask the questions begging to be asked. She walked through the arched doorway and into the loveliest room she'd seen in years, fires casting off warmth, the expanse of windows suggesting more of the spacious yard waited outside, the smell of cinnamon and the rich smell of honey hinting of something in the kitchen off to her right. And her attention finally focused on the people—startled surprise at the sight of the police chief here and then the lady with him.

"Hello, Marie."

The whispered words in the voice she had never forgotten . . . Marie froze; the pounding of her heart sounded so loud in her own ears, an awareness of such incredible shock running through her, that her mind wasn't sure how to move her limbs. She was aware, too, of Connor being the one gripping her arm so tightly she couldn't stumble even if her legs gave way. He had her safe and he had her here—here where Amanda stood, where Amanda was alive.

"Mandy—" She took one tentative step toward Amanda as she put all of it to-gether—the stress in her sister's face, the hair colored to deal with early gray, and the steady gaze perfectly matching the gaze she'd loved for so many years she could still see it in her dreams. Her sister, alive and well.

Marie began to smile as she rushed across the room. "Welcome home." She felt Amanda's arms close around her as she wrapped her own around the too-tall and too-thin frame and felt like heaven opened to smile at her, so great was the joy that welled up inside and turned her heart toward hope and joy.

All those years of prayers and the answer was so joyously better than anything she had ever hoped. "God brought you back. He brought you back."

"I'm sorry. I'm so sorry for everything," Mandy whispered.

"I wouldn't have stopped looking; I never should have stopped looking. They told me you were dead; they convinced me you were dead." The horror of having given up the search made the grief squeeze like a vise around Marie's heart, the pain of so many lost years incredibly intense.

"Sam had to help me convince you of that, honey; there was no other choice. You had to stop searching, for both you and Tracey's sake," Mandy whispered.

Marie eased back enough to touch her sister's face, knowing there was no way to understand that.

"I'll be able to explain some of it. I'm just so sorry you had to grieve for me as gone. Don't blame Sam. I didn't give him any options."

She wanted answers, wanted to cry why, but instead smiled through her tears. She wouldn't take the pain out toward Mandy, who had been her older sister and protector and confidante all her life. The reasons would be there and have left Mandy no choice; a lifetime together made Marie sure of that. "You're found now. You can't know how good this moment is or how much I've hoped."

"Better than a birthday surprise?"

Marie laughed, released from the tension by their shared memories. "Better."

"I owe you a few years' worth of birthday parties and Christmas presents and sloppily made breakfasts in bed and giggling girl talk."

"Yeah." Marie hugged her sister hard, afraid this moment would vanish on her, the tears breaking past her ability to control them. She tried to stop the sobs, and Mandy held on.

"I know, Marie. I know," Mandy whispered.

"Sorry." Marie fought back the tears and forced a smile. Mandy had the Kleenex pack already in her hand and shared. Marie could see her sister struggling to control her own emotions. She'd been afraid of this moment, Marie realized, surprised, Mandy afraid of the reception she would get when she appeared. "Explain it all later, Sis. For now I plan to celebrate and maybe tease you about coloring your hair. You never could stand the thought of that."

"Early gray runs in the family."

"Tell me about it," Marie agreed, softly laughing. She looked beyond Mandy's shoulder to where the chief of police stood near the fireplace, watching them, watching Amanda. "Thank you. However you managed this."

He smiled back. "You're welcome, Marie."

"Tracey's coming?"

"She'll be here with Marsh anytime."

Marie looked back at her sister. "When she shows, you'll be flooded with happy tears again and probably a joyfully screamed greeting."

"Oh, I hope so. She hasn't changed."

"No. Just grown up." She reached up to touch Mandy's face, trying to understand the changes in her sister, the years of stress showing where there should have just been years of joy had life turned out differently, and her emotions faltered. How much history had gone wrong for her sister to age her before her time, to make those beautiful blue eyes so clouded with stress. "I'm glad you're home. I missed you, Mandy." She wiped her sister's tears. "Come on; sit down. Talk to me." She settled beside her sister on the long couch.

"It's going to take a while, I'm afraid."

"I'm not planning to go anywhere," Marie

replied, smiling. She looked across at Connor. "You knew."

"A few days now," he softly replied.

A few days—before the turtle, before the call to ask for a date, before Sunday night and the help with the paintings and the casual talk about family and history. Her heart swelled over what he had done in the last few days for her and her family, and there wasn't going to be words to say thanks. She smiled. "I'll have to remember how well you can keep a secret."

"I'm getting drinks. What are you interested in having? Coffee? Hot chocolate? Something cold?" he offered, smiling back.

"Tea would be fine."

"What about you, Amy? Need a refill?"

"Coffee, thanks."

Lights passed across the windows, and Marie felt Mandy tense. She gripped her sister's hand.

"Marsh and Tracey," Connor confirmed, looking out the window.

"Do you think she's going to be mad?" Mandy whispered.

"A little. But a lot more overjoyed," Marie promised.

They heard Tracey laughing with Marsh

about something, and she came through the archway into the living room, slipping off her coat. Marie saw the first moment it hit, the way Tracey froze, and then she was running, jacket not off yet.

"Mandy!"

Marie leaned back with a laugh as Tracey about squashed her sister in a hug, her coat trailing behind her. "You're real; you're thin; I'm so envious; you're coloring your hair— oh man, that means I'm going to be doing it soon too. What happened? Where have you been? Why didn't you call me? Oh, you look good."

Mandy wrapped her arms around Tracey and just smiled. "I missed you too."

Tracey impatiently pushed aside the coat and sank onto the couch on the other side of Mandy. "Marsh, you should have warned me. I about had a heart attack."

"Hmm, I could have." He came around behind the couch and took the coat out of her way, then leaned over and kissed her. "You like surprises."

Marie laughed at the way Mandy was checking out Marsh. "He's a cop too, Connor's partner," she whispered.

"And I love him most of the time he's not

winding me up this way," Tracey added, pushing Marsh aside and turning back to her sister. "But we'll talk about him later. What happened? Start at the very, very beginning and don't leave out a comma."

Marie saw the stress Mandy was under reappear and squeezed her hand. "You want that coffee first?"

"I think I'd better."

Marie got up. "What do you want to drink, Tracey?"

"A soda is fine."

Connor had poured the coffee and the iced tea. He opened a soda for Tracey as Marie joined him to take the tray. She looked at him, at the steady gaze he gave her in return, at the quiet way he was watching the reunion, and she knew then something of what was coming. She was starting to think again and to put together the pieces. The most striking of which that the cops had felt this reunion needed to be held on a gated estate with rock walls well after dark.

"Thanks." She refused to let her smile change as she took the drinks back to her sisters. "Don't feel like you have to hurry with the answers, Mandy. I know they aren't going to be easy, and we've got all night. But why don't you start with what happened the night Greg was shot?"

Mandy smiled in thanks at the quiet opening and sipped her coffee before she moved to settle into the chair across from her sisters so she could face them both, and then she nodded. "Do you two remember where I used to live, the apartment block?"

Marie nodded.

"Greg lived north, more uptown, but we had a favorite restaurant that we went to on Friday nights down near my place," Mandy began, and Marie reached over to take Tracey's hand. One or both of them were going to end up crying before this was over—Marie just knew it. From the corner of her eye she saw Connor follow Marsh and the chief into the next room.

"We were talking about where we would live after we were married, laughing over our clashing styles for colors and carpet and my dislike of having a housekeeper. It was late when we finally paid the bill and walked back to the car. Greg drove me home." Mandy stopped her narrative, and Marie just waited.

"Did you see the shooter?" Tracey asked quietly.

"I think it's best if I not answer that," Mandy replied finally. "One of the bullets that hit Greg came through him and struck me in the side."

Marie closed her eyes. *God, don't let this go where I know it's going. She's not really back, is she?*

They talked about New York. They talked about the missing years. Marie listened to Mandy and to Tracey and couldn't find words to ease the ache in her own heart. So many years lost and gone forever.

"They want money; they can have the money," Tracey said, insistent, bitter, her anger growing.

"It's not going to be that simple, Tracey. Oh, how I wish it could be," Mandy replied. "Listen to the guys and stay within the protection they provide. Please don't take chances."

"You're not coming home."

"I can't, Tracey. The world thinks I'm dead, and it has to stay that way. For all our sakes."

"When will we see you again?" Marie whispered.

"I don't know," Mandy said quietly in return. "Tonight is already a huge risk."

"The cops can't do anything?" Tracey pushed.

"They've been working to make it better for a long time, and it is getting better. But it's more dangerous now than ever before as they try to bring it to an end. I don't want you two being dragged into my troubles."

"You should have called us; you should have let us help you. We're family," Tracey insisted, pacing away from the couch.

"I did what I thought was best."

"Like you are now, disappearing again? You're my sister; I want you in my life. You could have at least picked up the phone and called me once in a while."

Marie watched Mandy take the charge and saw the flicker of emotion cross her face before it went still. "There's more. Isn't there, Mandy? There's more than what you've told us."

She hesitated but finally nodded. "They killed a cop who had knowledge of where I was at. They beat him to death in his own home just to find out what he knew."

Tracey paled.

"I can't be in your life again, not until I can do it safely. I can't. My worst nightmare is that they go after the two of you to get to me."

Marie leaned forward. "We're not going to increase that burden on you, Mandy. We'll listen to the guys, and we'll follow their advice. You do not have to worry about us," she promised, knowing she'd push Tracey toward that somehow. "What do they have in mind to keep you safe? Is everything that can be done being done?"

"Yes."

"There must be some way we can safely see you and talk with you," Tracey persisted. "I don't care if we have to book a flight to Alaska and meet you in an igloo somewhere. It matters that we be able to see you again. The money ought to be able to buy us the means to do at least that much."

"The reporters around the new money make it risky for a while. When it calms down more—"

"Let the reporters—"

"Tracey!" Marie cut her off. She had been the one Marie thought would best be able to adapt, and she was absorbed in the anger of it, the unfairness of it, and the bitter hurt.

"Sorry," Tracey muttered, walking back over to the windows.

"I understand the anger and the pain of this," Mandy offered softly. "It's not what I want either. But caution is how I've learned to live, and that doesn't change easily."

Tracey turned, her arms folded across her chest. "So we see you a year from now, another night when the guys don't take us home, but instead take us to some out-of-the-way place where you are?"

"Maybe."

"You're my sister! I want my family back. Why don't we buy a secure house like this one and a small army of guys to secure the grounds and travel with us so we can be a family again? If the threat is that severe, then let's attack the problem, not just try to hide from it."

Marie found the thought appealing. "Could you consider that, Mandy? Coming home to somewhere very safe? I know you're worried about us, but there have to be options better than your disappearing again. Please, there have to be better options than that."

"I don't want to be burying one or both of you," Mandy cried, lifting her hands to cover her face for a moment and fighting for her composure, then tucking her hands back around her waist. "You have to understand Richard Wise. He wants money and he wants me dead. Anyone around me just becomes targets, and I can't live with that. I don't want to be gone and lonely like the last eight years, but I can't live with the fact my presence puts your lives at risk. Don't ask me for that."

"Then find something in the middle that works. Use the new money to find somewhere safe to stay and then let us come visit. It can't be that impossible to arrange for us to safely get to where you are. It can't be, Mandy. We're family and we're not going away this time. We're not letting you disappear."

Marie didn't want to be the one mediating between Mandy and Tracey. She wanted to be the one curled up in a chair crying over everything she'd heard and the pain Mandy had lived through in the last years and the tragedy of all those years on the run. But something had to give or she was going to watch her sisters tear each other apart. The emotions were too broken, the pain too deep, on both sides. She ached for Mandy while she understood and felt the same as Tracey.

"Talk to the chief, Mandy. You trust him? You must or he wouldn't have been able to set this up. Talk to the chief and see what he can work out. If the risk is too great, we'll stay away, we won't search to try and find you, and we'll let you go back into the shadows again. But if there is a way—please, you owe it to Tracey and me to try it and see. We need you in our lives. We love you so much, and our lives have been hollow with that void of your being gone. Don't ask us to endure that again if there is any way to avoid it."

Mandy gave in abruptly, a nod of consent, but clearly afraid. "I'll talk with the chief. But it's all I can promise, Marie. I can't put you two in danger even if that means I have to break your hearts."

Marie offered a broken smile and reached over to squeeze Mandy's hand. "I know, Sis." The dilemma Mandy was in was unsolvable, and Marie understood, even as it cut, why Mandy had stayed away so very long. "It's a plan then. We'll see what the guys say is possible." Marie looked around. Connor, Marsh, and the chief had not returned, but they had to be somewhere nearby.

Tracey came back over from the window and nudged Mandy to slide over on the chair more so she could sit on the armrest. "I'm getting engaged whenever Marsh finally gets around to asking, and I want you here to share that," she offered, trying hard to stop the pain they were both in and to explain the anger.

Mandy hugged her. "I love you. I desperately want to be here for that. Don't ever think I don't want to be here. It's just got to be safe; it's the only thing left I've got to give you."

Tracey cried and Mandy held on to her. Marie knew it was going to break Mandy's heart to walk away tonight, but she'd do it because she thought it had to be done. Somehow this had to turn out right again. They were family and it had to turn out right.

Tracey eased back. "I need a mop for my face."

Mandy laughed. "I think I do too." She rubbed at her own wet face.

Marie reached up and slid free the fine

chain and pendant she wore. "I've got something you might want to have back. This is yours, I think." She had given Mandy the locket before she entered the army, and Mandy had taken it with her everywhere she traveled and even worn it into combat. The locket had been a connection to home.

Marie slid the chain and locket back around her sister's neck and carefully latched the clasp. "I knew you never took it off, so it did its job. Sam used it to convince me you were really gone. I gave up looking after that. It's good to have it back where it belongs."

"I'm sorry, so sorry I had to do that."

"I understand now why you did."

Mandy hugged her hard. "Thank you, Marie."

"We're sharing the money with you equally—you do know that, Mandy, don't you? No half sister and other protests getting shoved toward us. We're a family, and it's going to be handled the way it should have been all along."

"You don't have to do that, please. I've lived with the reality that money has been the source of so many problems in my life that I honestly don't want it."

"It's not open for debate. Let it sit in trust for your kids if you like, but we'll be telling Daniel our decision tomorrow."

"No. For now, for lots of reasons, just let it be. To the world at large I'm dead, and it's easier to stay that way for now. I'll let you help with what I need and gratefully accept that, but we'll talk about anything else only after this situation is ended."

"It can sit for now, but know it's going to be there. I'm not going to wade through the dilemma of how to be wealthy without also watching you figure it out too."

Mandy smiled. "Tell me about college, Tracey. And about Marsh," she said, trying to shift the conversation.

Tracey moved to settle back into the couch cushions, not wanting to follow the change of conversation, but at Marie's soft look in warning, she picked up the topics. "School is school. I'd rather talk about Marsh," she offered lightly. "We met over at the college when he came to take a refresher course in criminal law. I overheard him registering and decided it was worth auditing the class."

"You did?" Marie asked, surprised, having not heard that before. "I thought you said you met him in class, that it was an elective that fit your schedule."

"So maybe it was a bit more than that . . . ," Tracey conceded.

Mandy laughed. "You never were one to hesitate when you thought a guy was interesting. How long before he invited you out?"

Tracey rolled her eyes. "Forever. I ended up taking Criminal Law II the next semester just to wear him down. He was nice and all and would buy me coffee at the breaks, but forget a date. He thought I was a nice college kid and half his age."

Mandy was having a hard time subduing her laughter. "Ten years between you?"

"Nine, but he's the only one counting."

"I gather you got past that eventually."

"He's not such a bad guy once he admits he likes you," Tracey replied, smiling.

Marie refilled her drink as she listened to Mandy and Tracey, and a smile lightened her mood. They were going to be fine. Somehow, they were going to be fine.

Two hours ago, God, I didn't know she was still alive. There aren't words for this joy. There aren't even emotions deep enough to touch it. Mandy is alive. I can't say an ade-

quate thanks. For the rest of it—I'm afraid we're in a situation that will take a miracle to resolve. She has to be safe.

"Tell her about your recent ski trip, Tracey," Marie suggested, folding herself back into the cushions of the couch. She didn't want this night to ever end.

Chapter Twelve

Marie hugged Mandy, trying to share a final time with a touch just how much her sister meant to her.

"I know," Mandy whispered.

Marie felt Connor's hand rest against her shoulder and reluctantly released her sister. "Good-bye, Mandy." Tracey had already left with Marsh, her farewell the hardest thing Marie had ever watched. She memorized her sister's face one last time and let herself step back.

"Good-bye, Marie," Mandy whispered.

Connor's hand urged her to step away. She lost sight of Mandy as they cleared the doorway and stepped outside, aware the chief had been moving across the room to join her sister.

"Marie?"

"Give me a minute," she choked out, fighting the tears wanting to consume her. She feared to the depth of her soul that she had just seen Mandy for the last time.

"She'll be okay. The chief is going to make sure of that."

The confidence Connor had in that man came through, and Marie let herself nod, let herself hope.

"We've got to be going. Anyone watching you and Tracey will be expecting the date to be over and you to be home soon. It's best not to disappoint them."

"Yes."

She walked with Connor to his car, and when he unlocked and held the door for her, she slipped inside.

●●●●●●

Marie cried for most of the trip back to town. Connor didn't know what to say that might help the situation so he didn't try to talk about it, just held Marie's hand to remind her she wasn't alone in this.

He'd sat with Marsh and the chief in the

great room while the sisters talked, and when the voices had raised, they'd heard enough to know the stress going on in the next room. The night had gone better than he expected in some ways and been so much harder in others. They hadn't been distant sisters in the early years; they had been the kind of sisters living in each other's space and doing it with shared love, together in the best way for sisters to be. Having Amy vanish from that had torn open so much of their lives. Having her return as she had—it hadn't ended the hurt; it had just opened a fresh new chapter.

"The apartment is the other way," Marie whispered. "And I don't think I can take another surprise tonight."

"I know." He turned east on Elm Drive. "You need a few minutes before you see Tracey, I think, and a few more minutes to catch your breath. We're going by my place."

He waited for a protest, for a problem with the intimacy of that so late in the night, but Marie didn't bother and part of him relaxed inside. She trusted him. In the midst of all this madness and chaos, Marie was trusting him without thinking about it first. That helped.

"When did you know?"

He swallowed before he answered, not sure how she'd handle the truth. "I recognized her photo—the one you have on your desk. She was in town three years ago keeping a quiet watch on you and Tracey, making sure you were okay and none of this trouble she was in had come to brush against either of you."

"Three years ago? She never got in touch, never wrote, never called, never said hello."

"She was honestly afraid you would be dead if she did come forward or be put in the situation where you had no recourse but to spend your life on the run as she had. She didn't want that, Marie. Not for you and Tracey. And I can't say I would have decided it differently than she did given the situation then."

"The oldest sister, protecting the rest of us."

"Yes."

"I wish she hadn't been so noble. Eight years of this—the best years of her life, all gone in an instant of madness."

"There's still time to recover some of it."

"Who did she call when she came back to town this time?"

"The chief. We were expecting her to get in touch with Sam, but there was some reason to think Sam might already have guys watching him. This worked out the cleanest, I think."

"How did she meet Granger?"

"That's an answer for another night. Please."

She nodded.

He could see the sharp fatigue overwhelming her, the sadness so deep it made the tears flow without her thinking of them. She wiped them away again, and he wished for a box of Kleenex in the car. She'd eaten a little from the buffet of food set out tonight, to give Amy a reason to eat, to give Tracey something to do with her hands, trying to mother the sisters a bit, and Connor understood it. Marie needed to be able to help, and there was so little she could do.

"Do you know where Mandy is staying tonight?"

"Granger will try and talk her into staying right where she's at, at least until she's had a few hours of sleep, but I doubt she'll agree. She hasn't told him what name she's using now, where she's been staying. And after so many emotions tonight I guess I'd rather have her stay in profile and go hibernate for a few days and just think. Your sister is a wise lady, Marie. Give her time to look at options."

"She was always good at planning."

"You need to stay close to Tom Bryce, listen to him, and to the other Silver Security guys that are around. It's really important over the next few days."

She turned toward him. "You know something else."

"Amy's had two guys following her, and they'll know she was heading back to this town. That's a dangerous combination. And no matter how much you want to share the news with someone, you can't mention to anyone the fact Amy is alive. Even when a reporter gets in your face and throws around questions, you've got to stay with the story you believed up until tonight."

"I can handle that; I know it's necessary."

Connor pulled into the parking lot where he had an apartment.

"I didn't know you lived on this side of town." She looked around in a bit of doubt at the apartment buildings that lined the street.

"Relax." Connor took her hand and eased her from the car. "I wasn't lying when I said I was well-off, and I can certainly afford better than this place. But there are occasions when being a single cop living in the area where you end up patrolling has its useful points, and the department is picking up half the rent for anyone willing to act as community-presence officers. It's meant more overtime and responding to the calls in my neighborhood, but it's had its good points too. There's not much happening on the streets that I don't hear the gossip about."

"I can understand that, and I wasn't judging; I was just wondering."

He led her up the flight of stairs rather than risk the elevator and any drunk who might be riding it up and down as his private amusement ride. "Crime is actually low in the area since so many officers are walking the streets now, targeting this zip code. We're shifting our focus more east now." He unlocked his door and turned on lights for her.

Inside the fact he was more affluent than his surroundings became apparent.

She walked into the living room, a stunned expression on her face even after all the emotions of her evening. "It's beautiful, Connor."

He smiled at her surprise. "The first year I replastered and repainted and put down new carpets. The second year I replaced all the fixtures and appliances. Management was fine with it when it was my money. I hear there is a waiting list of residents waiting to move up to this apartment after I move at the first of the month."

"You're moving? But you just got this perfect."

"There's a building three streets over that needs a presence more. We've got a couple of older ladies in that apartment complex having trouble with their in-laws. The apartment between them opened up, and it's an easy enough solution. No use having a domestic fight turned into a homicide on me, when I can move in and get spoiled by two grandmothers at once."

She laughed but understood. "You're a cop off the job as much as on."

He shrugged. "It's who I am, not just what

I do. And it's no hardship living in a spacious place I can fix up while half the rent is on the department's tab." He laid his coat and hers across one of the chairs. "Look around and make yourself at home. I'll get us something to drink and you a couple much-needed aspirins."

"Thanks."

He walked through to his kitchen. The message light was flashing, and he listened to his grandfather talk about a cabinet he had ready to pick up while he got Marie the two aspirins and poured them glasses of tea. He rejoined her.

"This is your family?" She was holding a picture, sorting out faces.

"My grandfather Peter, his wife, now deceased, my mom and dad, and the rest of the line are cousins."

"Are your parents still in town?"

"They have two homes, one here and one in Texas. They headed south about a month ago to spend the winter months."

"I like your family."

"I like yours too," he replied, offering her a glass.

"Is that where you went on vacation this year, to Texas?"

"For a long weekend. It's a nice way to catch up with the cousins as most of them came by. They live in the area near my parents' place."

He watched her swallow the aspirins, then wander farther around the room. Her expression turned closed again, and he knew it was hard to keep thoughts on the present rather than the words Amy had shared tonight. He didn't expect anything different. The only thing he did regret was the fact Daniel had not been there, for he thought it might have helped. Amy being a half sister would make no difference in reality for Marie or Tracey, but for Amy it was just another source of pain to deal with. It did affect their memories of their mother, their aunt, and the secrets that had haunted this family. Too many secrets, kept by too many people, all in the theory they were doing the right thing at the time.

"What did the chief say when he paged tonight?"

"You put that together."

She nodded. "It made sense afterward. You had known but not told me; Mandy is skittish. There was a good chance tonight wouldn't happen."

"His message just read 'it's on.' None of us wanted to build up your hopes, Tracey's, and then not be able to make the reunion happen."

"What if this Richard Wise finds Mandy? What if I lose her after I just found her again? Connor—" The fears came flooding back, the facts that scared her the most, and the tears returned.

He took the glass back and set it aside, then wrapped his arm around her. "It's going to be okay." He didn't know how, but it was something they would have to solve.

"I'm so afraid for her, so afraid," she whispered.

He let his hand linger on her hair, easing that pain the only way he could. Part of him worried incredibly about it not being okay, that her fears were founded in the real risks of trouble arriving. But there were limits of what worry could help.

Connor tipped up her chin. He leaned down. When she didn't lean away he took his time kissing her, feeling her hands come up to rest against his neck, feeling her weight shift and her head tilt to more easily welcome the kiss. She tasted of salt and tears, of sweetened tea, and of woman—he eased back to make a promise. "I'm not go-ing to let you walk through any of this alone. I care too much."

He felt the sigh rather than heard it. "Can I just lean against you awhile and keep my balance that way?"

He smiled gently. "As long as you like."

"My sister is home." There was the quiet satisfaction of a long-sought dream sud-denly true in the words. *"Thanks* doesn't seem like the right word tonight, and *relief* is not strong enough. Despite everything that came with it, she's home."

"*Joy* works."

"Yes."

She leaned back. "Connor, I need to know what is going on—all of it. The stuff Mandy can tell me and the stuff she can't. Would you keep me informed of what is really going on?"

He didn't know how to answer that, for he was torn between protecting her emotions and knowing she had the right to ask. "I promise to tell you as much as I can, the se-curity steps, the people we're trying to deal with. All of it that doesn't risk Amy or some-one else working the case."

"Thank you. It's so very, very hard being in the dark."

Connor stepped back. "Tracey is going to wonder where you have gotten yourself off to. I'd best take you home."

"Would you invite me back here one day so I can better appreciate your place?"

He laughed. "I could do that—hopefully before I end up packing everything."

"I'd enjoy helping."

She blushed and he laughed. "Don't go retreating on me now. I like this side of you." He reached for their coats. "I'm buying you breakfast today, before I go to work, before you wander down to work in the gallery."

"I'd like that a great deal."

He buttoned her coat up for her, then caught her hand, and opened his apartment door. "Let's take you home."

• • • • • •

Luke watched Amy circling the room after her sisters left, picking up glasses, plates, restoring order to the home. There was no need for her to do the cleanup, but he knew it was more to give her something to do while she thought than to particularly work.

"They've changed so much. Tracey—I remember her as being young, and she's a grown lady now and seriously dating a good guy. Marie looks tired, like the last few years, rather than just the last week, has pulled life from her. She's more quiet now and serious. That's my fault."

"There's no fault to place, Amy. You've coped with events and done the best you could; so has Marie."

She carried the dishes into the kitchen. "I've missed them so much; I didn't realize how much until they were both here."

Her sisters needed her, and even more, she needed her sisters. "Give me forty-eight hours to show you this can work, that you can safely come in from the cold," he asked as she came back into the room. She wanted to trust him. He could see the tears now back in her eyes and how badly she wanted to be able to say yes. "You can call me tomorrow or you could just come with me now. I'm fully prepared to make you safe from this moment on if you'll let me."

"I can't stay tonight."

"Then call me tomorrow and we'll arrange another time and place to meet. Give me a chance to at least show you what I'm thinking about. They need you in their lives again, Amy. And you need them."

"I'll call you," she whispered. "That's the best I can promise."

"You won't regret it."

Her hand touched the locket she now wore for a moment before she reached for her coat. "Please tell Connor and Marsh thanks for their help and Caroline. All of it is deeply appreciated."

"I will."

He didn't want to see her leaving, but she was preparing to go as she had come. On her own.

"Please don't try to tail me out tonight."

"I won't."

She nodded and moments later her car disappeared down the drive.

"What do you think, Caroline?" Luke looked over at his friend as they walked the estate grounds, finalizing the last check before they reset the security codes and left the place as they had found it.

"Amy is good at hiding. And this is a family in crisis."

"Would you take on her security?"

"Chief, I've got responsibilities and enough on my lap already."

"I know. But there are no other good options. She's not going to take a guy hanging around with her, not beyond deciding when and how she'll slip his protection and disappear for something she needs."

"She'll do that with me too."

"Not if you two agree to a simple fact that your loyalty is to her first and to me second. I don't want to know what she's doing, where's she's going, who she's seeing—I do want to know, but not enough to injure something I need more—someone with her to keep her alive."

"You need a retired secret service agent, not a retired cop. I don't think I could carry a weapon right now, let alone fire it, even to protect Amy."

"You would use the weapon if it was necessary to prevent someone dying," Luke replied, knowing when it came down to it that Caroline's training and instincts would do that job. He pushed his hand through his hair. "I want you back on the job, Caroline, but in this case, I need what you are better at than most people I know. You are one of the few people who might get Amy to trust and to talk; she needs someone hanging out with her, not just be protection around her. Just keep her company through this transition for a couple weeks. I'll talk with Jonathan about something more permanent after that."

"Where?" Caroline asked.

He smiled. "Got some ideas for me? We'll have to slip the sisters out of town to take them to see Amy in order to get away from the reporters. After a couple times doing that, the reporters are going to see it as a personal challenge to figure out where they are going. Even under the cover of a date with Connor and Marsh, it's going to be an ongoing game of cat and mouse."

"We'll need Daniel's help; he has to know now. It's going to take more than your personal financing for one thing, and I'll need Jonathan's guys for some specialized help."

"I'll be meeting with Daniel for breakfast tomorrow; he needs to know for a myriad of reasons, his own security just for starters."

Caroline nodded. "I'll help, Chief. But I don't have quite as much hope as you do that Amy is ready to settle down. She's been running an awfully long time."

"Thank you."

"I'll do my best." She smiled at him. "Do I get to tease you about having a girlfriend now?"

"Maybe later, much later. I'll settle for her simply telling me the name she's using. That will mark progress."

"Then I'll work on that for you."

He chuckled. "Do that."

"Admit it—the idea is growing on you."

"I'm old, set in my ways, and out of practice dating. It can wait awhile, I think."

"You'll do fine. I'll be in your corner."

"I don't know what that says about a guy, when a former date is the one smoothing his path for another lady. . . ."

She laughed and hugged him. "We'll just let that thought be. I like being that special lady in your past."

Chapter Thirteen

Luke took his personal car Saturday morning east of town to the roadside deli Amy had given him directions to. He pulled into the eighth spot east of the doors next to the Dumpster and a lumbering semi, and a minute later she tapped on his side window. He unlocked the door and she slid inside, locking it again behind her.

"Don't tell me you were out running this morning." She was dressed in sweats, the hood up, gloves on, breathing hard and still sweating under that sweat-suit jacket.

"Five miles or so. I thought I was going to be late." She braced her foot on his dash and tugged off her left tennis shoe to shake out a rock.

He shook his head at that and turned to back out of the spot. "You're okay with no transportation of your own?"

"Would you let me drive around if I had a car?"

"No."

"That's what I figured. And in a serious pinch I can get as resourceful as I need to be."

"Sam."

"I suppose I shouldn't tell you everything he taught me over the years."

"I don't suppose you should." He turned onto the interstate, watching his rearview mirror for any signs he had a tail this morning. It had looked clean on the way over, but he wasn't ready to say he was positive he wasn't being followed. He would be sure before he headed toward their final destination. "So tell me how the last couple days have been. You're not carrying luggage or any sign of that ledger you've been protecting."

"Just because I agreed to come in doesn't mean I'm shutting down the safe places I've got in the city. They're going dormant for a while is all. And you can feel free to stop at a local Wal-Mart so I can get the basics in clothes for a few days. Marie still has my wardrobe from New York in storage boxes she said, too sentimental to want to discard my things, and they should still fit. I bought great stuff after I got out of the army, and most of it is coming back in style again."

"We'll stop to buy a few days of casual clothes," he agreed. "Breakfast?"

"The nearest drive-thru would be great."

He smiled. "You sound like you're in a good mood."

She shrugged. "The decision is made. Until I make a different one, this is the new take on the days. I am nervous, Luke, that you haven't got things as prepared as you think you have, that I'll take a look around and say you have to take me back. But I'm giving you the benefit of the doubt."

"We'll know in about an hour then."

She turned to face him. "So what's been happening that I need to know about?"

"It's been remarkably quiet. There's been some talk in New York about your sisters, but the men we're most concerned about are still around their usual haunts; when they travel we should hear about it. Word on the streets here doesn't have anyone asking questions about you, so if your tails have arrived they are still laying low."

"And with Tracey and Marie? Any repercussions there?"

Luke smiled. "Besides calls wanting to know if you've made contact again? They're worried about you, excited you're alive, offering money, people, anything at all that might help out. I put Sam on it to try and slow them up. It's going to take a while before they can accept the patience that is needed right now."

"I saw the newspapers. There were photos of them getting back from their dates Thursday night—Marie and Connor, Tracey and Marsh. You can tell the guys were not pleased to have flashbulbs going off in their faces. Can't anything be done about the reporters bugging them?"

"A new, more interesting story will eventually show up; until then your sisters are the most interesting story around here. The newspapers have run a couple stories recently about Henry Benton, your aunt, and brought up some of the details about your apparent death in New York."

"You know it's only a matter of time before the headline reads 'Oldest Sister Still

Alive?' and they repeat the rumor mill out of New York. Marie will have her hands full when that happens."

"You can't stop a free press. If a newspaper reporter gets ambitious enough to run that story with rumors you are alive or goes to the lengths to see Richard Wise in prison, we'll cope with it when it happens."

"You'll have early word it's coming?"

"I see a faxed list of people who visit Richard Wise every day; the cops in New York are providing whatever they hear on the streets. But until you are ready to admit to the New York cops you are alive, there is only so much I can do under cover of protecting your sisters. You know they'll want you to testify against the shooter."

"I didn't see his face, just the jacket he wore and the center of his chest."

Luke looked over at her. "And I'll believe that when I think you don't have solid reasons to lie to me about it. You saw the shooter, Amy, either at the scene or during the attempt to escape him afterward. I won't push on that until I need to, since you don't want a material-witness warrant issued on you, but don't think I'll dodge that question forever."

He turned off the interstate to take his first detour through a subdivision, looking for any cars that might be following him through the turns. "You were hit in that shooting; where did you go to seek medical treatment?"

"Not a hospital."

She hadn't liked the warning he'd given about the shooter's ID; he accepted that but still thought it best to push. He didn't want buried secrets on him. "A less-than-reputable doctor then?"

"An army buddy helped me out," she admitted.

"How bad were you hurt?"

"Enough to know I never want to be shot again. It healed. Where are we going?"

"In circles at the moment." He pulled to the curb in front of a nice two-story colonial in a neighborhood of similar homes and watched the street behind him. "We'll eventually depart the other entrance to this subdivision, opposite of where we came in."

"You think you were followed?"

"No. But it's good practice for when I find I might be. Your sisters are practicing a good form of staying in plain sight and not going anywhere; that is going to get frustrating for whoever is watching them after a while. That will leave following the people your sisters see occasionally—their new cousin, Sam, Connor and Marsh, me."

"It was so much simpler when it was just me."

He smiled. "Only in some respects. You could be dead and the rest of us would just be furious with you for not letting us help." He pulled away from the curb. "How long do you need for doing your shopping?"

"Fifteen—twenty minutes, max."

He chose a store halfway to their final destination. "Pick me up a package of AA batteries too." He handed her an envelope. "Your sisters insisted, so don't jump on me about the cash. It's already yours."

"Fine." She pushed the envelope into her pocket. "I won't be long."

●●●●●●

Luke held the car door open for Amy. "Do you like the country?"

She glanced around before looking at him and smiling. "I guess I'm going to learn."

There was crushed gravel under their feet, the long driveway not paved, and still a long walk ahead to reach the house. Luke's dogs were already here and came racing to meet them. Two other German shepherds tagged along. "The shepherds are Zack and Obby and belong to Caroline."

Amy knelt to get acquainted. "More cop dogs. I should be relieved, but I think I'm getting surrounded."

Luke chuckled and ruffled Chester's fur while he tossed the ball Wilks had brought him. "They like the open territory to run."

"I didn't get to meet Caroline Thursday."

He looked around the property. "There she is." He nodded toward the barn, where Caroline was closing the large swinging doors. "I'll let her show you around the house; it apparently struck her fancy when she saw it."

"You're not into the big outdoors."

Luke smiled. "Not as much as I am the convenience of a grocery store and gas station a block away from my house. And winters out here can give you a lot of snow to shovel and push around."

She laughed and he relaxed. This was going to work out okay.

Caroline had been out somewhere on the property taking its measure, Luke thought. She still wore work gloves, and the farmer's coat was spotted with mud. And if he wasn't mistaken, that was her service revolver being worn on her belt and something of the cop's gaze he remembered as she walked over to join them, relaxed but alert. "Amy, I'd like you to meet Caroline St. James. Caroline, Amanda Griffin."

"Hello, Amy."

"Caroline. I've heard a lot about you."

They shook hands and it was a quiet sizing up. Caroline smiled and gestured to the house. "Come on in—let me show you around. We'll see what you think of this place."

She led the way up the stone walk path to the front door. It opened into a small closed-in porch that had several closets, pegs for coats, two brooms, snow shovels, and a place to sit and pull off boots.

Caroline stepped out of her shoes and hung up her coat. "The house is old, a farmhouse rebuilt over the years to incorporate central heating, a modern kitchen, and a spacious living room taking advantage of the original fireplace. The barn and additional buildings out back have been converted into a garage and self-contained heated workshop and private study. There are four bedrooms upstairs under the attic eaves, and the grounds cover a quarter section, about a hundred sixty acres. The nearest neighbors have places that are close to two hundred acres of tillable land with a stretch of woods along the river. Beyond a mailman and those two neighbors, it's a private road." She opened the door into the living area of the home and let Amy walk through to make her own impressions.

Luke stepped inside after her. He thought immediately that it was a good fit. Warm rugs, colorful fabric on seat cushions, ample seating, and a lot of polished hardwood floors that looked to be refurbished original boards. "The larger windows really brighten up the rooms."

Amy wandered through the door to the left, and Luke followed. It was a well-laid-out kitchen, with long countertops compensating for the fact there wasn't room for an island. The kitchen table was covered with a blue-checked tablecloth.

"How did you find this place?" Luke asked, looking back at Caroline.

"Family connections. They travel now they are retired and hate to have the place sit empty. He's a former arson investigator;

he understands it's more than a simple lodger needing a place to stay. We'll up the insurance policy to cover any unfortunate actions. Daniel already has the paperwork in place if you're comfortable saying yes."

"It's different than I expected," Amy remarked.

"You were thinking gated community and patrolled grounds and the controlled surroundings."

"Yes."

"I'd go stir-crazy," Caroline said, smiling. "I'll take forewarning that someone is coming and leave it at that. There are several places in this home you can actually disappear to if necessary. Somewhere way in the past the owner of this place must have run moonshine on the side or else been part of the Underground Railroad, because he's got the most elaborate network of storm cellars and storage drops on this property I've ever seen. I was checking out one of them when you arrived. I'll give you the tour of them later and keys to the various vehicles around here. I saw two all-terrain-type runabouts in the far building."

Amy looked at Luke. "Your dogs can stay?"

"They can."

"Then I guess I need to get my stuff out of the car."

Luke offered his keys. "I'll help you carry in a second."

Amy headed outside.

"Thanks, Caroline."

"I haven't done anything yet."

"You've read her right, on the need to keep her from feeling trapped in somewhere. You've got phone numbers for Jonathan if you need more help quietly on the side out here? There could be a few guys watching that private road, the back ways onto the land, without Amy ever knowing they are there."

"There's one already out there mapping the area for when that information is needed later. They'll have more guys around whenever you arrange for Marie and Tracey to be here. Can you stay for lunch?"

"I'd better pass. I've already disappeared for a few hours; it's best I show up at the office, and I'm overdue for stopping in to see my sister. I'll plan to come out for a late dinner tomorrow night and talk with Amy then about her sisters visiting."

"Why don't I plan to disappear about then

for a few hours and give you two some privacy?"

Luke smiled. "The relationship is hardly progressing past friends, Caroline. You won't be in the way."

"It's not ever going to progress that far if you don't give it room to do so. Amy and I will fix dinner together, and I'll have other things to do tomorrow night. Do you know if Marsh has given Tracey the ring yet? I don't want to be stepping into new news yet."

"Not the last I'd heard."

"What is with that man? He dithered something terrible on figuring out the right ring to buy and he keeps it stuck in his pocket? It's not like him."

"Money changes things."

"If it has, he's not being quite as bright as I would have thought. Go help Amy get her things; I'll show her the bedrooms and then unload my own luggage."

●●●●●●

Amy leaned her hand against the bedroom window and watched the wind stir the trees behind the house. The anonymity of her life on the run had been a blessing, no one knowing the truth beyond the basic fabric she told them. It wasn't going to be as easy as she had hoped to relax in this new world where people around her knew who she really was. But Caroline seemed like a nice-enough lady. A lot more interesting than Amy had expected for a cop. And it hadn't taken much time to see there was history between Caroline and Luke, a comfort that went beyond what she'd expect for a cop and the police chief.

She left the bedroom she had chosen—the corner room with the wedding-ring quilt on the bed and bookshelves tucked under the attic eaves and braided rugs over the hardwood floors—and walked downstairs. She found Caroline in the kitchen. "What did you do in the army?"

Caroline looked up from the ham she was slicing.

"Luke told me," Amy offered.

Caroline nodded. "Military intelligence. What about you?"

"Logistics."

"Miss it?"

"Yeah."

"So do I," Caroline confided. "Want one of these, or would you prefer turkey? I stopped at the deli on the way over."

"Ham is fine." Amy found the bread knife and sliced open a loaf of sourdough bread. "So what's the plan for today?"

"Television reception is not great, hence the stack of DVDs in the living room. I thought I'd take one of those four-wheel, all-terrain toys for a ride and see what kind of wildlife is around that the dogs haven't already spooked away. You're welcome to join me, or you could spend a couple hours exploring the house."

"I'll come along. I spend too much of my days inside as it is." Amy found the refrigerator fully stocked and got out sodas. "How's the security around here going to work?"

"I've got a small pocket phone for you to carry. Within about a hundred yards of this house when you touch number one it is automatically on intercom mode with mine. My actual phone number is speed-dial two and Granger's speed-dial three. The dogs are the primary warning for company, and we'll keep an eye out on the road. For vehicles we don't know—you disappear from sight and let me check them out. If trouble arrives—we make a deal now that you only run; I don't want any help. Either go to a safe hiding spot or grab a vehicle and go."

"I don't like that idea, but I'll agree to it."

"My job is to make sure someone coming after you has to go through me first, and whoever tries will find I'm more prepared for trouble than they expect." Caroline smiled. "I don't expect more than the mailman or maybe a neighbor out here. But the faster we both know these grounds like the back of our hands the better. I don't think we need gobs of security people around who will attract more attention than we need."

"Like the telephone guy working down on the east road."

"You noticed him?"

"Granger pointed him out as one of Jonathan's guys. I'm slowly learning the faces."

"He's tightening up phone service for me so it's not that easy to cut our communications, putting in a relay station for the cellular phones." Caroline stacked the sandwiches together. "What I could use is your taking a look at the photos from New York and telling me who you would consider as faces I should be watching for."

Amy knew the suggestion was really Luke's, another way to nibble at the identity of the shooter and what she had seen the night Greg was killed, but it was a reasonable and necessary request. "I can recognize a few of the people Greg did business with," she replied, "but the two that have been on my tail recently—they weren't from New York that I could tell."

"I think the feds hired them."

"What?"

"You've been appearing at random over the years to hand over information, which was making them some good cases and helping them get noticed and promoted; they wanted you to come in with everything you had and compel you to testify. Two investigators on your tail for twenty months— that's not Richard Wise—that's someone with rules they have to operate within. The cop you were working with probably had no say in the matter or even knew the tail was being planned."

She hadn't even seriously considered that option, but it was this cop's first opinion. "Maybe. I admit to being surprised I lived through our last encounter. They were waiting for me when I got home from work."

"What happened?"

"I have a habit of watching a place before

I enter, and one of them was too near a window even in the darkened house. Since they knew the location and probably had seen the safe houses I'd arranged in the area, I got out the hard way—hitchhiking cross country with a truck driver and his wife, even doing part of the driving for a stretch of Nebraska. A long state, Nebraska—you wake up to the sun and see it set all in the same state."

Caroline smiled. "Are you really ready to be back to stay?"

"No, but there aren't choices anymore. The money my sisters just walked into says they're in as much, if not more, danger than I am. Richard knows I've got only a few million of his cash left, if that, if he's assuming I spent part of it over the years."

"Why don't you turn in the last ledger and cash and at least clear away one item you carry? Your sisters—the gallery and apartment are going to be a secure fortress the way the guys are going."

"I've got the ledger tucked in a safe place a long way from here, and I don't want to have to leave for the week it would take to turn the ledgers in. And after what you said,

I don't think I'll be returning to Texas to make the drop either."

"We could fly out and get the book, and I could make the delivery for you. There's no need for you to become a material witness on cases they can make without you."

"New York will want me to testify about the shooting."

"Only if they get enough to convince them they can make the case against the shooter. A witness testimony but without the gun, without cooperating motive for who hired the shooter—it's your word against his, and a DA is not going to make that case when he has to deal with the fact you've been on the run for years with stolen money and books. The defense attorney will make waves that you were the one who hired the hit on Greg."

"And you begin to get the picture for why it was easier to just stay out there on my own this last stretch of time. Cops have more pushing on them than my welfare."

"I know. Luke gave me carte blanche, by the way, to not tell him stuff. Where you go, who you see, what you do—the only thing he expects is that I take the bullet if some-one starts shooting at us."

"Thanks for mucking with my head; that image isn't going to leave soon."

"Well, we'll have to compromise on it because I doubt I've got the reflexes to take the bullet for you. I'll do my best to make sure you're not in a place someone can easily shoot you. That's about my limit."

"Let's hope it never gets even close to that."

Caroline took her plate over to the table. "You want to borrow some boots for today? I think we're about the same size."

"Sure."

"Let's go explore while the sun is up and making it warmer. Tonight is forecast to be a bear of a cold front coming in, and tomorrow I doubt we want to move from the house."

Chapter Fourteen

Luke followed Amy into the house Sunday night, having been somewhat surprised to find her down at the barn upon his arrival, but after a second thought, not so surprised after all. She wasn't the type to like to be cooped up if there were options available to take her outside. "How are you settling in?"

"Better than I thought I would. It's going to take some time getting used to sleeping with the sounds of this old house in the night when the wind comes. I like Caroline."

"I thought you might." Luke pulled off his coat and used one of the open pegs to hang it up. "I can already smell dinner—I feel a bit guilty having you cook the meal," he teased.

Amy laughed and pushed the door open,

leading the way through to the kitchen. "As long as it doesn't affect your appetite, go ahead. It's swiss steak and mashed potatoes, simple but hot and hard to mess up. Ice cream and brownies for dessert."

"You'll find me a willing guest."

He pulled out one of the kitchen chairs as she moved to the stove to check the meal. She looked better today—more confident, less nerves showing—and her smile had been quick and reached her eyes. This had been the right move and seeing her confirmed it.

"Today was quiet?" she asked, glancing back at him.

He nodded. "I saw your sisters briefly at church. They know you're in the area—Marsh and Connor conveyed that message last night—and they know we'll set something up for Wednesday if possible."

"They didn't flood you with questions?"

"They're just glad to have you back. They'll be patient for a while now."

"How's the reporter problem?"

"Dispersing, thankfully. There were only two around the gallery this morning to shout questions and snap pictures as Marie and Tracey were leaving. Most have shifted to

interviewing friends of the family and trying
to arrange interviews through Daniel."

"I'm glad. Anything else happening in
your days? I know crime in this city didn't
stop just because I've been taking a slice of
your time."

He smiled, not minding she was asking
and finding it endearing. "An armed robbery
at a liquor store had me out late last night.
We're working two assaults, a domestic dis-
turbance, and a high-speed chase of a guy
who boosted a car off a dealer's lot. I'd say
it's been a typical weekend so far. Would
you like some help with setting the table?"

"Sure. Plates are that end, and glasses
near me."

He got up to work alongside her.
"Where's Caroline?"

"She's around somewhere, but the lady
likes to be discreet; she ate early even
though I protested it. I think she was talking
to Marsh last I heard. Something about a
ring. I can't believe my little sister is about to
be engaged."

"Let's hope Marsh finds the occasion to
give it to her soon; everyone is ready for it to
happen and he's stalling."

"I knew the money would be a problem. I just didn't figure it for this problem."

Luke chuckled. "They'll sort it out. He's older than her and now she's more wealthy than him too—it gets those reporters talking too much. You'll like Marsh, Amy. He's not that easy a guy to figure out, but he's solid."

"A wedding is going to be a challenge—they'll want me there and I'm going to have to refuse."

"Cross that bridge when we get there. You want regular knives or steak knives?"

"Regular should be fine."

The meal on the table, Luke held Amy's chair for her. "Would you like me to say grace?"

"Please."

He kept it simple, sorting out the emotions of several days into thankfulness that the sisters had met together safely and the pleasure of a nice meal. When he said amen, her head stayed bowed for a moment, and he turned his attention to the food to give her privacy.

She lifted her head, blinking hard. "I'm always weepy eyed these days. I don't know why."

"Stress letting off. You've been wound pretty tight for a long time."

"Probably. I used to pray for the next day to not bring trouble with it, and now—this place is pretty calm and it does surprisingly feel safe. My family is nearby. And that makes life so much easier. I used to always be running—now I know I'm planted, at least for a little while."

"We'll make it safe for it to be a very long while," Luke said. "I'm glad you fixed dinner—I would have been bringing something like fast-food fried chicken or the like. This is good."

"I'm glad you like it." Amy reached for the fruit salad. "Can I interest you in staying for a movie tonight? Caroline brought a huge stack of DVDs along."

"I can be tempted," Luke replied, smiling at her.

●●●●●●

Amy had already stacked wood in the fireplace, ready to strike a match and bring it to life. Luke moved to do that while Amy sorted out the DVDs. He listened and heard Caroline's car pull out. She'd passed by, mentioning a quick trip to meet Marsh as the reason, but he thought that was more of an excuse to give them not only privacy, but time. Luke wouldn't be leaving until she returned.

The fire going and beginning to draw so it wouldn't smoke, he watched it for a moment, then turned. He pushed back the coffee table and sat down on the floor to use the couch as a backrest.

"Hardwood floors are going to get hard on the tailbone after a while."

He laughed and patted the floor beside him. "Start the movie and come be a teenager again. We can pause it and move to the couch later."

She started the movie and adjusted the volume, then settled herself down beside him. "I'm too old for this, Luke. I was out riding on one of those four-wheelers yesterday, and I've got sore muscles that make me feel like I'm fifty."

He slid her a pillow for behind her back.

"Yeah, that helps."

He settled his hand over hers and interlaced their fingers. She fit him well, in age, in spirit, and he liked the look of her more every time he saw her. He wouldn't mind at all seeing this relationship finally slide past friendship to something more. She leaned her head against his shoulder to get comfortable. "So what are we watching?" he asked, amused.

"A legal thriller, I think. I'm so far behind what is out now that I don't even recognize titles."

"Want to make it a double feature?"

She chuckled and he felt it in his own ribs. "Only if we're sitting on the couch."

He smiled at her relaxed form and then turned his attention to the movie. His dogs were out here, his lady, a few more shifts in his schedule with his deputy chief's help and he'd figure out how to be out here more often too. It would make a good next few weeks.

Chapter Fifteen

Amy pulled a load of towels out of the dryer and pushed the door closed with her hip. It was nice to be able to do routine tasks without pausing to think about what might be around every door and waiting down every hallway. She carried the towels into her room and dropped them onto the bed to fold. She could feel the tension beginning to fade away after three days in this place. Luke had been right about that—the fact the stress level had been too high for too long.

Caroline had called with news the arriving car was Connor's; it would be good to have the boxes of clothes he was bringing out. Marie had promised to find the dresses as well as the winter clothes, and Amy about had closet space ready to hang them up; she'd found extra hangers in the guest bedroom.

The bedroom door burst open behind her. Amy turned, startled to see Tracey just before she was swallowed in a hug. Amy hugged her sister back, in turmoil over what it meant to have her here on an unplanned spur-of-the-moment visit.

"Marsh asked me to marry him!"

Amy leaned back to study her sister's smiling face and had to smile back. "Did he?"

Tracey held up her hand to show off the ring. "I had to tell you. He's taken so *incredibly* long to ask the question."

Her sister was beaming. Amy wrapped Tracey in another hug. "I'm glad for you. Really glad. I don't know if I'm ready for you to be marrying a cop," she teased. "You've had such a sheltered life and all."

Tracey laughed. "I know. We're going to fix up his place, and I'm going to still finish my degree. He's insistent about that. But maybe an early April wedding, so we can go south for our honeymoon and do some traveling together."

Tracey had come to the safe house without them being fully ready for it and possibly put herself at risk, but it had already happened. She was too excited to share the news to realize it, and Amy wasn't going to burst her bubble with a caution. She'd have that conversation with Connor shortly, if Caroline wasn't already doing so. Amy tugged her sister down on the bed beside her. "Let me see that ring again."

Tracey offered it and Amy fell in love with it too. Simple, nice diamonds, with a modern elegance to the flow of the gold. "Marsh has very good taste."

"He swears part of the delay in asking me was finding the ring. Caroline said Marsh pulled her along to see at least two hundred rings over the last couple months, half a dozen of them ones she would like herself, and he was never satisfied."

Amy laughed. "I love him already."

"Would you mind if he stayed around tomorrow night so you could really meet him? I know I wasn't supposed to come out with Connor today, but I begged so hard they finally gave in."

"Bring Marsh along Wednesday and see if Daniel would also like to come out for the evening. The guys can make sure no one is being followed, and that's the biggest risk short of someone saying something they shouldn't."

"They haven't given us a phone number to you yet, afraid one of the reporters might be listening in."

"I asked them to wait; being overheard really is a risk, Tracey."

"I'm disappointed, as I could keep you talking for hours, but I'll adjust." Tracey stood up and held out her hands. "Come on, say a brief hi to Connor, and I'll get out of here. Marie packed you like a gazillion clothes, and she already ironed every one. She hated the fact the guys insisted they get folded into plain boxes before they were carried out."

"I appreciate that," Amy replied, remembering one dress in particular she hoped Marie had packed. She wouldn't mind turning Luke's head if he came out Wednesday night too. "So if you're planning an April wedding, how's that going to affect the class schedule?"

"Marsh agreed I could cut back this semester to the hours I need to audit as prerequisites for the doctorate degree—that way I can stay with Marie while she's having to make so many decisions about the gallery, and I'll drive over for the two classes. I want time to prepare a proper wedding, and the house will take some planning together for what gets remodeled."

"It sounds like a good compromise."

"I can tell he was ready to get married when he listened to the ideas and said okay and didn't even fuss particularly hard about it being some of my money that went into expanding his study and building on another bedroom upstairs, so I can have a room to use as a home office too."

Amy followed Tracey downstairs, listening to the news, smiling at the joy she could hear in her sister's voice, and worrying about the rushed way she had come. Tracey wasn't dating Connor—any reporter would have picked up she had left the gallery with Connor, not Marsh. It was another reason to be curious, and that made reporters trouble.

●●●●●●

Daniel was an interesting man. Amy watched him move around the living room Wednesday evening, talking with Marsh, then lingering in a conversation with Caroline, and thought he made a good fit. She liked him. No one had brought up the half-sister fact, and it was beginning to sting less. She personally never wanted to know her father's name, and part of her was relieved she hadn't been asked to absorb that shock too.

She studied Caroline as she spoke with Daniel and saw a slight flush on her friend's face, animated in a really beautiful way. Caroline was elegant tonight and attracting attention from a guy wise enough to want to linger and get to know her better. They'd be a good couple, Amy thought, in a mind to think such thoughts. Marsh hadn't let Tracey get more than a few feet from him all evening, and Connor was doing a reasonably good job getting Marie out of the awkward phase of dating to being comfortable with him. Amy hadn't missed the way Connor had secured hold of her sister's hand early in the evening and simply not let go.

"You look content tonight."

She had a few seconds' warning before Luke's hands settled on her waist from behind.

She leaned against him. "I'm feeling very

much the oldest sister at the moment, watching my chicks find new homes."

He chuckled and leaned his head down beside hers. "Come for a walk. It's a clear night outside, and I'm inclined to remember how to enjoy moonlight with a pretty lady, but that's best done somewhere my cops are not going to notice."

She let her hand slide down to take his. "I like the sound of that."

Luke nodded to Caroline, and she nodded back. They stopped to get coats and then slipped outside.

"It's brisk tonight." Amy could see her breath, and her warm leather gloves became stiffer in the cold air.

"The moon makes up for it."

Luke reached for her hand, and Amy moved comfortably to his side. They walked down the drive toward the main road.

"It's been quiet out here so far?" Luke shined his torch over a couple rough bricks in the path.

"Yes. The place is beginning to feel like home. Caroline says we can use it another six weeks, if not ten. I'm going to miss it when it's time to move on."

"Your sisters certainly enjoyed the chance

to come out. The guys said they were both impatient with the convoluted drives to get here."

"They went separately to dinner and then diverted to here?"

"Yes. It seems best for security."

"I think so."

"I was thinking about options—if you'd like to take a trip next weekend. Maybe go over a county or two, do some driving for the day. We could start getting an idea of where might be a nice area to stay next."

"I'd like that."

He squeezed her hand. "Good. Are you getting used to the idea of Tracey getting married?"

Amy paused in their walk to look up at him. "Besides the fact she's so incredibly young? She's in her thirties, I know that, but inside she's still sixteen. She knows what she wants, and I do like Marsh."

"But?"

"Being a cop is just not that easy a profession on a wife—the waiting for a husband to get home when trouble has kept him late at the job, when the scanner chatter is about shots being fired."

"I know the risks are real in this job, but

being a cop also carries with it a partner at your side when that trouble arrives. For what it's worth, I think Tracey is good for Marsh. He's softer on the edges now; this job can push you toward being a cynic without that balance."

She shivered even with the warmth of the coat, and he saw and turned them back the way they had come. "What about you, Amy? Could you handle being married to a cop?"

She smiled. "I think that may be too straightforward of a question to ask right now."

He smiled back. "I know. Answer it anyway."

She thought about it and shrugged. "I don't know that I'm a cop's wife material either or anyone's wife material for that matter. You're talking about social functions and school gatherings and PTA meetings and suburban living."

He chuckled. "I'd say that's a pretty interesting idea of what suburban life is like."

"I was in the army for a decade, I've been playing hide-and-seek with real stakes for the years since, and for the next stage of my life I'm going to be a suburban housewife driving a minivan and trying to teach my kids not to shoot spitballs at the dogs? That image just doesn't connect."

He laughed at her words. "Spitballs at the dogs? Your own childhood is showing, I think. You worked as a retail associate at a mall jewelry store, and your friends from those years didn't see you as particularly discontent with your life. You also have a healthy need to not have any more major surprises in your life."

"Both true."

"I'll discount the concerns about suburban life then. What about the danger of the job?"

"Maybe it's because I know and have tasted living with danger that it's a different kind of burden to think about; not that a cop as a husband is such a big risk, but more that it will always be a risk. There is no peaceful expectation that a day will be quiet. You live life expecting trouble. I've been living that way for eight years."

"It wears on you," he said softly, understanding.

"Yes. This time the situation wasn't my choice—" She hesitated. "I guess I'm glad

I'm not being asked that decision right now. I don't know what I would decide."

They reached the rock path of the driveway, and Amy nodded to the left. "Let's walk over to the study." There was an enclosed study off the heated workshop, and she often retreated there during the afternoon to enjoy a book while she watched the dogs play together.

She unlocked the building, and they stepped back into warmth. A small light was on in the study, and she used it to cross over to the room and turn on the main lights. She slid off her coat and hung it on the coatrack. The book she'd been reading that afternoon still rested on the small table beside the leisure chairs, and the throw Caroline had used across her feet rested folded on the couch. It was a guy's study, lined with books and a nice desk against one wall, but also just comfortable space.

"So what was your reason for suggesting we sneak out again?" She settled her hands on Luke's shoulders and smiled at him, having to tip her head back but finding it nice.

His hands stilled hers. "You are dressed up tonight like a princess. I thought I'd mention that."

"I hoped you might have noticed," she replied, encouraged by the quiet pleasure she saw in his gaze.

"And if I'm not mistaken that is the same perfume you were wearing three years ago."

"I'm a creature of habit. Want to dance awhile? We could find some music."

"I think we're making our own at the moment, but we could try the dial on the radio," he teased.

She grinned and didn't bother to step away. "So are you going to kiss me or not?"

He laughed. "Probably. Someday. I'm thinking about it."

"Good. So am I." There was a deliberateness about him when it came to their relationship that she appreciated, even if the closest she'd get to a kiss tonight was the anticipation he'd take her up on the offer one day. They were destined to be either very good friends or something more than that, and she was enjoying the exploration. She took a half step back to study his face, leaving her hands in his. "We're awful different, Luke. You do realize that, don't you? How our lives have evolved. You're going to be working in the same job, the same town, until the day you retire, I predict. There might be a different house or two over the years, but the town and the job and the friends and the family are pretty much constants for as long as the eye can see into your future."

"All of which are good things, I think, and they would be for you as well. You need to see the lay of the land and stay with something that is stable for a while. Besides, a new job and new town aren't necessarily better even if it's more pay; new sometimes simply means more shallow. I want to hang out with the guys I went to grade school with. I know them and they know me. There isn't a need to be anything but who I am around them. There is power in that fact. And when you get to my age those kinds of friends are worth staying with."

"I envy you that. I've got Tracey and Marie and good friends from the military days spread around the globe. Beyond Sam and a few friends from high school, there aren't deep roots here."

"So we'll see if that can change in the future. I've got plenty of friends to share," he suggested, smiling. "What do you have to lose, Amy? I like you, and I'm safe, relatively. The rest is going to take care of itself."

"I'm old enough to take the plunge and close my eyes for the outcome to arrive." She knew the night was opening doors to a possible new future, and she found herself wanting to walk down that road with him. "So where do you want to go next weekend? I've a yen to see some snow."

"Snow we can stay right here and watch fall, if you believe the weatherman. I thought we'd take in some holiday lights and maybe a movie. We could do some early Christmas-gift shopping."

"A guy offering to go shopping . . . I'm remembering this, Luke. Just you and me, there's no need to take along security?"

"That's a call for the night before."

"Then yes, tentatively. Assuming Tracey and Marie haven't had a major hiccup in their lives I need to stay and worry about instead."

Luke laughed. "Deal, then. How long have we been hiding?"

"Long enough someone besides Caroline has realized we're gone."

"True. Five more minutes. I am the boss."

"I notice they still call you Chief, even off duty."

"They're teasing and rubbing in the age a bit and also accepting reality—I am the chief and nothing changes that in our relationship, even off duty."

"Respectful friends."

"Yeah. They know the decisions that come across my desk; I'm glad for that at times, the fact the respect stays even when it feels like I'm in over my head with the job. It helps, having cops like that working with me."

"You're a good police chief."

"Working to be. You'll like my secretary, by the way, and my sister. Both are sticklers for my work staying at work."

"How long, Luke, before it is safe to meet them? to come out of the shadows? You know as well as I do that we are heading to an impasse if this is still the way it is in six months, a year from now."

Her question turned him serious. "It won't continue as it is for months. I'm just hoping we get a few weeks of calm before trouble arrives. You need that time; your sisters do. But we both know there are too many pressures at work for this not to erupt some-where."

She sighed. "I know. Sometimes fantasy clashed something awful with reality; I so want to blink and find this was all a bad dream." She lifted her head to look at him. "Daniel's got better security around him?"

"Yes. It was a condition of his coming out tonight to meet you."

"Good. We'd better get back to the house, I think. Marie said something about getting out the picture albums tonight to compare notes on where Henry and Mom must have met and traveled together. I can't say I'm looking forward to it."

"They need the closure that facts can provide. Just listen. I'm sorry they aren't talking about your father too. I know that re-mains an awful hole for you."

"I never wanted to know and I still don't. I'm glad Henry was not my father."

He looked surprised by the intensity of her answer but chose not to probe that painful spot. He picked up their coats.

"I am glad you came out tonight, Luke. Very glad."

"I'm not planning to go anywhere for a long time," he reassured, helping her on with her coat and his hands resting for a moment on her shoulders before releasing her and slipping on his own coat.

He took her hand again for the walk back to the house.

"Until this danger passes: don't get too attached, Luke, please. When trouble comes—I'll do what I think is right and best. Even if that means leaving."

His gaze didn't shift from the path they were walking. "I know." He glanced over and smiled but with a hard, watchful look behind that gentleness. "You'll do what you think is best, just as I will. And if both our hearts get mangled in the process, but your sisters are safe, we'll still know it was the right decision."

"I thought you deserved to know."

"I haven't pushed for a promise that you'll stay not because I don't want it, but because I know you can't give it. There are risks now and ones that will wound us both if we're not careful. But I'm committed to seeing Marie and Tracey are safe, because they are the most important people in your life, and I'm committed to doing what I can to keep you safe too, with or without your cooperation when it comes down to the details."

She smiled. "I'm glad we both know that then. Don't be mad one day when I decide something you wouldn't have decided for me."

He tightened his grip on her hand. "I'll get mad, but I'll do my best to forgive you too. But you'll owe me a phone call or two this time—no more gone-forever-without-a-trace flights. You haunted my dreams for the last three years, you know."

"Did I?"

He smiled at the pleasure in her words. "I think we should plan an early start next weekend—say 6 a.m., and catch breakfast at one of the truck-stop diners that make the meal a feast. What do you think?"

"I think you're taking every minute you can get out of a yes, but sure, I'm game. Even if I do prefer to skip breakfast and catch the extra sleep."

"I'll be here early then."

"I don't know that I'll be telling Marie and Tracey where I'm going and who I'm going with just yet though."

"Chicken."

"You've only got one sister. Two is

tougher when they both decide to go for answers and giving advice. When can they
come out again?"

"It depends on how the press reacts to
their disappearance tonight. Basically, as
soon as it can safely be done, but not a day
earlier."

He held open the door to the house. Amy
paused, hearing music and laughter even
before they passed through the coatroom.
"Laughter. I've missed hearing them laugh
for so many years."

"I know." He smiled as he took her coat
for her, then nodded to the next door. "Go
enjoy it."

Chapter Sixteen

"So what time should I pick you up, Marie? Say 7 p.m.?" Connor showed his badge to the officer guarding the walk path that led up to a small bungalow off Eisenhower Boulevard and then slipped under the police tape. The idea of arranging a date while arriving at a crime scene didn't sit well as something he wanted her to know he was doing, but it had been such a headache last week trying to coordinate seeing her with the unpredictable hours of the job that he was taking a chance to talk with her whenever he could find an opening.

"Could you make it eight? With the shipment that just came in I'm going to need every minute I can get of Tracey's time to help me hang it, and she's around until seven. Eight will give me time to shower and change or else I'll be your date wearing packing dust and sweat."

He smiled at the thought. "I'll be there at eight," he promised.

"Thanks."

"Bye, Marie." He closed the phone and slid it in his pocket, catching the first breath of what awaited him in the house as he opened the screen door. He lifted an arm to cover his nose as he stepped inside. "So much for colder weather making this job easier. How long was it before he was found?"

The living room just off the entryway was small, more a place to sit and read a book than a place to have more than two people linger and talk. Marsh turned from where he crouched beside the body to look back at him. "I'm guessing two days plus. Monday's mail was brought in, and Tuesday's was still in the box."

Connor didn't have to ask cause of death. Stab wounds, deep and plentiful, the blood spray from artery wounds having hit the wall, furnishings, and turned the room into a horror show. Connor held back his initial reaction to the sight of the body out of respect for the dead. "Stabbing implies very personal."

"We'll look at the family first," Marsh agreed. "The front door wasn't forced, and the officer who walked around the house looking for signs of entry saw no immediate evidence of a forced screen or broken glass. Our victim appears to have let his attacker in, and our murderer inconveniently locked the doors on his way out. I had to shove out the lock to get inside."

Connor came around the sofa and stepped over the end table so he could get into the space beside the body without stepping somewhere soaked in blood. He pulled on latex gloves. "Do we have a name for him?"

"No wallet on him. A seventy-year-old retired gentleman, by appearance still in reasonably good physical shape: good muscle tone, fit, not wearing glasses or hearing aids, and with tennis shoes that look well used for walking. He would probably have lived to be a hundred if someone hadn't murdered him."

Connor absorbed the details while trying to block out the smell. The hands were still

in remarkably good shape given the decom-
position, no slices or broken bones. "No defensive wounds? That surprises me."

"Probably the blow to the side of the face
comes first, knocks him down, attacker
straddles him and stabs repeatedly . . . ,"
Marsh guessed, noting the angles.

"Yeah. You can see where the attacker's
legs protected the guy's slacks from the
blood splatter. Our doer must have looked a
mess on his way out of the house afterward
unless he changed clothes somewhere inside. There weren't blood drops on the front
walk that I saw. Arrived and departed by
car?"

"There's a door going out to the garage.
We'll check that direction. After dark, a
short walk to a parked car—neighbors
aren't going to be that nosy, but we'll see
what anyone happened to remember."

"He'll have bloody clothes, shoes, a
knife—at least it is something to find. Who
called it in?"

"The postman thought it odd the mail and
newspapers hadn't been picked up for a
couple days and mentioned it to an area patrol. Officers knocked on house doors on either side of here and across the street but

found no one home. I'm wagering we're looking at a retired guy living in a neighborhood of working couples and no one will remember seeing anything at all."

"It's easier to solve a murder in a community where crime is an occasional thing than a neighborhood absolutely shocked when it happens the first time," Connor agreed, hoping someone at least had a dog that had gone off barking for no reason at all and an owner observant enough to remember the cars on the street. He looked at his partner. Marsh had caught the call—this one was his. "Where do you want me?"

Marsh smiled and nodded toward the hall, letting him off the hook. "Work the office and bedroom and find us a name for him. If you can't find his wallet, a prescription bottle might do. It looks like he lives alone."

"Thanks."

"The next one is going to be yours. I'm betting it's an ice floater in one of the rivers."

"Don't even think it," Connor protested, remembering last year's winter discovery. He headed toward the bedroom to see if he could put a name to their victim. "We've got blood drops in the hallway," he called, noting the evidence. "Maybe cleaned up in the bathroom?"

He glanced in the open door on his left. "Oh yeah, blood in the bathroom. He tried to wash up in here." A bleach bottle sat with the cap still half off in the tub, suggesting the killer had been at least trying to destroy evidence of his own presence after the washup. The lab guys would be struggling to get prints on the guy, for the smeared blood still present looked like glove smears rather than fingerprints. Connor left that problem to the experts. He nudged open the medicine cabinet. He saw no prescription bottles, which surprised him, just Chap Stick, extra hand soap, a shaving kit, solitary toothbrush. Nothing in the room suggested a female lived here.

The room he thought would be the office turned out to be a spare bedroom. He opened the next room and found it to be the man's bedroom. The man kept a very neat home—that was Connor's first impression of the room. The bed was made with the spread tugged tight to remove folds, the pillows perfectly aligned. The furniture was clear of the usual miscellaneous items dumped from pockets: no spare change, matchbooks, toothpicks, pocket comb. A very nice watch sat on the dresser next to a cigar box. Connor pushed up the lid of the cigar box and found it full of coins, a couple dates on the dollar coins putting them at a hundred years old and solid silver. The watch and coins sitting out in plain sight, still here, said this wasn't an obvious robbery.

Connor opened the top dresser drawer and found the wallet in the same place his own grandfather kept his, top drawer left, next to the folded socks. He opened the thin worn leather. The driver's license gave him a name, and the photo was enough of a match to be the match they needed. "Nolan Price, seventy-one," he read aloud. Two hundred in cash still in the billfold.

He carried the wallet back with him to the living room. "I know this guy is going to prove to be former military, probably Korea. The house is tidy neat. I'm not seeing robbery as a motive—there's cash, coins, a nice watch, all within easy reach."

"I'll add another piece to it," Marsh said. "Look behind you, fourth picture down in that frame of snapshots."

Connor scanned the wallet photos arranged in the matted frame. "This is not good. Our victim, standing beside a Mr. Henry Benton." He lifted the frame down and worked the backing free. He slid out the wallet photo and then handed it to his partner. "That looks like a uniform to me."

"Chauffeur? It must be, given the car that is behind them. What is that, a Rolls?"

"Daniel doesn't use a chauffeur, but maybe his uncle did. The age would fit with this guy having retired recently."

"A coincidence? This particular guy turning up dead right now?"

"We've had stronger coincidences before," Connor replied, not wanting to get drawn somewhere the crime wasn't taking them yet. "Even if he still had something useful like keys to Henry Benton's estate, that kind of thing—Daniel doesn't live there, and a robbery isn't that simple. There are full-time security guards walking the grounds while the estate goes through probate. What's keeping forensics?"

Marsh stood. "They've got a fatal house fire over on the west side of town. I told them not to rush; our guy isn't going anywhere."

"True. Let's get outside a few minutes, Marsh. This is killing my sinuses."

"It's a little raw," Marsh conceded. "If it's family, we're probably looking for a nephew, I'm thinking." He grabbed Connor's arm, stopping him from passing the mirror. "How did we miss that?"

Connor saw the image too and turned to scan the room. "You're telling me."

The note was written in blood across the rich leather-bound books on the middle bookshelf, the note probably bright three days ago and now darkened into a stain in the books' leather. The sun passing free of clouds had briefly brightened the room and the contrast. He walked with Marsh around the body to get a closer look.

" 'I know . . .' Something else looks faded out," Marsh said.

" 'Family secret,' " Connor figured out, tracing but not touching the pattern from the other end of the shelf. " 'I know the family secret.' "

"What secret? A seventy-one-year-old guy has a family secret worth murdering over?" Marsh wondered aloud. "This victim is not Henry Benton giving away two hundred million in his will. What is going through this killer's messed-up head?"

"I don't think we're looking for someone particularly crazy," Connor said. "He used blood already at the scene and on a vertical canvas; that's a nice way to stop any match to handwriting. And writing on objects—forget fingerprints in this. This looks like a paper towel dipped in blood was used as a pen."

"The psychiatrist is going to love interpreting this one," Marsh agreed, writing the words down.

"You've got to admit, notes are pretty rare. What is this, our second one in six years?"

"I didn't like that case either," Marsh replied. "What else? Is that the extent of the message or did he try and write on something else strange when this line of books ran out?"

Connor looked around the room. "It's going to take hours to eliminate everything."

"The back of doors, the back of pictures, rolled-up blinds . . . not just what we see now, but what the killer might have selected as amusing at the time. What time are you meeting Marie tonight?"

"Eight."

"Don't expect to make it on time."

Connor took out his phone. "I knew it was going to be like this today, Marsh. Didn't I tell you just this morning while we were getting coffee that things were going too smooth with Marie?"

"You did."

"The third date and I'm already canceling one." Connor shook his head and walked away to have some privacy for the call.

"Don't tell her someone killed her father's former chauffeur, claiming to know a family secret," Marsh offered dryly, beginning the laborious process of turning over pictures on the wall one at a time to check for what might or might not appear behind them.

Connor scowled at his partner. "Marie? Connor. How's the picture unpacking going?"

He listened and smiled at her answer as he walked through into the kitchen to begin systematically opening and closing all the cabinet doors.

"You're not going to be able to come tonight after all," Marie guessed, speculating on why he had called back so soon.

"I'm afraid not. We've got a case that wants to be difficult."

"Dangerous?"

"Only to catching hepatitis B or some other blood-born bug. Forensics isn't here yet so the preliminary walk-through is on us." He covered the phone. "Marsh."

His partner came to join him.

Connor pointed to the inside of the pantry door. *I know the family secret* was painted in blood across the wood.

"He's getting neater. This must be the second attempt to write it."

"Prints," Connor suggested. "Maybe."

"A very slim maybe. But five will get you ten we find this message at least a couple more times."

"I'd take that bet."

"Connor?"

He uncovered the phone. "Sorry, Marie. I was talking to Marsh."

"You're at a murder scene?"

He opened the refrigerator, wondering if there would be a message written in blood inside it too. "I'm in a kitchen looking at a half-used carton of eggs," he replied, getting the image in her mind down to something more subdued than what he figured she was thinking. "Can I call you late tonight instead? Say around ten?"

"I'll still be up."

"Thanks, Marie. I'll talk to you then." Connor hung up the phone. "The reporters are going to have a field day with this crime-scene write-up."

"You know about the message; I do. We play bullies with the crime-scene folks— maybe we can keep it suppressed. At least the words of the message."

Connor shook his head. "There is no way reporters are not all over this as soon as the crime-scene photos are taken and our report written. It's not only a good story, it's a good *new* story. You know the news it is Henry's chauffeur will have it leading on page one of the society section tomorrow; it's *new* news that gives them a reason to repeat the Marie and Tracey story all over again. And when someone mentions what the message says, it's going to be announced in screaming headlines in a big, bold font."

"Then let's hope it really is some nephew that we find sitting at his kitchen table still wearing the bloody clothes three days later. Otherwise you might end up arresting me for confronting a reporter who splashed the investigation details across the evening news."

Connor smiled. "You want me to call the deputy chief?"

"I'll do it." Marsh pulled out his phone. "After that I'll call the chief himself. No use keeping the good news quiet. We'll need to interview Daniel tonight. He's the one who probably knows this guy and when he re- tired and who was listed as the next-of-kin contact in the employee file."

"On a Thursday evening—he'll be playing racquetball at the club."

"By chance do you know what Daniel was doing Monday evening?"

Connor frowned at his partner. "Helping me move furniture around, from five to after ten." His partner put Daniel on the list of folks to eliminate for doing the murder, and while he would have done the same, it was still an unpleasant thought to have had.

"Just asking." Marsh's attention turned to his call. "Yes, sir, I'm on scene now. Nolan Price, age seventy-one. A stabbing attack with rage features. There's a note left at the scene written in blood. We're going to need some special handling on this as I'd like to keep that quiet as long as possible." Marsh smiled. "My thoughts exactly. I'll keep you informed. Thank you, sir."

He closed the phone. "One copy of the case report and it goes directly to the deputy chief until this is wrapped; nothing gets filed through channels."

"The beat reporters are going to be burning you in effigy."

Marsh smiled. "That just leaves the forensics folks to keep quiet."

"Take names at the door and threaten bodily harm for who talks—I doubt it will work, but you can try."

"Give me a week with this message under wraps and I can use it to break the guy who did it. He's going to be begging for a chance to talk about his message when we get him into an interview room."

"The family secret is burning a hole in him, whatever it is," Connor agreed. He began opening drawers. "Do you see any knives missing from this kitchen? That wooden block on the counter looks full, and I'm not seeing a miscellaneous drawer with another knife or two lying around. The dishwasher is empty."

"Our killer brought his own weapon—that

doesn't often happen with a knife, not a slim-blade knife at least. Those wounds didn't look wide like a military knife."

"That was my thought too."

"So maybe not a family argument that flares, gets out of control, and the old man gets stabbed to death, but something a lot more premeditated."

"We don't get that many premeditated murders either." Connor closed drawers. "I'm glad this one is yours."

"Thanks a lot," Marsh replied dryly. "I'm calling the chief now. Unless you would like to do the honors?"

"I'd confirm that employment first and the fact this is indeed Henry's retired chauffeur. Maybe scan for tax returns in the office? I'm sure he's got them filed in chronological order, given how everything else is maintained. A copy of an old W-2 will do it."

"Good point." Marsh left the kitchen to go check.

Connor eased open the trash-can lid while holding his breath, afraid that he might be staring at the bloody knife or something else gut curdling attracting bugs. Just the remains of an omelet, too many days old, resting atop a folded newspaper and an opened can of chili. "When I die, God, please let my place burn down so someone isn't going through my trash afterward, wondering at how I lived," he whispered, gratefully closing the lid, and stepped away.

He turned toward the garage. Murder scenes always felt slightly off, like the details of life had gotten recolored with a touch of the horror in the house and made more starkly obvious that death pulled a person out of this life abruptly. Rich or poor, they left everything they had behind, even the last set of clothes they wore.

Marsh came back into the room. "Tax returns going back thirty-plus years show Benton Group as his sole employer. Granger wants us in his office for the 6 a.m. update."

Connor winced.

"Yeah, my thoughts too. He's in court at seven, the last round of that civil assignment board's lawsuit where he got pulled in as a witness. He did promise to bring real coffee."

"I'll crawl in with my eyes half open to be moral support," Connor promised. "Let's get those forensics guys working here and go find Daniel and a few people to interview."

"Already a step ahead." Marsh held up a manila folder. "Last year's Christmas cards complete with original envelopes. We'll start with the brother over on the north side of town. The guy sends a funny card and a fish photo of the two of them out on some rickety boat; the odds are good the two talked occasionally about what was going on in their lives."

"Anything show as recent phone records?"

"Just last month's bill; I'll have the phone company pull the recent calls. At least it looks like he was not into the twentieth century with a cell phone and e-mail, which makes this a bit easier. The calendar on his desk was a washout—two appointments in the last sixty days and both to the dentist."

"Better if it had been a barber," Connor agreed. "It's hard to gossip about things going on in life when you have a mouth full of instruments."

A white-paneled van pulled into the driveway. Marsh stepped to the door. "It looks like we caught Rachel and Joe for the forensics. That will be a plus."

Connor followed Marsh outside, relieved to get farther away from the smell. It was going to take a good hour under a hot shower to soak the traces of odor out of his skin and the clothes. It wouldn't be the first shirt he pitched as unrecoverable. The smell clung a lot harder than cigarette smoke ever did.

••••••

Daniel settled on the chair across from Connor and Marsh at a private table off the racquetball court, having come off the court to find the police waiting for him. In the first rush of adrenaline and fear he'd thought it was bad news about his cousins, but the reality felt just as rotten.

"Nolan Price worked for my uncle for thirty-four years. I finally talked him into retiring this spring when it was clear Henry would not be leaving the hospital for more than a few weeks at most and no longer coming into the office. As far as I know Nolan has lived in that bungalow most of those thirty-four years, and the closest I think he came to marrying someone was when he was courting one of the ladies who worked for my aunt as a part-time secretary.

This hurts, Connor. I remember the guy giving me one of my first driving lessons when I was so young I could barely reach the foot pedals."

Daniel tried to absorb the fact his friend had come from Nolan's murder scene, but the image wouldn't settle. It was hard at times, adjusting to the fact Connor was a homicide cop. Connor didn't look particularly comfortable at the moment, but not that stressed either. How did he walk away from blood and death and not carry it around with him?

"Nolan was Henry's chauffeur all that time? He got along with your uncle?" Marsh asked.

Daniel looked at his friend's partner and considered the question, trying to remember those details. "I think he may have been a handyman, a groundskeeper at first, but the last couple decades he's simply been Henry's chauffeur. Nolan was a nice man, very proper and punctual, and he treated those cars like they were his children. He would speak with me occasionally about Henry's health—'He seemed short of breath today, Mr. Daniel,' 'He seems tired today, Mr. Daniel'—that kind of comment, when I would meet my uncle arriving at the office. Nolan seemed genuinely fond of Henry."

"We spoke briefly with Nolan's brother."

"This news must have hit him awfully hard; I know he's in a nursing home now. It's one of the reasons Nolan agreed to the retirement; so he could spend more time with him."

"Were there any problems that you know of after Nolan retired?"

Daniel shook his head. "Nolan retired, but he still insisted on coming by the estate to start the cars every other day, keep them polished—they are destined to be museum pieces, and he wanted them in perfect condition. Nolan would stop and have coffee with the housekeeper who stayed on, then talk to the groundskeeper about the sports they both loved. He was over at the house two weeks ago Sunday when I showed Tracey and Marie around, and he proudly talked about where and when their dad had bought the various cars. I had the impression but for spending more time with his brother, Nolan hadn't settled on what he wanted to do with his time beyond exactly what he was already doing."

Marsh closed his notebook and pushed it

back into his pocket. "Any idea what that message might mean?"

" 'I know the family secret'—not a clue. To the best of my knowledge Nolan had no remaining family beyond his brother, and other than a few years spent in the service, had always lived in the area. Nolan wasn't the kind of guy to have a murdered wife buried under his house or kids of his own out of wedlock like my uncle did. His parents died of natural causes as far as I know, and he wasn't a drinker, didn't seem the type to gamble, rarely raised his voice. The household gossip would have brought things like that to my uncle's attention, and Henry had no tolerance for that kind of behavior in others, although he appears to have allowed it in his own life." Daniel shifted in his chair, aware that answer didn't settle well with the cops or with himself, for the note left at the murder scene clearly did mean something—*I know the family secret.* "Nolan's brother doesn't have an idea?"

"We'll talk to him again tomorrow."

Daniel nodded, understanding reality. The murder would have been a deep enough shock for one day. "As far as Nolan's ties as an employee to Henry—the only secret I'm aware my family had was what Henry revealed to the world in his will. There's no missing cash showing up as probate goes through, nothing unusual showing up in the independent audit of the Benton Group accounts, no second marriage Henry was covering up—there's nothing of interest that Nolan Price might have known about that I can guess at."

Daniel shook his head. "That's not to say there isn't something there; I've given up figuring out my uncle's behavior, but nothing has shown up to date. I'm just beginning to get through the extensive boxes of paper Henry kept stored in his home office—my uncle's retired bookkeeper kept receipts from having the draperies in the house cleaned twelve years ago to phone-call notes to the florist for the Christmas party at the house four years ago—but so far there's nothing that would be considered more than just a curiosity. You're welcome to look if you think it might help you. I'll give you a key to the estate and access to the papers Henry left."

"There's no need yet, but I would like to see where Nolan spent most of his time at the estate, if there were phone calls he made recently from there or a note he jotted down about meeting someone."

"Sure." Daniel pulled out his key ring. He slipped off the oval clip and handed it to Connor. "The housekeeper can show you around. Current phone bills—try the red in-box on the office desk. She tries to keep things that need my attention in that pile. I'll be glad to ask the phone company for the last couple weeks of records for you."

"It's appreciated, Daniel."

"I was helping you move Monday night while some guy was killing a former employee of my uncle's—that doesn't sit well."

"You know someone who drives a tan or beige Lincoln, maybe ten years old or so?" Marsh asked.

"No."

Marsh shrugged. "Maybe someone saw it at the scene, maybe not. The neighbors are not that clear on the matter. We'll be telling the estate security guys to keep an eye out for it as a precaution."

"You think this was someone Nolan knew from working at the estate or through the people who worked there?"

"When his life is his job it's the place you begin searching. Did he leave anything as far as next of kin in his retirement paper-work besides the brother?" Marsh asked.

"I don't think so, but I'll find the file and fax you whatever there is."

"I don't need to tell you, Daniel, that that note and the other details you heard tonight don't get repeated. Even to the sisters."

"I won't go beyond the basics, that I learned he had been killed and that you asked to see where he had worked on the estate."

Marsh nodded. "I'll keep you to that."

Connor got to his feet. "Sorry to interrupt your evening this way. We've got a few more stops to make tonight."

"You'll let me know when I can stop by and see the brother and maybe offer a hand with the funeral arrangements?"

"I will," Connor agreed.

Daniel rose and retrieved his gym bag. "I don't envy the day you two just had. You need anything else, however remote, to help solve this please call me."

"We will," Connor replied.

Daniel held up his hand in farewell and re-solved to clear his calendar for the weekend to try and make more progress on those files Henry had left behind. That message meant something. And the simple fact was Nolan Price had worked for Henry for thirty-four years, and there had been secrets kept by Henry in the past. The paperwork hadn't been as important as dealing with Marie and Tracey and getting them settled in with the new reality of being wealthy, but the priorities had just changed. He wanted no more surprises coming from his uncle's past that he didn't discover first.

●●●●●●

Connor knew he'd missed calling Marie as promised, but sometimes the best-laid plans fell apart. The eighth interview took them until the end of the late news, and in deference to the time, they stopped ringing doorbells.

"What do you think?"

Connor tossed his notebook on the car dash and looked at his partner. "I think we've been running in circles. Nolan's brother is in the early stages of Alzheimer's; you don't need a doctor to figure that out. Nolan had no other family according to the county birth and death records. There's no history in our records of family abuse between the two boys and their long-departed father. That message is a red herring. We just got spun by some schmuck who gets his jollies out of stabbing an old guy to death and sending the cops down a wild-goose chase."

"How many other stabbing deaths do we have open right now?"

"Only one, but it was a knife picked up in the middle of a barroom fight where the guy got his throat slit and bled to death. We know what happened, why; we just haven't found the guy that swung the knife. So mark that one off."

"We need to talk to the surrounding towns tomorrow."

"This could have been the first murder. He brings the knife with him; he's overly aggressive with the killing, leaving blood everywhere; he's thought to try and wash up afterward and use bleach, but he doesn't finish that cleanup. He has a message he wants to leave scattered around the house as a distraction but wants to write it in a clever way. I put all those pieces together and I get the picture of a young man wanting his fifteen minutes of fame with his crime across page one of the newspaper. Forget the fact Nolan was a retired chauf-

feur for Henry Benton—think old man, retired, living in a reasonably safe area of town
on his own, and not all that cautious about
strangers with a line to spin—I put our guy
as seeing a soft target he could go kill for
the thrill of it. And it was a full moon Monday night."

Marsh started the car. "Are you comfortable giving that assessment to Granger tomorrow morning?"

"It sure fits this case a lot better than
some buried family secret and somebody finally snapping and killing the old man.
About the only thing that might type that
way was if Nolan had a leaning toward boys
and had molested someone years before.
The fact he never married is a touch of a red
flag, but if that happened, there would be
more justification in that message the killer
left."

Marsh, the more cynical of the two of
them, Connor thought, for once shook his
head at the suggestion and dismissed it.
"The man who lived in that house was not
into boys. Look at what wasn't in that
house—nothing suggestive in the reading
material, no easy Internet access to suggestive materials, no questionable videos.

He was a solitary man who probably came back from the war not ready to talk about what he did in the service and chose to love his job and his cars as his life."

Marsh turned toward the side of town where Connor lived. "I'm with you. This was someone killing and wanting to make enough of a splash to get good news coverage of his crime. The neighborhood he chose, the victim, the message, the crime scene—maybe we should just feed this all to the reporters ourselves and see who laps it up and offers us information that might help us solve the case."

"Let the killer make contact with us."

Marsh nodded. "We fumble around not figuring out how to solve the case, whine to the press about no leads and the case going cold, annoy a couple reporters who are pestering us—" He smiled. "Our guy will show up somewhere to try to help us out or to gloat about how badly we are doing solving his spectacular crime. He thinks he got away with something—he wore the gloves, he used the bleach, he took the weapon with him, he got away unseen—he thinks he's smarter than the cops and that he's got his fame and his freedom."

"You wind up that image in his mind too far and he'll just kill again."

Marsh's smile disappeared. "Oh, he'll kill again. And I think he's already decided who. If this case doesn't lead very quickly to someone who knew Nolan and had an actual reason to kill him, then we are looking at someone who simply chose Nolan as his victim. You don't premeditate murder for a thrill and plan to do it just once. And that's what this is really beginning to feel like. A murder for a thrill."

"What do we tell Tracey and Marie? They're going to read the newspaper tomorrow and find out their father's former chauffeur was just murdered. They're going to be talking to Daniel."

"What we say to every neighbor and friend in cases like this—it's a coincidence that there is a connection between you and the victim. The six-degrees-of-separation-between-everyone theory applies again."

"I may mention it to Marie myself to head her off. She's wound up to worry about everything right now."

"I would."

Connor tried to shove the murder scene into the side of his mind marked "work" and let it go for a bit. "How's Tracey doing with Amy being back?"

Marsh smiled. "She's chomping at the bit for when she can next go out and see her again. It's been over a week and that's about Tracey's patience limit, I think."

"You want to suggest something for this weekend?"

"Let's see how this case unfolds first. I'd rather give short notice and be able to keep the appointment than schedule something that work just has us canceling." Marsh clicked on blinkers to turn toward Connor's apartment building. "You've been seeing a lot of Marie."

"I like her."

"Tracey's been inquiring on your intentions," Marsh offered.

"Has she?" Connor found the thought amusing. "Better Tracey than Granger. I think he's not so sure what to think these days, us dating sisters, and wealthy ones at that."

"He's afraid he's going to lose two homicide cops at the same time."

"Do you ever think about quitting or shifting over to administration after you and Tracey get married?"

Marsh snorted.

"That's what I thought. These hours are going to be killers on a wife though."

"We'll adjust." Marsh pulled up to the apartment door. "Don't forget to set the alarm; I don't plan to face the boss alone."

Connor looked around the area and then slid out of the car. "I'll be there."

●●●●●●

The alarm was not going off—that was the phone. Connor struggled to get his eyes open and groaned at the red digits blinking back at him: 4 a.m. This was brutal on his body and his mind. "Yeah?"

"The boss is already en route; he'll be at your door in ten minutes."

"Marsh?"

"Not the tooth fairy. We've got another murder, same MO."

"My feet are on the floor," Connor promised. "Where?"

"I'm struggling to find the address now. One of those pricey towers over by the lake. A resident complained about the smell, and the building super used a master to open the door. Now we've got complaining rich people annoyed to have cops walking around their building in the middle of the night. There it is. Forty-nine twelve Ulysses Street, the one with the square-cut balconies jutting into those triangular architectural features."

"I vaguely remember it. Why Granger?"

"Daniel called him after the building super called him. This one was Henry's retired personal bookkeeper."

Connor winced. "Tell me the boss isn't going to be working this personally."

"Granger? He'll let us do our jobs. But if he wants to run interference for us with the press, I'm all for it."

"True." Connor found slacks and a relatively clean shirt.

"Fill him in on every detail you can think of on the drive over here, as well as your speculation on this being a media thrill seeker. This second murder—we'll see if there is a note and what it says, but I'm leaning even more to someone trying to grab the sisters' fame and making it his springboard to a notoriety and infamy all his own. 'Sisters Haunted by Killer'—I can see it now, splashed all over the tabloids in bold headlines. 'The Blood Killer.' 'Revenge of All That Money'—"

"I get the idea." Connor stepped in on the headline writing. "You ought to warn Tracey and let her warn Marie before the reporters start shouting questions at them."

"You could warn Marie and let her warn Tracey," Marsh replied.

"I take it neither one of us likes this idea. I'll suggest Daniel go visit the gallery and tell them in person."

"That works for me. What about the sister Amy?"

"That is a no-brainer. Get Caroline on the phone and give her everything we have. I want her gut reaction to these killings anyway. She's got instincts anyone with any sense would respect."

Connor tugged his shirt on and hoped the chief would cut him some slack on the uniform. Getting to the dry cleaners hadn't been in the schedule this week. "What are you seeing at the scene?"

"Lots and lots of cop cars and people milling around and not a single person acting in charge. I'm going to go change that. I'll ring you back in five."

The phone went dead in Connor's hand, and he closed it and slid it into his pocket. He hated middle-of-the-night cases. Dinner hadn't happened because he'd just looked at a guy who had been dead for a few days, and if he was about to be looking at another dead guy, then breakfast was not going to stay down. No matter what they said about the fact you got used to the sight and smell, they were lying. You just learned to gag more tightly. He stuffed a piece of gum in his mouth to spit out when he got to the scene. At least it might help him forget the missed meals.

He picked up his wallet and keys and went to meet the chief.

● ● ● ● ● ●

"Nice neighborhood you live in, Connor. I keep forgetting you're tucked back here," Granger remarked, turning on lights but not the siren to remind a drunk staggering between cars that he was walking out into traffic and might want to rethink that.

"It does have its moments. And you're paying half the rent."

"The best money the department ever spent. You want to fill me in on what happened today?"

"Would you answer a question for me first?"

"Sure."

Connor picked up the jacket that he'd moved aside to take the passenger seat. "The perfume reminds me of someone I know." He said it with care, wanting to know as a friend without wanting to particularly cross the line that would have the chief switching to the look that would suggest he'd best shut up.

"She forgot the jacket last night."

"Okay. Just checking."

Granger smiled. "You'll walk yourself into a couple questions about Marie if you're not careful. Amy and I are warily sorting out the fact it's okay for her to trust a cop again. Her track record with our profession hasn't exactly made that an easy step for her to take. This afternoon—what happened with Nolan Price?"

Connor shifted back toward work without hesitation. "Marsh said to give you speculation as well as facts, and it's too early to sort out which is which in my mind, so let me just dump it all first."

"Okay."

Connor gave him the guts of the day's work and the dead ends they had chased so far.

Luke nodded. "Not bad for, what, ten hours so far? You need forensics to say they've got fingerprints or hair or blood from the killer, something to at least type him."

"They know it's as rushed a job as they can make it, but a phone call from you probably wouldn't hurt."

"I'll make that call."

"Thanks. How many other retired employees does Henry have out there?"

Granger nodded to the phone. "Daniel is speed-dial four. I'll want officers at every address he gives us just as soon as it's light. Let's make sure there isn't a third murder out there waiting to be found."

Connor picked up the phone and pulled out his notebook to write down whatever information Daniel had. "Daniel isn't on his way over to the bookkeeper's place?"

"I've got him going after the names of who might know where these two men live. The chauffeur had been at the same address for years, but the bookkeeper moved recently and had an unlisted phone number. It's not that difficult of information to locate, but still, for someone to have both names and addresses—somewhere you intersect with that estate paperwork, I think. The lawyer's office, retirement fund, health insurance company, somewhere both names are going to be listed along with current address information. Daniel was the one who could put that together the quickest."

"Good point." Connor turned his attention to the phone as the call was answered. "Daniel, Connor. Sorry about this start to your morning, man."

"I'm not believing the senselessness of this. Two old guys, retired, nothing to steal, no enemies I can imagine."

"I know." Connor passed on the question regarding other retired employees.

"Hold on. I've got names and addresses in a file on this desk. I just signed gift checks for everyone who worked for Henry in the last five years. Seemed a basic thing to do—give them a Christmas gift early enough they could use the funds before Christmas if they liked. My uncle should have been doing it years ago. Here we go. I've got fourteen names. You want them all or just the six who retired in the last year?"

"Give me those six first."

Connor wrote as Daniel read off the information on the fourteen employees. "Thanks."

"You'll make sure they are contacted? Or should I call and let them know what's happened?"

"Officers will make the first contacts," Connor reassured. "Marsh and I would like you to see Marie and Tracey for us this morning. Tell them the basics and try to brace them for the press stories coming. It's going to get tossed around and sensationalized even if the facts of the cases quoted turn out to be mostly fabrications and rumors."

"I can do that."

"Thanks, Daniel. I'll be back in touch in about an hour."

Connor closed the phone and read off the addresses to the chief. "Two are close enough to this area. I think we should check them first thing."

"Agreed. When we get on scene, if Marsh hasn't already cleared the floor of spectators—cops included—I'll handle it. Take your time on this one. I'll want answers when you have them, but I'm not going to be pressing. Two murders in roughly a three-day time period—we're after a guy who's pretty far out there on the sociopath scale."

"Marsh and I have already talked about alerting Caroline to what is going on and getting her read on what we have. She's better at getting into a killer's thoughts when it's the strange cases."

"I know; she's frighteningly gifted at that. I'll arrange to have someone stay with Amy while Caroline comes in and walks through the scenes if you think it will help. Let me know what you and Marsh decide."

"Thanks, Boss."

Connor saw the cop cars and reporters congregating at their destination and braced for the reality he was about to have flashbulbs going off in his face again. And his shirt wasn't all that clean.

The chief smiled. "You get used to managing them too."

"Sure you do," Connor agreed, reflecting on the fact that Luke had been wading into reporters for half his career now. "I've no desire to ever make a higher grade than lieutenant and detective."

Granger chuckled. "Want me to let you off at the back door?"

"Just park and get out first, Chief. They'll ignore me, thankfully, when they have you to swarm."

Luke parked beside Marsh's personal car. "First rule of handling the press: don't let them see you sweat."

"They didn't teach that part at the academy." Connor waited until the chief opened his door and stepped out of the car before pushing his open and using the doorframe to push two cameramen trying to get photos of the chief back far enough he could step out. The day was going to be full of this insanity, Connor knew.

Sykes got into his face with a handheld cassette recorder and a question Connor couldn't sort out from the mayhem around him, and instinct had him moving one hand around the reporter's wrist and the other toward his shoulder to force him back and out of his face. It was like getting pressed into a sardine can.

He broke free and straightened his shirt and wondered how his boss had ever learned to cope with it. He slipped his badge face out in his pocket and went to find Marsh.

The apartment was furnished more expensively than most homes, Connor decided, getting a taste of it from the inset stone in the entryway and the artwork facing him at eye level. "How did someone get past this security system?"

"Our victim let him in, same as with Nolan," Marsh replied, sitting on the steps leading to the second floor of the apartment and writing notes down on his pocket pad of paper. He glanced up. "How's the chief?"

"Saying a lot of words while saying little. He'll buy us some time. You cleared this floor?"

"Yep. Tossed everyone out that I didn't personally want to see at 4 a.m., and that was everyone. Joe and Rachel promised to wake up enough to work the scene for me since they have some experience with this guy's MO."

"Where's our victim?"

Marsh nodded to his right. "Staining an absolutely gorgeous and expensive rug in the living room."

Connor was in no hurry to follow the smell. "How long?"

"Probably killed after Nolan, just from the way the murder looks done, but probably also a Monday night hit. The decay looks about the same."

"Thanks, I needed that image. His name?"

"Sorry, I thought I said." Marsh handed over a driver's license.

Connor studied the photo. "Philip Rich, sixty-seven. He looks like the plastic-surgery type."

"It didn't help him die any prettier. Same knife attack with rage features, probably a blitz attack. Looks like the same kind of narrow blade, but that's a guess."

Connor reluctantly went to see the scene. He didn't react to the body, didn't let himself do it. Some things were just sights a person shouldn't see. The splattered blood had spotted a priceless chess set of ivory pieces and left streaks on the mirror above the fireplace. "No signs of robbery?" he asked quietly.

Marsh stopped beside him to also study the room. "No. I passed a few items that would fit in my pocket and clear a few thousand even with a fence taking most of the cash, and they're still sitting in plain sight."

"Someone knew this man, wanted him dead, and came with the intent to make very sure he was dead. Did he wash up again?"

"Yes. The downstairs bath—upstairs is a massive master-bedroom-and-bath suite, with a private sitting area, but it looks undisturbed. I'm guessing our killer brought a change of clothes to this one; there's a smear on the bathroom floor that looks like bloody fabric rested there, probably a pair of jeans from the texture captured in the stain."

"The knife?"

"No sign of it that I saw in the initial walk around."

Connor accepted reality and walked closer to the body. He pulled on latex gloves. "Again, no defensive wounds on the hands. Maybe the same stunning blow to the head and then straddle and start stabbing?"

"I think so."

"Philip Rich—Daniel said he retired almost eight months ago, before Henry had the last heart attack. He worked out at the estate most days, even though he had a business office downtown, and we know our chauffeur was around the estate most days. So it's pretty straightforward to assume our two victims knew each other. But I don't think from looking at this place and having seen Nolan's that the two men traveled in the same circles."

"Philip was a man desiring to be as wealthy as those he worked for," Marsh agreed.

"There's a message?"

Marsh turned and shined his light on the painting over the couch.

Pay me to go away was written in blood across a priceless work of art.

"Marie would cringe," Connor said softly, the first thought crossing his mind at the sight of all that blood on those nicely brushed layers of oil paints. "I'd say that is a definite demand."

"How much does he want, who does he want it from, where does he want it delivered . . . the note just raises all kinds of questions of its own."

"At least this guy is not crazy, as in ask us to stop the moon from rising or some such fantasy crazy."

"Two murders and one explicit blackmail demand . . . this guy is going to be twisted when we find him."

Connor shook his head. "No. He's the kind you meet, shake hands with, interview, and until forensics matches DNA and tells you that's the killer, you would swear he was just another interview in the files," he replied, beginning to worry for the first time about a case. This one was out of his league.

"It will crack the same way every case does, by shoe leather and persistence. And he's already made one mistake."

"What?"

Marsh walked over to the painting and studied the message, and when he turned it was a hard smile on his face, the kind Connor knew to be wary about. "He got greedy. A man who wants money—he won't disappear into the shadows and do his best to get away from here and his killings. No, he'll sit back and wait for the time to demand his payment. And we'll be waiting for him."

He nodded. "He did his two murders, left his notes, and he'll still be around."

Connor moved back to the doorway to get a sense of the room again and how the initial struggle must have gone down. "You don't ask a dead guy for money, so that leaves out our victims. You don't ask the cops for money, because that is a simple waste of your breath. So this guy is targeting the guy with the most money—that would be Daniel—and working his way through the employees, proving he's dangerous enough to Daniel that it is better to pay up than risk another person in that circle dying."

"That's the way I see it. Daniel is going to need better security. And everyone who worked at the estate in the last few years. Marie and Tracey—at least they're already pretty tightly covered."

"Granger is already looking at answering the most critical question—is there a third murder out there we just haven't discovered yet? It's possible the amount and the directions are already waiting for us at another crime scene."

"Let's hope that is a no; I want a full night's sleep first."

Connor let himself smile. "This is getting very, very old," he agreed. "You want the living room or the kitchen?"

"I'll take this room. Start on the kitchen, and when the forensics folks get here you and I will leave them to it and go see Granger, then begin the interviews. I think we've seen enough to go start asking people who aren't dead some questions."

Chapter Seventeen

Connor relaxed against the bench of the restaurant booth and considered the odds that pancakes might solve the odd mismatch of sensations in his stomach that had lingered for days. He felt like something the dog had brought in dead.

"You can't keep your eyes open."

He smiled at Marie or at least hoped that was what his expression came out looking like. "Not fully," Connor agreed. "But it's not dimmed my perceptive abilities. You look as lovely as ever."

She smiled but pushed the coffee toward him. "Drink it; they refill for free."

"Who's keeping the tabloid reporters at

bay? We've been sitting here five minutes with relative normalcy."

"A back-corner booth with Bryce at the next table over—it works most of the time. What are you thinking about trying?"

"Pancakes." It seemed to be one of the few words he could read. He was so tired he thought his eyes were going to swell shut just to get some darkness.

Marie signaled a waitress and they placed their orders.

"You should have canceled and gone to bed."

"I'm not canceling and standing you up more than three times in a row short of someone shooting me and there being a tube stuffed down my throat when I wake up." He put both hands around the coffee cup and thought the double vision might be one eye going to sleep on him.

"How long has it been since you really slept?"

He smiled. "Sixty hours, but who is counting? I'm not driving myself home; a patrol guy is taking pity on me. I think the bed is still at the old apartment, but every-thing else got moved to the new one. At this point I don't care. I'll sleep on the floor somewhere."

"Where's Marsh?"

"Comatose in his own bed, I expect," Connor replied, pleased the coffee actually tasted like coffee to his spinning senses. "Let's not talk about my work—you'll see it all in the paper anyway. Let's talk about you and me going out somewhere for dinner."

Marie smiled. "We'll see if you can manage breakfast at four in the afternoon first. You really should have just gone home, Connor."

He looked at her over the coffee cup and let his smile fade. His gaze held hers, and he let the last day show in his eyes, just a bit, never more than a bit, and told her the truth. "I wanted a better image in my mind to drift to sleep on."

She blinked, gave a very slight nod, and then smiled at him. "Want me to sing you a bedtime song over the phone so you can listen to me too?"

He chuckled but thought he might push her to do exactly that later on. "It's been a brutal couple days."

She reached over and touched his hand, for her, quite a shift to be the one reaching out first, and it felt nice as her hand settled firmly on his. "Eat, sleep. Tomorrow the world will still be insanely crazy, but you'll be back standing upright to face it."

"Exactly." He nodded at the waitress's offer of more coffee. "I left the chief at the office where he planned to shut the door on his office and catnap on the couch, and Marsh at home, threatening the world at large if anyone bothered him in the next eight hours. I figured half an hour for food and twelve hours of comatose time and I might figure out what day of the week it is again."

He yawned and it cracked his jaw. "Talk to me, Marie, and I don't care about what. I'm just going to sit here and wilt some more while I eat and enjoy looking at you."

She dumped a packet of sugar in her coffee, and he would put her on a full blush starting, but she gamely nodded and took up the challenge. "The paintings came in as magnificent as I expected. I think Tracey is going to take the lake painting as a gift for Marsh as she loved it on sight. And I think I might give Daniel that Gibson you knew he would like so I can make room for this really gorgeous study in the color red. It's cubes and squares and firework bursts, and it reaches out and grabs you from across the gallery."

Connor listened and smiled and thought about having a future with her one day, the idea growing stronger with every moment together. She was a hole filler in his life, a hole that had needed to be filled for a very long time.

"What?" She paused her chatting to smile at him, the blush growing.

"Our breakfast is here."

"That was not what you were thinking."

"I know." He shifted aside his coffee and ice-water glass to accept the plate, suddenly feeling a smidgen more awake. "Eat."

"Connor."

He just smiled at her. "You want to share those strawberries? They look good."

She'd ordered a cheeseburger and a fruit bowl. She set the bowl between them. "You're going to tell me what you're thinking."

"Not right now I'm not." He smiled at her, because she amused him and pleased him and he liked looking at her over breakfast foods. "I told the patrol guy to pick me up in forty minutes. Tell the rest of the stuff about the paintings."

She unfolded her napkin. "Do you like art?"

"I will by the time you tell me all the reasons you love it." He picked up his coffee and smiled at her. "Going to keep the Denart?"

"It's already been moved upstairs to the apartment," she admitted.

"I knew it. What else was in the recent shipment?"

She talked and he ate and he thought about maybe next week . . . that would be a good time to talk with Marsh about the two of them starting to double-date. Nothing too hard to sort out, just two sisters, two partners, figuring out how to shove the job aside for long enough to do some courting in proper fashion.

● ● ● ● ● ●

Marsh held out the second coffee mug he carried and stepped back to let Connor enter his home Sunday afternoon. "You don't look that much more awake than when I left you yesterday. You were supposed to sleep, remember?"

"I went to share a midafternoon breakfast with Marie first," Connor admitted. "But the rest of the time I was flat and out of it. Not that I wouldn't have taken another week of sleep if it were offered."

Marsh smiled, not entirely surprised at the answer. He walked back to the dining-room table. "Have you seen the newspapers?"

"No."

"Sykes is doing a magnificent job. He's got the text of the first note and a really great photo of the blood running down the living-room wall at Nolan's place."

"You're kidding."

Marsh handed over the paper.

"How the . . . ?" Connor turned a darker shade of red as he got angry, and Marsh watched him push away the reaction and then look up, his gaze hard. "Who's the leak?"

"That's what I've been trying to figure out," Marsh replied, impressed with the control his partner was learning. When he had seen the photo, he'd slammed down a mug on his counter so hard he'd split it into three pieces. "To get the photo—that says someone in the chain of evidence in the lab.

A negative gets exposed to make two prints instead of one, that kind of thing."

"Sykes doesn't have the second message?"

"Not yet. But you'll figure he's working everyone who might have stepped into that living room and been there to see it. I figure the building super is already leaking the full details for a wad of cash. From the phone call to 911 to the first cop securing that apartment door—I'd make it five minutes for the super and at least one or two nosy neighbors to have seen more than we would like."

"So much for burying the information. Reverse tactics and play cold case now? Push the information we have out to the press and see who comes back to nibble at it?"

"Granger can figure that out. It's going to be Monday before forensics gives up enough to run with. I'm taking the rest of today, such as it is, off."

"No disagreement here. Someone is pulling phone records, bank records for us?"

"Yes."

"Monday is early enough then. Granger has us on for the 6 a.m. update again?"

"Seven, he said. I think he wants some sleep too."

"At least no one else on the list of Henry's employees turned up dead. I'm hoping the next note is simply a nice simple fax to Daniel's office."

Connor set down the paper, having skimmed the article. "I came by to see if you want to maybe do a double date two weeks from Tuesday night, take the sisters out to a concert. I've got tickets for the nine o'clock show at the fairgrounds. It's a big enough crowd we might be able to blend in and enjoy some privacy such as there is in a crowd of five thousand."

Marsh reached for his wallet. "I'll pick up half."

Connor waved it away. "You can buy the dinner. Want me to ask them both?"

"If Marie says yes, Tracey is going to jump on the offer. She's been dropping hints for the last week about you two."

"It's just a date." But Connor smiled as he said it, and Marsh could read the way the wind blew. "Marie's a nice lady," he observed. "Calm and private and contained in her world. It's a nice world to slip into, I'd be thinking."

"I'll learn to appreciate the art." Connor finished the coffee. "You need a new coffeemaker or at least a new filter and grounds; this is awful."

Marsh laughed. "Get going, Connor. I'd say you have a lady to see before she makes plans for her evening."

His partner headed out with a nod, and Marsh let himself relax back into the chair and consider the changes. Connor dating was a good thing. Dating Marie . . . she wasn't dating material; she was the marrying kind. He wasn't so sure about that idea, for Connor had never even drifted that way before, but Marsh thought the idea would grow on him with time.

The coffee really was awful. Marsh dumped his out in the sink and risked pulling out the basket on the coffeemaker. He couldn't remember when he'd dumped those grounds in there. He made a fresh pot of coffee and pulled out the remains of a deli sandwich to eat as he worked. The pad of paper and the pens were sitting there on the table waiting for the inspiration of what to write, but so far they were blank. Marsh sat at the table and went back to contemplating the crime scenes in his mind's eye and thinking about what still bugged him about what he had seen. He picked up his pen and doodled.

When the coffee was done, he got up and poured himself a full mug. *Better,* he thought, appreciating the difference. He slipped a lid on the mug and he picked up his phone. "Chief, you got a minute?" Marsh had taken a chance and called him at home. "I've got an idea I want to run past you." He picked up the newspaper and took it with him as he headed to his car, the photo circled in a bright red pen.

●●●●●●

Luke found the afternoon unexpectedly warm and appreciated again the fact he'd built the backyard deck as a place he could linger on the sunny winter days. "Sam, you were the one running background checks for Henry on the staff he hired. Was there anything at all in the background check of Philip Rich that suggested trouble?"

Luke leaned back against the railing of the deck and studied his friend, trying to pull anything of use out of the guy's memory without having to come right out and explain Marsh's idea. It was far-fetched but still the kind of thing he paid his officers to sense, and Marsh was convinced he had something. Luke was too.

Sam relaxed in the deck chair he'd chosen. "Philip was not a guy you want to spend time with—an hour with him reminded me of a root canal—but he was precise at his job, competent to make money recommendations, and he knew the proper way to keep a person's finances away from an IRS audit. If he got paid a little too much and reported more hours worked when he had some lower-paid staffer actually doing the work—it wasn't so far across the line that Henry bothered to care about it."

"The bookkeeper and the chauffeur have one thing in common; they both knew Henry Benton," Luke offered. "And Henry was definitely keeping a couple secrets for the last three decades. The bookkeeper knew something; the chauffeur saw something—and someone out there put two and two together and figured out Henry's secret."

"If it's not the fact he had two daughters, then what? Another affair? Henry is dead—he's not going to care," Sam noted.

"Daniel would; the sisters would."

"But that kind of thing is a blackmail fax, not two murders. Why shut up two retired guys who apparently didn't know they knew something? Philip at least would have been hitting Daniel for a monetary fee if there was something that smelled not quite right in Henry's affairs and should be best left swept under the rug. He'd stay silent for a price, but he was the kind of guy who would want to be paid for his silence."

"Nothing like that was going down," Luke replied.

Sam rubbed the back of his neck. "You mind if I make a suggestion?"

"Go ahead."

"You and your guys, you're seeing this nice and logical and from the crime scenes working your way out. Why don't you just step back a minute and see the big picture? It looks different from where I'm sitting."

Luke sensed another turn coming his way. "I'm listening."

"Amy's shooter out of New York disappeared a week ago; it took at least four days before the cops up there noticed the old man was not around, as in gone and three more for them to conclude he wasn't sleeping off a hangover somewhere in their own backyard. That's what I came over to tell you this fine evening. And he currently drives an old tan Lincoln."

Luke slapped the railing of the deck as the pieces of information fit together. " '*Pay me to go away*'—he's hunting down a list of people who get him ever tighter and closer to Daniel and the sisters."

"Seems like a reasonable fact to me. These two gents—they were easy targets for a guy like that, easy to approach, simple to kill. The family secret is staring you in the face, Luke. *Amy is alive.* That's the family secret. The fact these two guys were chosen as the place to leave the messages— six degrees of separation is all. They were convenient ways to get Daniel's and the sisters' attention. This guy couldn't care less about Henry and his dalliances over the last decades and who else the guy might have been seeing—and yes, those ladies are definitely out there because a guy like Henry never changes his stripes, but they are just background noise to this. The chauffeur and the bookkeeper were chosen to simply get the attention of the man with the money. '*Pay me to go away*'—I'm guessing he's got a figure around forty million in mind, given Richard Wise's sense of interest payments."

"Amy is the real target," Luke said with rising dread; trouble had come and found the lady he cared a great deal about.

Sam nodded. "And if the New York shooter is here and doing the hunting, you can bet he's not leaving without his personal problem solved. Amy had to have seen him that night, no matter what she says. He'll have a personal reason to want her dead."

"So do we work these two murders to find this guy?"

"There won't be evidence to find, I'll wager. He's careful in his own overkilling style. And it served his purpose this time to do the extreme overkill with a knife rather than a gun. He's making sure the press are hungry for every detail of the cases and doing the digging for him. One of those reporters will one day get a hint that Amy may not be dead, and this will burst open on you. The shooter may even plant that rumor to help have dozens of eager reporters searching for where Amy is hiding out."

"This doesn't ever get easier, does it? Big picture or small, I've still got the same problem. Amy to protect, two murders to solve, and Richard Wise out there wanting to make trouble for this family until the day he gets what he wants."

"I think the money will always be his scorecard of who is winning and who is losing, but the end of this—he'll want Amy dead. And as long as there is someone willing to pick up that assignment there is going to be trouble." Sam got to his feet. "You want me to talk to Jonathan? have a few more guys out watching Amy?"

He would love to build a brick wall around her, but he shook his head. "Not yet. Amy's got the senses of a cornered alley cat—she knows when there is more than Caroline around the property. Don't ask me how, but she's pegged when Jonathan's people were out there three out of four times now. The circle of people who know that location is small enough; I think we can keep it locked-down knowledge. For now I'll just warn Caroline which guy we think has shown up in town. Put your focus on finding that car he's driving and where the guy is staying. There has to be something being whispered on the streets that will help us find the guy."

"I'll do that."

"Thanks, Sam."

"Always glad to help the police," Sam replied, smiling a bit too dryly for Luke to take him seriously. The man didn't respect authority as much as he accepted the fact it existed. But he was the good kind of friend to have around, regardless.

"Don't take too many chances," Luke requested. "I like my friends living long enough to bug me."

Sam laughed and disappeared out the backyard gate.

Luke sighed. Nothing about this case set well right now, from the thought of the New York shooter prowling around his town to the idea Marsh had brought him earlier in the evening. It didn't particularly matter which theory was right; trouble was here. Figuring out how to stand in front of it was the challenge.

He'd go see Amy once dark fell—he owed her that.

●●●●●●

Amy settled into the couch across from the blazing fire, holding a mug of hot chocolate between her hands and staying too calm for Luke's tastes; he'd rather see fear than a quiet resolve that said Amy was deciding something he might not like.

"Do you have a sense of where this man might stay in town, if he has arrived?"

Luke shook his head and just watched her think.

"I'd like Caroline to see the scenes and the photographs of the victims," Amy said. "You said her loyalties would be to me first, then you. I need a firsthand sense of what this guy did and how he did it. I'll trust her perspective."

"Everything but the photos," Luke agreed. "Both guys were stabbed; it was vicious. I'd like her opinion on this guy's behavior too, but the rawest stuff can be skipped. Marsh and Connor dealing with the images is enough." Luke hesitated. "You're surprised he used a knife."

"The man I remember seeing occasionally around Greg, doing business with him, was one of the calmest, coldest guys I ever met. If you're right that this was the man who shot Greg, then I'm not going to dispute it. I didn't see who shot him that night. But the man I remember meeting briefly with Greg wouldn't use a knife, not if the situation allowed him to use a gun."

She sounded very certain of that conclusion, and Luke wasn't going to dismiss that impression easily. But if it wasn't the guy from New York who had done the crimes, they were after a freelance killer who struck twice in one night for a reason entirely of his own creation. "The family secret being the fact you are alive, the demand he be paid to go away—it makes sense given what you feared would occur."

"Yes."

"Do you want me to arrange more security out here? Do you want me to move you somewhere else farther away?"

"No. You were right. The harder I am to approach, the more my sisters become the easier targets. Daniel isn't thinking of paying this guy, is he?"

Luke had hoped she wouldn't ask that question. "Daniel cares a great deal about the three of you," he replied carefully.

"You know you feed money to a madman, he eventually comes back for more. It won't change anything about this situation for the better."

"I've conveyed that too."

Amy pushed a pillow behind her back, her attention shifting more into her thoughts than on the present. She finally sighed. "When do you think his next message arrives? How much he wants and where he wants it delivered?"

"I don't know. He could be waiting for us to use the press to send him a message that we agree to his conditions. He could be just sitting back considering striking again to drive his point home. We've warned those we think might be at risk, improved their security, put more people on the streets in the vicinity of the gallery block."

"Defense is hard."

He nodded. "Offense is always the easier way to run a case. I've got feelers out on the street for where this guy might have landed. That car of his is a vulnerability we should be able to exploit."

"It will have been dumped by now; it simply helped set his ID in your head. He'd need to do that if he's trying to make sure you knew it was a message coming from Richard Wise without actually tipping his hand that it was Richard behind this. Who's been to see Richard recently?"

"His lawyers, two from his family, and one guy you may remember, Lewis O'Dell."

"Yeah, I remember O'Dell. He'd be the one holding the door for Richard Wise."

"He's still doing basically that, as best the New York cops can tell. Still loyal and probably the one carrying the messages from Richard out to the old crew."

"For a price loyalty is not that hard to achieve. So what do you think happens next?"

"I need something from the forensics at the scenes to point us solidly at an imported talent being the killer, or I need to figure out what killer grew up in my own backyard. That's the priority right now. And hopefully preventing the next message from arriving at the end of a knife."

"Tell Daniel from me that he can't pay; no matter the pressure of what is happening. Money is not going to solve this."

"Is there anything in that oldest ledger that might help us put this suspected shooter behind bars? anything that would make another case against him if we can't make this one stick?"

She shook her head. "No. I'm not opposed to turning in the last ledger, Luke. It will likely put Greg's father behind bars, but I've accepted that fact. I just don't think we need another front opening right now. There were two men on my trail before I arrived in this town, and there is no indication they have gone away either. I'm worried about them sitting out there too, watching my sisters, trying to trail them to locate me. Don't focus on New York as the only threat."

"Connor and Marsh aren't going to let a tail stay on them when they come out this way. It drives your sisters up a wall to go all around the county before actually coming here, but it's working. They'll make sure it keeps working."

"One slip and someone has this location."

"I know." He smiled. "I've gotten accustomed to seeing you comfortable and somewhere I can find you; I'm not going to let events change that if it's something we can control. If you want Caroline to see the scenes, we'll need to set something else up for a period of time while she's gone."

"Jonathan's guy can babysit me for a few hours, and I promise to not duck out on him."

"Good. Where is Caroline?"

Amy nodded to the window. "See that small hill beyond the fence? She spotted quail out there. You arrived and she headed out to take advantage of the window of time while you were the one babysitting me to watch them."

"Somehow her impression of our relationship isn't exactly how it tends to run, but I get your point." He walked over to the window and followed Amy's directions to study the land. "I never did figure out how Caroline survived in the city. She's in her element when the land is open and the sky expanse is above her."

"She enjoys the city too, but in a different way." Amy got up from the couch to join him. "You look tired, Luke."

"I am. The press has been intense as they look for facts. They think these killings are related to the will, Henry's past, and your sisters' new money."

"I know. There's some security in the fact they aren't yet focused on the idea I might be alive. You're keeping the press far from Marie and Tracey?"

"Yes."

"They know they can't try to come out for a while? that it's best we stay apart for now?"

"Yes." He reached out a hand to rub her

arm, reassuring with a touch. "Your sisters need your phone number; it's hard on them, not being able to talk with you."

"Not yet."

"You could call them when they are at Marsh's place. We can arrange it so it's a step removed from where people might normally be probing."

"I'll think about it; that's the best I can offer. Phones worry me, Luke; too many conversations go farther than you hoped." She forced a smile. "You'll have a long day tomorrow. You'd best be getting home to get some sleep."

"I should." He considered her. "You want a hug?"

She slid into his arms. "I do."

It felt good to hold her, to know that somewhere in this she was at least beginning to trust him. "I hate leaving you out here, way too far away for my tastes."

"It's going to end one day."

It was the first time she sounded confident about that fact in her own mind. Luke noted the change and tightened his arms for a moment before stepping back. "I'm not kissing you today either; I'll never get out of here if I do."

She laughed. "True. I'm walking you to your car."

He settled his arm across her shoulders. "I'd like that."

Chapter Eighteen

"It's too quiet." Connor dropped the stir stick for his coffee into the trash bag at his feet and thought about calling it a night.

"The report was solid. It's a tan Lincoln, nine years old," Marsh replied, shifting the notebook he was updating into his briefcase and glancing back at the parked vehicle they were watching.

"A car that hasn't moved in the last three days." They had spotted it Sunday night, and now it was Wednesday. The initial hope that their killer would return to his car had so far proven a dead end. He could be sleeping off a bad couple days drinking in one of the rooms around this depressed block and thus not venturing out into the world. He could but after three days he was either drunk enough to kill himself or not planning to come back for the car. "Our guy left it for us to watch."

"Probably."

"I vote we have it pulled in tomorrow morning for parking violations or something."

"I doubt our knife was left in the vehicle, or the next note we're waiting for him to drop on us."

"You still think this is the red herring, that it's a local guy doing the killings, not some imported talent from New York?"

"I do."

"Why?"

"An absurd hunch," Marsh replied. "I told the chief the idea. No offense, but I don't want to be looking stupid twice in as many days. I'll tell you if I find something that makes me right."

"That's a lot of partner trust for you when it doesn't extend to so much as an explanation."

Marsh smiled. "How did last night go?"

Connor frowned. "Why are women so hard to figure out?"

"I'll take that as a 'not so well.' "

"Marie was beautiful, chatty, engaged, her normal perfect self."

"You haven't dated long enough; that's for sure. No lady is perfect."

"Okay, so she has this annoying habit of worrying, but on the whole I'm not knocking that as such a bad thing, given she's in the middle of two sisters whose lives are turning in circles. Tracey marrying you is a big deal, as is Amy in hiding. No, last night Marie was perplexing."

"How so?"

"Haven't I made it perfectly clear in a thousand ways I like her?"

"I got the message."

Connor shoved his coffee back into the holder. "She hasn't. She was trying too hard to be likable last night. It's been driving me crazy the more I think about it. What is it about women and the fact they never figure out how to relax around a guy? I felt like I was seeing the polite-behavior Marie when I just wanted to hang out with her for the evening."

"On an official date, dressed up, and a nice restaurant. Bad territory when you want relaxed."

"Well, I'm not likely to invite her to my new

place—it's barely above a rattrap right now with the walls being prepped to replaster— and I'm not going to get invited to her place above the gallery as long as getting there is a wall of reporters to wade through. She doesn't mind chatting on the phone, but she doesn't really like it for personal conversations, and the job hasn't exactly been kind on the work hours."

"You've got a problem."

"I already know I've got a problem, thank you. Let's not talk about women; the subject frustrates me."

"I'm not talking," Marsh agreed, smiling.

"You're engaged. What do you remember about dating, anyway?" Connor muttered, reaching back for his jacket. "I'm walking the block again. You want a sandwich this time?"

"Get me something that was shipped from the manufacturer already sealed. It's not that dark that I can't tell from here the cleanliness, or lack of it, in that shop."

"The coffee was hot," Connor replied, "and I doubt the rest kills me. Five minutes."

Marsh nodded and shifted to pick up the binoculars, watching the shadows for signs there was actually someone willing to move on a cold night like this.

••••••

"You look busy."

Luke turned to see his sister in the doorway to his office Thursday morning, and his concentration on the report in his hands turned into a smile of welcome. "Never too busy for you. What brings you downtown?"

"You haven't been home for a few days it seems, so I thought I'd bring over the tickets to the concert next Tuesday night. You mentioned taking the kids."

He smiled. "I haven't forgotten; Margaret has it written on my calendar with block letters, meaning I change it at risk of her resigning. I gather they are looking forward to the evening?"

"It's all they've talked about lately." Susan set down her purse and jacket on the chair and studied him. "Too many work hours lately, I think; you look exhausted. I saw the newspaper."

Luke grimaced. "Sykes is getting inside information from somewhere. It's making it difficult, defending against the press while trying to work an investigation."

Susan reached back and closed the door behind her. "Sam bumped into me at the grocery store, while I was picking out strawberries for the fruit plate tonight, of all things. The guy looks very much out of place with a mango in his hand, like he's not sure what exactly it is."

Luke walked around his desk. "This isn't good."

"I guess he figured I would be seeing you in a reasonable time. His office got broken into, nothing displaced, just skimmed, he said. But he'll assume he's being followed now, and he knows his phone has been tapped; he thought you should hear it sooner versus later."

"We were expecting something of the sort. I didn't put Sam on using you as the messenger though; I'm sorry about that."

She smiled. "I haven't been your sister for such a short time that I haven't figured out the extra duties which come with being the police chief's closest relative. This is not the first message passed to you via me, and it won't be the last." Her smiled faded. "This is still three-year-ago stuff reappearing, isn't it? You've been . . . absent . . . more than usual recently."

"I know. Yes, it's the same problem."

"She came back."

He merely lifted an eyebrow.

"Give me some common sense, please. You don't hire Sam to find you information; you hire him to find someone. And lately you've had a lady's jacket in your car and haven't mentioned you were seeing someone. You always mention when you date, because it keeps me off your back about if and when you're ever going to see someone and settle down. Sam working for you three years ago, being back in your life now in a serious way on something unrelated to your official job—it's personal, Luke. Give me the common sense to figure that out."

Luke had begun to smile partway through her words, and as she finished, he just relaxed in a chair and let his smile broaden. "Since you've already shut the door, you want to have a seat for a few minutes. You'll like her, Sis; she's a nice lady."

"I figured that much out on my own. She's got trouble?"

"Yes. The Griffin sisters in the news lately? Amy is the oldest that everyone talks about as having been murdered in New York years before. She's still alive."

Susan sank down in a seat and a few moments later closed her mouth. "All right, I got my shell-shock moment in. She's okay? Safe, I mean?"

"As best we can arrange. Someone wants her dead so she's not coming out of the shadows for a while as this plays out."

"Why tell me?"

"Because I like her more than a little," Luke finally replied. "And I promised a long time ago that there was one person I wouldn't keep secrets from when it became really personal."

"You could have bent that promise to me and I would have understood. Still . . . you really like her?"

"I do."

"And it's going to be forever and an age before I get to meet her."

"I'm afraid so."

Susan smiled at him. "I'll grow into that idea. It explains why you've been disappearing."

"And if Sam is getting followed, I may soon be as well. So if I'm more paranoid in the next few weeks, driving in circles, ignore it. We'll get this guy sooner or later."

"The killings . . ."

"I don't know, Sis. Probably related, but it's just hunches all around for what is going on."

"You know I like Daniel a lot; I always have, and the sister I met, Marie—I hope you can resolve it soon. I'd hate to think of more trouble showing up in their lives."

"I do too." He got up and offered his hand. "Come on; you have to meet Marsh for a minute while you are here and tease him about getting engaged. The man turns positively embarrassed in the nicest kind of way."

She slid her hand into his. "You're enjoying that part of it, aren't you? Seeing him finally settling down."

"As proud as a chief could get. I've seen all the relationships that didn't pan out, so it's nice to watch one working for a change," he admitted. He walked with her back through the bull pen, and spotting Marsh perched on the corner of Connor's desk in a serious exchange, he cleared his throat to give his guys two seconds to shift gears before Susan reached them.

"So tell me what you two were debating," Luke suggested to Marsh, finding the copy of the report he had been reading when Susan appeared and passing it to Connor for his attention. The two cops looked somewhat ill at ease being back in his office again, but Luke figured they would grow out of the problem eventually. One day he expected one of them to be sitting in his chair and running this place.

"The car. The VIN numbers show the Lincoln is New York registered, and the plates have been proven to be stolen. So the car is his, but the drop spot—maybe he paid someone in town to do his work for him, because either by pure luck or help, he chose one of the three spots in town I would dump it if I wanted it to be an interesting find for the cops. There is enough come-and-go housing in those blocks to make it a plausible area he might have settled."

"They towed the car in last night."

"Yes. The crime-lab guys found nothing, not even a partial print. He'd cleaned it out and left it for us."

"He was probably watching the car too, to see who would come and watch it before it got hauled away," Luke added. "He'll have made you and Connor for sure."

"A bother, but not so unexpected," Marsh

replied with a shrug. "We're already all over the news thanks to that pack of reporters, and he could get our photos off a search of the newspaper archives if he wished. You've got to assume this guy stayed in town."

"Sam's place got slipped into—neatly, but files ruffled. So he's searching for information wherever he can get it."

"Okay, that's news. Sam want us to take a look?"

Luke smiled at Connor and his detective grimaced. "Forget I asked. Did he get any prints?"

"He would have remarked if he had. You've got the recent photos on this guy that New York sent down?"

"Copies taped to the visor in all the vehicles and an extra copy in my wallet. We'll know him on sight, Boss."

"Let word slide down through the ranks that I'll personally thank the guy that radios in a confirmed sighting. I don't want an officer out on his own trying to stop this guy without backup, but I want him off the streets as a priority."

"I think Marsh and I have already passed that message out," Connor replied. "It's going to cost us a couple nice game tickets, but that kind of offer tends to get some guys willing to work some overtime off the books. If there is something to hear—or see—out there, I expect we'll have it."

"Good." Luke looked between the men. "Anything else catching your interest in the lab reports? I've seen the results coming in. Pretty thin so far."

"A few hairs they haven't been able to identify pulled from a blood spot on the bookkeeper's body and a couple partial smudge marks from the bathrooms that might be sweat. It's not a lot of evidence to match to a killer. The knife is consistent to both victims, including the busted tip on the blade. We're back at both scenes this afternoon to give Caroline a look at them."

"Keep it toned down a bit, okay? You two having nightmares is enough."

"I'm not pushing photos her way," Marsh concurred. "You want to hear her thoughts?"

"Anything glimmers at all, call me. This guy got both victims to let him inside, and they apparently didn't sense danger until it was too late. I'd love to know how he managed that."

"We're talking to the neighbors for a third time tomorrow, hoping to get something new, and we're going back through the interviews of people who knew the two of them, looking for someone they had in common recently. To just arrive, meet them, and kill them—he's using quite a story."

"Or someone they both already trusted had made the introductions," Connor offered, "not realizing what was being set up."

"Yeah, that fits. If you get an idea for how you want to try and push this guy, let me know. I'll do the press work for you."

"Appreciate it, Boss. I had a reporter leaning against my car this morning, waiting for me at 5 a.m. That's not the way to start the day."

Luke smiled. "Tell me about it. Tell Caroline hi for me and that I still want her back on the job. She's going to get tired of being away one of these days."

"I might even weave her a story or two about how much she's missed," Marsh said, smiling back. He nodded his partner toward the door. "We'll call in."

Chapter Nineteen

The moon was far enough up in the sky that looking out her studio window Marie could see it rising between buildings, bright in the clear night sky. She hummed to herself as she worked on the painting before her and listened to the apartment for sounds of Tracey and Marsh leaving. Tracey was on the way back to campus for a Thursday night lecture, and Marsh had promised to take her back and forth. Marie would go say good night, but she'd already said it once and thought giving the two of them some privacy was a better idea. Tracey had been too subdued lately with everything going on, and she needed Marsh around to smooth that out again.

"Daniel?"

"I'm still here." The phone on the table was set to speaker mode; they were keeping each other company long distance tonight.

"Why don't you call it a night and get back to work on the problem tomorrow?"

"I counted boxes, and there are another thirty-eight to go through. My uncle's bookkeeper kept everything; I haven't got to the boxes my uncle filed himself. I'm sure they are here too."

"I could help out."

"It's just methodical work, scanning every page for something that might be important and marking the rest to be shredded once this settles down again. How's the painting coming?"

"About done. I like this one." She was trying hard to capture from a photograph a walk path and bridge she had visited last summer. It had been a good day with her sister, and she could remember the day well enough to try and get it onto canvas.

"I liked the last attempt."

"Too many shadows in the trees; they looked sinister rather than peaceful."

"Did Tracey leave for school?"

"Just." She'd heard the distinctive sound of the outer door closing. "She needs the drive time with Marsh to shake away a few cobwebs. It's been gloomy around here the last few days."

"Same here. I talked the housekeeper into taking a couple days off; she'd known the two guys for years. This age of life you expect to hear heart attack not murder."

"I know." Marie didn't want to think about it, didn't want to talk about it. Especially didn't want to reflect too long on the fact it was Connor who had stood over the bodies, worked the scenes, and now led the search with Marsh to find the killer. "Would you like to come over to the gallery tomorrow and take a look at that seascape that came in? It's pretty special."

"Lunchtime? I've got an appointment out your way."

"Sure."

"It's a date then. Any more thoughts on what the lawyer sent over?"

"Tracey already has her will signed and notarized. I'll read the final copy on mine tomorrow. Shifting everything to Amy is a simple step, but if Amy and Tracey have both passed away—I'm not sure who should get asked to absorb this stress. Being wealthy is nice when it comes to living easier, but the rest of it—"

"Leave it to be paid out over time to your church; it's got to go somewhere since you won't be taking it with you."

"Very true. Why do you talk so easily about heaven for others, Daniel, and yet not believe in God?"

"Do I have to answer that?"

"I already know your uncle was not exactly a good role model for what being a Christian is like. But the chief—he lives the same way he believes."

"I know. Luke and I have talked a lot about God over the years; he can be persuasive when he needs to be."

"But you still don't believe."

"I think God lets people in power do too much damage, that He cares about the big picture and bringing down nations and raising up others; but get down to a finer level where intervention would matter in justice between people and He doesn't do enough. The Bible talks a lot about taking care of the poor and the widows, and God doesn't seem to be that interested in changing the fact the poor just get poorer and the powerful more abusive in societies. God should be the cop walking the block, not a supreme court justice where it takes a decade for a legitimate grievance to get heard."

"Maybe Christians are supposed to be doing the work to lift up the poor and oppressed."

"Then God inspires very little loyalty to His cause. When was the last time you gave a gift to someone who was poor?"

The question caught her off guard. "The church missions group gives a lot and part of that would be my gifts, but that dodges your question. I don't know anyone who is really poor; that's sad, isn't it? I'm in a downtown that used to be the run-down part of town, and now it's too wealthy for those who used to live here."

"We're too comfortable in our own little worlds to actually connect with those who might need some help."

"So that's God's fault?"

"I'd like to think someone was taking responsibility for the problem, and He says He sees it and feels their hurt."

She thought about it and painted some more. "You feel guilty being rich."

"Don't you?"

"Yeah, some." She sighed. "Not enough to go back to not having money. Identifying with the poor by being one of them may make it easier to connect and empathize, but it's a lousy way to help."

"So we'll give away a few checks to try and feel better about ourselves and share some of the money around. I don't want a religion that hopes for heaven because it's the wealthy, prosperous place to be in the future. I want heaven to mean something more than a place; I want it to be a relationship. And so far the God I see and hear about—let's just say He and I haven't squared away what kind of relationship He's talking about."

"A love one, Daniel. Jesus looks at you and sees you and loves you. For all your money and things you worry and care about."

"Henry sure didn't see Christianity as that; he viewed it as a tithe to the penny and an appearance of the right actions, and the rest of life's decisions—that was just business."

"I'm sad for him now and the coldness of that and for you. It doesn't have to be that."

"So I'll think about it some more in my

own fashion, but not enough to believe like you do yet. It's not a taboo topic, Marie, just one I see differently than you."

"Okay." Marie bit her paintbrush handle and studied the scene before her. Too dark again. "Remember God is looking for a love relationship next time you ponder it: trust, loyalty, discipline, closeness—all that a love relationship implies. I don't model that all that well, but I know it's what He wants." She set aside the canvas to start another one. "Change of subject—I was thinking more about the wedding gift for Tracey and Marsh."

"Any ideas?"

"Maybe." She flipped through the notebook on the table. "They are planning to add on to the house to give them more space, and Tracey is a better decorator than I am. But they aren't going to be around the house all their lives, and while I can't plan trips for them, I could find out some things they would enjoy getting out to do together. Marsh loves to ski, and Connor mentioned Marsh is also a pretty avid fisherman. If the family had access to a boat and launch slip at the lake, it's something Mandy could even join us to do, spending a day out on the water, that kind of thing."

"It's got possibilities."

"Marsh would never accept it outright as a wedding gift, I don't think, but as a gift that is part of a larger something else? Maybe."

"You want me to find you a house to buy on the lake? It shouldn't be that hard."

"I was thinking more about you," she admitted.

He laughed. "You really didn't like my apartment, did you?"

"It's nice enough and all, but you live inside the office all day and go home to live inside an apartment at night. There's no outdoors in your life beyond your spectacular rose-filled walkway. You need a real house in the city, not some place outside of town you go to stay once every couple months. You ought to think about it, Daniel. You've got family now to help you mess up more space. And the thought of your moving into your uncle's place—it gives me the shudders. It's beautiful if you like a museum feel, but it's not somewhere for you."

"I'll admit I'd enjoy having a boat."

"See? The idea is already growing on you."

"Have they set a date for the wedding yet?"

Marie picked up the phone and walked out of the studio and into the kitchen to get herself something to drink. "They're talking about April, I think. Tracey likes the thought of having her anniversaries in the decades to come during that month." She eyed the closed garbage sack that reminded her it was garbage pickup in the morning, and she didn't plan to have the flopped tuna salad she'd thrown away stinking up the house for another day. "Let's talk more about a boat tomorrow. I think you should do that with me."

"You've got a deal."

"I'm going to go do chores and think about Connor maybe calling me later. You should stop working now."

"I'll admit to feeling stiff enough it's time to take a break from sitting at this table. I'll finish this box and call it a night. It was good talking with you while I worked; the time passed quickly."

"I think so too. Good night, Daniel."

"Night, Marie."

She closed the phone and thought not for the first time that he was a really nice man. Not so easy to get to know, but nice. She picked up the trash bag and slid her keys into her pocket.

The security cameras showed all was quiet out on the street, and the rain had thankfully eased off. Marie walked outside and put the trash into the Dumpster behind the building and went back into the gallery, turning on the low-track lighting and walking through to her office. Bryce was around—he was always around—but she was beginning to find that presence a background comfort rather than an intrusion.

Her office was neat but the trash overflowed, and she gathered it together along with the trash from the front checkout desk. The new display of paintings looked sharp together, she thought with pleasure, doing a walk around to see what else could be dealt with tonight. The front window needed to be wiped down inside again; it collected dust from the overhead heating more than most of the other windows, and she liked it to sparkle. Another month and this gallery would have new heating and lighting and a brand-new drop ceiling. Peter had promised a showcase, and he had ideas to make the architecture of the place itself become a beautiful thing.

She unlocked the door and took the last trash out. Maybe while Peter was working in the gallery she'd see if it was possible to refurbish the interior brick on the building and make it a rich, rough background for some of the more interesting pieces of art where the color contrast would be an asset. There was only so much that could be done with a white display wall.

An arm grabbed tight around her throat, her hair tangled by a hand and yanked back, bringing her face to the sky, and something cold touched her skin. "Don't move." She felt a knife blade against her throat and didn't try to even breathe. "They should have paid me; you'll mention that to them. They should have paid me."

She felt something hot and wet swung into her hands, and he was gone. She struggled to blink away choking tears and looked down.

The guy had eviscerated a cat.

She dropped it. She didn't throw up or stagger or faint. The rushing in her ears removed the present from her thoughts, and the next time she blinked Bryce was standing in front of her.

"Saw him, couldn't stop you, couldn't reach him." She could hear the anger in his quiet words and the tenseness in the man as he became the only thing in her world. The man had big hands, tough hands, and they were wiping junk off hers without appearing to be brisk about it, but the blood was going away. He was using his shirttails, she vaguely realized.

"Take a breath."

The words settled inside deep enough she did so.

"That's the way." His face looked like a boxer's might about the time his eyes narrowed and he punched straight into your face, but he still smiled at her. Not angry with her, incredibly, not angry with her for walking into this mess.

"Sorry, Bryce. Taking the trash out was stupid," she tried to whisper, only to find her voice hoarse.

He ignored the words and finished with the basics of his task. "Good enough to get you under a hot tap to take care of the rest." His arm settled around her waist before he let her try to take a step. "Remember the stairs."

"Yeah."

She wasn't fully ready to be out of that shock, she realized as she misjudged the doorway and hit the doorpost.

Bryce was punching in security codes behind her on the pad and then walking her toward the downstairs restroom. "Towels?"

"The narrow closet, where we keep the cleaning supplies."

She didn't look toward a mirror, nudging it open so as not to be able to see an image of herself afraid, nor did she look at her hands under a stream of hot water turning red with remaining traces of the cat. She just closed her eyes and used the soap.

"Good. Use this." Bryce pushed a washcloth into her hands, and while she soaped it, his rough hands pushed back her hair and wiped at traces of the tears. "Hold still, Marie. This will sting a bit." He wiped something across her face that came as a cold shock and then a bitter smell.

"What?"

"All done."

The guy hadn't cut her, she was sure of it,

but something had been on his coat sleeve pressed in tight to her face. "Thanks."

"Connor's coming."

She thought herself too shaky to want that attention but nodded. "Okay."

She wrapped her hands in another dry towel and tried to smile at Bryce. "I'm going to go change and drink some coffee and forget that just happened."

"You won't, but it's a good first few steps. You want me to come up?"

"Better to know you're down here making sure no one else does."

"I'm coding the doors so you can't step outside on me again without an alarm blaring at you to rethink it."

"A good plan."

He knew. He knew something had been said. He knew a lot more had happened in those seconds than she had said. He knew but wasn't even nibbling to find out; he'd just called Connor. She squeezed his arm and went toward the narrow stairway, glad now that it took hands against both walls as she walked upstairs.

"Let me see."

Marie turned her hand for Connor to see

the bruise spreading across the side. She'd broken two fingernails. She'd gouged the man, she thought, in the first-instinct move as the arm came around her neck. She'd reached up to grab him and didn't remember doing it.

Connor, sitting on the footstool in front of her chair, looked all cop as he held her hand and inspected the bruise. His expression had changed in those first few moments when he had seen her from an intense emotion to the pulled-back care he was taking now. She was relieved, part of her, that she wasn't being asked to swim in his heavy emotion right now too. She couldn't absorb any more.

"The clothes you changed out of?"

"On the towel in the bathroom. It registered enough that you might want them so I didn't throw them away." Her voice sounded tired, she thought, listening to herself, and a bit too calm, like it had happened last year instead of less than half an hour ago.

Connor brushed back the hair that kept sliding forward to cover her face and held her gaze with his. "You've got to start at the beginning and tell me every sound and smell and movement you remember. Everything matters, Marie. No matter how farfetched the thought you had."

"It was fast and without hesitation. He had every move planned, I think. A thick heavy coat, not those new lightweight-fabric thermal coats, but an old heavy fabric, bulky. He had an arm around my neck and a handful of my hair pulling my head back, and I could still feel all that fabric smothering me."

"A sense of the coat's color?"

"Dark, I'd suppose, because I had no sensation someone was even there before he was already behind me. The Dumpster lid kind of echoes in that brick alley and maybe I didn't hear what I should have, but the movement—I didn't see him coming, didn't sense him. He was just there."

"Taller than you?"

"No more than an inch or two, he was pulling my head back and into him, so his shoulders were right behind mine. Kind of tall, thin, I think, under that coat, and strong in the arms, young. I remember smelling what I thought of as metal and something bitter and maybe grit. The knife he held had to be already covered in the cat's blood, I guess. My eyes burned when he let me go, irritated, like there was grit in them. It was fast, Connor. Bryce was already there before I was even blinking and seeing again."

"Young in his voice, his build?"

"Just an impression from all the energy, the speed of it, and maybe the voice."

"He said something."

She struggled to keep her gaze on his. "I didn't understand it."

"Tell me anyway. Word for word if you can."

"I won't be forgetting it. He was angry as he said it. He said don't move and then he said—" she took a breath and quoted— " 'they should have paid me; you'll mention that to them. They should have paid me.' "

Connor paled, she realized in the part of her mind that was watching him watch her, and she pushed away the memory of the alley to focus again fully on him. "That means something to you."

"Yes. It does." His hand raised to brush swiftly along her cheek. "Thanks for the quote; that will help. Do you have any other impression of him, of his voice, of how he moved or carried himself?"

"Just that he seemed tense and angry

and maybe very revved up. His voice was hard. . . ." She bit her lip.

"What, Marie?"

"I'm not going to say I've heard it before, but it was familiar to me—you know what I mean? Like I had heard it before and felt mad before too. Not a memory of the voice but an emotional reaction to it."

"Recently?"

She shook her head. "I'm sorry; that's probably scrambled brains talking right now. I'm not sure what it is I need to convey about the voice. But I remember reacting to it and not just the words. Who was supposed to pay him, Connor? The cops? Daniel? Who am I supposed to tell?"

"Marie . . ."

"You promised to tell me what was going on."

"I'm sorry. I can't, not about this, even now. Not without risking other people."

"The guy who is after Mandy wants to be paid; that's what this is all about."

"I'm seriously sorry, but I can't answer that." He leaned forward and wrapped his arms around her, bringing her toward the edge of the seat. "You need to go soak in a hot tub awhile—you're still cold, and I need to make some calls. Then you and I are going to go out for a long drive and push this back a ways."

Her hands tightened hard around his. "You can't tell Mandy. Connor, if you tell her someone got through to touch me, she'll disappear and I'll never see her again. You know she will; she'll run to try and take the trouble with her. You know that is what she's going to do."

"Easy. Amy's not going to run."

"Please. Spin it any way you have to, but you can't tell Mandy what really happened. A robbery attempt, anything else. Silence about this is the only thing that I can offer to help her right now."

"I'll talk to the chief," Connor reassured. "That's the best I can promise."

She bit her lip again and nodded. "I am awfully cold. If you'll take those clothes away and the towel, I'll take a hot shower. I want to wash my hair again."

"I'll go do that now." He kissed her forehead. "I'm sorry, Marie. That I wasn't here. That we didn't stop it."

She leaned against him and hugged him back. "I'm okay."

When he had dealt with the clothes she

had left for him, she stepped under the hottest shower she thought she could handle and let herself cry.

●●●●●●

Connor paced Marie's kitchen, waiting for Marsh to find some privacy. He wasn't about to let Tracey overhear this conversation.

"I'm alone."

"He sent his message through Marie, angry, ticked—he grabbed her in the back alley and put a knife to her throat."

"Where are you, at the hospital?" Marsh asked sharply.

"Her place. Bryce was on it within seconds, and Marie walked away from it badly shaken. She'd stepped outside to take out the trash of all things." Connor felt his words breaking at the anger of that.

"Don't bash your hand against one of those brick walls right now; remember she's in one piece. Start talking. I need the details."

Connor took a deep breath and nodded. He read the quote from his notes to get the message exact. "Marie said a little taller than herself, thin, and young. She's pretty certain about the fact he was young. This isn't our New York hitter; she didn't describe a fifty-year-old guy with an accent. Marsh, what was your working idea?"

"That there was a third kid out there of Henry Benton, a son."

Connor sat down on the nearest chair.

"This trouble comes rolling in coincident to the will, and who would know about a boy Henry fathered but the chauffeur who probably drove him to where he was seeing the mother and the bookkeeper who probably paid off the lady just like Henry did with Marie and Tracey's mom. The killings could be that of a very angry man who didn't get recognized in that will and wants his cut of the money too."

"What triggered the idea?"

"Your comment that stabbings are very personal crimes. The message claiming a family secret. If the guy is young, impulsive, very angry—I could see a knife attack on the two retired guys who knew the truth and never came forward to state the fact a son also existed."

"And it explains why he might be let into their homes; they knew him," Connor realized.

"Henry kept track of the girls—you don't think he might keep track of a boy? He knew enough not to want to claim him, but to instead leave Daniel as his major heir. Connor, I may just be chasing a phantom that doesn't exist. Nothing yet says there is a son out there, let alone one that would commit two murders like this and attack Marie."

"But it explains why you've been going back through the phone calls the sisters have received, the mail—looking for signs he made contact with them after that press conference."

"For what it's worth, Sam doesn't see it as likely. He investigated everyone else in Henry's past over the years, including keeping track of the two sisters, and Sam can't imagine Henry having a son that he didn't get asked to check out and keep tabs on too. As far as Sam knows Marie and Tracey are Henry's only children."

"Which takes us back to theory one—'I know the family secret' is the fact Amy is alive, and 'pay me to go away' is Richard Wise laying down the marker for how ugly this is going to get if he's not fully paid off."

"There is evidence our New York shooter

is in town; we've got his car, and Sam's place got searched," Marsh reminded him.

"And opposite of that theory two—Henry has another kid out there not recognized in the will, and he wants money from the family to go away. He killed the two people who could identify him as a way to deliver his demand. Whoever grabbed Marie tonight was thin, young, and did not have a New York accent. He was definitely angry he hadn't been paid. And we both know that while the reporters are clamoring for that second message, they don't have it yet. This guy tonight knew something that only the killer would know."

"I don't know, Connor. If all the pieces were fitting in place, we'd have this solved. We need fingerprints, blood work, trace evidence from one of the crime scenes— something to help sort this out. It keeps coming back to not enough facts. If there is a son out there, we have next to nothing right now to point us in a direction to search to even confirm he exists."

Connor heard Marie shut off the water. "I'll pick you up first thing tomorrow morning and bring whatever Bryce can add to this. We're going back to those crime scenes to canvas neighbors again."

"I'll be expecting you. Tell Marie from me that I'm very grateful she's okay."

"You'll have Tracey prepped not to push for details tonight?"

"She'll handle it smart."

"Thanks, Marsh."

Connor closed the phone and knew he needed to call the chief. But first he just forced himself to take a couple more deep breaths and get past the last half hour. Bryce's call had shaken him harder than any message he'd ever answered, and the reality of that was going to take some time to absorb. Marie would come through this okay even if he had to stand and take a bullet for her; he couldn't handle her getting hurt any more by this.

He stepped toward the hallway door and pushed in numbers. One thing at a time. The first was just to survive tonight.

"Chief? It's Connor. There's been trouble at the gallery."

●●●●●●

"You can't pay him," Luke said, watching Daniel prowl around Henry's former home office like a caged cat. His call had caught Daniel just getting ready to leave for the night, and Luke had come over to deliver the news in person. Daniel had been talking to Marie less than half an hour before the attack; that had made this reaction all the more intense, and Luke was hoping he could defuse it.

"Two former employees dead, Marie terrorized, don't tell me what I can't do with the money, Luke. Frankly right now I'd like to light a bonfire and use it as kindling."

Luke held up his hand and offered reality. "If this is a young guy thinking the family owes him money, he's already disturbed enough to do two brutal murders. Handing him money and having him disappear would be to set up someone else to be dead in the future. A guy doesn't kill twice in one night and become a saint for the rest of his life.

"Second—if it's our guy from New York who did the killings, then he's after Amy, and regardless of whether Richard Wise gets his money the hatred has gone on too long—he'll stay on it until he has Amy dead, and if he goes through her sisters to make that happen he won't care. I'm not going to be surprised to find our New York shooter has co-opted some local talent to help him out, maybe even to do the killings for him. Getting into Sam's place, following the sisters, killing the two employees, dumping his car, staying out of sight of the local cops who have a fairly recent photo of him—that is a lot of ground for one person to manage in a city he doesn't know well. So he's probably arranged local help. He wants Amy; that is the job he'll sit back to handle himself. The rest is just details."

Daniel finally sat back down. "How do you sleep at night?"

"I don't," Luke replied. "I need to know if Henry Benton had another child, and I need to know that by any means you can dream up to find out."

Daniel tapped a pen on the desk, thinking. "Was there anything in the book-keeper's effects that might have been from his period of time working here? Any other file boxes in storage, a ledger, anything in a safe-deposit box?"

"He kept every receipt in his life, the same as he did for Henry, but so far nothing is popping up as being something more than his own personal papers," Luke replied, having checked with the officer sorting through the files.

"Then if Henry knew he had a son, the evidence will be somewhere in this house and in his personal records."

"Is it possible Henry had a son he didn't know existed?"

"Sure. If an affair led to a pregnancy and the lady wasn't inclined to come get more money out of Henry than he offered when they split up. But you'd think either the mom or at least the son would have made contact over the years. We're assuming if this son exists he's younger than Tracey and Marie, not older?"

"A guess, but probably in his late twenties."

"If he's not a minor and his mother kept anything at all around the house of the letters Henry liked to write or spoke at all of who his father was, the trail back to Henry wouldn't be difficult for someone to push against and follow. There should have been contact with Henry at some point."

"Assume there was a payoff to the mother fifteen to twenty-five years ago. Would it have gone through the Benton Group accounts?"

"No. Henry kept a bright line between private and public business. It would have been a cash payment taken from a private account. One his personal bookkeeper would have probably handled and his chauffeur went along to deliver." Daniel grimaced just saying it.

Luke nodded. "It's a working theory we need to either prove or knock down so we quit chasing it. For what it's worth, Sam doesn't think a son exists. Henry would have wanted to know about him and would have kept track of him."

"I'd agree with Sam." Daniel pulled out a ring of keys. "Come on; I'll show you what there is to work with."

He led the way through the house and opened the file-storage room. The boxes were neat, orderly, and shelved floor to ceiling. "I've eliminated the boxes on the left, and when everything has sorted itself out the plan is to have them shredded. These thirty boxes—I'm finding everything in them from receipts to phone-message notes. Henry apparently asked his personal bookkeeper to take care of all the paper, and so it was just filed away as it got created. The personal bank accounts—most Henry closed years ago and rolled into the Benton Group—but the canceled checks are still here filed in among all the other papers. I'm guessing we are not going to find one actually made out to the lady involved. It will be for something else and converted to the cash Henry needed. It wouldn't have been uncommon for his wife to be going through the receipts or the mail as it came in. The last payment to Marie and Tracey's aunt that I found had *florist* scrawled at the bottom."

"A lot of flowers."

"Yes." Daniel shut off the light. "I'll have my assistant come help with the search; if the evidence is here, we should be able to find it."

"Henry never mentioned anything that might cause you to think back and wonder if he was talking about a son?"

"There's nothing I can recall that even glimmers at more children than Marie and Tracey."

Luke picked up his coat, and Daniel walked outside with him.

"Take reasonable precautions the next few weeks, Daniel, no jogging alone, buzzing people into the apartment, leaving car doors unlocked—"

Daniel smiled. "Don't worry about me. There's security all over this place, the office, and they've been rolling by the apartment building regularly. I'm covered."

"Let's keep it that way." Luke started his car. "I'll be in touch."

"You'll be my first call if I find anything," Daniel promised.

Chapter Twenty

Caroline lifted a hand to Marsh, sliding into a seat in the restaurant that put her near the window and traffic flowing in and out and far enough away from the table with Marie and Tracey and the two cops not to interrupt their lunch. She ordered just the day's special, a bowl of soup, knowing it would be served quickly, and then settled back to observe.

Marie looked better.

Amy had sent her with the precise request to report back a firsthand impression of how Marie was doing four days after she had a knife at her throat. Given the state Amy was in over the incident, Caroline thought the request reasonable. She'd left

Amy with one of Jonathan's guys and come to town to get her an answer.

Watching Marie, Caroline put her at a little nervous, not enough sleep, but doing a good job of staying with the conversation around her at the table. Connor, sitting beside Marie, didn't look like he'd slept much better. Beyond a glance over and a smile, he'd otherwise shown no sign he had seen her come in. *Better that way,* Caroline thought. The cops knew what was in the manila envelope she carried; let them finish their meals with their ladies and enjoy the slice of normalcy before business returned.

The waitress brought her soup.

Ah, there was Bryce. She'd missed him in the first scan of the room, but he was here eating lunch and watching the crowd too.

Caroline didn't know if anything in the envelope she carried would help, but it was full of photos Amy had marked and annotated with memories from New York. At least it was another set of faces to watch for in an otherwise wait-and-see game for who might be around. Amy, more than anyone else, needed to know if the two murders and the knife attack represented new trouble appearing or a wave of old business relating to herself now reaching out toward her sisters.

Connor had been smart to get Marie back out in public, if not relaxing, then at least getting settled and okay with being in a crowd. Sykes had plastered Marie's photo on the front page again, and Marie's instinct would be to hide in the gallery flat and not venture out. Going shopping together, then stopping at a restaurant for lunch had been good first choices for Connor to make.

Sykes had sources. Caroline didn't particularly like what he wrote, but the facts were solid. The story of its being a robbery had shifted toward its being more a mugging. Not perfect with all the facts, but close enough someone had talked to Sykes before he wrote that piece. Someone inside. They were seeing crime-scene details and photos in the newspaper before the reports were being finished, now this breach—the chief was going to fire someone just as soon as he figured out the leak and probably do it in a spectacular fashion.

Caroline ate her lunch and thought about her own Christmas shopping. She knew Amy had started hers on that last trip with Luke, and from the looks of the sacks

around Marie and Tracey they had also begun theirs this morning. Maybe Amy could
get talked into going a town over and
spending a day at the mall—the excursion
would do them both good. They couldn't
help solve these two murders, and sitting
around and waiting for a face to appear in
the crowd was not a good option.

The group at the table rose, Marsh holding the chair for Tracey, Connor helping
Marie with her packages. Making the quick
decision that it was best to be ahead of
them on this walk, Caroline tucked money
for her lunch on the bill, left with her drink
refill, and slipped on her coat. The group
would be a minute or two just getting their
things gathered together. The sisters would
want to ask about Amy, and Caroline wasn't
comfortable doing that here. She caught
Marsh's eye and nodded to the door, then
headed out ahead of them.

●●●●●●

Marsh paid at the counter to put all the
meals on his charge card, and he smiled at
the image Caroline made as she moved
past the crowd at the exit: bold red hat, long
black coat, gloves, a pretty little thing in the

way guys appreciated such things. She disappeared into the crowd of pedestrian traffic on the sidewalk, heading north toward the gallery and where they had parked the squad car. She needed someone special in her life, and he wasn't above trying to make an introduction, but for the life of him he couldn't think of someone special enough to do. He knew the folder she brought was business, and he didn't particularly want that part of his day to return yet. He pulled on his gloves.

Tracey joined him. "They had exactly one left. It's perfect." She held up a baby mug with a colorful balloon bouquet formed into the ceramic sides she'd bought at the restaurant gift shop and then slid it back into the sack. "My extended list Christmas shopping is officially done."

He held her coat for her. "You're absolutely sure? No second cousin of your hairdresser's mother you've forgotten on your list?" he teased.

She hit him for the teasing and then slipped into her coat. "Admit it, you enjoyed this morning."

He smiled at her. "I'll admit shopping with you is an experience."

"And one you come back to enjoy every year." She pulled on her gloves and beamed at him. "Let's go find dessert."

"Tracey—"

She laughed and picked up the sack with her final purchase, and he held the restaurant door open for her. "You've got ten minutes, don't you? Time enough to slip into the candy shop for a piece of homemade fudge?"

"I suppose Connor can take that long to say good-bye." He was aware of Connor lingering behind them at the table with Marie and Bryce, and he purposely gave them privacy for a few more minutes. He steered Tracey around a group of teens on the sidewalk. "I need one more gift for the chief's sister, Susan, so let's also stop at the department store you like and see—"

Shots rang out. One slapped into the fender of the car parked at the curb right behind them, and a second shattered a display window ahead of them.

Before the glass could be pulled downward by gravity Marsh had Tracey covered and moving toward the only shelter reachable, a gray sedan parked at the curb ahead of them, shielding her head with his arms and blocking her body with his.

Pedestrians screamed, scattered.

The back car window above them exploded as two bullets slapped into it. Something hit brick. Something hit people. He could see people falling. Tires squealed as the shooter tore away from the scene.

He could feel adrenaline stretching his nerves to the point his heart wanted to explode. "Tracey, stay—"

He realized his gloves were covered in blood.

"Tracey—"

Her eyes were open and blank, and that was her blood washing over his coat sleeves. His hands searched frantically. Back of the neck, into her brain, already gone . . . his mind put together the realization she was dead, but the word didn't have a meaning with it.

"She okay, buddy?"

A hand rested on his shoulder, and the light blocked as a guy leaned over him to see. "Oh, man. That's three he hit."

Three.

The shakes made it hard for him to release her to lay her back on the sidewalk; he rapidly shoved together his scarf and gloves to provide a cushion for her head. Not even a final breath or a whispered word, just gone. "Tracey—" He choked on tears as he tried to untangle the way they'd fallen and moved to sit up beside her.

Her mug had spilled from the sack and cracked into three pieces. The new silk scarf she'd bought that morning tied loosely at her neck had knotted to one side and gotten dirty. A hard fist in his chest made breathing labored, and his hand kept shaking as he touched under that scarf. No pulse at all. She was still pretty; he closed her eyes so she wouldn't keep looking at him.

"Don't move me."

The cried words behind him registered, and he realized the commotion around him now was crying and pleas, and while he didn't want to care, he turned his head to look and saw a sidewalk deserted but for injured and those who had braved coming back to help. Cuts, broken arm, twisted knee, the perils of the stampede to move away . . . and shooting victims.

He struggled to his feet and walked north down the path of the gunfire and saw the man who had stopped by him working to help a young man shot in the leg.

Red hat. He saw the color resting against the bookstore building brick wall and angled that direction. Caroline sat against the building, one leg bent, her arms lax at her sides.

"Hey, lady," he offered softly.

Awake, eyes focusing on him, but not moving on her own.

He struggled to kneel without falling. He shifted her coat to see. Her blouse was covered with blood. Struck in the chest up toward her left shoulder, a few inches over and the bullet would have hit her heart. "Hold on, Caroline." He tried using her scarf to make a pressure bandage, but the material was too thick and not solid enough. He pulled over one of the shopping bags littering the sidewalk and tugged out a yellow silk blouse. She groaned as he pressed it tight against the bleeding. "I know it hurts."

Her head rolled toward him, her eyes clear as they looked into his. "Bloody Irishman, he shot right into the crowd not bothering to aim beyond shoving the gun out the window and yanking the trigger while he drove with the other hand."

"You saw him?"

"Tall guy, Irish, the curly side of red hair; had this crazy four-leaf clover hanging from his rearview mirror. Driving a cab. Looked right at me." Her eyes began to drift from focusing on him. She tried to smile. "Funny the things you remember when a guy points a gun in your direction."

She coughed and her eyes closed against the pain. He saw the alarming sign of blood at the corner of her mouth. Her breathing began to shallow out.

"Stay with me." He tried to ease her down to lay on her side, knowing at least one lung was filling up with blood.

In an instant she'd drifted away from him.

"Paramedics are coming." His Good Samaritan knelt beside them and shoved around a coat he had brought over to give her some protection from laying on the concrete.

"I need them here first; she's hit in the lung."

"The kid that got hit in the leg will make it. The lady with you, your wife?"

"Fiancée," he choked out.

"I just wanted you to know there's a nun with her."

He nodded because there weren't words to say.

Cabdriver. Irish. Tracey was dead. Caroline was dying. He heard the sound of sirens finally approaching. *Cabdriver, Irish, curly red hair*—he was going to regret the fact he'd missed him.

"Marsh, hold still. Are you hit?"

Connor wasn't taking his shake of his head as an answer and tugged at the coat, searching for himself. There was so much blood on him now Marsh wasn't even sure himself anymore that none of it was his own. Everything hurt.

Marsh leaned against one of the parked cars, and he watched the nun sitting with Tracey, holding her hand, being more comfort than he'd been able to be to her. Tracey wasn't Catholic, but if she'd been alive she would have liked the fact the lady cared enough to say a prayer for her. "Marie?"

"Bryce has her. Shots took out the window of the restaurant, but we were still too far back inside."

"Tell me someone spotted the cab." His voice sounded odd to him, old, hollow. He should be feeling anger, but he wasn't feeling much of anything beyond the hurt.

"Irish guy, four-leaf clover hanging from the rearview mirror; every cab in the area is being stopped. I wish she'd been able to tell you which cab company; there are a lot of cabs downtown today."

"He was shooting at me."

"I know; you said. I think it was broader, partner." Connor pressed hard on a gash on Marsh's arm. "Put your hand here and keep pressure on it. You've got some flying-glass cuts."

He obeyed but wondered why he should bother. "Caroline's not going to make it."

Connor looked over his shoulder at the ambulance, where paramedics were rushing to lift the stretcher inside, lights already going. "Don't bet against her. Come on, buddy; you're going to the hospital where a doc is going to bless you with a look-see."

"No. I'm staying with Tracey."

Connor's gloved hand turned his head so that Marsh was forced to look at him. "No, you're going to the hospital. I'm going to make sure she gets the best of care with all the dignity a shooting victim can still get; that's my word. But you're not staying to see it. Go get checked out, get changed, and join me at the precinct in two hours."

"I have to stay and help." Marsh knew he was in the way here, in the way of the man-hunt, in the way of treating the injured, but leaving was something that would just make this situation worse, permanent. He was leaning against a car parked along the street, and he tried to stand.

Connor caught his arm to steady him. "Way too much happened in the last few minutes for you to be trying to help me yet. Two hours, Marsh, then we're working this together."

"We're going to find the shooter today," Marsh said, settling it in his mind.

"We're sure going to try," his partner promised, his voice choking a bit as he said it. Connor nodded to the paramedic who had been standing a discreet distance back. "Get him to the hospital in one piece."

●●●●●●

"He was shooting to take out both sisters, Chief. Two into the restaurant glass, he caught Marsh and Tracey in the open; Car-oline got hit at the end of the exchange," Connor explained, trying to not get caught by the glare of lights now reflecting off window glass as television trucks beamed lights from the end of the block. Too many spectators, too many people around.

"Where's Marie?"

"Bryce took her out the back way and won't stop until they make that safe house on the other side of town. She doesn't know, Chief, about Tracey. Marie doesn't know yet." He struggled against tears. "I didn't see it coming, not like this."

"Marsh?"

"Too deep in shock to put it together yet; he thinks they were just shooting at him. I put him on the second ambulance heading to Mercy General."

The pressure of Luke's hand on his shoulder tightened. "Okay. The deputy chief and I have got the scene. Where do you most want to be?"

"Cab hunting. I promised Marsh we'd find that cab."

"You and Mayfield, pull in as many guys as you can use. Stop every single cab and then pull every logbook and hack license in the city if you have to. I'll push through the warrants. Tall guy, Irish, the curly side of red hair—he's not unique for a cabdriver in this town, but he's close."

Connor nodded his thanks. "I told Marsh two hours, and I'd meet him at the station."

"Keep him moving today, okay? Whatever you have to do. Don't give him a lot of time to think. You took his sidearm?"

"When I was searching him over for bullet holes of his own. It's locked in the gun box of the first arriving officer."

"I'll handle it from there. And, Connor—I'll tell Marie about Tracey personally."

"I appreciate it." He fought to keep his voice together. "Sorry, Chief. I just can't do it."

"I'm sending my sister to step in with Marsh; she can nag him into listening to the doctors. The chaplain is on the way to meet Caroline. Just focus on the task in front of you, and let the thinking about it come later, okay?"

"Yeah." Connor found the guts to look down the sidewalk at where a white sheet covered Tracey. "They were getting married, Chief."

Luke squeezed his shoulder. "Go find Mayfield. He was over at the communications van a few minutes ago."

Connor nodded and took a deep breath as he turned that way. He wished like crazy it was one of the guys under that sheet instead of Tracey; anything would be an easier loss to absorb than losing Tracey.

"Connor." He followed the shout and found Mayfield waiting for him. "Sorry, man."

"Yeah. We're going after that cab."

"An all points is already out; they're stopping every cab in the city. You want to put emergency traffic stops on the outbound interstate lanes?"

"There, and a couple patrol cars sitting on the airport entrance and anywhere else we can think of as exit points where he's going to try and dump the vehicle." Connor climbed into the van beside Mayfield and tried to focus on remembering the street names he normally knew without thinking about them.

●●●●●●

Who wanted him dead?

The question rattled around the tired focus of his thoughts as Marsh accepted the scrip the emergency doc wrote him for pain pills and stuffed it in his shirt pocket.

"Your personal doc can take those stitches out in about ten days. Any redness or extra heat in the injury, see him before then."

"Sure, Doc."

The ER still bustled with staff coming and going between curtained-off cubicles, and Marsh was left alone again. One of the guys in the squad had brought over the shirt and slacks from his work locker. Marsh buttoned the uniform shirt, relieved to have something clean.

The curtain moved, and where the doctor had disappeared a lady reappeared. "They said you can go now?"

Marsh offered the chief's sister a partial smile. "Yeah. I don't think they want to particularly keep me. This hospital and I go way back." He'd been shot twice in his career, and both times had ended up here with him staring at the ceiling and getting asked inane questions by doctors about hands and toes and names of presidents.

"I remember." Susan was at his side to help when he shifted off the bedside to stand, but he wasn't nearly as wobbly on his feet now after they shoved nearly three sports-drink bottles full of some awful sweet stuff into him.

"Your headache is pounding?"

"Like a full-blown parade drum section is camped out in there," he agreed.

"You would think they could do better than aspirin in a place like this."

"They could; I passed." He slipped on his sunglasses to slash the light he had to deal with in half and cover the fact tears were too close to the surface for comfort. "That helps."

She offered what she had brought with her. "The coat is probably a size too big, but the gloves should be right."

He accepted the coat. "I appreciate your thinking of it."

"Connor did. He said—" She bit her lip.

"It's okay, Susan. I was wearing that other coat. I know what it ended up looking like."

"Yes, well, it's not a memory you should have." She gathered up the papers that had become his admission records and nodded toward the center aisle. "They'll need you to sign out at the desk."

"Of course, one more signature on one more form."

She smiled and with one arm around his

waist hugged him. "I'm buying you some good strong coffee before I take you to the station."

"Connor's there now?"

"Yes."

He didn't ask about Tracey, and she didn't offer. He knew what had already been done. The medical examiner's staff had put her in a body bag and taken her to the morgue and started taking X rays so they could take the slug that killed her out of her and into evidence. Tracey was dead, and the evidence needed to convict her killer was still in her.

He took a troubled breath and refused to let himself think about that reality. He needed to work; he needed to do something.

●●●●●●

The police-department desks were busy with guys—that was the odd realization Marsh had as he walked through the bull pen of desks toward Connor's and found guys who were off duty now back on duty. Susan knew the building layout as well as he did, but he still kept a hand on her arm to escort her, not wanting to break that thin line of comfort yet in having her with him.

"I'm sorry, Marsh."

He nodded at the officer's condolence, the words repeating over and over as he made his way toward Connor's desk.

Connor set down his phone and got up to lean against the side of the desk as Marsh pulled out an adjoining chair. "The mayor and the rest of the city council are here. I've got the squad union rep running interference to keep them out of your space for at least another half hour so you can hear what we have first."

"I appreciate it."

Connor handed Susan his notepad. "Can you—?"

She glanced at the note, at Marsh, and nodded. "I'll use Beth's phone." She headed over to join the unit's secretary.

"Your extended family heard the news; Susan can handle the initial call."

"Thanks." Marsh and his second cousins had ceased to be more than blood relations a long time ago, their opinion of his job vocally expressed at family gatherings, something that had been the final straw. They were a thousand miles away and not likely to come to the funeral.

"We haven't found either the cab or the driver yet. We're stopping every vehicle that is seen, but nothing so far. We've got a pretty good overview from the company dispatchers where cabs should have been during that slice of time. We've also got a list of cabs that were not on duty but where the vehicles were out with their drivers, most parked at home in preparation for weekend shifts."

"The cab is going to be difficult—an Irish cabdriver, maybe not quite so tough."

"There are officers going through cab hack licenses looking for possible matches based on the description. Others making sure there isn't a stolen cab somewhere in the mix. It's going to speed things up if we are able to get a sketch we can release to the public."

"Susan hadn't heard—how's Caroline doing?"

"Still in surgery. Another two hours minimum before she makes the recovery room. She lost a lot of blood, Marsh. I don't know."

She'd be dead and he'd have that on his

conscience too. "Anyone else at the scene proving to be a good witness?"

"A lot more general and contradictory information than what Caroline gave us—cabdriver, no it was a cab passenger; middle-age, no kind of young; white hair, no dark; some insist it was a woman driving—"

"That's probably a glimpse of the red hair getting remembered."

"Exactly. I'll trust Caroline's memory as probably the most accurate description we'll get from the scene." Connor ran his hand across his face and shook his head, trying to shake off the fatigue gripping him, then looked over at him.

Marsh understood the inspection going on—his partner was trying to get a read on how he was really doing behind the calm exterior. Tracey was dead, he was bleeding inside, and it felt like a Mack truck had run him over. He wanted the guy who did this. Marsh didn't bother to say it. "What else do we have?"

"We know there were eleven shots fired, and the area hit covers about a quarter of a block. The technicians tracking down the shots are finding all kinds of angles. We're assuming at this point that the cab tried to come from the center lane over to the lane nearest the restaurant and opened fire as he straightened out, fired while he was driving past, then sped up through the intersection and out of the area."

Marsh didn't remember the cab and wished he'd been turned even slightly more toward the street to have been able to see something useful; as it was, there were only the memories. "The first shot—it hit the car behind us, then a display window, then the shot that hit Tracey . . ."

"Two early ones hit the restaurant window, then the car behind you," Connor suggested. "Two others shattered the back car window, one hit a pedestrian in the leg, a miss that hit brick, and the last hit Caroline."

"Do we know yet if the gun was in the system from a prior crime?"

"The lab is still working on it; we'll have that answer soon. I doubt it was a local piece. He probably brought it with him."

"I don't remember an Irish guy in those New York pictures, do you?"

"There was one in the envelope Caroline carried with her. Maybe she comes out of surgery and can give us a positive ID that it was the guy she saw."

"Marie?"

"The chief told her; Daniel's with her now."

"You need to go see her."

"I've got to have something to tell her, Marsh." Connor's voice broke. "News that we have this guy at least. Something."

Marsh nodded, not able to say much to that but to agree. "It looks busy around here."

"If it can be thought of to try, we're trying it. The deputy chief is managing things for a while; the chief went to see Amy."

"This is going to tear her up."

"I know."

"Where do you need me most?"

"We're trying to sort out security cameras in the area and see if any of them caught a snapshot of that cab. The lab just called that they got the bank tapes in-house."

Marsh pushed himself to his feet. "Let's go see what they can give us."

Chapter Twenty-One

Luke slowed as he approached the private farmhouse, the vehicle partly blocking the last stretch of the road enough to tell him the reality. He rolled to a stop and halted beside the truck. "What happened, Jonathan?"

"Amy bolted within minutes of the breaking news flash. By the time my guy got from his truck where he was patrolling the road back to the house she had taken her coat and we think a backpack and disappeared. I've got twenty guys searching the area trying to get a clue of the direction she took. I've even got a bird in the air, but she's good at this and she's gone. My guess she had a vehicle tucked away as a precaution somewhere in the area or else she hot-wired something to borrow. She was smart enough not to take one of the vehicles on the property."

"You had transmitters planted?"

"On anything that could move, including the tractor. She's carrying that phone Caroline gave her, so maybe we'll get a break. She uses it, I'll know where she's standing to within a meter. But I'm not hopeful. They got through to Marie; now her sister Tracey is dead; Amy's not only afraid—she's angry. She's not going to make the more obvious mistakes. And unless Caroline took it with her, her backup piece is missing. She had it tucked under the stack of kitchen towels by the back door. Amy would have known that." Jonathan shook his head. "Bad day all the way around. Anything we can do for you in town?"

"Marie is safe, and I've got Daniel with her so he's covered by proxy. What do you think Amy is going to do?"

"I don't know the lady. I've just read the army personnel file on her. I think she's going to hunt down the guy that killed her sister and do your job for you."

"She's not leaving the area."

"I'll put money on the fact she's heading back into town, not away from it."

The thought didn't settle well; none of today did. "I'm going up to the house to look around, then head back to see Sam. I could use a couple guys to watch the gallery tonight so I can leave Bryce with Marie."

"You'll have them," Jonathan promised. "I'm sorry for this, Luke. They seemed like a nice family, the sisters."

"They are." Telling Marie about Tracey had been close to the hardest thing he had ever done in his life. He just wished someone had been able to tell Amy the news in person, rather than have it be a media announcement.

He drove toward the house. *Amy, I know you're hurting, honey. I know you're grieving. But you have to let me help you. You've got to call me.*

●●●●●●

The hospital recovery room had lights dimmed to half wattage to make it easier on patients coming out of the drugged coma of surgery. Marsh felt clumsy trying to walk quietly in his work shoes. "Thanks for this." It was incredibly late, edging toward midnight, for the surgery had lasted six hours and the recovery even longer.

The nurse escorting him smiled as she tied the mask for him. "Five minutes and not a word to her doctor. She's been asking for you."

He lifted one eyebrow at that but nodded, and the nurse directed him toward the third curtained cubicle. They still had Caroline on heart monitors and IV lines and what looked like an emergency transfusion line taped in place on her right arm.

He rested a hand on the raised handrail and leaned down to speak softly. "Hey, Caroline. It's Marsh. How are you doing?"

Her eyes had moved toward him as she realized she had company. She tried her best to smile. "It hurts like you know what."

He eased down the mask just for a moment so she could see his answering smile. "I'm sorry about that. They should have good drugs here though to help with that."

"Yeah. Remembered something."

He moved the mask back in place and carefully slid his hand under her limp one at her side as he waited for her to form her words.

She tried to lick her lips as she breathed

in. "The cab—it had these three big white stripes down the side. I forgot to tell you that."

He made sure he didn't tighten his hand around hers more than a fraction as the news sank in. It made the cab one of the Speedy Yellow Cab Company's vehicles. "Thank you. That will help. Do you remember if the shooter was old, young, thin, heavyset?"

She fought to think and shook her head. "Sorry."

He'd come to simply make sure with his own eyes that when they said she would make it they hadn't been trying to soften the number of deaths on his conscience today; now she'd changed the search they were on and helped them out in a huge fashion. He could see the battle going on to stay alert against the pain. "Let me get the nurse and a bunch of painkillers for you. We'll be around when you wake up next," he promised.

"Thanks."

A brief word with the nurse and she nodded and moved to join Caroline while he stripped off his mask and the paper gown they required for this room. He left the recovery room.

"How's she doing?" Connor asked, pushing away from the wall by the elevator.

"Better than anyone could have expected. Three white stripes on the cab; we're looking for a Speedy Yellow Cab Company car."

"Hallelujah. There are less than a hundred in the city. I'm on it. You want to ride with me?"

"I'm staying for a bit."

Connor hesitated as the reason registered. "You'll let Susan stay with you?"

A couple minutes sitting with Tracey's body in the morgue and he'd need someone else to be doing the driving when they left here. He forced a smile at his partner. "Yes. Go find that Speedy cab. It's the best thing you can do for me tonight."

"I'll call you just as soon as we know anything."

Marsh nodded, glad Connor had the job to focus on, that it kept him moving and hopefully gave him something to tell Marie. Marsh waited for the elevator with Connor to close and then punched the button for one to take him to the basement. He thought he was still breathing but wasn't sure. It would be so much easier to have been the one who had died.

● ● ● ● ● ●

Caroline struggled to open her eyes and then focus on her guest. "You are here."

Amy turned from the window and the dark night outside and came toward the hospital bed. "Yes."

"I thought I was dreaming."

"I'm not here officially. I kind of had to sneak in. I wanted to make sure—" Amy touched the back of her lax hand. "How are you doing?"

"All in one piece and moving my fingers and my toes." She tried to smile. "It's okay, friend. I'll make it. I am so, so sorry about your sister."

"They shot her on the street while she was walking with Marsh. No warning, no reason, just because she was my sister."

Caroline nudged a finger against her friend's and wished it could be a hug instead. "Much loved, much grieved. You haven't slept yet."

"No."

"I don't think I would have been able to

either in your place." Caroline struggled to realize where she was at. ICU, yeah, this would be ICU. And the night outside looked like the middle of the earliest morning hours. "Luke bring you?"

"I'm traveling alone for now. I just had to know for sure. . . ." Amy brushed at her tears. "Thanks for being there, Caroline. At least you were there."

Caroline hurt, hard, as the reality connected, and she turned her hand to grip Amy's. Her friend was running. "Marie needs you; call her; head there."

Amy's hand tightened on hers, but she didn't reply. "Thanks, friend. I owe you."

"Pray for a cute doctor to show up for the rehab," Caroline suggested, trying to smile and reconnect with the past she needed Amy to remember, to the friendship they had forged. "The last one looked like my former drill sergeant."

Amy laughed.

Caroline tightened her hand. "You run, I'm going to be mad," she whispered.

"I won't run."

Caroline nodded, accepting the soft words. She closed her eyes, breathing in shallowly against the pain and knowing she also didn't like the way those words had been a promise. Amy wasn't running, and that meant she was already on a course of action.

Caroline came alert enough to realize Amy had slipped away on her as softly as she had come. She wished she were going with her. Tracey dead—that reality was going to mess up Marsh too.

"How are you feeling?"

Caroline thought she had been sleeping but stirred at the chief's words, forcing her eyes open. She'd asked the nurse to call him but couldn't remember how long ago that had been. Being shot was turning out to be harder than she thought for staying with a sense of time. "About as well as I look, I'm afraid."

"Pretty beautiful around the edges but for a few bruises."

She smiled just a bit; then her eyes turned serious. "I'm so sorry about Tracey."

His hand covered hers. "I know."

"How's Marie? Marsh?"

"Marsh has me worried; Marie is still

pretty dazed. Connor is pushing through and carrying a lot of what has to be done." He squeezed her hand. "Amy is gone; she bolted when she heard the news."

Caroline closed her eyes, fighting with a fierce headache. "She was here."

She felt Luke jolt at the words. "Amy?"

"I promised her she had my loyalty first but forget that promise," she whispered. "She's got to be heading to her prior safe houses because she's not running. Maybe Sam has an idea where in town she has them. She's probably got at least two if not three. Where did you pick her up that day you brought her to the farm?"

"East of town. She'd been running for a few miles she said, looking pretty sweaty and winded."

"She was probably able to see the diner from where she was staying and saw you arrive. Run in place for a while, and you can say you've been for a twenty-mile hike and it will get believed. Check the area; it's worth a shot at least."

"Thanks, Caroline. I've been at a loss for where to start."

"Amy grieving for Tracey—there's no

telling what she'll do, Chief. She was fighting for her composure while she was here."

"Okay. I'll deal with it; I'll find her."

"I know you will." She struggled to wet her lips. "I froze, Chief. I heard the shots, and I just stood there until one of them knocked me down."

"There were zero places you could have gone to get out of the line of fire," he replied softly after absorbing the pain she was in over that memory.

She didn't bother to answer that. "Just so you know: getting shot is not something I plan to do again. It hurts."

He gently smiled. "I'm glad to hear it. I don't want you telling the doc you feel fine so you can get out of here early; stay put and let them sort you out."

"Since I don't have the strength to lift my head at the moment, that's a simple promise to make."

He squeezed her hand. "We haven't been able to locate the shooter even with everything you've been able to tell us. Do you think you can help us with a sketch?"

"I'll certainly try."

"After the doctor comes by we'll bring in a sketch artist to talk with you and bring copies of the photos we have from New York."

"I got a good look at him; he looked right at me. I'll get you a good sketch if we don't have his photo," she promised.

Chapter Twenty-Two

The nurses seemed pleased with how quickly Caroline was coming out of the lingering sedation from the surgery, but Connor didn't think she looked much better than she had an hour after she had been shot. He hated the fact they needed to push for more information so soon rather than give her more time to rest, but she gamely waved the sketch artist over to the bedside. Connor stayed back out of the way while the sketch artist worked with her, his chair pulled near her bedside and the sketchbook held so she could see it being developed.

"That's not perfect, but it's as close as I can figure out how to describe," Caroline finally said, looking from the sketch over to him.

Connor came closer to see it. The face did indeed look Irish, and he could almost see the red in the hair even though it was a black-and-white drawing. He'd been hoping to recognize the face but drew a blank when he saw the drawing. "It's a solid sketch we can work from, Caroline." They would have it plastered all over the city within the hour.

She'd given him everything she had for concentration; he could see the exhaustion clouding her face. She worked the morphine drip again to help keep down the pain.

He moved around to the other side of the bed while the sketch artist collected his equipment. "It's time for us to get out of here and let you try to sleep."

Her hand turned to catch his. "Can you arrange for me to see Marsh, please?"

He could lie to make it easier on her, but that wouldn't do either of them any good in the long run. "I'm not sure where he is, Caroline. He was gone from his place when I went to pick him up this morning."

"No word?"

"He called the station shortly after midnight to confirm he had the latest news, and that was the last anyone heard from him. He sat with Tracey for a while last night in the morgue, went to see Marie after that, then went home. He refused my request to stay with him."

"He'll be wanting a private place to say his good-byes to Tracey. The funeral isn't going to be the place to do that, not with all the press around it. Try that place he and Tracey liked up by the lake."

"I'll check there, thanks."

"He'll be okay," Caroline whispered. "He loved her too much to not stay and deal with finding who killed her."

Connor tightened his hand on hers. "I'll bring him by here later today to see you."

"I'll take that as a promise."

● ● ● ● ● ●

One of Jonathan's men stood outside the doorway to Daniel's apartment, and Luke found it reassuring as he walked down the hall after stepping from the elevator. "Has the press been a problem so far?"

"We're stopping most in the lobby," the man replied.

Daniel opened the door before Luke

could knock. He was dressed conservatively in a suit, but his tie was loose and there was a kitchen towel in his hands. "Thanks for responding so quickly."

"I was on this side of town," Luke reassured. "How's Marie?"

"Still sleeping." Daniel nodded toward the kitchen. "I'm fixing a late omelet; would you join me?"

"I'm okay, but I'll take some coffee."

"Help yourself; it's ready."

Luke poured himself a mug. "Thanks for this, having Marie here. It will be easier than the gallery flat, I think."

"She can stay here indefinitely, Luke. It's not a problem at all. I just wish it was under different circumstances."

"Your message sounded urgent."

Daniel picked up a file from the counter and handed it over. "Short answer—yes, there is a brother out there not recognized in the will."

Luke felt the first breaking piece of news slide into place. He opened the folder. He hadn't thought it could be proven. He scanned an old lab test.

"That shows father paternity to be a match," Daniel said. "There's no reference number on the lab work, the only identifying fact on the second party sample the notation that it was a blood sample. But the father paternity is a match to a male, the signature on the payment voucher is Henry's, and it's an old enough piece of paper it fits what you thought might be the case. Sam had never seen that document or heard of the lab which was used."

"The tests were run six years ago; and there's no clue from this how old the son was when the test was made."

"Nothing there suggests the son's age or name. He could have been two years old or forty. For what it's worth, I went back to my own personal calendars for that period of time six years ago. Two days after Henry received that lab-test result, he called and made me an offer I couldn't refuse to come in as a partner in the Benton Group. It seems clear that Henry never intended his biological son to be his heir."

"So let's assume it was a surprise to Henry to hear he had a son and the boy was at least in his late teens when this test was run. What would Henry have done?"

Daniel slid his omelet onto a plate. "Since Henry paid to have the claim checked out, and it confirmed he did have a son, he had to do something with that knowledge. My guess he paid either the mother or the boy off. That was his pattern."

"Any sign of the payment?"

"I'm still looking. Now that I have an approximate date I should be able to find it."

Luke thought it through a step further. "What if it wasn't just one payoff, but a series of them? Only six years later Henry dies, the money stops, and there is one angry relative out there who didn't get recognized in the will. *Pay me to go away*—maybe it's more accurate a message to say *continue to pay me to stay away*?"

"I'm leaning that way." Daniel rubbed his face. "We'll pay him, Luke. If he shows up again somewhere or makes contact. That piece of paper says he's Henry's child. I'm not going to weigh it further than that. You can catch the guy whenever you can for the murders, but until then we pay him. It's necessary to try to protect Marie at this point."

"I won't fight you on it," Luke replied, knowing this changed things and put a focus to some of the anger out there. "We'll have to prove the connection from this test result to the two murders, but it does give a motive. It means the street shooting and the murders may be entirely separate threats." He sighed, thinking about the growing complexities. Both theories were proving to be right. "To get in to see Henry just to make this claim of being his son—that couldn't have been that easy to do. We need to find Henry's schedule books, phone calls, anything for this time that might give a lead on someone who was persistent in trying to get a face-to-face meeting. And if Henry saw him long enough to have blood work drawn and this test run, you can be sure there was at least one more meeting shortly after the date of this test."

"I've got my assistant at the house searching for anything in that time period, six months before and after that date. Maybe there is finally some luck and we get a name for this relative. I've just realized I've got a cousin who may be a murderer. You have to admit my pedigree seems to be getting significantly worse with time."

"Have you told Marie?"

"At this point keeping secrets from her seems like a waste of time. Connor was by last night to tell her what they had been able to find out about the cabdriver, to break the news about Amy having left."

"You're prepared for the possibility Amy will appear here or call Marie?"

"I'm hoping she does. We'll arrange a quiet, private place for them to meet, and I'll call you. Marie really needs to see Amy and know for absolute certain that she's alive and okay."

"Is the shock passing?"

Daniel shook his head. "Marie's too quiet and contained even under normal circumstances to get that good of a read on how she's doing now. Connor helped, got her talking a bit more, but you can tell the sadness is beginning to really take hold. I'm hoping she stays a touch numb to it all for a few more days while this plays out. Tomorrow is going to be early enough to talk about funeral arrangements."

"I'd like to be here for that and have at least Connor here if not Marsh. If Marsh shows up here, keep him here, would you, until Connor or I can come over?"

"He's got you worried."

"He lost his fiancée. He's got cause to react however it's going to hit him. I'd just prefer to be hanging out with him as it happens than have him out on his own."

"I'll call you, Luke," Daniel reassured.

Luke set aside his coffee. "I'll slip out before Marie wakes up, and I have to say there is no news. I'll call later with whatever update I've got."

"Okay." Daniel walked with him to the door. "Don't worry about the time tonight, for when you call or come by. You'll be welcome, as will Connor and Marsh."

"Thanks."

Luke walked back to his car and checked with the dispatcher for messages, then stood and watched the drifting clouds in the clear, cold sky. He wasn't cut out to carry the weight of being the police chief, not on days like these. He hadn't tried to say a prayer in the last forty-eight hours—sometimes the words were just too shallow. He could feel himself pushing the weight on his shoulders from himself to God and wordlessly handing it on to stronger hands. Too many people grieving today. Too many people grieving.

He got in and started the car. He had to find Amy. He would have another death to deal with if she stayed out there on her own;

he couldn't handle it. Marie couldn't handle it. *Where did you go, Amy? Where did you decide was safe?*

●●●●●●

Marsh wasn't moving much, just sitting watching ducks land on the water and bundled-up joggers traverse the paths around the park. Amy sat down on the ground beside him and pulled up her knees to rest her chin on her folded arms and thick coat sleeves.

"You hung back long enough I wasn't sure you would come over," Marsh said.

"Connor is looking for you."

"I know," Marsh said tiredly, stripping another twig of leaves. "You called. I'm here. How can I help you, Amy?"

"Don't feel so sad. Tracey was happy until that last moment she died. How many people get to be so lucky in life? She slipped into heaven laughing with you about Christmas gifts."

He wiped away a tear but said nothing.

"I can't come to the funeral," she whispered. "Someone has to break that news to Marie. Someone has to be with her."

"She's staying with Daniel."

"I guessed that when she didn't return to the gallery last night."

"You okay for cash?"

"Yes. It's just easier to do what I need to do without company."

"You can't find this guy on your own, Amy. The entire police force wants him—let them find him first."

"Someone sent him, and after him there will be another. The shadows are going to be safer for a while. Will you take care of Marie for me? really make sure she gets through this okay?"

"Connor will do that for you; he's falling in love with her, I think, even though he hasn't said it in so many words."

She picked up a blade of grass from the cold ground and shredded it. "And you? What are you going to do?"

He shrugged.

"Caroline could use some help getting back on her feet. She's been a good friend to me. She didn't deserve to get clipped just because she was helping me out."

"I thought she looked so cute as she left the restaurant ahead of us: bold red hat, long black coat, those twirly earrings she loved. She gets shot, and the only people pacing the hall to make sure she's pulling through are cops, an uncle, and a few friends. It didn't seem right."

"I thought the same thing. Go see her for me, Marsh; she needs a friend around. And go see Marie. There wasn't anything you could have done to prevent this. Tracey was in God's hands, and He decided it was time."

He wiped at tears that turned the lake into a washed-out pool of color.

"You can't wish for it to have been you," Amy said softly. "You can't carry that wish around with you for the next decade of your life, letting yourself die slowly because you didn't die quickly on a sidewalk instead of Tracey."

"Let up, okay? It's my right to have wanted to be the one to protect her, and I failed her that. The most important thing I needed to do, and I failed at it."

Amy leaned her head against his shoulder and then took a deep breath. "I know. I brought the trouble her way to begin with." She got to her feet. "Tell Connor I said hi."

"And the chief?"

Amy dropped the blade of grass she had shredded. "It's not that big a town; he'll find me before long. I just wanted to say how sorry I am, Marsh. Tracey loved you a lot."

He nodded.

Amy rested her hand on his shoulder for a hard moment and then was gone.

●●●●●●

"You want to stop for something to eat?" Connor asked, feeling out what Marsh was thinking behind the silence. Marsh had shown up at Daniel's to see Marie shortly after 4 p.m., and Connor had driven over to meet him there.

"Maybe a sandwich after we see Caroline," he replied.

Connor didn't like the quiet or the grief. His friend had changed from cop to someone more focused on his own thoughts of the past than caring about the case that had to be solved. Connor needed him focused, despite the loss, despite the pain, because there was no one better at putting the pieces together than Marsh, and Connor needed that help right now. Too many threads of the murders and the shooting were piling up, and he was drowning in the details knowing he wasn't putting them together as quickly as he should to see the big picture.

"I could use you at the office for a few minutes to take a look at the phone-call reports coming in. The sketch Caroline gave us went out to the public shortly after 10 a.m."

"Tomorrow, after the funeral arrangements are made."

"You heard from the chief, that your hunch about Henry's having a son was right?"

"Not now, Connor. Right now it just doesn't matter."

Connor racked his memory for some clue Marsh might have said in the past about where he kept his backup piece. The man wasn't ready to go through another midnight on his own. It didn't matter if this was tiredness or grief; it was simply the fact Marsh was no longer acting in predictable ways. He'd disappeared for over twelve hours and never said where he had been. Connor couldn't take another slice of the worry. Not about Marsh. He pulled into the hospital parking lot. "I'm coming up with you."

Marsh nodded. "How was she, Caroline, when you saw her earlier?"

"Tired beyond words, pretty weak. But you wouldn't know it for her eyes and the way she wanted to know answers to her questions."

Marsh gave a small smile. "That's true to form."

"Hold on." Connor stopped his partner and opened the back door. He lifted out a big bunch of flowers. "They're from you. I already stuffed another dozen roses into the vases around her room earlier. She got a kick out of them."

"Thanks, Connor."

He squeezed his partner's shoulder. "Rag on me, get angry, even sweat a few tears, but just don't go disappearing again, okay? I've been around you too long—I don't know what to do when you're not there to bug me."

Marsh blinked, then smiled. "Yeah, that would be a bummer. Tomorrow afternoon, Connor. I'll look at everything you've been able to tug together."

"I'm holding you to it."

Connor knew the way to Caroline's room and punched buttons on the elevator.

"Watch out if she offers to let you taste what Scott brought her. Whatever he smuggled in would put a guy back into the hospital. Some mint sugar thing that would make your eyes roll back it's so sweet."

Marsh chuckled and shifted the flowers to straighten his jacket and turn back the collar on his shirt.

"You look okay, like you slept in the clothes, but okay."

"Thanks a lot, buddy; they were clean and from the closet this morning."

"Then you don't look so good."

Marsh snorted and pointedly waited for Connor to exit the elevator first. "I hate hospitals."

"I seem to remember," Connor replied, relieved to hear the complaint return.

●●●●●●

Marsh leaned over the bed to kiss Caroline's cheek. "You look like paste, friend. What are they doing to you in here?"

She smiled up at him. "You should look in the mirror. Thanks for coming; I ordered Connor to bring you by."

"He did. These are for you." He rested the stack of flowers on her chest so she could enjoy them without moving her head. "Amy's worried about you, but I told her you had steel in your insides and the bullet kind of bounced back out."

She giggled and groaned. "You're as bad for me as you ever were. You doing okay?"

"Getting smothered with that question," he replied without replying and took a good look at her. She'd been a lot closer to dead than anyone had been putting into words. There wasn't much life in her body beyond the eyes, too much blood lost, too much weakness. He just held her cold hand and smiled at her. "It's not doing you any good to pretend you are laying here unable to get up when we both know you could be out dancing a waltz right now. You want me to bring over breakfast in the morning so you don't have to eat the hospital concoction you get offered and maybe whip you in a game of checkers while we ignore the morning news?"

Her eyes laughed. "Just don't bring one of your spicy skillet creations and have me stuck here an extra week." Her hand tightened on his. "Yes, come over. I need to see your craggily face annoying me." She coughed and closed her eyes against the pain.

"Bullets are a pain in the—"

She interrupted his words with a laugh. "I think it was the surgeon's knife that hurts more." She looked over his shoulder. "Take him home, Connor, after you feed him something, and shove a couple sleeping pills down his throat."

"Right, as if anyone would dare try." Connor smiled back at her as he dropped a heavy hand on Marsh's shoulder. "We're going and you're going to get some sleep."

"Probably. I like the drugs they have here. Sleep gets to be more floating," she remarked, smiling even as her eyes closed again.

"Come on," Connor said softly.

Marsh waited for one more minute until he was sure Caroline had slid back toward a sleep that wasn't full of bad images, then kissed the back of her cold hand and picked up the flowers to slide them into a vase. Old friends couldn't die on a guy; it was too much of a pain to say good-bye. At least Caroline was surviving this.

Chapter Twenty-Three

"Show me the call-in log again, Connor." Marsh held out his hand for the binder, trying to focus on the overall picture of the last forty-eight hours while keeping one ear on the television newscast.

SWAT had busted down the door of the place the guy had been staying two days ago only to find the apartment cleaned out. They were at least getting closer to the man in time.

His head hurt from crying too much, and his heart was too heavy to take a conversation on what was coming next after having spent an hour with Marie on the funeral arrangements. Three days, and he was going to be putting Tracey into the ground. He didn't think he'd be eating in the next two days the way the nausea of that thought lingered.

"What time did you say that call came in on the room they went and raided?"

Connor flipped back a sheet. "Eight twenty-two."

"There's another one in here roughly the same time; a grocery store clerk thought she saw a guy matching the description buying a two liter of soda and a can of peanuts. She remarked that he crossed the street after he left rather than getting in a car."

"Where?"

"Marble Road. That's what, northeast?"

Connor reached for his coat. "Let's go ask in person. I'm going brain-dead reading this stuff."

Marsh considered the idea a wild-goose chase but reached for his own coat. Connor had been doing all the shoving on this case for the last forty-eight hours; it was time he saw some fresh air even if the lead wasn't all that solid.

●●●●●●

"Where is she?" Luke asked softly, taking a seat on the cold city bench of a bus stop next to Sam.

His friend merely shifted the newspaper he was reading. "You'll see her coming down the fire escape at that brownstone east of the bank in about two minutes, I think."

"What did you do?"

"Had one of my guys go knock on the door as a deliveryman. She won't answer it, but she'll rightly assume she might not want to be there in the next few minutes."

"Interesting place she chooses as a safe house, dead in the center of town and within walking distance of the gallery."

Sam smiled. "She's got moxie. I'll give her that. And it cost me a clean five hundred to get that much of a lead on her. She's inspired some loyalty on the street."

"She's not going to be pleased to see me, so you might as well head on."

Sam winced. "Forget it; we just got spotted and lost her at the same time."

Luke turned to see a jogger turning the corner at the end of the block.

"So much for her using conventional exits. She must have gone up to the roof and over to another building before coming down." Sam picked up his radio. "Anybody want to tell me they have her?"

"You didn't mention she used to run track," one of his men complained back. "She's heading over two streets toward the park."

Sam looked at Luke.

"Let her go," Luke replied.

"Let her go and come on back in," Sam repeated for those on the radio loop. "You want me to join you?"

"No. I've a hunch where she might go eventually, and if not there, a reasonable guess for where one of her other safe houses is located. At least if she's uptown she's not prowling the lower east side looking for our Irishman."

"Don't underestimate the hurt she's feeling over Tracey; Amy may in the end simply put out word where she is and intentionally let the Irishman find her."

"I know, and I'm not sure who would be the last one standing in that confrontation." Luke checked his watch and then turned up the collar of his coat. "Call me if you spot her again or if she makes contact. She's spoken with Caroline and Marsh so far—I'm

guessing she sees her sister Marie sometime soon."

"She's going to call you."

Luke shook his head. "No. Not this time.
Not until she's settled everything she wants
to settle on her own." They might be friends,
and maybe a lot more than friends, but she
wasn't going to trust him with this part of
her world yet, and he wasn't going to be
able to set aside the fact he was the chief of
police long enough to look the other way.
But there was no reason to chase her at this
moment and just make it harder on both of
them.

"Thanks, Sam." He headed back toward
his car.

●●●●●●

Caroline was beginning to expect the
slipped-in visit when the nurses thought she
was asleep. "Do you want me to call the
chief for you?" she asked Amy softly, worried at the stress on her friend's face, at the
lack of sleep she could see.

"Calling him just makes this harder. Luke
has his own ideas for how this should play
out, and I'm tired enough not to want to
fight him over it."

Caroline eased a breath in against the heaviness in her chest. "It's the same guy, isn't it, the shooter here and the man who shot Greg?"

"Maybe. Eight years kind of changes someone's appearance. Your sketch was close, but it wasn't an immediate that's-him reaction."

"So maybe I got part of the face wrong," Caroline whispered, not surprised if that turned out to be the case.

"You're tired. I'd better be going."

Caroline touched her hand to stop her. "Call Luke, please. He cares an awful lot about you. You know that, don't you?"

"I know." Amy squeezed her hand. "I see Marie in the morning; Daniel's arranging it for me. Anything you want me to pass on to him?"

"Daniel?" Caroline asked, looking puzzled at her friend.

"He'll be asking to stop by and see you, I think."

Caroline smiled. "Sure he will; he's a nice guy. Luke doesn't have friends who aren't basically nice guys."

"Well, maybe it's time you let one of those

nice guys get close enough to be the one pacing the halls when you're in here."

"He's not a cop; it doesn't work unless it's another cop," Caroline whispered, appreciating the thought though.

"Maybe true." Amy smiled. "You can tell Luke that he can call me. He'll understand."

Caroline frowned at her, confused by the message. "Where, what number?"

"He'll figure it out," Amy replied. She leaned over and offered a gentle hug. "I'll see you later, friend. That's a promise."

● ● ● ● ● ●

Because there were certain days in his life being the chief of police was simply too hard a burden to bear, Luke watched Amy walk across the hospital parking lot and turn back toward downtown, and he let her go without stopping her. The car dashboard clock showed minutes after 3 a.m. He had figured she would come to see Caroline, that she would eventually make arrangements to see Marie, and so far he was two for two.

He finished his coffee and wearily wondered if Amy was staying somewhere reasonably safe and if she'd ever decide it was simply time to trust him and call him. The shooter would get picked up sooner or later, and if Henry's son out there had done the two murders—it was only a matter of time before they figured out his name. This wasn't settled by any means, but the pieces were moving around on the board. All that remained was the learning to live with the reality that had come. But it looked like he had lost Amy, nearly as permanently as Marsh had lost Tracey. He just hoped Connor and Marie managed to survive this together.

He started the car and let it idle again to warm. Another couple hours and he'd visit Caroline too, then head over to see Daniel.

"55-14."

He reached for his radio. "10-2."

"DMV records for that plate shows a Hampton Road address, 754, Apartment A, registered name Ivan Graves."

"754 Hampton Road, Apartment A." He thought about it a moment and put the car in drive. "Mark me 10-8, same address."

"Yes, sir."

It was a long night of playing hunches, but there were only so many ways the reporter dogging his investigators could get inside information to run in screaming head-lines above the fold on page one. Sykes had made news with too many stories to make it simply good reporting. And since Luke couldn't put an inside source on the most serious of the leaks, that meant the reporter had another source. He wasn't above ad-mitting a reporter had better contacts than the cops when it became obvious he did. Luke would start with what he had. Ten min-utes ago Sykes had walked out of the hos-pital, over to a car owned by Ivan Graves, and slipped into the passenger seat. Who had been driving was a mystery, but the deadline for a story in tomorrow's paper was thirty minutes from now and Sykes was still working—that was enough to get a chief's interest.

In the middle of the night there was time for a chief to follow a very slim hunch.

Chapter Twenty-Four

"Come sit down, Marie," Daniel encouraged. "Amy won't be late. She just said she was walking over, and it's a cold morning out there. Give her a few minutes."

"I know." Marie walked back over to the couch in the living room. She smiled. "I changed my mind; your apartment does kind of grow on a person over time."

He offered the pillow she'd taken to sliding behind her back to ease the ache. "You can help with more of the artwork if you like. It still needs a lighter touch, I think."

"Maybe the seascape," she offered, having thought that before. Her smile faded into the weight of waiting for Mandy. Days had passed, and she still didn't know what to say. She'd stayed behind at the restaurant to ask Connor about Christmas plans with Mandy being able to join them, and moments later glass had rained down and she had ceased to be thinking.

"Don't cry. Not before she comes," Daniel said softly, offering his handkerchief.

"Some guest I turn out to be, walking around in slippers and carrying a box of Kleenex and sleeping the majority of the days."

"The rest of those pills from the doctor are going to get used too and without protest. Another five or six days and you may be standing upright without weaving on me, but until then you're sleeping some more."

She rested her head back against the couch and thought again that she was glad she liked him, this cousin she had never known she had. "Tracey would have never wanted all this, the manhunt, the hiding, the fact her photo is headlining newspapers."

"She's safe in heaven; the rest of us will shift and cope with that," Daniel replied. "Are you okay with what you want to tell Amy?"

"Yes. She's not coming to the funeral. I

can absorb that. The rest of it—" She didn't let herself think about the rest of it. "Will Luke be here, to see her too?"

"He knows she's coming, but I think he's giving her room instead. Room to decide what she wants to do most."

"Yes, Luke would want to be fair that way. Mandy doesn't trust him yet, not really, completely. Kind of like you, how you don't trust God. All the pieces are there, but it just never nudges across the line to take the risk."

"She's afraid of getting hurt."

"We all are."

Marie listened for a soft knock on the door and wished Connor had been able to come and see her this morning. Not that she would do anything more than cry on his shoulder like she had done last night, but it would be nice to have him here to lean against. He'd just wrapped her in a hug and said he was sorry over and over again, and she hadn't been able to think of anything to reply but to hug him and be glad he was there. It wasn't Connor's fault, and it wasn't Amy's, but both carried the hurt as if it were their tragedy to prevent and they had failed.

The knock came on the door, and Daniel got to his feet.

"Stay with us, Daniel, please."

He squeezed her shoulder as he passed behind the couch and went to answer the door.

● ● ● ● ● ●

Traffic had picked up while Luke was visiting Caroline in the hospital. He turned east out of the parking lot and headed toward Daniel's place. A night following the tracks of a reporter had been a bad trade-off for the amount of sleep he hadn't gotten—watching who the reporter was meeting was a sound idea; assigning himself to do it not so sound. Maybe a quiet word to the traffic detail and they could start sourcing addresses where they spotted Sykes' car over the next week—that might give him a lead. The guy was getting his information somewhere.

Luke covered a yawn and checked the time again. He didn't want to arrive at Daniel's so early that Marie and Amy were in the early stages of grieving with each other, nor arrive so late that he missed seeing Amy.

"Have him call me," Amy had said. The message Amy had left for him with Caroline circled around and around in his thoughts and didn't make sense. He wondered if Caroline had remembered it properly, or if he was simply too tired to understand the message.

Then he knew.

He reached for his pocket phone and opened it; he called directory assistance. "Park Heights, the Radisson Hotel, please."

He listened as the operator dialed and then the front desk answered.

"Ann Walsh, please."

"One moment, I'll connect you to her room."

Luke listened to the phone ring, knowing Amy was at Daniel's right now, and heard the room answering service pick up. He closed the phone without leaving a message.

He took a right at the next light. Three hours, he'd give Amy three hours with Marie while he cleared away what he could on his desk and left the manhunt in the hands of his deputy chief, and then he was going to go knock on a hotel-room door. Amy wasn't coming in from the cold, but she'd stopped running. That was enough for now.

●●●●●●

Thirty hours without sleep—Luke rested his head against his arm and hoped someone took mercy on him today and kept new crises for tomorrow. He needed shut-eye time and soon. Amy answered the hotel-room door on his third knock.

"No food this time, but an offer to take you out for a bite if you would like," Luke said softly, studying a face so stressed he knew her time with Marie had not gone well.

"I don't think I could eat right now," Amy replied, studying his face as he was studying her and relaxing as she absorbed the fact he had zero desire to push her right now. She stepped back to let him enter the room. "You figured out the message."

"Yes."

He looked around the room, but other than signs she'd stretched out on one of the beds to catch a nap there was nothing in the room to show it as being occupied. He took a seat at the round table, and she paused by the ice bucket to retrieve a couple sodas keeping cold in the melting ice before sitting near him rather than across the table. He accepted the one she handed him, relieved it was caffeine free. "Thanks."

"Would it help if I turned in the ledger and told the New York cops everything I can remember from that night?"

He blinked. "Yes," he replied simply.

"Then set it up for me, please. One of Jonathan's guys can pick up the ledger for me if I give him detailed enough instructions on how to find it."

"Give me four or five days. We'll make sure you have a lawyer of your own in on the discussions so they can't bring you into the trial without your testimony being screened off and aliased." He reached over to touch her face, seeing ten years of age in the last few days. "I'm sorry, Amy. I'm so sorry about Tracey."

Tears drenched his hand, but she held his gaze. "It may have been the same shooter that killed Greg. I'm sorry; I just don't know for certain."

She didn't know; she really didn't know who had shot Greg. "We're close enough on his trail—we will find him. Caroline can make the case in court. She's good on the stand, solid, credible, and she did see him.

Please don't feel guilty for not remembering the face of who killed Greg."

"It was dark that night and wet, and I should have seen enough to remember because he chased me for blocks, but I never saw enough to remember a face. . . ." Her emotions were tumbling on him, the calm of this lady long ago broken.

Luke slipped a hand around her neck and moved to bring her into his chest and hold her.

"Marie didn't blame me. She just wanted me to come home."

The sobs broke his heart, and Luke closed his eyes. "You can safely come home, Amy. We'll make it safe," he whispered.

Too much grief, too many hurts, too much running. She had come to a full stop with him, and he knew the running was over. He shook a bit, knowing the grief she carried and the risks that would now bottle her into one place. "I've got a place arranged in the next county over with a sheriff friend who will help us out. You and Marie can spend as much time there together as you like and not worry about here."

"What if this shooter leaves town and no

one pays for killing Tracey? How does that get absorbed and swallowed and lived with? I want to stay and walk the streets and find him and make sure he can't get away. . . ."

Luke wondered all those things too, how long it would be before he could find justice for them, where this would end. God had let a wonderful lady get shot and killed, and there was a bitter taste to accepting that fact.

He rested his head against hers and let Amy cry, and his heart broke with the pain she was in. There were no words he could say, no certainty he could offer. Just a promise that she was no longer dealing with this alone.

Chapter Twenty-Five

"I don't know, Chief. I must have contaminated the murder scene that night," Connor said, entering Luke's office with a file in his hand from the second murder scene. "The hair they took off the bookkeeper's sleeve turns out to be that of the reporter Sykes. I did a couple shoving rounds with him in the parking lot that night when they surrounded the car, and it must have been on my jacket when I got upstairs. They had his DNA in the system from a bar brawl a few years back, the one where they were trying to figure out who bit someone's ear."

"Sounds like Sykes." Luke skimmed the lab report Connor had brought him and then tossed it on the stack of paperwork already on his desk. "Don't worry about it. Write up what happened that night, ask the local station for an uncut copy of their interview with me in the parking lot since you're probably in the background on that tape, and leave it for the district attorney to deal with when this case eventually gets to trial. It's not the first time a trace fiber got explained to a jury, and it won't be the last."

"Thanks." Connor hesitated in the doorway.

Luke looked up to study his detective more carefully. "You want to shut the door, go ahead," he offered softly.

Connor shut the door and slid into a seat across from the desk. "I'd like a slice of time off."

Luke didn't let himself react. He'd been expecting something of the sort for a few days now. "How much time and when?"

"Tomorrow after the funeral. Maybe a week, maybe two."

"Granted."

Connor lifted his hand. "I'm not . . . I'm not walking the line to resigning like Marsh is. I know I'm not. But I look at those photos of the knife attacks and I see Marie being one of them and I . . ." He shoved his arms back across his chest and just took a deep breath.

"You've talked to the chaplain?"

"And the department shrink. Thing is, in the old days I would have thought it was something to mention to Tracey and maybe have her push me out of it, and she's not around and that makes it come full circle with the pain."

"I know."

"Are you worrying about Amy this way?"

"Yes."

"So I think I'd better take some time before I have to catch a new case and have to work it along with Tracey's murder . . . you'll be shorthanded with Marsh off and Caroline not coming back. . . ."

"I've been shorthanded before, and that's a problem for this side of the desk, not that side, so don't worry about it. You'll take a week, two, and if you need more you'll say so. I want you around for the next decade. I'm not worried about the next month. I've been a cop a long time, and I haven't seen murders like those two more than a couple times in my career. It was evil in action and it's sticking. Give it time to slide to the side."

"Thanks, Chief."

"You're escorting Marie to the funeral tomorrow?"

"Yes. Marsh wouldn't hear of riding with us, with Daniel. He's coming, but coming alone."

"Sometimes the drive is the only thing that lets the thoughts settle. You'll be with him for the service and the graveside—he'll know he's not alone."

"Most of the department is turning out," Connor said. "Amy?"

"I don't know. I'm still working the problem."

"If I can help, or Marsh—"

"I'll ask," Luke promised, pleased at the offer. "It isn't that Amy doesn't want to desperately be there, but bringing trouble to her sister's funeral—I think that would kill her if it happened."

"I know, but she needs to come. Marie seemed steadier today, like the shock is drifting off. Sad, but okay. She said heaven makes a difference right now."

"I know it does. Tracey was happy to the last moment of her life; that helps with the memories too. Anything I can do for you and Marie?"

"Bryce gave us the details on the place

you're thinking of for Amy to stay. It will take a burden off Marie, being able to stay with Amy, and being away from the gallery will help too. Bryce said he'd have security ready tomorrow, so Marie is going to leave Daniel's on Sunday and let me drive her over there."

"Take Marie's studio things over with her too. Nathan said we can have the property as long as we need it, and he's the kind of sheriff who makes that offer and means it literally. It will be home for them until this is fully wrapped."

"I appreciate it, Chief." Connor moved to the doorway. "Would it be okay for the service if I have Marie not arrive particularly early? She'll have enough condolence words after the graveside service to not want her dealing with a lot before the funeral too."

"Five minutes before it starts is going to be plenty early."

Connor still hesitated. "I bought Tracey a bunch of daisies, not all that original, but I thought she needed something that wasn't traditional mourning flowers."

Luke smiled. "That's good instincts.

Marsh and Marie are going to appreciate it too."

"I don't plan to tell Marsh," Connor remarked, half smiling for the first time. "He knocks my flower choices. I'll see you tomorrow, Chief, unless something else breaks in the case overnight."

Luke watched his officer leave. He thought back through the emotions he'd seen in Connor and nodded to himself. They were on the money, not too far into the pain side to not be countered by the steel that formed with this job. Connor needed the couple weeks off, but he'd absorb this and make it back. The job was always pushing a man. Connor was holding. Luke wasn't so sure Marsh would make that turn, but he was hoping and watching. He needed both men back and able to handle the job that was still ahead.

●●●●●●

Luke was pleased to see the funeral service turnout of officers to support Marsh was close to every officer off duty. Luke watched Marie from where he stood off to the side of the sanctuary. The shock was slipping into the past, and the transition to coping with the loss was settling in. That was a good thing to see. Marsh had hold of Marie's hand, and that was steadying them both, Luke thought.

Daniel rose to introduce a friend of Tracey's from college to do a reading. Daniel had assumed the public role for Marie to give her the space she needed, and Luke thought Daniel was keeping the right light touch to the service. The minister had done a remarkable job of capturing all that was best in the lady they celebrated without minimizing the loss. Daniel was doing his best to end this service on that same note.

Luke shifted his gaze back to the casket as the final hymn music began and people moved to stand. He owed Tracey justice. Somehow he had to find her that justice.

The service drew to a close, and pallbearers came forward to lift the casket, Marsh and Connor and Daniel forming the lead of the group. Luke moved toward where Marie stood and slipped her hand under his arm to escort her.

"Thank you, Luke."

He covered her hand with his. "Amy's here—left of the balcony, in the choir prep room. Connor's going to slip you away before the short walk to the cemetery and bring you back here afterward."

Her eyes filled with tears at his quiet words, and she simply nodded.

He didn't release her hand until they had left the sanctuary and ushers were going forward to orderly dismiss the crowd row by row, and then it was only to leave her in Susan's keeping while Connor completed his task. There would be a police parade-rest line forming between the church and cemetery grounds, and Luke thought Marsh might need some company for that solitary walk. It was the one place that was going to hit him most hard.

Luke walked by Bryce and got a solemn nod that arrangements were in place for Amy, and then he went to join the minister and arrange a seamless ten-minute delay before the cemetery walk began.

● ● ● ● ● ●

The graveside service was mercifully short. Luke nodded to Connor once Marie was safely in Susan's keeping and taking the condolence of friends, and his officer crossed to join him. A cemetery was not the place to talk business, but Luke didn't think in this instance Tracey would mind.

"The service—Tracey would have approved," Connor said.

"I think so too." Luke pushed his hand into his pocket and retrieved a note he had written to himself during the graveside service. "I'm sorry to bring business up in this setting, but I need you to consider something for a minute. That newspaper story Sykes ran this morning came with details I know we never released even in-house. What if our killer is talking to our favorite reporter?"

Connor blinked before a flash of anger crossed his face, and then a serious intensity took its place. "I noticed the details too. We never said a word about that knife tip being broken off, and the medical examiner purposely filed a restricted report direct to the deputy chief just to keep it out of the general knowledge pool. Hold on, Chief." Connor walked away and minutes later returned with Marsh. "The chief has a hunch you need to hear; just listen a minute."

"The information that the knife tip was broken off was severely restricted, but Sykes had it this morning. He's also got the location and objects right for where the messages were left—the books, the painting. What if our reporter is talking to our killer?"

Marsh studied the grass at his feet for a moment, then lifted his head and nodded. "Yes. Sykes is not that good a reporter; we all know it. And he's been breaking news since that very first story."

Luke waited, wanting to hear what Marsh thought should be done. His officer smiled. "Put a tail on the reporter. We're not likely to get wiretaps authorized by any sitting judge I know of, but a discreet tail—there's enough to warrant it based on that story this morning. We can always argue we were investigating an internal leak of privileged material and the reporter was tangential to an internal probe. Better to put internal inspectors on the tail to back up that argument. Connor and I can do some backtracking with the people the reporter has been quoting in his articles and see who else he's been mentioning as names for second- and third-confirmation sources to get folks to talk to him. There's nothing that says we can't talk to the same people he is."

Luke studied Marsh and weighed the offer. "You two know these cases backward and forward, and we're looking for something subtle that was at the scenes but not in internal notes. Give me another twenty-four hours and just see if it's worth pursuing. The time off still stands for as long as you need it, but I could use a little more time first."

"It's an idea, Chief. They've been few and far between. We'll be at the 6 a.m. update with whatever we find," Marsh promised.

Chapter Twenty-Six

"Chief."

Luke looked up from the phone messages in hand. It was not yet 5 a.m., and the office was as busy as it ever became by midday let alone for a weekend shift. His officers wanted this street shooting solved and were working it 24-7 to make it happen. The district attorney stood in his doorway, and the fact the man had come over rather than calling said a great deal for how this was becoming an all-hands case.

"I've got you a warrant on the blood sample Henry sent in for testing. The lab didn't use it all in that paternity test, and Daniel twisted arms and got some incredibly good lawyers to argue the rest of the submitted sample still frozen at the lab is the possession of the estate. We've got the remaining blood sample of Henry's son being flown from the clinic to our lab. They promise a profile in twenty-four hours, and if there's a hit in the systems from this guy we're going to have it by noon tomorrow."

"An ID on the son takes us one very large step toward a possible killer."

"I'm not leaving the office in the next forty-eight hours. You get a name, I'll give you whatever assistance I can on making motive alone enough for a search warrant."

"I'll try to bring you something else to dress it up once we have the name. Thanks."

The district attorney nodded and left.

Luke lifted the phone. "Margaret, are Connor and Marsh in early?"

"They never went home as best I can tell. They're using the deputy chief's conference room for whiteboard space."

"I'll find them. When the mayor calls, tell him it will be an hour before I can get back to him."

"Yes, sir."

Luke pushed the phone messages into his shirt pocket and picked up his jacket.

He'd left Connor and Marsh chasing a lead, and when they got something solid they were not the kind of guys to let go of it.

The conference room was littered with folders and binders and the sharp smell of old pizza with anchovies on it.

"The reporter isn't talking to the people he's quoting; he's making large parts of the stories up, Chief," Marsh said, as Luke pulled out a seat and sat down to listen to what they had. "We worked the phones for hours yesterday, backtracking Sykes' stories. He has most of his facts right, even the sequence of things that happen are right, but he's putting that knowledge as coming from people he's quoting as his sources, and those sources are saying they never talked to him.

"I've got confirmation that the medical examiner quoted in the article Friday morning was in a court deposition and not available by phone. Connor has two people quoted in Thursday's article who were driving back from Florida and insist that they took no calls, let alone talked to a reporter named Sykes. There are four factual items mentioned in the articles we can't source to reports filed in-house. They are mentioned in private notes filed direct to the deputy chief, and no one accesses his office and his safe but him. So in my opinion the answer is yes, this reporter is trying to make his jump from local daily to national newspaper, and he's doing it with the help of the killer passing him information."

"What are we thinking? Phone calls? Meetings? How's the information getting passed?"

"With any other reporter I would say it would have to be anonymous phone calls or faxes coming in that the reporter is exploiting for these articles, but with Sykes—I wouldn't put it past the guy to be doing middle-of-the-night, dark-garage meetings with the killer himself. I type him as liking the drama of that kind of danger; Sykes is aggressive, fidgety, everywhere we turn, and wants attention on how great a reporter he is."

"Sykes was the first to go after Henry's affair and repeat the Amy murder story in any depth," Connor added, "and both sounded slanted and sordid in the telling. Marie was really hot about that first one, I remember. So Sykes has enough information on this family to wonder where it all is coming from in such a short research time frame. I put him as having had more than a few conversations with whoever killed the chauffeur and bookkeeper and went after Marie. Does he know he's talking to the killer? At this point you have to believe he does."

"What about the story on the street shooting?" Luke asked. "I can buy him talking to our knife killer, but what about the shooting? He knew details on it faster than anyone else did. I'd love to be able to explain that."

Marsh chewed on his coffee stirrer and nodded. "Sam. He said his place got ruffled and speculated it was our New York guy looking for a lead on Amy as he had done before."

"Yes."

"Where else would you go looking for information if you really wanted to be comprehensive about it and had money to spend?"

"The streets, you'd buy it."

Marsh nodded. "And offer some of that cash to the reporters working the stories. Our New York shooter arrives in town, spreads a little money around, says he's with a national paper and will pay for a tip and a lead and maybe help with a reference down the line as a thanks for the help, and we've suddenly got Sykes calling the shooter when he gets a rumor on where the sisters are going to be, or where they have been and who they have been with. Sykes is probably getting paid to hand over an early copy of his articles before they show up in print the next morning."

Luke saw Connor beginning to nod. "Yeah, Sykes would be jumping on that kind of opportunity. Cash and a foot in the door to a national paper—he'd cooperate with a guy that he didn't see as local competition. Info he had in exchange for cash and maybe info the shooter thought worth passing back to him."

"We need more guys tailing Sykes," Marsh repeated. "And I don't care how tough that wiretap warrant is to get; we need it."

Luke agreed. "Give me your raw notes on everything that can serve as ammunition; then get enough guys together and build me a 24-7 surveillance plan on Sykes. Even if we can't get the warrant I want to know and have photos of everyone the guy even shares a hello with during the next week."

"The newspaper office will be a problem."

"I'll have an undercover sitting a desk away from Sykes by this time tomorrow. We'll know who he sees and who he talks to."

"How?"

"Call it a chief's persuasion. And the fact the editor in chief owes me a favor the size of this state and has for over a decade. I'd say it's time to make that account square." Luke liked the thought of calling in that marker, and it would serve a double purpose this time.

He looked at Connor, then Marsh. "I came bearing news of my own. We may have an inside way to get us the identity of Henry's son." Luke repeated what the district attorney had passed on. "Once he's identified, if we can connect him to having talked to Sykes, the case for a search warrant gets a lot stronger."

"I don't think he got rid of the knife," Marsh remarked, "not when he took the trouble to bring it to both scenes. That knife means something to him for some reason for him to have held on to it after that tip broke off and to have chosen it for the crimes. We'll get enough for the search warrant, and we'll find the knife."

"I want in on that interview, Chief," Connor requested.

Luke looked at Marsh.

"Yes."

Luke nodded. "Your lead on the case, it's your interview if you want it. But if he's quick to lawyer up you're going to be facing a dry well to sort back through and prove he was the one doing the killings."

"If he lawyers up rather than confesses, we'll still make the case. There will be some trace of him at the scenes. The sweat stains they haven't identified from the bathrooms, a couple of the unidentified trace hair fibers. You can't swing a knife like he did for that long and not leave a trace of yourself behind."

Luke looked at the clock. "Noon tomorrow. It may be a long day once we have news, so get some sleep today. That's an order."

Connor smiled. "Yes, sir."

Marsh just nodded, but Luke would take it as a promise. "Good job tracking this back. Get me the raw notes, and I'll push for the wiretaps. And I think I'm going to enjoy waking up the editor in chief for this request. Marie will be okay with staying put another day?" he asked Connor, aware plans had been to take Marie to the safe house Nathan had offered as a long-term place for Amy and Marie to stay.

"She'll stay at Daniel's another day. Amy?"

"She's with Sam today. He thinks he may have identified the two guys who had been tailing her since Minnesota; they've apparently been asking questions about her around town and asking them of people more inclined to call Sam than answer the questions. Sam wanted to get a visual confirmation from Amy before he pays the two men a visit."

"Who are they?"

"A couple guys from New York who were around during the days Greg was working for Richard Wise. They'll be after the cash, I'm guessing."

"Any idea how they got onto Amy's location in Minnesota?"

"None, and I doubt Sam asks when he walks up to their table at a restaurant and suggests this town is a dangerous place for them to remain."

"That's not going to eliminate the trouble they represent. They'll be back."

"Once Sam has their faces and names confirmed, it won't matter. They won't be able to go anywhere in this town without Sam knowing about it, and that kind of pressure will end their search for Amy."

Luke hoped Amy confirmed they were indeed the two men who had tailed her on and off since Minnesota—it would be another problem contained. If he couldn't remove the danger she faced, then containing it was the next best option.

He got to his feet. "Get your notes together I can use for the wiretap warrants. If the lab has success with that blood sample, we're going to have a busy day tomorrow."

They nodded, and he headed back to his office to place a call to the newspaper editor.

Chapter Twenty-Seven

"Chief."

The head of the lab was in his doorway, and he was closing the door behind him.

Luke hung up on the mayor. "What do you have?"

"Henry Benton's son—DNA came back with a match in the database. Kevin Sykes. The reporter isn't talking to Henry's son; the reporter is Henry's son."

Luke scanned the sheet of paper to see it in black and white as he strode back to his door to pull it open. He stepped out into the outer office. "Margaret!"

She was halfway across the office toward the elevator and immediately turned.

"Connor and Marsh, as fast as you can

find them. Then get me the deputy chief."
He looked back at his lab chief and smiled.
"Tell me where you want that meal, and you
and your wife are eating at the best restaurant in town tonight."

"Sargetti's."

"Done." Luke flipped around the phone
on Margaret's desk and punched in the
number of the SWAT commander.

●●●●●●

Luke eased into the cluster of officers a
block away from Sykes' home. SWAT had
deployed to give them a quiet look at the
house from all angles. "Someone tell me
this guy is at home."

The SWAT communications officer listening in to the radio traffic shook his head.
"Sorry, Chief, everything inside is too quiet
and his car is not here. Thermal doesn't
show a heat source big enough to be a person."

"The newspaper office downtown?"

Marsh shook his head. "He's not there.
The deputy chief just sent enough officers
into the newspaper's offices to walk the pit
aisles and into every restroom and break
room before the editor in chief could protest

our arrival and toss us out, and they confirm that Sykes is not at the office. We've got men watching every entrance to that building if he does show up. He's on the street somewhere."

"We put him as being Henry's son and doing two murders; he's not going to be sitting idly waiting for us to show up and arrest him. Anyone else we need to worry about him going after with a knife right now? Daniel? Marie?" Luke asked.

"Covered. Amy too. And we've got officers at the Benton estate and the Benton Group offices as another layer of precaution. Where else?" Marsh replied.

"We don't know enough about Sykes, his parents, places he vacations, friends. Find those facts and assume he'll be trying to slip away and leave town. We need his phone records."

"An officer is standing at the shoulder of the employee running them as we speak."

● ● ● ● ● ●

"Chief, there are lots of calls to a number over on Barry Road," the officer handling retrieving Sykes' phone records called in. "I'm looking back sixty days. The calls start a day before the murders and have been steady since then, most between 2 and 4 a.m. This isn't some sweetheart he's calling, not in that area of town. And it's incredibly close to where that Lincoln was found parked: two, three blocks north."

"He was calling our New York shooter and selling previews of his next day's news article?" Connor suggested.

Luke nodded. "We need something else as a match before we send SWAT to knock down a door. Review the phone-tip lines for sightings in that area, get a photo spread together, and put a couple plainclothes on the street showing it around. I don't want a visible cop presence in the area until we are ready to seal the area and go knock on a door. What time was the most recent call?"

"Three this morning."

"Yes, I think Sykes just led us to our shooter, and he was at that number this morning. Watch the details, people, and the security. Let's get this guy on the first try. Marsh, Connor—you're with me. I want a long-distance look at that building while we get the facts in place to go breaking down another door."

The SWAT team began to reassemble,

and officers stationed to watch Sykes' home for his possible return fanned out. Luke began to feel hope that this was coming to a close. "Connor, you drive. I remember the last time I offered the keys to Marsh."

His officer smiled but took the key ring.

They would find Sykes by day's end, Luke thought, if only because he had too visible a face to hide. People thought reporters were someone to notice. And to get the shooter the same day—it would be sweet. Change locations, get SWAT set up, study the layout to confirm where the shooter's room was at, and go in and take him down.

Sykes was their guy: it explained the depth of his knowledge about Henry and the sisters in his early news stories; it answered the question how he had the crime-scene photos and knowledge of the note text when they hadn't been able to find a leak within the department. Sykes' contact with the shooter out of New York also explained why they hadn't been able to locate word of him on the street. He'd been able to lay low and still have everything he needed to know about the sisters' movements fed to him.

All of it because of money. Money Richard Wise wanted to stop Amy from turning into the authorities; money Sykes thought was his due as Henry's son. Daniel's comment that on some days he just wanted to burn the cash and be rid of it fit what Luke was feeling now. This had all been senseless. But it would be over soon. They would get the New York shooter, and they would locate Sykes. Hopefully without another officer ending up shot.

Luke turned to the SWAT leader as they moved back to their vehicles. "Let's get a couple SWAT officers watching this address on Barry Road immediately. I don't want our shooter slipping out of town before we're set up to go in and get him. News of our search for Sykes is going to be on the air soon, and our New York shooter will know his location is blown."

"I had the same thought. I've got two spotters already on the way over there now."

●●●●●●

"Chief, I've got Kevin Sykes exiting the back door of that apartment building and walking west." The remark from the SWAT officer watching the building with a spotter scope electrified the gathered cops preparing to make a move in on the apartment. They were half a block away, taking advantage of the fact abandoned buildings were common on this block.

"He drives a blue four-door Chevy or a white Dodge company car," Marsh alerted the officer.

"White Dodge, east side of the street; he just unlocked doors," the SWAT officer confirmed. "He's going to be heading west on Park Avenue, and that will put him into one-way traffic at Lincoln Avenue. You'd best stop him before that merge or he'll be able to use the heavy off-ramp traffic to his advantage."

"Mayfield, take him as soon as he passes Piedmont Road," Luke ordered.

"10-4."

Luke looked at his SWAT leader. "Move inside the apartment building and take that room as soon as you're in position."

"Yes, sir."

Luke moved forward with the communications officer to the SWAT departure point and watched the team slip into the apartment building and head for the third floor.

The waiting began. *Four minutes,* Luke thought, able to think through the moves he had made so many times himself in the past.

Shots rang out.

Irishman, that was Luke's first impression, and the second, overwhelming relief. There wasn't an officer down.

"He was shooting before we popped the lock on the door—two through the wall, four into the door as it opened. Frank took him down with one shot to the chest. Sorry, Boss. He's not going to be able to help us identify his employer."

Luke's own assessment of the scene was showing more personal courage than that concise review wanted to assign. The men had not hesitated to deal with the incoming fire and respond as a unit; that spoke of solid leadership and honed teamwork. "You did the job with dispatch and no one else hurt. I'd say that was a solid success. Tell your guys to debrief separately with the deputy chief, then stand down; they've got my personal thanks."

"Yes, sir."

"And, Jim?"

"Sir?"

"Tell them to give me their personal wish lists on equipment and training. I might as well use the mayor's coming praise for the success as a way to push for a dollar-amount thank-you in the budget."

Jim smiled. "Yes, sir."

Luke took the smile in the way it was intended. He'd been co-opted to the politics of the job, but it no longer felt like a burden—it was a necessary part of the job. He was beginning to feel comfortable being the chief. Sending the SWAT guys in had been his weight knowing one might take a bullet, and dealing with the politics of the shooting was also his job. Maybe Amy would understand when he tried to explain it to her tonight. He thought she might. He figured she was right—it would take a forced retirement one day due to old age to get him to leave the job.

"Marsh, Connor, where are you?"

"Watching the doors, sir."

"Don't grouse at me, Marsh. I let you stay within a city block as promised. Join me back at the station. You've got a conversation to have with Kevin Sykes, and I intend to be on the other side of the interview glass when you do."

"Yes, sir."

"I thought that would make your day. You have a plan in mind?"

"Psych him out, sir. I know more information about what has been going down the last month than he does. A reporter will never be able to stand it."

"Thank you. For a while there I wasn't sure you were ready for this."

"Born ready, sir. Born a cop."

Luke smiled at the reply. "Let Connor drive while you write your notes. You go in as soon as Sykes comes through processing."

Luke clicked off his radio. "Glad to have you back, Marsh," he said softly. Luke turned to locate his evidence chief and put a plan in place to process this scene. Marsh might have taken a big loss, but he was going to survive it as a cop. That mattered. There were friends on the force to help him pick up the pieces and deal with Tracey's being gone.

"Someone have a suggestion for who gets to write this scene up?"

Several officers near enough to hear the question groaned, but one bravely raised a hand. "Fields, sir. I'll take coordinating it."

"Good. The officers with you just became your deputies for the day."

Fields smiled but nodded. "Thank you, sir. They'll make my life miserable."

"Command always does that. Jim, where are you?"

"The roof, sir. I think I just figured out how he focused in to plan that street shooting. I can see the restaurant through the scope."

"I'm on my way to you." He headed for the stairs and the roof. For the first time there was true relief that they had this contained.

God, there isn't a word to express the relief. Two killers located and contained—it's not much justice for Tracey or an end to the troubles Amy faces, but it is progress. What next, God? I'm too tired to think right now, much less pray with eloquence. Carry me. Carry Marsh and Marie and Amy dealing with a grief so deep I can't find words to express in sympathy. The need just gets bigger to have You guiding our lives. It hurts so much, the losses that have to be accepted. There are some days I don't know how to

keep moving with any optimism for the fu-
ture. This is one of those days.

Luke stepped onto the roof, where Jim
was kneeling by the edge and studying the
streets around them.

"The shooter could see the restaurant
from here and watch the sisters come and
go. And standing at the right spot, he could
watch the Lincoln he had parked," Jim
noted. "You wonder if he really thought he
could get back the money Richard Wise
wanted, or if he just came to deal with the
fact Amy could ID him as the one who killed
Greg. Killing the sisters would bring Amy
into the open—maybe that was his entire
plan."

"I doubt we'll ever know." Luke walked
over to where Jim stood and studied the
area. "At least the one man not currently in
jail who has the most motive to want Amy
dead is now removed from the equation."
Luke thought about the pieces still in play;
he looked around the area one last time,
then nodded to Jim. "The scene is yours;
I'm heading back to the department to meet
up with Sykes."

"Yes, sir."

Chapter Twenty-Eight

The interview of Kevin Sykes had been going on for five hours now, still without the reporter requesting a lawyer. Luke watched through the glass as his officers worked, Marsh and Connor switching around the conversation with the ease of being able to read each other's thoughts, putting Sykes on videotape walking back over himself on details only the killer would know without ever trying to get him to directly confess. That would come, Luke knew, but not before they had the man so twisting in the wind he couldn't remember what lie he had told to cover another. They would get him talking about the knife he had used soon. If he wasn't the police chief and if those weren't two of his own officers, he would be trying to hire them in an instant.

"They're good."

He glanced over at his deputy chief. "I was just thinking the same thing." Luke drank more of his coffee. "Do we have room to move them up another pay grade?"

"I don't think either one would see a promotion to head of major cases as a move up, even with the increased rank. And Marsh is going to get dragged into administration when the time comes."

"Elliot is ready for something bigger than head of homicide—I plan to move him up to criminal investigations as a whole at his next review. Maybe move both Marsh and Connor up to share head of homicide? Goodness knows the job needs two people to cover the hours. Marsh is going to grieve Tracey by pouring himself more into the job—we might as well use that reality and give him more territory to handle. It will be harder to think about a personal loss when he's grousing at 6 a.m. update meetings and hand-holding rookies learning homicide. We'll let Connor make sure Marsh doesn't end up firing the entire lot of detectives under him."

The deputy chief smiled, thought about it, and nodded. "I'm for the move; it's solid. Elliot's been dealing with the narcotics murders, and it would be good to have that background in the overall criminal-investigations slot. And the detectives reporting up to Connor and Marsh will take the move to be a good one, promoting from within the group." He nodded to the interview going on. "How long do you think it takes before the whole story comes spilling out?"

Luke watched them work. "Look at Connor. He's begun to do his two-steps-forward, two-steps-back, lean-against-the-wall pacing. You can see Connor using Marsh's questions like a one-two setup, five questions from Marsh, one from Connor, and always a new fact getting pushed with each group of questions. An hour tops, and they'll have Sykes confessing to the two murders and then writing it all down—his one last great journalist coup—he'll write his own arrest story and his unveiling as Henry Benton's son."

"Think Connor will spin it that way?"

Luke smiled. "I would. And they think like me."

"There's a compliment in there, I think."

"I miss being down in the trenches. You?"

"I'll always have a fondness for traffic duty. Crashes and chases and lots of drunk drivers, but it was my turf as a rookie. I was keeping the streets safe and proud of it." The deputy chief watched the interview for a few more minutes, then nodded to the clock. "Want me to take the nine o'clock press briefing?"

Luke glanced at the time and figured he could let the press wait another two minutes. "I'll do it. I want to do some public congratulating of the SWAT group; they did a nice job today. And this—" Luke nodded to the interview and let himself shrug—"reporters will love nothing more than tearing apart one of their own in custody, but I can do the dance around with no comment for an hour and get away with it while Marsh and Connor get everything on tape. You can call that press conference in the morning to announce the arrest and the charges against Sykes. I'm planning to sleep in."

The deputy chief smiled. "Thanks."

"You'll have to do it without Marsh and Connor too, I'm afraid. I'll give them twenty minutes after the interview concludes to scrawl together their report, and then they are going to give me the good-bye salute and take two weeks' vacation and probably call in and request to make it three."

"Let them have it; then promote them when they return."

Luke laughed. "I like how you think. Page me when it looks like this is wrapping up. I'll go fence words with the press for a while."

"Sure thing, Chief."

Chapter Twenty-Nine

"You look pleased with yourself tonight."

Luke smiled at Amy as she joined him, sliding down into the cushions at the other end of the couch in Daniel's living room. She'd talked him into letting her stay in town one more day, with Marie, with Daniel, and he'd been in the mood to be convinced. The fire Daniel had left burning in the grate had turned to bright coals and steady heat, and Luke was enjoying watching the occasional blue flame flicker between the logs. Occasionally life needed to burn like that, quiet, hot, and comfortable after blazing flames and popping bark. The tasks of the last few weeks were wrapping up, and he was in no hurry to move into tomorrow.

"Not thinking much, just enjoying."

He settled her feet closer to his leg and tugged the throw blanket down to keep her warm. The floors were too chilly when she persisted in walking around barefoot.

"Connor came by?"

"He arrived a few minutes ago. Marie slipped downstairs to talk with him rather than invite him up. I can wager a guess why she was interested in the privacy."

Luke smiled, able to guess as well. A cold night for walking, but he didn't know that he'd particularly mind if he was Connor coming calling to see his girl. They would make it as a couple, he thought, despite the awful toll of the last few days. Marsh had told him he was heading out to ski again, and Luke had been relieved to hear it. Marsh was willing to walk back into the memories he'd shared with Tracey, and there was healing in that.

"What are you thinking about?"

He turned to study Amy. "How much I like being the chief on a night like this."

She tucked a pillow behind her to turn more on the couch to face him. "Because you're smart enough to come upstairs to see your girl rather than huddle in coats on a cold boardwalk and steal a few minutes of late conversation?"

He tweaked her bare toe. "That too. Glad to have Connor as one of my guys. Marsh. They did more than their jobs today—they made things a bit more right in the world."

"I worry about Marsh. He was always the quiet one when I met him before, but now . . . he looks out at life and you wonder how many miles of emotion are pooled behind those calm blue eyes."

"He'll say good-bye to Tracey in his own time and find a way to make life work again. You'll help, I think, and Marie, just being able to share Tracey with him. You can't undo the fact life can brutally hurt at times."

She wiped at tears. "Maybe they weren't all the way married, but they were, you know? Tracey chose Marsh as her other half, and he's still her other half."

"I know."

"I'm going to miss her so incredibly much." Amy bit her lip but looked at him. "Tracey left Marsh her money."

"Daniel told me."

"Well, Daniel hasn't told Marsh yet; it didn't make sense to drop it on him while the manhunt was absorbing him. Marie and

I both expect a fight with Marsh trying to refuse it. We don't plan to let him. We don't want the money, and it was Tracey's last decision. We're going to honor it even when Marsh gets mad at us for insisting on it."

"Good."

"You think Marsh will take it?"

"You'll have a fight on your hands bigger than you can imagine, but Daniel assures me there is no way Marsh can say no. He can give the money away if he wants, and probably will, but he can't refuse the gift. And that fight will do him good. I'm promoting him and Connor when they get back from this break, and he's going to fight that idea too. It's hard to ignore living and get stuck in grief when life is piling on aggravations around you. I'd never want to take that tack with the majority of people I know, but Marsh is not most people. He'll make it through this painful stretch better with responsibility and pressure than with the sympathy. So I'll feel for him and care and push him as hard as I think he needs to be pushed."

"Connor's going to hesitate to ever propose to Marie after all that has happened. I don't put him as superstitious, but what happened to Marsh is going to be setting heavy in his mind."

"Marie prefers to move at a slower, more deliberate pace by her nature. Their relationship can handle it and thrive." He smiled. "You, however, are soon to be a suburban-living, bored lady if the New York cops have any say in the matter. Word on the street has very few takers interested in working for Richard Wise now. If you do, you end up in jail or dead, and that's a pretty good deterrent among a crowd more interested in their own future than an old score to settle."

"It's not closed yet, but going that way," she agreed. "So where are we going with this relationship next? I find I don't mind being stationary in one place, but I do get bored."

"We'll start with your settling in one place and giving me your phone number. I've been searching around to find you way too much for my liking since I met you. It makes it kind of hard to call and ask you out to dinner."

"I'd like to meet your sister."

He blinked at that request. "Would you?"

"I bet she'd like to meet me too."

Luke laughed. "Honey, I think that's a given." He let the smile slide to something serious to ask softly, "You want to move into the gallery flat at some point?"

She shook her head. "Marie wants to move, to start over somewhere else in town. She's too in tune to the memories there; what she paints in that studio now would be sad paintings. She needs somewhere that makes it easier to smile, and I'm inclined to agree with her."

"What are you thinking about?"

"We'll stay at your friend Nathan's place long enough to be absolutely sure life is returning to quiet. Six months maybe, a year. I don't want to get overconfident and assume this is the end of the trouble, but I'm growing hopeful for the first time in a long time. Once the books are turned in and Richard Wise is confirmed to be less of a threat—then Marie and I will find a new place to move to." She looked at him and attempted to hide a smile. "Maybe a little place I know for sale over on Sandstorm Avenue. A place on a big corner lot with a fence around the backyard and lots of roses growing around an inground pool. I hear it's got five bedrooms and original wallpaper in the attic room."

"Original plumbing I suspect too. You don't think it's a little obvious moving into a place four houses away from the police chief?"

"Is it? Fancy that. You can come use our pool and Connor can turn red saying sir all day."

"Just ask Peter to walk through it before you buy it, okay? Make sure there's nothing in it he can't fix."

"He already promised that there was nothing money can't fix when it comes to plumbing, heating, roof, and walls. The decorating—he said that was our job."

"Why do I get the feeling I'm being told about this after you bought it?"

She just smiled.

"Come here then, neighbor. I haven't had a hug tonight, and I find I miss it."

She obligingly shifted around on the couch to share his space. "Do you think we'll ever look back on this time and be okay with it?"

"I'm not even going to try: eight years of your life gone, Tracey's death, Marie and Marsh walking around with broken hearts.

But I guess I'd rather be a survivor of it than not. We'll look back at this night and remember, and sometimes remembering is better than anything else that could be added to it."

"Life flows swiftly by and sometimes through tragedies, but it keeps flowing on."

"I wouldn't have put it so philosophically. Life happens."

She leaned back. "You want to stay and watch the sunrise with me? Or should I kick you out to go get some sleep?"

"I can't stay right here and do both?"

"No. That would be rude to your girl."

"Oh." He smiled. This was going to take getting use to, but there were times in life patience got rewarded. He rubbed her bare arm and wished she'd pulled on a sweatshirt rather than be beautifully dressed and cold. "Why don't I come back and take you out to breakfast? You need some sleep."

She leaned back and looked at him. "Promise?"

"Promise." He tipped up her chin and leaned down to kiss her. She tasted a bit like coffee and honey, and her eyes were open through the kiss, enjoying the sight of him too.

"I'm out of practice," she said softly, her hand tracing his mouth.

"A fact which pleases me," he replied, settling his hand over hers and interlacing their fingers. "I'll have breakfast every day with you for the rest of our lives if you'll behave yourself. I like the dating bit and the flirting and the courting. . . ."

She laughed. "Okay. I'm walking you to your car so morning can get here faster."

"Only if you put on shoes. I'm seeing frostbite in your future the way you keep tempting fate."

"It gets your sympathy so it has its rewards. We might accidentally bump into Connor and Marie though."

"I'm not whispering to warn them we're coming," he replied, amused at the thought. "Come on, up. Let's go say good night at the car so I can properly say good-bye again."

She moved away with a soft laugh but pulled on her boots and a coat and let him take her hand for the short elevator ride downstairs. "I wonder what Daniel will think, his guests sneaking in and out on him in the middle of the night."

"If he's smart, he'll think he's missing

something in life spending it just babysitting all that money and making it grow into more money." Luke eased her into his arms for a final hug at his car. "You're okay until morning? No nightmares to chase away or gremlins to swat down for you?"

She hugged him back. "I'll be remembering a kiss and thinking about breakfast."

"I like that thought," he replied, watching over Amy's shoulder as Connor slipped Marie back inside the building. He bit back a smile and slid his glance back to Amy. "Would you like to start a new tradition tomorrow? Maybe a kiss good morning to add to a kiss good night?"

"Sounds promising."

"I think so." He rested his forehead against hers and decided she had pretty eyelashes. "I'm going to miss you for the next few hours."

His pager began to beep, but he ignored it.

"Maybe six, or would you prefer seven?" he offered.

"No earlier than eight or I'll have icky teeth, and my hair will look like a rat's nest still."

He smiled and kissed her one last lingering time. "Eight."

"Answer your pager; you're the chief."

"The next twenty years of this . . . at some point remind me to smash the thing."

She smiled and slipped from his arms. "Don't be late."

"I wouldn't dream of it." He watched until she walked back into the building and gave him one last wave before letting himself look at the beeper. The text scrolling by said *hospital: two bb cvd*. He ached to hear civilians were hurt to the point of broken bones, knew the drunk-driver tag would be the cause, and felt honest relief to not see the capital *C* which would mean a cop was among the injured. The department had absorbed all it could for a while.

He reached into the car and picked up the radio. "55-14. Mark me 10-8 to Mercy General."

He watched a light come on in Daniel's guest bedroom as he started the car to let it idle and warm up. Amy would sleep and he'd do his job—there was comfort in that. "Night, Connor."

"Night, Chief."

Luke smiled as he reversed out of the

parking spot and turned toward the hospital. The man was learning. There hadn't been any discomfort in that quiet reply. He'd have Connor as deputy-chief material yet.

The midnight pages for the top cop's assistance were rare; probably one of the city councilmen had been driving the car; those drunk-driving arrests his officers preferred the chief to make. Luke shifted the radio volume up a notch and listened to the flow of the dispatcher's voice. The town was quiet tonight overall. A good quiet.

About the Author

Dee Henderson is the author of twelve best-selling novels, including the acclaimed O'Malley series and the Uncommon Heroes series. As a leader in the inspirational romantic suspense category, her books have won or been nominated for several prestigious industry awards including the RWA's RITA award, the Christy Award, the ECPA Gold Medallion, the Holt Medallion, the National Readers' Choice Award, and the Golden Quill. Dee is a lifelong resident of Illinois and is active online. Visit her at www.deehenderson.com.

Book Discussion Guide
The Witness

1. As the book opens, Lukie shows authority, skill, and a take-charge attitude in his
work. Do you think he's happy? In his drive
to see justice done, what kinds of sacrifices
has he made in his life?

2. Imagine what it would be like to live your
life constantly on the run, like Amy. What
would be the hardest part? What would you
miss most about your current life?

3. Does the idea of starting over somewhere
with a completely new identity ever sound
appealing to you? If so, why? Do you think
it would solve some problems, or merely
create new ones?

4. What are the character traits that sustain Amy when another woman might have caved in to the pressure? What keeps her from giving up?

5. Does Amy stay on the run simply for self-preservation, or does she have other motives to remain in hiding?

6. In chapter three Amy says, "Freedom is worth more than any amount of money when it's the one thing you don't have." Discuss the relationship between freedom and money for the various characters, especially Amy, Marie, Tracey, and Daniel.

7. How do Marie and Tracey react to the news about their father's identity and their inheritance? What do their reactions say about their values? How do you think you might have reacted to similar news?

8. What do you think it would be like to become rich overnight? What are some of the problems the sisters encounter with sudden wealth?

9. Why would Tracey's wealth make Marsh reluctant to propose to her? Is this a valid concern?

10. The question of trust is threaded throughout *The Witness*. Luke must earn Amy's trust, which she's not eager to give. How does he go about doing this?

11. How do you think Amy maintains her trust in God when she doesn't trust people?

12. Why does Daniel have such a hard time trusting God? If you were Daniel's friend, what would you tell him about God's true nature?

13. Discuss Connor and Marie's relationship. What qualities draw them to each other? Do you think they make a good match?

14. What qualities make Caroline a particularly good friend for Amy at this point in her life?

15. Discuss how Marsh deals with his grief over Tracey's death. How do his friends support him?

16. Was the identity of Tracey's murderer a surprise to you? Why or why not?

17. Do you think Amy and Luke will eventually get married? Do you think that they will live happily ever after, putting the terrors of the past behind them? Why or why not?